ORB HUNTERS

ORB HUNTERS

HEADSPACE

BOOK 3

J. D. EDWIN

STORY CARTEL PRESS

This book is dedicated to all the writing software I said I would use and then didn't.

"If you think this Universe is bad, you should see some of the others."

—Philip K. Dick

CONTENTS

CHAPTER 1

THE ORB ARRIVED ON A BRIGHT MORNING. NO ONE KNEW WHERE it came from or how it came to sit dead center in Radley Cove. In fact, no one even noticed it until the fishermen rose to untie their boats and head out for their morning catch. It was, by all accounts, a significant and monumental event. One that I completely and utterly missed.

Rosi snuck into my room early, not an easy feat considering her room was clear on the other side of the house and Kit, the housekeeper, was already banging around in the kitchen, singing her throaty tunes. Mother didn't like for us to get out of bed before sunlight peeked through the windows, but in our entire twelve cycles as twins, that had never stopped Rosi once.

"Kova," she whispered. "Look at this."

I squeezed my eyes shut. She hopped onto my bed, dragged herself over the sheets, and climbed under the blankets next to me.

"Kova?"

She flicked me on the forehead. I yelped and sat up, rubbing the sore spot. She grinned at me from under a messy nest of white hair.

"That hurt," I complained. "Why are you out of bed? Mother's going to give you the evil eye again if you don't get yourself right for breakfast."

Rosi waved me off. "Look what I've got!" she exclaimed, holding out one hand as a pale gray shape slithered over it. She grabbed it just before it could disappear into the folds of the sheets. It struggled briefly, then relented, blinking at me with wide, wet yellow eyes. I was suddenly wide awake.

"Is that a pebble lizard?" I exclaimed. "Where did you get that?"

"Found it on the back porch," she declared proudly. "It was being chased by a gull, but I saved it. It lost a foot and I wasn't sure it was going to make it, but it's looking alright now."

"Can I hold it?"

Rosi dumped the lizard into my cupped hands, but it snapped its jaw and scraped me with its tiny, sharp talons. I dropped it and it scrambled across my bed. I dove after it. For having only three of its four legs, it was awfully fast. It found a spot near the headboard and faced me, hissing.

"I'll get it!" I started to dive for it again, but Rosi grabbed my arm.

"You're scaring it," she said, half scolding. "It's just a little lizard."

"Well, *you* grab it, then," I huffed. "If it gets under the bed, we're going to have to dig it out with a broom."

"You can't just *grab* it. You have to make it feel safe so it doesn't run."

"How do I do that?"

"I've been reading up on it," Rosi said with a hint of smugness. "You just act like you're one of them. Like this."

She got on all fours on the bed, skinny arms propping herself up, then bent her elbows and lowered her body down to the sheets. I watched her weave her spine back and forth, doing her best to emulate a slithering lizard and looking absolutely ridiculous. She opened her mouth slightly and made a low hum as she moved, unhurried, toward the lizard.

It stared at her, tense and watchful, but did not run as she got closer. Rosi reached out, moving her hand slowly, and scooped it up. It lay on its belly on her palm, calm and steady as a rock.

"See?" She brandished the lizard at me. I rolled my eyes despite being secretly impressed.

"Great, you got it," I said. "What now? Mother's going to have your hide if she sees that thing. Why did you bring it into the house?"

Rosi pressed her lips into an exaggerated pout. "I wanted you to see it."

"It's like the leaf snake all over again."

"I let the snake go."

"Only after Mother found it nestled in her slipper. She nearly stomped that poor thing to death."

"I'll find a place for it." Rosi bounced restlessly on the bed, the lizard still in one hand. It wasn't the first forbidden thing she'd brought into the house, and it wouldn't be last. Everything fascinated Rosi. Even little pebbles and weeds were sources of endless excitement for my sister.

The sound of my bedroom door unlatching made us both whip around. Rosi thrust the lizard behind her back as Kit stuck her head inside. She glanced at the two of us, frozen in place on the bed like dumbstruck mice.

"There you are," she chided. "And you aren't even dressed for breakfast! What would the matron say if she saw you messing about with Kova again?"

"I have time," Rosi protested. "It's still early. I just wanted to say good morning."

"Well, we will both catch your mother's mean streak if you don't get yourself right," Kit scoffed, looking Rosi up and down. "Don't forget to comb out that nest on your head, and wear what I set out for you this time, not whatever comes to your mind. If you look a mess again . . ."

"She won't," I interrupted, sliding across the sheets and off the bed. I tried to push Kit out of the doorway. "Quit fussing. She'll be right for breakfast."

Kit shook her head. "She better. I swear she enjoys making the matron angry."

"Just go!" I said. Behind me, Rosi smiled her best smile of innocence. "Hurry up. I have to brush my hair."

Kit gave me a mistrustful look and pulled out of the room. I could hear her stomping down the hall, muttering that these "Onasi urchins" would be the death of her. Rosi and I stifled ourselves until she was out of earshot before collapsing into a fit of laughter.

"Oh wow," I said, gasping for breath. "I really thought she was going to catch on. I swear, she's on top of you more than Mother." I peeked out to make sure Kit was safely out of sight. "You better get dressed before she comes back again." I nodded toward the lizard in her hand. "And let that thing go. You can't keep it in the house for long."

"I wanted to wait till its foot grew back. I heard the pebble lizards can regrow their feet if they don't lose the whole leg."

"Stash it somewhere safe, then," I said as she snuck out of my room. "Don't get on Mother's bad side again."

She gave me a mock salute with her free hand. "Yes, captain."

I returned it and hurried to get myself dressed for the day. Despite our quips and banter, Mother's wrath was anything but a joke.

UTTAM AND PRIN were already at the table when I arrived, dressed in the expensive dark silk tunics that Mother was partial to, white hair laid neatly against their heads. Despite being old enough to have been invigorated into their chosen genders, our older brother and sister were far more adept at acting the part of the obedient children than Rosi and I. Prin, the eldest child at four cycles older than us, was wearing a string of black pearls in an effort to appear more grown up. Uttam, the second eldest at two cycles older, had just gone through his invigoration ceremony two seasons ago and had taken the exit from his genderless childhood with a seriousness that bordered on ridiculous. He spoke with strain to make his voice as deep as possible, mimicked the posture and fashion of men far older than him, and took great care to plaster his hair down with as much greasy gel as he could manage, the only way to get his unruly locks to lay still. His hair was busy and stiff like Rosi's, a fact that I knew he resented, not the least because Mother and Prin kept reminding him of it. Personally, I was partial to his natural hair, as the gel looked wet and disgusting.

I'd taken care to comb back my long red mane, parted evenly in the middle and pinned in place with pairs of pearl-adorned barrettes, two on each side. This was how Mother liked me to set my hair and I'd done it the same way for as long as I could remember. I wore the autumn-red tunic Kit had set out for me, though I was not a fan of the color. Against the red of my hair, it was brazen and flashy. But I knew it was what Mother wanted. My hand still bore a pink welt where the lizard had scratched me, but luckily it wasn't terribly noticeable. I took my usual place at the right-hand side of the head seat, though I couldn't help looking longingly at the end of the table, past Uttam and Prin, at Rosi's spot.

Meals in the Onasi household were a ritualistic affair. Mother's seat was at the head of the table and mine was at her right-hand side. To her left was Father's seat. Uttam sat next to Father, and Prin next to me. Then, next to Prin but a conspicuous distance away, the odd one out, was Rosi.

Mother had a way of doing everything. Mealtime seating was always the same. Certain colors were only worn for certain seasons. If we went out as a family, she always held my hand while Father and the other children walked behind us. Visiting company were to sit on the wide couch in the family room, with Mother in the large armchair and the children on the long bench, always placing me in the corner closest to the guests. Everything in the house was arranged with a logic and rhythm not to be deviated from. From dishes and cups in the cupboards to the paintings on the walls to the shoes lined by the doors to the way my hair sat on my head, everything had a way, and everyone followed.

Well, almost everyone.

Rosi's seat was empty. The children of the family were supposed to be seated at the table before our parents arrived. Uttam, Prin, and I always observed this rule without fail.

Uttam kicked me under the table. I tucked my feet underneath my chair and pretended it didn't hurt.

Mother entered the dining room, trailed by Father. She was a tall woman, with severe features and long, straight, impossibly stiff hair. Uttam and Prin straightened their backs and smiled lovingly at her, but I was the only one she raked her gaze over as she approached the table. Seeing my hair and clothing in place, she gave a small nod of approval and took her seat.

"I see Rosi is late," she said as Kit began to serve. "Again."

"She'll be here soon," I said quietly. She turned to me, and her gaze softened. She reached out and stroked my long red hair, sliding her fingers between the smooth strands.

"You look lovely in red," she said. "Did you remember to oil your hair?"

I hadn't, but I nodded anyway. The oils made my scalp itch. Despite Mother's claim that she could tell the difference, she had never done so. She just needed the reassurance that I was doing as I was told.

"Red is lucky," she went on. Uttam tried to kick me again and missed. "Remember that. It's a symbol of prosperity."

I nodded again. These were words I'd grown accustomed to hearing. Red was lucky. Red was the symbol of good things to come. Some wore red. Some adorned their homes with it.

And one in a hundred million, like me, was born red. There were many names for the rare ones like me, but the most common name for those born with red hair was "beacon." A beacon of red among a sea of white. Many tried to dye their hair to achieve the red color artificially, but no matter the chemical or technique applied, the naturally white hair of Fiinians simply couldn't match the exact shade and luster the beacons possessed. To be born a beacon was a real and true privilege.

Or so I was told.

A soft patter around the corner. Rosi appeared. I was about to let out a sigh of relief when I spotted her feet. To her credit, she had *almost* dressed herself appropriately this time, in a tan tunic with her hair back and flat brown shoes. But on her feet were two mismatched socks, one of beige lace, which Mother most had likely had Kit set out for her, and the other thick and bright orange, bunched messily at the ankle. She plopped down into her seat. Uttam and Prin exchanged a look that told me they were already gleefully anticipating Mother's reaction.

"You look lovely today as well, Mother," I said quickly, distracting her.

"Why thank you, dear," she said, smiling. Across from me, I saw Father relax ever so slightly. Many cycles his wife's elder, Father was a quiet, timid man who shied away in the shadows while Mother ran the house. I often caught him letting out sighs of relief when conflict could be avoided. Kit entered with a laden tray and began to dole out porridge. There was to be no more conversation once food was served. Mother preferred mealtimes to be quiet and "dignified" and we were only to speak on the rare occasions when she spoke to us first.

Rosi picked up her spoon but did not immediately begin eating. She clinked it around her plate, then studied its reflection. Her leg jiggled in place rapidly, rocking the table.

"Rosi," Mother said, and Rosi quickly stopped at the sound of her chilly voice. She shoved a spoonful of porridge and dried fish in her mouth, then became distracted by the light reflecting from her plate before she could start chewing.

Rosi had this way about her, and unfortunately it was the direct opposite of Mother's. While Mother strived for order and consistency in all things, Rosi thrived on the new and unpredictable. Every little thing caught her eye, from the refracting light on a shiny surface to the tiniest splinter of wood on an old tree. Her energy never ceased and her steps never slowed. She sat with fiddling fingers and jittery legs, eyes darting to every motion that crossed her sight. She spoke without thinking and acted with every impulse. While the rest of us lived by Mother's orderly playbook, Rosi could never quite stay on script. Her very existence was a challenge to Mother's carefully crafted plan for the household, from her mismatched socks to her nonstop movement to her wide-eyed, uncaring stare when punishment inevitably fell. Every day she seemed to find a new way to dissatisfy Mother, and every day she failed to learn. Rosi complicated a house that was supposed to be neat, simple, and tidy, and though I would never admit this out loud to the rest of the family, she made it more interesting as well.

Even her birth was beyond plans and expectations. Like me, Rosi was a rarity, but of a different type. Children born with the birth defect of being gendered were far less desirable than beacons.

Rosi glanced at me. When Mother shot her a sharp look, she quickly turned back to her plate, but the second Mother looked away, she looked toward me again. I pretended not to see.

She coughed. No one looked at her. I knew she was trying to get my attention.

What? I tried to mouth to her, but it wasn't necessary, because as she leaned forward, I saw the movement in her front pocket.

Prin shrieked as the lizard leaped onto the table and made a mad dash across it, zigzagging in between plates and bowls.

Rosi dove to catch it. She missed the lizard but did not miss the jug of fruit juice. It crashed spectacularly as her elbow struck it, showering Uttam's lap with its sticky contents. I winced and was glad Kit had chosen to use the metal jug today instead of the fragile, ornate glass one. Uttam jumped out of his seat, knocking over his plate. Globs of vegetable mash, bits of dried fish, and pickled berries scattered all over the table. Prin pushed her chair aside abruptly as the river of red juice cascaded toward her. Her backside struck me hard. I wobbled and tumbled in a graceless heap to the floor just as the lizard made its way to my end of the table and hopped off, right into my outstretched palm. I stuffed it into my pocket and hurried to my feet, hoping no one had seen.

In just a few blinks' time, the carefully arranged breakfast table lay in shambles.

Mother hadn't spoken a word yet, but everyone in the house knew that Mother's silence was far more fearsome than her wrath. Rosi was still half sprawled on the table. Her eyes met mine as Father pulled her away from the mess of food and plates. Blood thumped in my ear. Even Uttam, dripping with juice from the waist down, didn't dare move as we all held our breath and looked toward Mother.

"Kit," Mother said. The maid hurried forward. "Find that thing and kill it."

"Ma'am . . ."

"Go."

Kit hurried off. The lizard wriggled in my pocket. I pressed a hand over it to keep it still. The fact that no one had seen it drop into my hand amidst the chaos was sheer luck. But that luck was about to run out. Mother cleared her throat. Every eye in the room darted back and forth between her and Rosi, who was busy staring at her feet.

"Mother," I said in a small voice. "I'm sure Ro—"

"Kova," she said. "This isn't your business."

"But—"

"Silence." I shrank back, bracing myself as Mother leveled her gaze on Rosi. "And you. You just never learn, do you?"

Rosi gave a little shrug and kept looking down. I pressed my lips together so tightly they felt numb. Behind me, I heard Kit banging around the kitchen, searching for the lizard wriggling in my pocket.

"Maybe if you went without a few meals, you would finally learn."

Rosi was terribly good at keeping a straight face. I struggled to keep silent as Mother's voice rose.

"Leave the table. There will be no meals for you for the rest of the day."

Rosi shuffled her feet back and forth.

"You disrespectful, feral, impudent—"

I cringed. My mouth began to open. I had to say something, even though I had no idea what.

"ARE YOU READY?"

Silence.

I paused. Had those words come out of me?

"ARE. YOU. READY??"

Everything vibrated. It blared simultaneously from the windows and the walls and echoed off every surface. My teeth chattered. Never in my life had I ever felt so assaulted by three simple words.

For a long, strange moment, no one knew what to say. Our parents exchanged glances, as if each expecting the other to provide a plausible explanation. Mother looked to be struggling between confusion and irritation at being interrupted in the middle of her speech. Then, just as we all began to think it was over, it came again.

"I SAID. *ARE. YOU. READY?*"

"It's on the screens!" Kit exclaimed from the kitchen. She was frantically pointing toward the family room. Mother and Father began to leave the table, followed by Uttam and Prin. I caught Rosi's eyes as she peeked up from the floor. She extended her right hand slightly in front of her, all five fingers splayed. I did the same.

"What is that?" Father said as he headed toward the family room. Rosi folded one of the fingers against her palm, then another.

Five. Four. Three. Two. One.

As we both pulled back our last finger, I ran around the table, grabbed her by the arm, and ran down the hall together toward her room. I heard Prin shout to us, but everyone else was too distracted. We ran into her room and slammed the door shut.

"Did you catch it?" Rosi asked me breathlessly.

"I did." I pulled the lizard out of my pocket. "Why'd you take it to the table?"

"I didn't mean to," she protested. "I tried to hide it, then Kit came and told me I had to come eat *now*, and I had to tuck it in my top. How was I to know it would run?"

"Well, Uttam deserved getting all that juice dumped on him," I said. "He was kicking me again. Wish it hit Prin, too. Maybe next time."

"Next time?"

"Plenty of lizards by the cove."

We were lost to a fit of laughter. Outside the door, the rest of the family could be heard clamoring over something or other. I flopped myself down on Rosi's narrow bed covered in old, hole-filled sheets.

"Listen," I said, "I'll bring food for you tonight. After everyone's asleep. I don't know what I'll be able to get from the kitchen, but I'll try."

"Don't worry about it." Rosi shrugged and went to the window, where she peeked out with one knee on her chair. For having only a bed, chair, and table with chipped paint, Rosi was rather crafty at rearranging her tiny room. Less than a bynight ago, she'd had the table and chair by the window and the bed against the far wall. Now the bed and table had switched, and the chair sat with its back against the window. Despite having little to work with, Rosi found endless ways to change the little world around her.

"I will," I insisted. "It's not right for her to starve you. It was only a little lizard."

Rosi didn't answer. She stared outside the window.

"Rosi?"

"Look," she said.

"What is it?"

"Come here."

I pushed up next to her, pressing my face against the glass. Through it, I could just about see Radley Cove to the east, sitting under the clear green sky. I craned my neck as hard as I could.

"Can you see it?"

I squinted and—yes, I could. Though the window frame cut it in half, I could make out the round black shape in the center of Radley Cove. It was huge, easily filling up at least half the space of the cove and taller than even the municipal buildings at the town square.

"What do you think it is?" she asked, though I had no better idea than she did.

"Maybe something they're putting up for the winter festival."

"But the rosalit flowers haven't bloomed." She peered down to the streets. "That's a lot of people there."

"They're just excited." I pulled on her arm. "Come on, let's find a place to hide the lizard before Mother remembers how much trouble you're in."

I turned away from the black orb, but Rosi lingered. On that bright morning, the world was small and simple. It was made up of our laughter, that tiny bedroom with its narrow window, and the little lizard that scurried through the holes on Rosi's sheets. I watched Rosi's fascinated expression and wondered, not for the first time, how the world looked through her eyes.

CHAPTER 2

THE THUNDEROUS VOICE GRATED ITS WAY THROUGH WHAT turned out to be every active electronic device on the planet, as well as a good portion of inactive ones as reported by multiple sources who worked or lived near landfills. Supposedly, it also translated itself based on whatever language or dialect was used locally to the device.

It lasted for most of the first day, repeating itself time and again, leaving just enough time in between for one to think maybe it was finally over before starting again. My lessons with the home instructors on that day were canceled, which would have been a welcome occurrence if it weren't for the fact that the voice pestered us incessantly. Rosi and I huddled together and packed our ears with scraps of fabric.

As evening fell, the voice finally fell silent, but our quiet town of Radley had become a frenzied circus. Not only did government vehicles arrive in droves, but the media had latched onto our town like the stubborn summer vines that made their way up the corners of our garden wall. Every channel on my pixel screen was filled with "*the news that rocked all of Fiina,*" "*find out the latest on the invasion,*" and "*watch our round-the-clock coverage on the alien orb.*"

Thirteen days—just over a full bynight—passed before the

next broadcast began.

It started with a black screen, then white began to appear in the corners and the black shrank until it became a solid circle in the center of a white screen. Next, a figure appeared. It was long and thin and made entirely of light. Standing before the black sphere, it had no discernable facial features and moved with a strange grace.

"People of Fiina," it purred. Its voice, both feminine and masculine at the same time, was accompanied by a gentle rumble that was almost a pleasant sensation to the ears, making it difficult to turn away. And like the first voice, it spoke the local language. *"We have come from the stars in search of* you."

Here it stepped aside and lifted one hand gracefully, holding it flat so the black sphere floated just above it. Then, the circle began to spin slowly, becoming a smooth, three-dimensional form as it did. The screen dimmed around the edges, leaving a faint halo around the sphere and the figure. Here, the experience varied from viewer to viewer. Some reported feeling a strange chill as they stared at the spinning sphere. Some claimed they felt a sense of suddenly falling, a vertigo that came swiftly and departed the same way. Some reported voices speaking an unknown language, though no one could replicate any of the sounds made.

"The gods have smiled upon Fiina," the being said to no one in particular. *"You are the chosen ones, upon the chosen planet. You are being given the rarest of opportunities, to prove yourselves, to show you are worthy, to earn a chance to stand at the side of the true masters of the universe."*

A pause here. Then, the black orb shrank away, growing smaller and smaller until it disappeared. The figure turned to face the audience—or so I assumed; for all I knew, it was turning its back to us.

"Welcome," it said, *"to Headspace."*

This was the end. The screen faded to black. After a count of five, it began once more.

In the days that followed, the video became a staple in every household, playing over and over on every available screen, looping and looping day and night through its own mysterious channel. Changing the channel was an option, but inevitably, when you next turned on your device, it was back. I told myself each time that I would switch off the channel the moment it came on, but I couldn't bring myself to. No one could. We all watched, transfixed, mesmerized by the being made of white light and the black sphere.

Despite the commotion just outside our window, life in the Onasi house went on as normal. The chilly beach around Radley Cove, nicknamed "Prickle Beach" for its jagged white rocks and pinch-happy sand crawlers, was usually deserted during the winter months. Now, it was filled with gawkers, news reporters, and military personnel both day and night. Rosi and I could see them easily outside of her window. Knowing this, Mother forbade me from spending time in her room. My lessons were doubled and there was scarcely a time during the day when I wasn't occupied learning music, arts, etiquette, sciences, or calculations, all things deemed more fitting to fill my time. The children were also forbidden from watching the orb's channel on the screens in the family room, but that didn't prevent me from sneaking into Rosi's room at night, where we hid under her covers, watching the video over and over on her blurry, outdated pixel tablet.

Mother was determined to let nothing disturb the rituals of the family. A single misstep, she said, even a single delay, could affect my future like a ripple in a pond.

"We have no need for rumors and sensationalism," she said nearly every morning as she combed my long hair with meticulous care. Since the lizard incident, she had taken to personally seeing me through my morning routines. She said it was to ensure everything was done properly, but I knew it was to prevent me from hanging around Rosi. "Make sure you pay attention to your lessons. They are what will serve you well when you grow up."

I nodded along, holding still as she pulled my hair painfully in an effort to make every strand lay just right. I went through my lessons, practiced my tunes, and did my calculations. But at night, I kept myself awake by staring out the window overlooking the garden, waiting for the house to fall silent. As the winter drew near, the rosalit flowers were just beginning to bloom. This cycle they were white and large, quite a bit different from the small, yellow petals they had sported the previous cycle. Some said it was due to all the rain we had gotten during the warmer seasons; some said it was the acidity of the soil in Radley. I adored rosalit flowers even though most regarded them as a weed, which I supposed was reasonable for the only plant on Fiina that stubbornly grew and thrived without fail in every region, adapting itself to whatever climate that happened to surround it. I'd even heard of towns in the western region that had discovered rosalit flowers with multicolored petals.

I counted them as the moons rose. Here in Radley, they blanketed the hillside at the start of every winter. I waited for the sound of Kit's heavy footsteps retreating to her room after her nightly chores. Then I opened my door, tiptoed past Uttam and Prin's rooms, across the house, once again toward the far wing.

Rosi was rearranging her room again, which she had been doing almost compulsively since the orb's arrival. Her meager possessions changed places almost daily. I closed the door behind me and squeezed myself against the hinge to get out of her way as she carried her only chair to her bedside and grabbed her pixel tablet. It was on its last legs and almost half the pixels were dead and black, but that was probably why

Mother hadn't bothered to take it away. The newer models belonging to Uttam, Prin, and me had been removed from our rooms within a day of the orb's arrival.

The tablet flickered to life as I turned it on. Rosi hopped onto the bed next to me as the familiar video began to play.

"People of Fiina, we have come from the stars in search of you."

Rosi was restless tonight. Before the video cycled even one full time around, she got off the bed, peeked out the window, then came back and sat down on the floor, if twisting her arms under her legs to contort herself could be called sitting. "I saw silver stars again."

I set the tablet down and slid onto the floor next to her, watching her rock back and forth on her back, skinny legs waving in the air.

"Don't talk about that. You know it makes Mother mad."

Rosi rocked into a seated position. "But I saw them. In my dream. They're . . . oh, I wish I could show you, Kova. They're amazing."

"All that banging around is turning your brain to mush." I flicked her forehead. She laughed loudly, then quickly slapped her hands over her mouth. We turned out the lights and climbed under the sheets, huddled together as we watched the video over and over until we fell asleep nestled against each other.

No one noticed the first ones who went. They were chalked up to the usual "unsolved mysteries," the run-of-the-mill kidnappings, runaways, lost adventure seekers, and such.

But then the stories began. People disappeared without a trace, and the details were identical—one moment they were there; the next they were not. No fanfare, flashes of light, or shiny waves of energy accompanied their disappearances. Not even a "pop." They simply went away.

Mother shut down all talk of the orb, but Uttam and Prin,

who attended school outside the house, whispered between themselves of things they'd heard from their friends and acquaintances.

The military had considered some sort of strike, Uttam said, but it was temporarily holding off out of concern for civilians around the cove—us.

Prin's friend's aunt disappeared shortly after the video broadcast started. The orb took her, or that was what they believed.

Uttam said old man Neeli, who had owned a fishing boat out on the cove since Mother's mother was a child, tried to wade into the cove one night to fire his wide-barrel hunting gun at the orb, but the military guards stopped him. He was not compliant, and they dragged him away by force. His wife had disappeared a bynight after the orb came, and his husband had followed the day after. His neighbors all heard him wailing his sorrow like a mountain hound.

I didn't worry about any of this. My world remained the walls of Mother's house, lessons, and nights spent in Rosi's room.

Once in a while someone would knock on our door. Sometimes they wore uniforms. Sometimes they had recorders and cameras. I had no idea what they wanted, but it usually had to do with the orb or the people who disappeared. Mother or Kit turned them away as Rosi and I hid in the hall around the corner to peek at these strange visitors, trying to guess what kind of questions they wanted to ask. None of them ever made it inside.

Mother never mentioned the orb, the rumors, or the visitors to us aside from the occasional warning not to speak of them. But more than once, as I lay awake at night waiting for my chance to sneak out, I saw her sneak past my bedroom door and peer in. Then, a soft sigh as she retreated, as if relieved that I was still there.

. . .

Despite her best efforts to keep me inside since the orb's arrival, even Mother knew she couldn't keep me cooped up forever. After much begging, fussing, and a little extra tantrum I threw on top for good measure, she finally allowed me outside with Rosi, with the caveat that we stayed on the side of the hill facing the house where she could easily see me. This, of course, meant that we climbed as high on the hill as we could, toeing that line between being visible to her sightline and not. The higher we went, the better we could see the orb sitting in the cove.

"They don't even let people over anymore," Rosi said, hopping on one foot over a line of pebbles.

"Over where?"

"On Prickle Beach. It's blocked. I tried going there and they told me to go away."

"Mother let you go?"

"I didn't ask." She wobbled and fell on her rear. I winced. She would get no dinner again if she came home with dirt and twigs all over her clothes. "I went a couple times. I almost snuck through once, but they found me."

"You're going to get in trouble."

Rosi ignored me. She plucked a handful of rosalit flowers and held them out to me. "Look," she said, thrusting the petals under my nose, "they're getting big. And they smell different this year, too. Did you notice?"

I nudged her away. The pollen tickled my nose. "I'm serious," I said. "You shouldn't go running to that thing. What do you think is going to happen if the lawmen haul you back home? You'll never leave your room again."

"I have a window." She sat down again. Her white pants rubbed against the damp soil and mashed flower petals. "I saw them again."

"Mother said not to let the neighbors hear you talk about that stuff."

"They're silver," Rosi continued, as if not hearing me at all, her fingers picking absently at the ground. "This one is black, but there are silver ones."

"What if it really took all those people?"

"If it did, don't you want to find out what it's doing with them?"

"Maybe they're taking all the freaks."

I spun around at the voice. Three figures descended the hill toward us.

"But if that's true, they would've taken her," the one leading the group said. They appeared to be the oldest, white hair set in gelled spikes, the way Uttam used to set his when he was younger. The other two chuckled.

I eyed them uneasily and got to my feet. Rosi, however, only smiled.

"Hey, Vasi," she said brightly.

Vasi picked up a small rock and threw it at Rosi. She ducked and it narrowly missed her shoulder, but her smile didn't falter.

"Hey!" I exclaimed. Rosi tugged my sleeve.

"It's fine," she said. "They're just from my school."

"I thought she was the only freak in your family," Vasi said, eyeing me with a smirk. "Didn't know she had a fire-scalp sibling, too. Are all the kids in your family freaks?"

"Nah," Rosi replied cheerfully. "Kova's a beacon."

The other kids picked up rocks and whipped them in our direction. I stepped in front of Rosi and lifted my arms to block her.

"Come on," I said, pulling her to her feet. "Let's go."

"Where you going, fire-scalp?" Vasi called. I ignored them. A rock hit my back and I quickened my step, dragging Rosi with me and hoping the other kids wouldn't follow.

"Bye, Vasi!" Rosi called back. "See you at school."

"Don't talk to them!" I snapped. Behind us, I could hear shuffling steps. Another rock struck me.

"Run, freaks!" one of the kids yelled.

"It's okay, Kova," Rosi said.

A rock hit her shoulder and she let out a small yelp.

"We'll get you tomorrow," called Vasi. "Watch yourself, *girl*."

I stopped. Rosi stumbled as I nearly pulled her over. I turned around.

"Say that again," I said.

"Kova." Rosi pulled on my hand. I yanked out of her grip. Vasi and their cronies grinned darkly.

"I'm not talking to you, fire-scalp," Vasi said as they advanced on Rosi and me.

"I don't care," I said.

"It's fine, Kova. Let's just go."

I pushed Rosi away as Vasi stepped in front of me.

"Say it."

"I'm talking to the g—"

The sensation of my fist meeting their teeth was even more satisfying than I expected.

MOTHER WAS LIVID.

In fact, I couldn't remember a time in my life when I'd seen her angrier. Not even the time Rosi spilled an entire jar of pickled sugar berries all over her new holiday tunic.

All things considered, I didn't think I had done too badly. My clothes were stained, but against the red and orange patterns it really wasn't all that obvious. Besides, not all the blood was even mine and I was quite proud of that fact, a pride that was short-lived when Mother discovered the bloody spot on the side of my head where Vasi had yanked out a good chunk of hair.

"My Kova, my poor Kova," she kept saying as she applied pungent, stinging disinfectants to my wounds, giving extra attention to the spot on my head.

"I'm fine," I said, though I knew it would be a good while before she stopped fussing over me.

"I can't believe Rosi got you into a scrape like this," she said.

"That child needs serious discipline. I do *not* know what to do with her."

"It wasn't her fault. It was that kid from her school. They called her a *girl*, Mother."

The mention of the slur gave her slight pause, but she recovered quickly. "That is *no* reason for you to get yourself banged up like this. She should not have hung around children like that in the first place. That child needs to learn to keep better company. And those children's parents will be hearing from *me*." I flinched as she cleaned flakes of blood out of my hair, stroking my long locks sadly. "Look at this. Look at your lovely hair. What if this part doesn't grow back?"

Then I'll be bald, I thought but did not say.

"Maybe we ought to tie your hair up from now on." She wound a thick strand of hair around her finger, as if imagining how it would look. "A thicker braid would not have been pulled out like this. You must be more careful."

I fought my irritation. I was tired of talking about my hair.

"We'll cover this spot for now," Mother said, occupied with her own thoughts. "Hopefully it grows back. If it doesn't, we'll style it. Don't worry."

I wasn't worried. I sat in silence as she meticulously cleaned my hair and went on and on about how it could be laid so that no one would notice the spot. For a moment, I wished that Vasi had yanked the whole damned thing out.

ROSI WAS KNEELING on her chair at the window when I snuck into her room. I was a little surprised she was still awake since Mother had kept an extra close eye on me after the fight and I'd had to wait until everyone was completely and soundly asleep before I could sneak out of my room. I lifted my shirt and removed the snacks and bread rolls I'd snuck from the kitchen for her, but she didn't turn around.

"What are you doing?"

She gestured for me to join her. “They’ve put more lights around it. You can see it really clear now.”

“I don’t want to look at that thing,” I said, sitting down on her bed and pushing a roll toward her. “Aren’t you hungry? You didn’t get dinner.”

She stuffed it into her mouth absently. For how much of Mother’s anger she’d endured earlier in the day, she didn’t seem the least bit fazed.

“That kid’s a jerk,” I said. “You need to tell them to lay off. What if they hit you in the head with those rocks? I can’t always be there.”

“I’ll be fine,” Rosi said absently, breaking the bread into tiny pieces and allowing the crumbs to fall onto the floor.

“Watch that. You’ll get in even more trouble.” I hopped off the bed and began to gather the crumbs on the floor.

“Don’t worry about it,” she said, taking another bite of bread. “You don’t have to keep me out of trouble.”

“Like I didn’t need to today?” I snapped.

“You wouldn’t have gotten your hair torn out if you didn’t,” Rosi said, and something about her tone annoyed me. She wasn’t scolding or lecturing me but stating a fact as simply as saying the cove smelled like fish.

“You sat there smiling at that idiot like they weren’t about to beat up on you!” I shouted, then quickly closed my mouth when I remembered everyone else was asleep.

“I didn’t ask you to fight them.”

I got to my feet in a huff and threw the breadcrumbs onto her bed. “Fine!” I said. “Get in your own fight next time, then!”

I stormed out of her room and didn’t care that the door slammed shut just a little too loudly. I went back into my own room, pulled the blankets over my head, and screamed into the nearest pillow.

. . .

Outside our walls, there was much going on. But mealtimes in the Onasi house remained the same quiet, ritualistic affair they had always been. And it was during one of these silent dinners that it finally happened.

I sat at Mother's right hand, keenly aware that she was watching me out of the corner of her eye to make sure I was holding my soup spoon at the right angle, placing it on the correct side of the plate, and chewing each bite without making my cheeks pooch outward in an unattractive manner. Next to me, Prin was making an exaggerated show of her own table manners, daintily placing each bite into her mouth as if she was putting on some pantomime show.

I was still sore with Rosi after our argument, so I made a pointed display of not looking at her. I'd snubbed her the last few days and was irritated that I couldn't tell whether it bothered her or not. When she came to meals in mismatched clothes or disrupted quiet evening hours with her incessant chattering and wiggling, I kept silent and tried not to listen to Mother's harsh words raining upon her head. When she ran to me in the halls, eager to show me the latest trinket or pebble or mud cricket that she'd pilfered from the beach, I turned my nose up and looked away, ignoring her hurt and confused expression. I still snuck pilfered food to her when her meals were taken away, but I only opened her door wide enough to throw them in, then closed it with a louder bang than I had to, just to make sure she knew I was still angry.

Rosi sat in her usual spot, swinging her feet and occasionally kicking the table leg. Mother had grown tired of lecturing her about her feet and could at times overlook it when she was in a decent enough mood. But Rosi's restlessness was above and beyond her norm tonight. She clinked her spoon around her bowl in a circle.

Clink, clink, clink.

Mother's face twitched with every clink. Father cleared his throat and Rosi stopped, then almost immediately started again as if unable to stop herself. The spoon went around and around, carving a perfect circular path in her vegetable mash.

Clink, clink, clink.

"Rosi," Mother said. I dipped my head low and took a bite of my own dinner.

"Rosi," she said again. "That's *quite* enough. I would expect even you to remember the most basic rule of the table."

Rosi looked up blankly. Her hand continued to clink around the bowl.

"I'm thinking," she said. "About the silver stars."

"Stop this nonsense," Mother said sharply. "I will have no more of this in the house. It's bad enough that the town is flooded with these loons sprouting their crazy conspiracies. I won't hear it from you, too."

I kept my head down, shoved a spoonful of food into my mouth, and chewed resolutely.

"But they're there," Rosi said. "I see them when I sleep."

Mother's palm struck the table and all the dishes jumped. "That is *enough*!" she barked. "You are losing your mind. If you cannot get yourself under better control, we will have to send you somewhere where you can. Now stop talking nonsense immediately."

Rosi finally met her eyes directly. Though she broke the rules diligently and with great frequency, I had never seen her stare down Mother like this.

"No," she said, very quietly and very firmly.

Mother rose to her feet. Every fiber of my being itched to break the tension, to distract Mother before she really decided to send Rosi away from our home. But our argument played in my head, and I hesitated.

Rosi looked toward me. Our eyes met, and that's when it happened.

And all I could think was, *it's true. They really do just disappear.*

CHAPTER 3

THE DAYS FOLLOWING ROSI'S DISAPPEARANCE WERE A BLUR. THE tutors came and went, but I remembered nothing of what they tried to teach me. The music lessons all sounded like noise. Several of them told me to stop rocking my chair as they taught, and one told me to stop pinching the skin on my arm. Once I stopped doing those things, they informed me they couldn't teach me anything if I insisted on crying hysterically.

At night, my room became vast and endless, like I was drifting untethered in space. I began to sleep in my closet, on a nest of clothes and blankets, with the door shut and sheets tucked under the door to keep out some unidentified threat. It was uncomfortable, stuffy, and suffocating, but that was a small price to pay to pretend I was hiding from something that I could be magically protected from by a thin panel of wood. I couldn't eat. I was empty. The world was somehow duller, as if someone had wiped away a layer of color with a dirty rag. Without Rosi next to me, pointing out every spark of light shimmering on the window and the different shade of each blade of grass, everything ran together in a haze. I hadn't been without Rosi's presence for a single day since I was born. She was the lens through which I saw a world made up of more than just the rituals and rules of the Onasi household. The hole inside me was deep, raw, and shaped like her.

Outside my room, things went on as usual. In fact, they went better than usual. There were no more delays leaving the house because Rosi was dawdling about in her room, fixated on a loose string or strap. No more meals interrupted to keep Rosi from kicking the table. Lectures on how to dress and how to act were a thing of the past. With Rosi gone, the household was a well-oiled machine, following its routines and rhythms, never straying a single beat. I even saw Mother smile to members of the household besides me. If I hadn't known better, I might've thought she was happy. But how could she be? She couldn't possibly, not with one of her children gone like this.

I spotted Kit wiping away a tear when Father mentioned Rosi's name in a quiet corner of the kitchen, but she shooed me away when I tried to ask. And so I drifted through each day, utterly alone in a house full of people and yet terrifyingly empty.

"I'M SO SORRY. This will never happen again."

I sat on the floor in the family room, listening to Mother apologize to my principal tutor, Daris. For the tenth day in a row, I had failed to repeat the tune she'd tried to teach me, and for the tenth day, she had chided me for my lack of focus. She was an expensive tutor who commanded a very prestigious name in the community. And today, when she had smacked my hand for the tenth day in a row, I had bitten her very prestigious fingers.

"I am willing to overlook this," Daris was saying. She had a nasal voice that grated on my nerves on the best days. Maybe I ought to have bitten off that hook nose of hers. "But if it repeats, you better consider muzzling that feral child if you want me in this house again."

"It absolutely will not," Mother answered. "You must

forgive my Kova. They had a sibling who was a terrible influence on them."

I bit my lip.

"I hope you have the good sense to separate them, then," Daris said, her voice full of disapproval. "It would be a shame for a beacon to waste their future."

"You won't have to worry about that. That child has run off."

"Good riddance if you ask me."

I slammed a fist into the wall behind me and on the other side, I knew Mother heard it. But she carried on without missing a beat.

"Oh, yes." There was a smile in her voice. "I quite agree."

Pushing to my feet, I stormed toward the family room door, but before I could even make it around the corner, a firm hand on my arm stopped me. I spun around to see Uttam standing over me.

"Let go," I said.

"What do you think you're doing?" he said. His eyes were full of derision. "The whole house heard that woman hollering when you bit her. You do *not* need to show your face right now."

I wrenched my arm out of his grasp. "She's telling people Rosi ran away. That's a lie. We all saw it. That thing took her. The orb. It too—"

Uttam's fist connected with my forehead, and I stumbled backward. Before I could react, he grabbed my arm, kicked my feet out from under me, and pinned my face against the cold floor. I struggled and he bent my arm behind me painfully.

"Don't worry," he said, holding me down with a knee on my back. "I'm not going to do anything to the *beacon*."

I tried to buck under him, but he was much larger and heavier. He raked a hand through my hair, then gripped it and gave it a hard yank.

"You're an idiot," he said. "You better start acting the part, because if you don't play your cards right, someone just *might* rip all this pretty hair out some day. Then you'll be worth nothing like the rest of us."

With that, he gave me another shove into the floor for good measure, got up, and walked away. Daris had long left, and if Mother had any clue of the commotion that just took place, she gave no sign. I sat up. Humiliated tears threatened to spill out. I wanted to yell and shout and scream. At Uttam. At Mother. At myself. At the whole world. Instead, I slowly rose to my feet, went to my room, and shut myself in the stuffy closet.

I FIRST MISTOOK the sound of the window opening for the squawk of the black jay birds that nested by the cove in early winter. Adjusting myself on the pile of blankets, I turned my back to the door and tried to will myself back to sleep.

"Kova?"

I pulled the nearest blanket over my head.

"Kova."

The closet door opened. For a moment I thought my dreams were invading my reality. Then I thought Mother was checking up on me again. I wasn't sure which I dreaded more. But a familiar face under a pile of white hair appeared and all traces of sleep dissipated.

"Rosi!"

She grinned as I scrambled out of my nest and dove into her embrace. Part of me was terrified that she would crumble to dust as I touched her. But she was solid between my arms. Her hair tickled my face as I squeezed her as tightly as I could.

"Oh, Kova," she said. "You're hurting me."

I pulled back reluctantly, unable to stop touching her face and hair. She was here. My sister was back. She was still wearing the same oversized gray top and baggy pants she'd had on when she'd disappeared two bynights ago. But something was different. I reached past her and felt for a switch. The dim yellow bulb on the wall of the closet flickered on.

I had no doubt that the person before me was Rosi, and yet, when the light hit her, I didn't recognize her for a moment. As I studied her face, trying to figure out what else had changed, she grinned and cupped my face in her warm hands. There was a strange look of disbelief in her eyes, as if seeing something she'd thought she had lost long ago.

I WAS FULL OF QUESTIONS, but Rosi wasn't terribly interested in answering them. Before I had even fully processed the reality of our reunion, she dragged me out of the closet by the hand, down the dark hall, to her bedroom, where she fumbled around, searching until she came away with a scrap of paper and a half-dried pen, which she uncapped with such enthusiasm that it was almost desperation.

"I want to tell you about it, Kova," she said. "Oh, I wanted to show you." I cringed at the sound of her smoothing out the wrinkled paper roughly with her hands against the floor. The shuffling and crinkling were very loud in the quiet night, and I glanced nervously toward the door, though I wasn't sure what I was afraid of. Surely the family would be thrilled to have her back. By the time I looked back, she was already scribbling away.

"What are you doing?"

"I have to show you," she said again as she wrote furiously. "The silver ones are the ones they use to talk. And the little ones. You put your hand in and they move. The blocks will fly when you tell them to." She raised a hand and waved it through the air, fingers wagging as if mimicking a bird flying. "The black ones. Oh, Kova, the black ones. They create worlds. Can you even imagine?"

"What?" I stammered. "What are you talking about?"

She didn't answer. The pile of papers in front of her was quickly growing. She was drawing the same image over and over, scratching it out each time she was dissatisfied and then restarting.

"Rosi?"

No response. The sound of pencil against paper sounded terribly loud.

"Rosi!"

She lifted her head, as if just noticing me. I quickly dropped to my knees at her eye level before she could look away again.

"Where have you been?"

Rosi blinked and looked through me. Then, she burst out laughing. I quickly clapped a hand over her mouth to muffle the sound. If Mother woke to find her in this delirious state, she might really ship her off somewhere and I'd never be able to find her again.

"You look the same," she said. "I don't know why I thought you'd look different."

"What are you *talking* about? What happened to you?"

"I will show you." She shoved her final drawing at my chest, nearly pushing me over. "Her name is *E-V*."

"What?"

"I'll *show* you," she repeated, urgency creeping into her voice. "You have to see it, Kova. I can't just tell you about it. I *have* to show you."

"Show me what?"

She smiled in a way that I could only describe as exhausted. But I saw relief as well as she reached out, wrapped her arms around my neck, and pulled me close.

"I missed you," she whispered in my ear. "Everywhere I went, I still missed *you*."

SOMEONE WAS SHOUTING, and it took a moment to realize it was my own voice. Several hands held me down. I struggled and sputtered. The lights turned on and Mother and Father's faces swam into view.

"Kova," Mother's voice said. My ears felt like they were full of wet cotton. "Kova. Wake up."

I blinked hard, gasping for breath. The sensation of Rosi's body was still on my skin, as if it had left an imprint. My hands searched for her frantically, pawing at whatever was in their path. Mother grabbed my fingers and held them still.

"You're dreaming," she said. "It was only a dream. It's alright."

I couldn't catch my breath. "Where is she?" I blurted out. "Where's Rosi? She was here."

"Rosi is gone," she said matter-of-factly. I turned to Father, who glanced at Mother, then nodded slowly. In this light, he looked terribly tired and old. "She's not here. You had a nightmare."

"I . . ." *It wasn't a nightmare,* I wanted to say, but something on Mother's face stopped me. I couldn't describe her expression as anything but fearful. Why? I had only been dreaming. But then her eyes flickered downward and I followed her gaze.

My arms were covered in angry pink welts, as if someone had sunk their nails into my skin and dragged hard. Had I done this to myself? For a moment I was too stunned to speak, but another thought entered my mind: I had been in Rosi's room only a moment ago. She had entrusted me with something.

I looked around for the scrap of paper, digging through the sheets desperately.

"Are you alright?"

I nodded distractedly, feeling frantic as I searched my bed. Mother grabbed my hands and stopped me.

"You had a bad dream," she said. "It's alright. Let's go put something on your arms."

I stared at her blankly. Sadness and disappointment gnawed at me. My arms stung like mad, but all I wanted was to be left alone. I yanked out of her grip and pulled the covers over my head.

"Go away," I muttered. I heard Mother and Father speak to

each other. One of them tried to pull the sheet from me, but I held tight. I couldn't stand to be comforted or touched by them. After a while, they put out the light and left.

I stayed under the blankets, sobbing as quietly as I could manage. I wanted to return to the dream so I could find Rosi once more, but sleep eluded me. I lay awake, staring at the ceiling as tears carved their paths down my face.

I rose with the sun and trudged to the washroom to start yet another listless day. As I reached up to clean my face, I saw it.

The palm of my right hand was covered in red marks. The skin rose as if someone had pressed into it with something hard and sharp. But unlike the wild scratches coating my arms, I could make out a distinct shape and design— a large oval and several smaller dots in the middle.

I held my hand up to the light. The image was clear in my mind. The scraps of paper, the pattern she had tried again and again to get just perfect. I must have done this to myself, carved it into my palm as I dreamed of Rosi.

I ran to my desk and copied the pattern onto the first piece of paper I could find. I might never know if it meant anything or was just wishful thinking born from my own grief, but I couldn't simply let it go. When it was done, I tucked it carefully into the corner of my bottom drawer, where it stayed for the remainder of my lonely childhood.

CHAPTER 4

"KOVA?"

I blinked and for a moment wondered if I had gone blind. Fumbling around in the dark, I shoved the blankets away from the bottom of the closet door. As I'd gotten taller, maneuvering around the closet floor had become more difficult. My neck was sore from sleeping in an awkward scrunched position all night. A sliver of light peeked in. I reached up and pulled the door open by the handle, squinting against the morning sun just as Kit stuck her head through my bedroom door.

"Miss Kova?" she called, shaking her head chidingly as she saw me half stumble, half crawl out of the closet, my nightshirt bunched awkwardly around my waist. "You're sleeping in the closet again? The matron doesn't like that."

I pushed strands of red hair out of my face. "She doesn't have to know."

"You better get ready for breakfast if you don't *want* her to know."

"I will, I will."

I changed out of my nightclothes, washed my face, and sat down in front of the dresser mirror, where I grabbed a brush with my right hand and dipped my left hand in the dish of oil

I'd set out the night before. I ran the brush and my oiled fingers through my hair in turn, taking care to lay flat loose strands. The whole routine took less than two minutes. I had become so well-versed in Mother's lessons in grooming that I could do it in my sleep.

Outside my window, Radley had changed.

There was hearsay and gossip, but with Mother doing her best to keep it out of the house. I knew very little. I'd heard the orb had opened. The way it had happened had been surprisingly anticlimactic. A hatch had fallen away into the water, as if simply tired of holding on. What had come out of it was hotly debated. I'd heard talks of bodies. I'd heard whispers of strange objects. There had been talk of government-seized artifacts and tech. I never had figured it out, being too busy screaming at and biting every expert Mother had paraded through the door to "help" me. But as I grew older, I understood that the opening of the orb was an event described as "transformational" for the entire world of Fiina. A ripple of changes came from it, strides made in technological advances, communication methods, and standards of living, all stemming from our little town.

In the cove, the orb still sat, where it had stayed for the last seven cycles. Radley had changed around it, nearly unrecognizable from the modest fishing town of my childhood. Businesses had sprung up overnight. Lights and bustling activities had filled the streets. The size of the town had doubled cycle by cycle. Foreigners with deep pockets had made their way to our hilly country and brought with them their trades and wares. The locals referred to the boom as the blessing of the black orb. No one had known we existed before it arrived. The orb put us on the map.

Many were thrilled to see the changes around town. I had never quite made up my mind about it. Seeing the new replace the old piece by piece was strange. More than once I'd stood out here, looking down on the little city below and wondering when exactly the Radley I knew had disappeared. The orb had become a fixture of the town, a mysterious eyesore that went from being a threat from the unknown space to a symbol of hope and prosperity.

I finished dressing myself, gave my hair one last check in the mirror, and headed out of the room. I needed to be on time for breakfast—no matter what happened around us, the gears of the Onasi household turned the exact same way they always did.

Father was already at the breakfast table when I arrived. He looked up when I approached and I saw the fog in front of his eyes for a moment as he looked surprised at my arrival, then confused as he wondered why he couldn't remember my name, then angry at his own frustration. Then the fog cleared, and he smiled at me.

"Good morning, Kova," he said.

I bent and gave him a kiss on the cheek, pretending that I hadn't stood in front of him, patiently waiting for him to sort out his clouded thoughts.

"Good morning, Father," I said.

He started to say something else, possibly to comment on the weather or my choice of clothing, but then the fog came over him again and he forgot his words. The fog was coming more and more frequently lately. Some days it was faint, as insignificant as forgetting a name. Some days he looked lost. I'd caught him standing in the middle of the house more than once, looking around as if wondering not only how he got there but how his entire life had led up to that particular moment.

Kit entered with a pitcher of juice. She poured the liquid into five cups, all of which were set on the left side of their respective place settings. As she finished the last one—Father's—she moved it to his right without a word. Sometimes he knocked it over on his left side. She had been doing more things like that lately. Little nudges that guided him through his days.

Prin arrived a moment later, smiling ear to ear and draped in a loose, ruffled blouse of green silk and two layers of black pearls. The whole getup was garish, but then I supposed the bride had a right to be garish in the days leading up to her wedding. Mother followed and took her seat at the head table. I saw her cast a rare smile at Prin, who beamed back proudly.

Uttam arrived last. Contrary to Prin, he wore a shapeless dark gray shirt and the blank, unimpressed expression that had become his default in recent cycles. As he took his seat next to me, I saw Father tilt his head slightly toward the end of the table and frown, as if looking for something missing but unable to recall what it was.

There had once been six place settings. Now there were five of us at the table. But life went on, both in and outside the Onasi household.

MY LIFE HAD a ritual and a rhythm. Every detail was planned, and every movement was routine. I woke to meticulously prepared meals, ate with well-practiced manners, dressed in outfits laid out in the same spot, and waited for Daris to arrive with my schedule for the day. I was trained daily in arts, literature, sums, current events, and most importantly, grooming. Clothes, gems, powder, hair. Being intelligent and charming wasn't enough. I had to glow, radiate beauty and poise, and turn heads in a crowded room, which was a challenge since I was as plain as the day was long and would not earn a second look from anyone if it weren't for my thick red mane.

But there was safety in routine. To dance to the same sheet music every day also meant never having to stray a single step. And never straying was the only way to ensure a perfect performance, in life and in all else.

At least that's what I'd been taught.

My life before the routine had been chaotic. I couldn't remember—or rather I was well trained not to remember—most of it. There had been screaming, and crying, and frequent hitting and biting. I had dreamed, or hallucinated, or both. There had been a name and a face that I had obsessed over to debilitating levels.

In the end, Daris had been the one who fixed me. She hadn't so much gotten through to me as figured out a way to build a slipshod wall around the darker parts of me. It wasn't easy. I still shuddered sometimes, when my body remembered the sensation of my hands being whipped when I stepped out of place or let my mind wander to where it shouldn't go.

Watch your step. Follow the path. Listen to your elders.

I would cradle the welts on my hands and repeat the mantras.

Watch. Follow. Listen.

Again and again.

Watch. Follow. Listen.

They worked.

Slowly, steadily, the mantras had taken hold. Repeating them became easy. They shut out the name, the face, the memories and dark thoughts. Days became bynights and bynights became cycles. Words became habits became routine. Mother and Daris laid my path before me and I walked it, reciting those mantras to myself.

Watch. Follow. Listen.

The ritual and rhythm of life for the last seven cycles. I repeated them as I slowly pulled the pieces together. I repeated them as I grew, as I invigorated, as I changed from a child to a young woman. So long as I listened, I could shut out the voices. So long as I followed, I could almost forget. If I never looked away from the path, I never had to think about the bad things. Sticking to the playbook meant I could live a life happy, full, and productive without wasting my energy on things not worth dwelling on.

Or so I was taught.

"I'M SO proud of our Prin."

I looked up. Next to me, Uttam did not.

"She is leaving to join a household of her own very soon," Mother continued. Prin glowed at her compliments. "I just know she's going to be a wonderful wife to her spouses."

I had no doubt of this. Mother had found Prin a nice, well-endowed household. Her husband and wife were at least twenty cycles her senior and had no children. They would dote on any child she bore, and she would want for nothing.

"It's all because of your teachings, Mother," she cooed. Her saccharine tone made my teeth itch. Uttam made a sound next to me that was either a scoff or a cough.

"But we mustn't dawdle," Mother continued, turning her attention to me. "Our Kova will be ready for her debut any day now, and *that* is a moment we must prepare for with extra care."

Prin's smile faltered but did not fall. She was nothing if not well trained.

Mother moved a strand of loose hair off my shoulder. My hair had grown long, almost reaching my hips. "I'm sure you're impatient for your turn," she said. I smiled and nodded, as was expected. "I promise, once I find a suitable mate or mates for Uttam, I will devote all of my attention to—"

"Start now."

Mother paused.

"Excuse me?" she asked.

"I said start now," Uttam said. He hadn't lifted his gaze and was methodically eating his meal as if unaware of the attention leveled on him. "I don't need spouses. Start on Kova. Find her someone rich. That's what you want, isn't it?"

"Uttam," Mother said, biting his name. Uttam still didn't look up. He put a piece of bread into his mouth and chewed as if he was punishing it.

"Make us pretty, marry us off, get us out of the way so you can focus on the beacon. She'll bag a wealthy one for sure, won't she? People will pay anything for that red hair."

Prin and I tensed. Father frowned, though he looked confused instead of angry. It was no secret that Uttam had less to say with each cycle that passed, least of all to me and Mother. There were times when he went days without saying a word to me aside from nudging me out of the way with a grunt. He dressed in dark, somber clothing, neglected his lessons, and in the past season, he had even given up putting gel in his hair, letting his messy white locks fall where they might. We all attributed it to typical teenage solemnness, and if Mother hadn't been so preoccupied with Prin's upcoming nuptials, she might have had more to say about it.

But even with his sulky silence and unpleasant attitude, Uttam had known better than to mouth off to Mother. Until now.

"Leave the table," Mother said. I could tell this was the last out she was going to give him. If he excused himself and apologized, the day could still be salvaged.

Uttam didn't move. He took another bite of bread and refused to meet anyone's eye.

"I said *leave* the table," Mother repeated. "You are obviously poorly this morning, if not in body then in manners. And I will not have you ruining everyone's morning."

"Poorly?" Uttam let out a dry laugh and pushed his chair away from the table. "I am having a poorly *life*."

"Uttam!"

"*What?*" he snapped, interrupting her again. Anger and shock alternated on Mother's face as Uttam stood and finally faced her. Out of the corner of my eye, I saw Kit approach the table and gently guide Father away from the commotion. "Am I being rude? Is this bad table manners? Is it going to make me harder to marry off? Are the rich slats you drag us to meet going to be upset? Am I damaged goods now because I can't keep my tongue still? Guess you better tape my mouth shut when it's time for the auction."

Mother rose to her feet. Prin and I instinctively rose as well and vacated the tense air between Mother and Uttam.

"How dare you?" Mother seethed. "How dare you speak to me like that? I have sacrificed everything for you, you ungrateful child. You have food on the table and clothes on your back because of me! You ought to be grateful to have a home and a future instead of living on the streets!"

"I'd *rather* live on the streets!" Uttam shot back as he stood out of his seat. His gruff movement knocked the chair back and it clattered loudly against the dining room floor. Prin flinched. "I'm sick of this! Sick of everything. Sick of *you*."

He spat that last word as if it were venom. The shock on Mother's face was palpable. Her usually stately features twisted into anger.

"Get out," she said.

Uttam met her cold eyes, unwavering.

"Get out of this house. If you want to live on the street, then do so. You can come back when you're ready to apologize for this horrendous behavior. *Get out!*"

Uttam started to open his mouth, but instead of speaking, I saw the corner of his mouth twitch, almost as if he was suppressing a smile. With all eyes on his back, he walked away from the table without a word.

Mother sat. Prin and I followed suit after a brief hesitation. Kit brought Father back to the table and picked up the chair Uttam had knocked over. There was a moment of discomforting silence.

"Sit up straight, Kova," Mother said. "When you have your own household, you must always hold yourself like a proper mistress of the home."

. . .

THE REST of the meal lasted an eternity. I finished eating as quickly as I could without compromising my good manners, then excused myself to get ready for my lesson. But I went to Uttam's room instead and found him packing with a fervor I hadn't seen before.

"Don't say anything, Kova," he said as he threw a handful of clothes into a garment bag. "I'm not going to change my mind."

I watched him move around his room, opening and closing drawers, pushing their contents around with a rough hand. From the looks of it, he had deemed very few things worth taking.

"You don't have to do this," I said. "It was only an argument."

Uttam stopped. He regarded me with an expression that I had become long accustomed to getting from him, one that told me he thought I was an unbelievable idiot.

"An argument?" he said pointedly. "Is that what you think this is? Just an argument?"

"You had a bad morning. Just apologize. She won't hold it against you."

"No, she wouldn't hold it against *you*. Not the beacon who can do no wrong."

He took his hand out of the drawer he was rummaging through and slammed it shut. The sound made me jump. Uttam grabbed his bag and began to walk out. There was such determination and finality in his step that a familiar wisp of fear coursed through me. No matter our differences, no matter his treatment of me, the thought of watching him leave and possibly never return filled me with cold dread. I stepped into his way and blocked him.

"Move."

"No," I said. "Don't leave. It was just a mistake."

"It wasn't a mistake. I did it on purpose."

I blinked. "What?"

A hint of pride crept across his face. "You think I picked a fight with Mother on impulse? You really haven't grown up at all." He tried to push me out of the way, but I refused to budge.

"Why would you do that? Why would you get yourself kicked out of the house?"

"Because I'm tired."

"Tired?"

"Tired, Kova!" I started at his raised voice. "I'm tired! I'm tired of watching what I say, how I dress, what I do. I'm tired of being told there's a plan for me to follow, a path for me to walk, a role for me to play. I'm tired of living this way. It's like being putty, having someone cram me into a box, then push down on me so I can fit in all the nooks crannies."

He tried to move past me again, but I blocked his way once more.

"Where are you going to go?"

"I've been talking to a fisherman on the wharf. He needs a hired hand and he's going out to sea today. I'm going with him."

"And then what?"

"No idea." A glint flickered in Uttam's eyes. "That's the exciting part."

He pushed me. I pushed back.

"Just go apologize to Mother. You're not going on some fishing boat!"

He grabbed me by the wrist, dragged me into his room, and flung me against the nearest wall. Even though we were now almost the same height, Uttam had always been stronger. He pinned me against the wall with his arm across my neck. I gasped for breath as he leaned toward me. I expected him to get angry with me, or sneer at my helplessness, but was surprised to see the expression on his face.

"Aren't *you* tired of this?" he asked, and for a moment he looked almost sad. But it went away as quickly as it came, and he released me. I rubbed my sore neck as he slung his bag over his shoulder. "Have a nice life, *beacon*."

With that, he left. I went after him just in time to see him walk out the front door without a word to the rest of the family. From the window I watched his retreating form descend the hill just outside the house, surrounded by red rosalit flowers, toward Radley Cove where the black orb sat.

CHAPTER 5

"KOVA!"

I flinched and nearly dropped the cup of fruit wine in my hand. Daris's fingers tightened around my upper arm as she gave me a severe, scolding look. I instinctively straightened my back and squared my shoulders.

"Are you listening?" she hissed. I quickly nodded. She pointed to a rotund gentleman surrounded by a gaggle of young men and women. "That's Belox Mo. He has two wives and a husband but is looking for someone with a little more business acumen to run his estate. Be sure to mention your private education when you talk to him."

"Yes, ma'am," I replied stiffly.

"And there's Persa Uuntag," she said, pointing me toward a confused-looking older woman with sagging skin dangling from her neck and cheeks. "She just lost her last spouse and from what I hear, she only intends to wed once more, if at all. If you could catch her eye, your position as the favored spouse is guaranteed."

Which eye was I supposed to catch, the milky one or the one that wouldn't stop shaking?

"Smile," Daris whispered, and I pulled the corners of my lips

as close to my ears as I could manage, though no one was looking at me in the sea of bodies.

"Are you a real beacon?" asked a new voice.

I started.

"She is," Daris said, her stern voice suddenly sweet and silky. The newcomer appeared annoyed at her for butting in, but he said nothing. "Your home is lovely."

"Yes, thank you." He gave her the same once-over he gave me, though not quite as thoroughly. "I am Galen."

"Oh yes, we know," Daris quipped. "And may I say you do a wonderful job keeping up this beautiful household."

Galen did not acknowledge her compliment. I knew him, though we had never met in person. His was one of many names and faces I'd been made to memorize for this very important night. His mouth smiled but his eyes did not. At a glance, he didn't look more than ten cycles older than me, though I suspected his apparent youth was deceptive, as even the servants of the wealthy were adept at camouflaging the markings of age. His skin was smooth as marble, not a single blemish in sight. The shimmery silks of his tunic traveled seamlessly down his body. He looked me up and down with a flicker of his dark eyes and I could almost hear him ticking off boxes in his head.

Galen was the butler of the house, the one who kept the gears of the abode turning when its mistress was busy with her many ventures. He studied me in the same manner a fisherman might eye a fresh catch to deem if it was worth keeping for market or should be thrown back. I tried not to squirm under his gaze.

"Forgive me," he said dryly. "There are many who color their hair these days to pass themselves off as beacons. Of course," he glanced at the crowd, "they all claim to be real."

"Kova is a true beacon," Daris said. "A genuine rarity."

Galen chuckled. "If you say so," he said lightly, already

walking away. Daris shook her head as he disappeared into the crowd.

"He will be a tough one to get past," she said. "But it's alright. We're not here to aim as high as the mistress of the house. Being realistic is key. You should go talk to Persa."

I didn't move. I was an animal caught in bright lights. A young woman—a fellow suitor—bumped into me. She turned and gave my face and clothing a disdainful look.

"I guess they really just let anyone with red hair in," she said under her breath.

My face froze in its rigid smile. My insides seized up. I tried to turn away and smacked face first into a servant carrying a tray of fruit wine. Every eye in the vicinity was on me as glasses shattered on the floor all around my feet, splashing my shoes and pant legs with sticky fluid.

Daris gasped. "Kova!"

I practically ran from her side.

I WAS TWENTY-TWO.

At my age, Prin had been engaged to be married. She had two children now with her husband and wife. Mother had expected that I would be married by now, or at least secured to a well-endowed suitor. Being a beacon, after all, ought to mean I was highly desirable as a partner, especially for the wealthy investors and industrialists who had descended upon Radley in the past ten cycles.

But I was as far from married as I could be. Mother was worried, though I had to admit she did a fair job at not letting it show. She fawned over me, encouraged me, and told me endlessly that I had simply not found the one worthy of me. I smiled and nodded, but deep down I knew the truth.

I was ordinary.

Aside from my red hair, I was neither beautiful nor charismatic. My face was easily forgettable, I was awkward in front of strangers, and I possessed little to no talent in the creative arts. My banter was dull compared to the numerous other suitors who attended these matchmaking events, and I had a bad habit of seizing up in silence when the occasion called for wit and charm. As a marriage candidate, I was completely and utterly unremarkable.

Distancing myself from the guests and serving staff took a while, but I finally found an empty washroom on the third floor of the house and was about to splash water on my face when I remembered that with the amount of powder on my skin, I would end up covered in an unattractive paste. Sighing, I dabbed the water around my neck instead.

A woman with perfectly laid red hair and a miserable expression looked back at me from the mirror. Staring at her, I thought once again of the last question Uttam had asked me.

Aren't you tired of this?

Despite our tumultuous relationship, I struggled with his absence. The house was bigger, emptier, and quieter without him shuffling around. Mother had moved on without missing a beat. The breakfast table had been set with only four chairs the next day, and no one had mentioned Uttam. It was unspoken among the rest of us that so long as Mother did not say his name, we didn't either. And before we knew it, three cycles had passed, and we hadn't spoken of him once.

I tried to smile and my muscles ached as if resisting the mask I was trying to force onto it. My hair was plastered to my head with extra gel to cover the bald spot that had never quite grown back after a particular tussle I'd gotten into in my youth. I was a fake, a pretender. Galen was right to look at me like he did. I didn't want to be here. I would much rather stay in this washroom for the rest of the evening. But then what? Mother was home, eagerly waiting to hear about my success or failure from tonight. She'd gone to great lengths to have me admitted to this event—the socializing opportunity of a lifetime, at the home of the great Meli Veti. If I spent the entire night hiding, I would never hear the end of it. Gritting my teeth, I pushed open the door and relented to my fate.

From a balcony overlooking the main hall, I spotted Daris searching for me. The spilled wine had been cleaned up and the party had resumed. I scanned the attendees from above. The guests were divided into two groups—those seeking a first spouse and those seeking a last one. The first group was young, eager, beautiful, and almost all of them wore prism stones or crystals on their cheeks. They batted their eyes and smiled, while the friends or kin who accompanied them sang their praises and steered them toward the most eligible potential suitors within the second, much smaller group. There were far fewer here seeking a last spouse. They were older, slower, and looked generally bored with what life had to offer. These were the ones who came because they had yet to find The One, that favored spouse who would win the height of their favor and be left the king's share of their estate upon their passing. Counting the hostess, Meli Veti, there were only six of these coveted persons present tonight.

Growing up, I'd always assumed based on Mother's high expectations of me that our family was one of affluence, at least by the standards of the locals. Now, in the home of one of the very few wealthy elites of Radley, I realized we were little more than common peasants playing pretend. Being a beacon meant approximately nothing in this sea of powder and dye.

A HUBBUB on the ground floor. The eyes of the guests turned almost as one to the red-carpeted spiral staircase in the main hall as the hostess and lady of the evening appeared. The sight of her snapped me out of my trance.

Meli Veti was the closest thing Radley had to capitalist royalty. She commanded attention no matter where she went, and until recently I'd only seen her face on screens. As she reached the bottom of the stairs, she lifted her gaze and smiled.

Her hair, instead of the common dull white, was a shimmery silver, and I couldn't help admiring her stylish red-and-black scarf and dark gray shift, having no sense of fashion myself. From a distance, she could be mistaken for a much younger woman. The only things that betrayed her age were her warm gray eyes and the soft wrinkles curving playfully around the corners of her lips.

But the most interesting thing about her, at least to this gathered crowd, was that unlike the majority of those who were of her station and age, she had never wed.

The bolder young suitors immediately pushed themselves forward. Galen stood in the corner and even from here I could read the disapproval and disgust in his body language at the sight of the young men and women fawning over his mistress. I ought to be among them, smiling and running my fingers through my vibrant red hair, and conveniently mentioning in conversation that why yes, I was indeed a real beacon.

The thought nearly made me gag. On the best of days, I would not—nor would I want to—warrant a second look from a woman like Meli Veti.

Beauty. Poise. Efficiency.

Watch. Follow. Listen.

I repeated these mantras dully in my mind—Daris had taught me many over the cycles past. They did little to ease the dread that gnawed at my chest, but at least they kept me from imagining a hundred ways in which I could humiliate myself if I rejoined the crowd below. My shoes and pants were still stained with wine. I wanted nothing more than to go home and hide under a pile of blankets in the closet.

I milled about the higher floors of the house. Though well aware that I was only delaying the inevitable, I couldn't help lingering just a little longer. Meli's home was above and beyond anything I'd ever seen or imagined. Expensive red fabrics draped from every window, barely touching polished, flawless stone floors. Music played from places unseen and crystal fixtures dangled from the ceiling of every room. Intricate adornments braided from hair-thin strands of shimmery gold metal hung from the walls, many sporting polished red stones, one of which was probably worth more than my entire home.

I peeked into each open room to distract myself. A few servants came and went, giving me curious or suspicious glances, but thankfully none told me to return to the party. I saw a few modest-looking guest quarters, a small den, and a closed room at the end of the hall that was most likely Meli's private quarters. I paced mindlessly until a single door caught my eye.

Off to the side of Meli's quarters was what appeared to be a study at first. I hadn't paid much attention to it until the light bounced off the surface of a glass display case inside. Once I paused my pacing, I realized it was one of many.

Carefully, I stepped into the doorway.

Two rows of glass display cases sat in the center of the room, surrounded by neatly organized shelves that lined the walls. I stepped up to the nearest one, taking care not to touch anything.

The case was filled with carvings made from an aquamarine-colored stone, which I recognized as an expensive and rare sea rock that could sometimes be found in the seas just beyond Radley Cove, though I'd never seen any so large. A small, intricate plaque contained a line of text that dated the carvings to be at least three hundred cycles in age.

The next case contained a variety of coins and currencies from what must've been every country and continent on Fiina. I had no doubt that Meli had obtained them personally from each location. To be able to see so many places in one lifetime was unfathomable to me, who had never been outside of Radley.

Each case and shelf contained increasingly fascinating contents, from paintings by famous artists to historic artifacts to meticulously mounted specimens of rare insects and small mammals. I lingered over them, enthralled by Meli's collection.

I moved on to the shelves. Among the rare books and ornate carvings, my eyes glossed over a drab-looking object. When I glanced toward it again, the word on the plaque before it caught my eye and nearly took my breath away.

Orb.

I stopped.

The plaque stared back at me.

Cycle 2112. Radley Cove. Artifact from the black orb.

I looked closer.

At first glance, the block directly behind the plaque looked like a simple piece of industrial metal, but as I peered closer, I saw that it was a strange, complex shade of gray. When the light caught it just right, it shimmered every color under the suns, and yet, together, they mixed into an odd colorlessness. The surface of the block was rough, jutting out here and there as if it had been poorly cut. But when I squinted, I could see that the pieces sticking out of its otherwise smooth surface were in the shapes of perfect cubes. In fact, the entire surface of the block was divided into neat, perfect cubes, almost too tiny for the eye to see. Their edges vanished and reappeared depending on the angle I looked at them from. The longer I looked, the more tiny squares I seemed to see. I stared at it, mesmerized.

"Amazing, isn't it?"

I nearly jumped out of my skin as I yanked myself back from the shelf. I spun around and found myself face to face with Meli Veti. She gave me an amused look and walked into the little makeshift museum.

"I'm sorry," I said quickly, completely losing any shred of poise that Daris had instilled in me. Suddenly, I was very worried that she would look down and see the wine stains on my shoes. "I didn't mean to come in here. I—"

"It's quite alright," she said. "I needed a little quiet from the noise myself." She stepped next to me. "It's a lot heavier than it looks."

"I-is it?" I stammered.

Meli reached up, took the strange cube between her fingers, and held it out to me. "Here," she said. "I will show you."

I will show you.

I froze at those words. Meli took my reaction for hesitance. "Go on," she insisted. "You won't hurt it."

I held out my hands. She dropped the cube into my open palms. She was right—it was heavier than I expected. A *lot* heavier. And though I couldn't see inside it, I could sense that it was incredibly dense. I held it in one hand and slid my other hand over its surface.

A strange vibration coursed through me. It went as quickly as it came, and by the time it faded, I wasn't certain I'd felt it at all.

"What do you think?" Meli asked, watching me as if waiting for a reaction.

"It's . . ." I couldn't find the right words. Meli smiled her graceful smile, took the cube from me, and put it back in its place.

"I've had it scanned," she said. "It's built of those tiny blocks. In fact, the tiny blocks are made of even tinier blocks, too small to be seen by the naked eye. But the truly miraculous thing is, there's nothing holding them together. Logic dictates that they should fall apart, but they don't."

"That's incredible," I said, incredulous. "Did it . . ."

Something in me stopped me from asking the question on the tip of my tongue. I'd been taught—trained—to not think about or speak of certain things, and even now, it was a hard habit to break. Thankfully, Meli seemed to read my mind.

"Did it really come from the orb?" She winked. "Yes. Certain things are better kept out of the eye of the public. I went to great trouble to obtain that little item, among other things."

"Other things?"

"I have a bit of a fascination with the orb," she said. "I collected a number of things from it through various channels and at great cost, though I have no more understanding of them than anyone else. I even moved my home to Radley just to be able to see the orb. I've always loved rarities and oddities. I can't explain it—just looking at it fills me with . . . wonder, I suppose is the word." Meli looked me up and down. "You grew up here, didn't you?"

I nodded. "Yes."

"You remember when the orb came, then?"

"A little. I was young and it was . . . chaotic." I thought for a moment. "I live on the hill facing the cove. We can see the orb from most of our windows."

"What did you say your name was?"

I started, suddenly realizing that I had not even properly introduced myself. "K-Kova," I stammered. "Kova Onasi."

"Onasi," Meli repeated. "That's a lovely name."

"Thank you," I said quietly, trying hard to keep my fingers from fidgeting. My mind tried to play every scenario that Mother and Daris trained me for, but this fit none of them.

"Was it difficult, growing up as a beacon?"

The question startled me. I stared at her blankly.

"No need to be nervous," she said with a smile and stepped closer to me, gingerly taking a strand of my long hair between her fingers and examining it. "I learned long ago how to spot the real thing from the fake. It's been quite some time since I met a genuine beacon."

"Thank you," I muttered, unable to think of anything else to say.

Meli studied my face. I couldn't help but think that she looked at me the same way she looked at the cube on the shelf. Before I could start squirming in discomfort, she had stepped back.

"When you grow bored of this lot," she said, gesturing around at the displays, "come back and join the party."

And with that, she was gone. I stood in place numbly, trying to comprehend what had just happened.

Mother was silent after Daris debriefed her on the events of the evening, but her disappointment was loud. By the time I had returned to the party, Meli had already been surrounded by a gaggle of suitors. I had not mentioned the odd encounter to Daris, which was just as well because Meli had not acknowledged me again. I had spent the final hour of the party awkwardly wandering about, thinking of the mysterious cube in Meli's museum.

"The chance of a lifetime," Mother lamented quietly, "chance of a lifetime." I couldn't tell if she was talking to me or herself.

I knew what she was thinking. With every cycle that passed, I was a little older while younger, fresher faces entered the scene and the quality of hair dye improved. Soon beacons would be nothing to bat an eye at, and then what? She might have to admit that her golden child was drab and awkward, with no real prospects for fame or fortune. The hopes and dreams she had piled on me since childhood were slowly being quashed.

"Maybe someone saw you," Mother said wistfully. "Maybe they'll remember you after the party."

"Maybe," I said, trying to sound hopeful. That seemed enough to pick her up for the moment.

"Next cycle we'll find someone," she said, patting my knee. "I believe in you, dear. You are special."

We had arrived home late. Kit had likely already seen my father to bed. After comforting both me and herself, Mother bid me good night and retreated to her room. I was grateful she had chosen to wallow in her disappointment alone rather than attempt to commiserate with me.

I snuck one of Kit's smokeweed sticks from the kitchen and lit it on the stove. Back in my room, I stripped off the jewels and satin and opened the window. I sat with one arm hanging out in the cool night air and smoked. The dry, bitter smoke filled my throat and nose and made me a little lightheaded. I didn't enjoy smoking, but I did it nonetheless. Once a rebellious act, now even this useless vice had become a habit that gave me no satisfaction save for the comfort of sticking to a familiar, repeatable act. I dragged deeply, blew the smoke out of the window, and listened to the sound of the waves in the distance.

I couldn't see the orb from my window, but I knew it was there. The temporary lights put in place during the early days of its arrival had been replaced with expensive mood lighting that changed with the seasons. Tourists came and went all the time, but there was always a major influx during the winter festival, an event I had once relished as a child but hadn't attended in many cycles.

My eyes flickered to that bottom drawer of my desk, then quickly tore away again. I ought to throw that thing out, the final lingering piece of my childhood delusions. If Daris or Mother knew, they would certainly insist on it. But I couldn't bring myself to. Instead, I simply did not allow myself to think about it. I'd gotten quite good at ignoring it. There were days when I could almost forget it existed.

I snuffed out the smokeweed and tossed it out the window.

I had become very good at almost forgetting. I'd been taught to forget many things. Bad habits, traumatic events, and people who no longer lived here, just as a few examples. A face or a voice or a name sometimes threatened to bubble up and I pushed it down as if it was second nature, a simple part of life. Fiina had grown accustomed to the orb's presence and moved on, and I did as well.

Until I had laid eyes on the gray cube.

I stared at the drawer. It beckoned to me. I thought about getting ready for bed but couldn't convince myself to move.

What mantra could break me out of this?

Beauty. Poise. Efficiency.

Watch. Follow. Listen.

See nothing. Hear nothing. Speak nothing.

I repeated this last one to myself. This was Daris's mantra for me whenever I tried to bring up the orb.

It will do nothing for you to dwell on that thing. You must refuse. Refuse to see it, refuse to hear of it, and refuse to speak of it.

I turned out the lights and sat on my bed, staring at the shadows playing on the ceiling. It was over, this single moment of weakness. I had nearly been steered off the path by an unexpected encounter that would never repeat itself. I would never see Meli or that cube again.

A KNOCK on my door woke me. I had no idea when I'd fallen asleep. The window was still open, and I was still in my underwear, never having gotten around to putting on my nightclothes.

"Yes?" I called as I hurried to close the window and pull the covers around me.

"Something just came for you," came Mother's voice. "A delivery." There was a strange giddiness in her voice. The door opened and she stuck her head in, and I could tell she was straining to keep from smiling. "You sneaky child. Why didn't you tell me?"

I looked at her blankly. "What?"

"You didn't tell me you had spent your evening charming Meli Veti."

"Meli Veti?" I echoed in confusion.

Mother opened the door the rest of the way. In her hand was a small white stone pot filled with dark brown dirt. From the dirt sprouted a single, slender stalk, topped with large, loose petals white as newly fallen snow.

"Is that . . ."

Mother placed the pot in my hands, sat down on the bed, and gave me a loud kiss on my cheek. "My clever Kova. I never should've doubted you."

I stared at the flower in disbelief. It was a rosalit, but an extremely rare, out-of-season one. It must've cost a fortune to breed in a nursery with controlled climate. A line of delicate text was written on the pot, words from an old Fiinian poem.

Serve the rare ones gifts as rare as themselves.

Mother threw an arm around my shoulders and gave me a tight squeeze. "I bet she saw good stock in you. I'm going to have Kit lay out a special breakfast for us. This is a day to be celebrated."

Then, like a whirlwind, she was gone. I sat numbly in bed, holding the inexplicable flowerpot.

CHAPTER 6

My second visit to Meli's house was vastly different from the first. Emptied of guests, its halls were practically cavernous.

Mother had spent the last bynight preparing me for this day—my first private visit with Meli. I'd stayed up late memorizing her entire family tree, the careers and hobbies of each of her extended family members, and the founding history of the manufacturing and construction empire that had led to her current position of wealth, as well as a number of hearsay articles on how she preferred to progress her courtships.

Truthfully, I had no idea if any of this would be of any help to me. My interaction with her had been limited to one brief conversation. She had suitors far more attractive, educated, and articulate. I couldn't imagine what she wanted with me.

The doorman showed me inside and left me, as if expecting that I would know where to go. I stood awkwardly, dressed in the flowy red skirt and black top Mother had carefully selected for me. Modest but flirtatious, she had claimed, then had spent an insufferable amount of time debating whether I should add a few prism stones under my eye, only to decide at the last moment that it would be best for me to remain "casual." I had no doubt that she had already planned out my outfits and scripted conversations for every future interaction with Meli.

Walking into a woman's house with a script was not exactly my idea of romance, though romance was the farthest thing from my mind as I stood on Meli's polished stone floor. The moment I set foot into the house, my gaze pulled toward the main hall and the stairs that led to the study.

"Welcome back."

I nearly jumped out of my skin. I had never even heard Galen approach. I instinctively shrank at the sight of him.

"Th-thank you," I stammered.

"Thank the lady of the house, who saw fit to invite you back." He raked his gaze over me. "Though I don't quite understand why."

That makes two of us.

"I will," I stammered. "Thank her, I mean. I will."

Galen walked a slow circle around me. "So," he said lightly. "What's so special about you? Go ahead, tell me. I can count on one hand the number of people Meli has been interested in. What exactly have you done to gain her attention?"

"N-nothing," I replied uncomfortably, wondering if it would be construed as impolite if I ran out the front door before Meli was alerted to my presence.

"Kova!"

I looked up in relief to see Meli hurrying down the stairs. She was dressed casually today in a cream-colored blouse and a long, loose skirt. Galen's expression warmed. He took her hand and kissed it as she approached.

"I was just greeting our guest," he said. "But she's in excellent company now, so I'll leave you two alone."

"Thank you, love," Meli said, beaming. But as Galen passed behind her, I saw him give me a look that could only be described as bitter before disappearing down the nearest hall.

Meli took my arm in hers. I mentally ran through several things to start our conversation—her latest success in business, the new art she had acquired while overseas, the lovely qualities of her family members, the books I'd read that just "happened" to be among her favorites. . . . But Meli beat me to it as she led me back toward the stairs.

"Come," she said. "I thought we could pick up where we left off the other night."

My heart skipped a beat at the memory of her little museum.

"Yes," I said. "Please."

I HAD EXPECTED to be shown the room on the third floor again, so to be let into Meli's private quarters was a surprise. The suite was expensively but tastefully decorated, with dark red couches covered in buttery leather and thick matching curtains. I was very careful not to touch anything as Meli led me inside and gestured for me to join her at a small shelf next to the window.

Every tier on the shelf was filled with knickknacks of various sizes and shapes, all made of the same strange, iridescent gray metal. The nearest item to me was a small knife. Or rather, half of one. One end of it was a sharp, well-defined blade, but a finger's length down the shape distorted, as if whatever force held its form together was losing its grip. Where the handle ought to be was instead a spray of tiny blocks, connected to each other only by edges and corners. Whether the tiny blocks were in the process of forming the knife or coming apart, I couldn't tell. It looked like a paused video; a moment frozen in time. The next item was a round cup. It was better formed than the knife, but I could still make out the rough edges sticking out of its surface. The next item was barely formed, resembling a cluster of tiny blocks rather than anything identifiable.

"This is my private collection," Meli said with a hint of pride. "I have shared it with a very privileged few."

My heart pounded. The sight before me was too strange to comprehend, and yet undeniably gripping.

"It's unusual to encounter anyone with true interest in rarities," Meli continued. "Especially you younger folks. But you were different. I could tell."

"Could you?" I asked in what I hoped was a coy, flirtatious tone.

"Out of all the suitors, all the guests there to land themselves a rich spouse, you alone found your way to the only room in the house that held anything of true interest. That makes you a rarity in more ways than one."

There was that word again. *Rarity*. A word that seemed to accompany me everywhere.

"Tell me," Meli said, "what do you remember of the day it arrived?"

For a moment I drew a blank.

"There was a lot of chaos," I said slowly. "People in the streets, looking at it. The military came. Then government officials. The broadcast started and for a while no one could shut it off."

"Ah yes, the broadcast." Meli nodded thoughtfully. "I have many recordings of it, in different languages depending on where it was played. Marvelous, wasn't it? I can't count the number of times I've watched it. Did you watch it often?"

"When I could. My mother said it was a distraction."

"But you still found a way?"

"I did."

"Curiosity. It's a hard thing to fight, isn't it? What else do you remember?"

"People disappeared. The old man who lived next to us lost both of his spouses."

"He must've been distraught." Meli shook her head sadly. "Many good people were lost to the orb. Do you recall the day it opened?"

I didn't.

"They say they found people inside," she went on. "Poor souls who had passed not long ago. Rumor had it they died from wounds that looked self-inflicted. Though some say that was only dramatization and that they really found nothing, and no one knew what happened to those people. The government kept it hush. Ghastly business if it was true."

I couldn't think of a response to this, but thankfully she didn't seem to expect one. She took my arm in hers again, and though her grip was warm and friendly, I couldn't help stiffening at her touch every time.

"Come," she said. "I have one more thing I think you'll find very interesting."

Meli led me through the lower floors to the back of the house, where we exited into the garden. Passing a garden full of foreign flowers and an ornate pond filled with fish I couldn't name, we arrived at a windowless structure with a thick door bearing a sophisticated lock, a building I mistook for a guest house at first. Meli unlocked it using the fingerprint scanner and keypad.

"This," she said, "is the crown jewel of my collection."

At first I saw nothing but darkness. Then the door closed behind me and bright overhead lights burst on. I blinked hard, shielding my eyes. When they adjusted, I drew a sharp breath and couldn't figure out how to let it out. Meli gave me a conspiratorial smile, pleased at my reaction.

"Amazing, isn't it?" she said. "There's nothing like it in the world."

Except there was, and I'd seen it. As I stared at the large object before me, brown with rust and completely metal, there wasn't a doubt in my mind. I took a careful step toward it and touched its surface gingerly. The moment my skin connected to it, I heard it.

A humming. A steady vibration that reached my core.

I walked around the structure, running my finger along it, listening to the hum that was almost a melody. As I reached the other side, I spotted a wide rectangular shape. I traced its outline carefully.

"It's a door," Meli said, coming up beside me. "At least, that's the theory."

"Does it open?" I asked, though my eyes were already on the tiny square at its center.

"Believe me, I've tried." Meli sighed. "It's airtight. There are a few glass panes. I assume they're windows, but they're completely black and opaque. Getting my hands on this thing was not easy, so I hesitate to use any means that might damage it." She smiled secretively. "Although I have a feeling it wouldn't budge or break so easily."

I ran my fingers over the square on the door. It was covered in protruding buttons arranged in loose concentric circles. When I pushed one, I could feel a little give.

"There might be a code," Meli said. "But there are too many combinations to go through."

"Uh-huh," I muttered, struggling to keep myself steady. "It's . . . incredible."

"Isn't it?" Meli sounded terribly pleased. She put a hand over mine, tracing gently up my arm and to my long hair. She slid her fingers through the smooth red strands and suddenly, I understood. "I've always had a penchant for rarities."

She kissed me. I stood there woodenly as her lips massaged mine. When she pulled away, my face smiled its practiced smile and I hated myself for it. She smiled back and gave me a peck on the cheek.

"You would look absolutely lovely," she said, as if describing a piece of furniture or a new trinket about to be added to her display case, "walking the halls of this house."

I LEFT Meli's house in a daze. Mother was on the edge of her seat when I returned home, wanting to know all about our encounter. I told her it had gone well, then shut myself in my room to "rest."

What happened?

I thought of the way Meli looked at me, like a knickknack to be added to her collection. The beacon. The rarity. Sitting pretty in her house amidst her shelves, another addition to her collection. I gripped a handful of the maddening, frustrating red hair. If I just yanked it out, this would all be over. I would be worthless as a suitor. Meli Veti would never let me set foot in her house again. And I would never . . .

I stopped.

The bottom drawer stared back at me, beckoning me as it had for all those seasons. I dropped to my knees and pulled it open before I could change my mind.

There it was.

My hands trembled as I retrieved the scrap of paper tucked carefully into the far corner. Even holding it, I still wondered if it was blank, that maybe the dream all those cycles ago was just a delusion, that maybe what was on this paper was nothing but a bunch of incoherent scribbles. Maybe I had never kept that scrap of paper in my memory and this was just another piece of meaningless garbage that I was making out to be more than what it was. I took a deep breath and unfolded it.

It looked just how I remembered it. No matter how hard I'd tried to convince myself I'd forgotten it, it was etched into my mind. The large oval shape was exactly the same as the metal structure in Meli's vault. The smaller dots in the middle had once looked like just a random jumble, but I now recognized them forming a very specific and meticulous pattern.

Like a code on a keypad.

CHAPTER 7

I COULDN'T QUITE SAY WHEN I STOPPED PAYING ATTENTION TO Mother's lessons and notes. Perhaps it was after my third date with Meli, when she gifted me with an expensive pin made of rare gray pearls collected from Radley Cove. Perhaps it was when she invited me to have dinner in public for the first time. Perhaps it was when she started casually putting her hand on my waist when we perused her collection, which we did on nearly every date.

Or perhaps it was when I realized that the "delusion" I'd carried with me all these cycles wasn't so delusional after all. It was a fragile thought, like a thin flake of ice poised to melt at a puff of warm breath. I carried it with me carefully, propped up on a delicate scaffold in my mind, fearful of it dropping and collapsing the bubble of hope thin as blown sugar.

Mother and Daris continued to educate me on how to properly woo Meli. The lessons became longer and more detailed after each date, and Mother was becoming increasingly restless, as if the closer I grew to Meli, the more she was unnerved by the possibility that something could go wrong. I reassured her again and again that I was following her playbook exactly, laughing at all the right times, talking about all the right things, and initiating physical contact at all the right opportunities. She had no reason not to believe me. After all, the intervals between my visits with Meli were decreasing in length and the gifts were increasing in value.

The truth was the moment I stepped into Meli's house, all of her advice was forgotten. I spent nearly every visit in Meli's study. Occasionally she might have a new item, and we poured over these together, guessing their purpose and examining every detail. She caressed my hair in a manner all too similar to Mother, and I couldn't tell whether she enjoyed discussing her treasures with me or if she just liked having a preview of what it was like to have me among her collectibles.

But despite my increased discomfort, I found myself smiling and flirting, unable to resist any chance to be near the artifacts and to hear what Meli knew about the orb. Every chance I had, I asked to see the metal structure. Meli referred to it as "the egg," which I supposed was as accurate a description as any. We whiled away many afternoons and evenings in the stuffy vault, trading theories about the thing, examining its surface a hair's length at a time. I would've hardly noticed the days passing if not for Mother's obsessive time keeping, counting how many days I'd been able to keep Meli interested. The seasons turned warmer and were on their way to becoming cold again when Meli brought up marriage.

I didn't say no.

FIINA HAD AN OLD SAYING. It went something along the lines of *mirrors lie, but it is a lie we love, because we can put on a face for mirrors, but not ourselves.* As a child, I had never quite understood it. But now, staring at myself in the mirror, I couldn't stop thinking about it. With my hair wound into tight curls and tied back with cream-colored ribbons, my blemishes and moles covered with powder, and the rest of me draped in wedding greens, I barely recognized the reflection in the mirror. It felt like a lie and looked like one as well.

Mother smiled ear to ear for days. Everything was finally going according to plan. I was going to marry a wealthy spouse who might someday leave me a sizable fortune that I could use later in life to head up my own household. My relatives and offspring could live in luxury. At last, I was fulfilling my destiny of prosperity and fortune.

I ran my fingers over the meticulous curls in my hair. Meli was excited to wed me. She was eager to have me in her house.

And in her collection.

Beauticians and hairdressers came and went. Almost all of them told me to stop biting myself as they went to work transforming me into Meli's perfect bride. I tried my best, but the moment they turned their backs, I found myself gnawing on the joints of my fingers again. My right leg couldn't stop bouncing up and down and I felt like I was standing on a very tall ledge, looking down at the dizzying drop below as I prepared to plunge to my death.

Aren't you tired of this?

I drew a deep breath.

This was the path laid out for me by Mother. This was where I was meant to be. I knew nothing else, and I was not brave enough to depart from it. I was a coward, and I was afraid. Now I was about to embark on a new path sure to be laid out for me by my wife, one that revolved around being displayed and shown off as the newest prized addition to her collection.

A rarity, like everything else on her shelf.

THE DAY of my wedding was a mirage, a film clip of someone else's life. Faces disappeared and reappeared in front of me—well-wishers, gift bearers, and favor seekers. The heavy beats of wedding drums echoed in my ears. I'd eaten, though I couldn't remember the taste. I'd danced, though I couldn't remember how. I'd smiled and laughed when Mother prompted me to. Without her, I would've drifted through the day like a dead-eyed fish.

Now, with the ceremony done, I stared wide eyed into the darkness. The night was silent save for Meli's rhythmic breathing next to me.

Even here in my wedding bed, my mother was ever present. She'd lectured me on all the ways to pleasure my mate with calculated precision. I wasn't exactly a newcomer to the tricks of the bedroom. A pretty girl with warm lips and a rebellious streak from Daris's etiquette class had initiated me to the ways of physical pleasure, and a boy from the docks needing a place to sleep had kept me warm on a handful of cold nights. Not long after, I had heard him bragging to his cohorts about bedding a beacon and had never allowed him into my bed again. But whatever I had learned from those encounters plus Mother's teaching must've worked, because Meli certainly seemed both pleased and pleasured. I lay listening to her breathe.

Was I going to spend every night from now on methodically pleasuring a woman who saw me as a collectible?

I sat up, careful not to disturb Meli. She was a skillful lover. But every time she touched me, I recalled the way she caressed the objects in her study. In the morning, when we opened our eyes and saw each other, we would be officially cemented in marriage.

I got out of bed as quietly as I could manage and paced the length of Meli's luxurious bedroom barefoot.

Our bedroom. It was our bedroom now. Hers and mine. I would come back to this bed tomorrow. And the day after. And the day after that. This was my home now.

Meli sighed and turned her back to me, deep in sleep. I stared at her as if seeing her for the very first time.

My wife.

My *life*.

I couldn't catch my breath. I needed air. Wearing only my nightgown and house slippers, I snuck out of the bedroom, leaving the door unlatched behind me to avoid the noise it might make.

The house was completely dark save for the light of the garden lamps seeping through the side windows. I found my way downstairs, turned down the first hall, went two rooms further, crossed into a different wing, and quickly found the door I was looking for. I grasped the doorknob, bracing myself for the creaking noise it might make. Thankfully it turned smoothly, and I stepped out into the side courtyard.

The damp salty air tickled my face. I inhaled deeply, let it out, and pictured myself standing out here every night after Meli fell asleep, drinking in the scent of the sea.

For the rest of my life, or at least hers.

The vault loomed in the darkness. Despite the silent night, I could somehow hear the hum of the thing inside. Almost like a melody, singing to me.

I went to it.

The door was locked, but the scanner had been coded to recognize my fingerprint. Meli had given me free rein to her entire collection as a marriage gift. The bright lights overhead made me squint, and I quickly closed the door behind me in case anyone in the house happened to peek out of their window, though I wasn't sure what I was trying to hide.

The metal egg sat with its unspoken secrets. I circled it. Once. Twice. On the third time around, I stopped at the hatch, in front of the keypad.

My fingers slid over the buttons. I'd felt them countless times and memorized every bump and imperfection on their surface. When Meli wasn't looking, I'd mimed my fingers over them as well, pretending to enter a certain pattern that had committed itself to memory despite Mother's and Daris's best efforts. But never once had I dared to push those buttons down.

I touched those buttons again. I knew exactly what the pattern was.

I pressed them, a little harder this time.

If I entered that pattern, pushed those little buttons all the way down, then what?

I feared discovering the answer. I was scared that it would reveal something to me, but more scared that it wouldn't. At least when I didn't know, I still had blind hope on my side.

I touched the buttons, pushing a little harder. I could still walk away and allow myself to retain a shred of hope. Not knowing was better than being proven a fool. Because if it gave me nothing, then . . .

Then I would have to go back to bed, wake up in the morning, and start the first day of the rest of my life. Somehow, that thought instilled more fear in me than any other possibility.

I gambled everything.

My entire life, tied to this house, to one woman, so I could pursue a grief-driven hallucination from my childhood.

I pushed the first button down before I could change my mind. Then the next, then the next, until the buttons on the square panel were pushed in the exact same formation as the message from the dream I'd held on to for the last ten cycles. As the last one went down, my heart jerked upward like a restless mountain mouse. I stepped back.

Nothing happened.

Despair descended over me, and my knees nearly gave out. I slumped against the metal door. The walls pushed in at me and the ground pulled me down, as if tying me to this life I'd agreed to.

Nothing. It was all for nothing.

I slammed a fist against the door. It opened with a hiss.

I jumped. The hatch had moved inward a finger's length. I stared at it, terrified that it was an illusion created by my own hysterical mind. It wasn't. I put a hand on it and pushed it to one side. It slid open with surprising ease. Swallowing hard, I stepped inside.

The interior was cold, narrow, and made entirely of metal. The air was stale but smelled strangely clean, as if it had been freshly sterilized. I shivered and rubbed my bare arms, wishing I'd put on something warmer. The majority of the space was partitioned into smaller rooms and corridors. A ladder led up to a crawl space, and another led down to a storage compartment. I walked through the space carefully, apprehensive that I might run into its past occupants—or what was left of them, though excitement was welling up inside me with every move I made.

I passed a small common room with a table and a small bench. A tight space that might be a washroom followed. Beyond that, the hallway opened up to a wide, circular area. Benches lined the walls and a number of rectangular screens were mounted over them. They looked like the pixel screens common to Fiina, but thinner, flatter, and with no dials or buttons.

At the other end of the hall was a sizable living space. Like the rest of the place, it was sparsely furnished, with a writing surface, two small screens mounted on the wall, and a bed just wide enough for two average Fiinians. A metal cabinet was mounted near the door. I nudged it open and found a set of loose, thin clothing that might be some sort of uniform, as well as what looked like a loose, dark blue top. A colorful patchwork blanket was rolled up and put away toward the bottom.

I have to show you.

I examined every detail in the enclosed space, seeking something that stood out or caught my attention. But I found nothing. As the initial fascination began to wear off, I felt disappointment set in.

Was this what I had been waiting for? It looked like an abandoned hut. If it had ever housed anything or anyone alive and interesting, they were long gone.

Dejected, I returned to the circular space lined with benches. In the center of the room was a strange object—a round cylinder, about as high as my belly. As I drew closer, I saw that it had no buttons, dials, or gears. Its top surface appeared to be covered in a green, gel-like substance.

You put your hand in and they move.

I hadn't allowed myself to remember that voice in a very long time. I raised one hand, fingers splayed, and held it over the green gel. As I did, I heard the humming, the same one I had heard the day Meli first showed this thing to me. The same humming I had noticed—now that I thought about it—when the door opened.

I hesitated. What if the green gel was toxic? What if it melted the skin off my fingers? I stood there, hand held barely a hair's length over the console. I wasn't certain I was brave enough to test my luck. And yet, having found nothing else of interest in the egg, I couldn't deny that something told me this was my last shot at—

At what?

I didn't know. But I had to find out.

I gritted my teeth and plunged in. The gel enveloped my skin instantly and the screens around me blinked to life. I watched, alarmed, as they lit up one by one, bathing me in an eerie blue-green glow.

A voice startled me. It spoke so suddenly that I jerked my hand out of the green gel and spun around, expecting to find some strange alien creature behind me. But there was no one. The voice spoke again, a language I could not understand.

"What?" I stammered.

"Calibrating," it said in East Fiinian dialect, emitting from every surface around me. It was a female voice, but with an odd mechanical quality. I turned and turned and couldn't find the source. **"Lan. Language. Set."** A pause. **"Hello."**

"H-hello," I said.

"Wel. Come."

I took a step backward toward the door.

"Running d-diagnostic. Capsule functioning at f-fifty percent capacity."

"Who are you?" I asked, though no answers came. I glanced behind me, half expecting someone to appear, but the computerized voice simply went about its business.

"Loading d-destination."

"Do you know Rosi?"

No answer. I took another step toward the door when it slammed shut with a thunderous *bang.* I jumped in surprise. Suddenly, none of this felt like a good idea.

"Did you close the door?" I asked, fear welling up inside my chest.

"Sealing chamber."

I rushed down the hallway and pushed the door, then hammered on it with both fists. It didn't budge.

"You. R-return?"

"Open the door!" I shouted. "Open it!"

"Home?"

"Yes!" I said. "Home! I want to go home!"

"Return p-path. On," the voice said. **"Prepare for t-ke off."**

"Prepare for what?" I cried. "Wait!" I rushed back to the control console, but nothing changed no matter how much I stuck my hand into the green goo or wiggled my fingers. Confusion, terror, and regret, fought for space inside my chest. A large rectangular area on the far wall, initially completely opaque, began to fade to transparency. "Hold on!"

"Tak-taking off."

A thunderous crash outside. Debris clattered against the outside walls. Suddenly, I saw Radley from above. I pressed myself against the broad window. Below me, Meli's estate grew smaller and smaller. Radley Cove, with the black orb in its center, stared back at me like an enormous eye. The town looked increasingly like a toy model as we gained altitude. Then it disappeared beneath thick layers of clouds.

I fell heavily to the cold metal floor, still dressed in my night slip and house shoes.

"Hi," the voice said cheerily. **"Wel. Come. Aboard. I am. Ee. Vee."**

CHAPTER 8

I SCREAMED.

I cried. I hammered on the door and clawed at it until my hands were bruised and bleeding. I shrieked at the faceless entity called E-V to shut up as she attempted to engage me with pleasantries. She was certainly persistent. Even as I sat on the floor, hyperventilating with angry tears streaming down my face, she continued to attempt chitchat with her short, broken sentences.

I sobbed, my body jerking uncontrollably. Just a few minutes ago I had stepped into this mysterious chamber, thinking I was one step closer to Rosi. Now I was hurtling toward the sky as the metal egg—the *capsule*, as E-V called it—ascended further and further. I wished I had stayed in bed. I wished I hadn't let curiosity get the better of me. I wished more than anything that I'd left the strange green stuff be.

Watch. Follow. Listen.

Beauty. Poise. Efficiency.

I pushed the mantras away angrily, even though they tried to invade my mind over and over. There was no one here to impress, no one to praise me for how I spoke and acted. I was completely and utterly alone.

We left Fiina's atmosphere. I watched the land below me

disappear; then the curve of the horizon came into view, then the entire planet. It was like a movie, one of the many geographical films my tutors had showed me as part of my lessons. I slapped and pinched myself, trying to wake up from this nightmare. I paced the narrow hall, telling myself I was going to open my eyes at any second to find myself back in Meli's bed, or back in bed at home, or back in time, twelve cycles old, and the black orb had been a dream all along.

None of those things happened. I closed my eyes, then opened them to find nothing changed.

Defeated, I slumped heavily onto a bench near the large window on the capsule's front. Fiina grew smaller and smaller in the distance. I was among the stars in nothing but my slip.

Had Meli discovered her collapsed vault yet? This was going to be hard to explain when I returned.

IF I returned.

The thought drove new fear into my heart. I hugged myself so tightly my hands began to grow numb. I had no idea where this thing was going, or how long it was going to take. No one could come after me. There was no food or water that I could see, and ever since leaving the atmosphere, the interior had become downright frigid.

"Col-?"

I lifted my head at E-V's voice.

"Cold?" she repeated.

"Yes," I snapped. "I'm cold. I don't have any clothes."

"Clothes," she said. **"Locker. You. Wear."**

Clothes. I remembered the metal cabinet. Seeing no other options, I pushed myself off the bench, went to the bedroom, and riffled through it. The gray uniform was flimsy and light to the touch. I couldn't imagine it would provide much warmth, but it was better than hurtling through space in a nightgown. I undressed and reluctantly pulled the thin, loose material over myself.

The moment I straightened, I felt a tiny, brief sting all over my body as the fabric tightened automatically to fit my torso and limbs. It pushed my back straight and my shoulders back, supporting my every bone and joint. The bone-chilling cold of the capsule suddenly became a pleasant coolness.

"Better?" E-V asked. She sounded pleased with herself.

"Yeah," I said, slowly turning my arms as I studied the material in wonder. "Better."

"Shoes. Top."

I reached over the top tier of the cabinet, which I had neglected to examine before, and came away with a pair of strange-looking, thick black socks, or so I thought. But after the uniform, I had a feeling I shouldn't underestimate them. I took off my house slippers, put one of my feet in, and immediately felt the same sensation—a pinprick that came as quickly as it went—then the "sock" stiffened and took the shape of a short boot that reached halfway up my calves. I put the other one on and it did the same. Standing, I tried walking around and found my ankles completely supported and the soles heavy and comfortable. I slipped the blue top over my torso and took the patchwork blanket as well.

By the time I returned to the control room, Fiina was little more than a faint green dot in the distance. I stood in front of the window and watched it disappear.

It was beautiful.

The realization surprised me. The sight of a planet disappearing among a vast blanket of sparkling stars was something I'd never imagined. Had Uttam felt this way when he had boarded that fishing boat, inhaled lungfuls of salty air, and looked out to the distant horizon? I touched the cold glass. On the other side of it was endless space.

A strange sensation washed over me, as if I was letting out a breath I'd been holding for most of my life. My shoulders lowered as if they'd been held up by strings that were suddenly cut.

Rosi.

Her name was Rosi.

I had gone so long without being allowed to think about her, or even say her name. But there was no one here. No one to tell me what to do or stay on a path. No one to tell me not to miss or cry over her. My world had felt so small in the last ten cycles without her by my side, eager to show me every detail of the world.

Her name is E-V.

It wasn't a delusion. I had been right all along even though the whole world—along with myself—had tried to convince me I wasn't. It *was* a message. This thing—the capsule, as E-V called it—had always been here, waiting for *me*.

I wrapped the blanket around myself and sat in front of the window, leaning my forehead against the window separating me and the stars. My hair fell to one side, uncovering the bald spot I'd spent countless hours hiding growing up. No one was going to comment on it now. It was not a scar to hide. It was my badge of honor.

For the first time in a long time, despite being surrounded by nothing but emptiness and stars, and drawing farther and farther from everything I ever knew, the fear that gnawed at me subsided.

I'm going to see it, Rosi. Whatever you wanted to show me, I'm finally going to see it.

A JOLT WOKE ME. My back and neck ached from lying on the hard bench. Sitting up groggily, I saw nothing but blackness out the wide front window. The stars and planets had vanished. Not a single light remained to be seen.

"E-V?" I called. *"E-V!"*

No answer. I pushed the blanket off my body and stood, slowly turning my sore neck just as the door to the capsule opened with a soft hiss. My entire body tensed. A slew of horrible images invaded my mind. I pictured myself strung up by a race of strange-looking aliens and put on display as a slave, being examined and fondled by prospective buyers from a slew of oddly colored planets. I held my breath and waited.

Nothing.

I took a cautious step toward the door and waited again. No alien creature entered. In fact, there was not a single sound outside the door. Cautiously, I grabbed the door and slid it aside.

A whoosh of air rushed in. Just outside was a platform, not much wider than I was tall. I stepped onto it gingerly. The air was breathable, a fact I was grateful for as I realized I'd stepped out of the protective walls of the craft without checking if I was about to be sucked into the vacuum of space. All around me was silent darkness save for a single open door from which white light was pouring through. Between it and me were a series of blocky platforms, seemingly supported by nothing. Upon closer examination, I saw they were made of the same familiar gray metal as the baubles in Meli's collection. And like her collection, they were frozen in a strange state of decay, crumbling into smaller and smaller cubes that stayed floating in the air, barely connected at the corners.

"E-V?"

Still nothing. I bit my lip. Nowhere to go but forward. I touched my foot to the first platform. It held firm. I stepped onto it, fearing it might drop into oblivion and my journey would end right there. But it didn't. I stepped onto the next one, keeping my eyes on the light ahead of me and trying hard not to think about the bottomless black beneath me until I finally stepped through the door.

The sight that greeted me was breathtaking. I was standing on a long, suspended walkway. Looking up, I saw many others just like it, crisscrossing back and forth like a web. I looked down and saw the same. The distances to the floor and ceiling were so great that I could not find either. I'd never seen anything like this on Fiina, and I could not imagine the skill and technology that had gone into creating a structure so incredibly vast.

As I ventured farther inside, I saw that whatever this place was, it had been left neglected for a long time. Many walkways were broken. Debris of metal and stone lay in piles. Parts of it had gone dark, though I couldn't find a single light source to begin with. The light inside appeared to simply exist, like the air. The walkways all led to a central structure, but I couldn't tell what it used to be. At the moment, it was little more than a fallen jumble of wires, metal, and rock.

The air in the center was different, denser. Or was it my imagination? I couldn't quite tell. Though there was nothing there to see, I couldn't shake the feeling that it had once been something very different. Very significant. Now fallen to disuse.

Was this what Rosi wanted to show me?

A shape darted across my line of sight before I could formulate an answer. I flinched. It landed right in front of me, square in the center of the walkway.

Piercing blue eyes staring into mine. Its body was small and slender, like an emaciated child, and entirely white save for a large, uneven patch of black on its chest. Its features, aside from its eyes, were barely present, mere indents on its smooth face, and it was missing one hand. Taken all together, it resembled a broken mannequin. Spotting me, it arched its back—an alarmed pose, and moved on all three of its remaining limbs backwards, away from me.

Before I could react, another sound came from above—a heavy thud like something landing. The creature immediately darted behind the nearest pile of debris and hid. I scrambled to do the same. The thud came again. Something was moving overhead and drawing closer. Blood pounded in my ears. I had forgotten for a moment that I was on an alien world, ignorant and defenseless with no way to protect myself. I cowered in my hiding place, afraid to move even a finger. The thudding grew louder. Then closer. Then stopped.

A figure dropped heavily onto the walkway. From where I was, I couldn't tell if it was a person or a machine, but their black armor and heavy footsteps sent shivers down my spine. If they had a face, it was hidden behind a black, featureless mask. Their back was to me as they looked around slowly. In one of their hands was a blade shaped in a crescent curve that ended in a sharp tip, almost like an animal claw. In the other hand was something thin and white, and I suppressed a gag as I realized it was the remainder of the creature's severed arm. The figure in black paced the walkway slowly, spinning the curved blade around their fingers. After a moment, they threw the dead limb over the edge and began to methodically search the piles of debris.

I didn't dare move a hair, or breathe. From where I hid behind a half-rotten metal panel, I could see the wounded creature cowering, just out of sight of the hunter in black. It curled up as small as possible and stayed still. The hunter kicked a pile of rubble, and I heard metal and stone tumble over the side of the walkway, echoing against the surfaces beneath. They moved onto the next pile, eliminating every possible hiding place. It was only a matter of time before they found the creature.

Or me.

I trembled and the air hummed.

Another pile of rubble went over the edge. The sound of heavy footsteps approaching sent fear coursing through my body.

The humming grew louder.

The creature leapt from its hiding spot onto the hunter's back. I heard the ensuing struggle and saw a tumble of metal and debris fall over the side of the walkway. The hunter shouted in a language I couldn't understand, followed quickly by the creature's shriek. I didn't dare move from my crouch behind the metal panel, the only thing that separated me from the altercation.

Something hit the ground hard. The walkway shook. I closed my eyes and tried to find a mantra to calm myself, but nothing worked. Everything I'd been taught my entire life suddenly felt like complete and utter drivel.

The panel rattled loudly, followed by a pained whimper. I saw movement through a small crack. The white creature was on the other side. It slid off, tried to stand, and failed. The black hunter was approaching, weapon drawn.

The humming vibrated through me, though I wasn't sure if the sensation was manifested from my own terror. I pictured that curved blade slicing through my body. Fear drowned me like water, forcing its way inside me until I couldn't draw another breath.

I'm going to die.

Like air from a popped balloon, it burst from me. The hard surfaces around me rippled. I heard the black hunter utter a surprised grunt. Their footsteps stumbled and then suddenly fell quiet.

I stood.

The silence around me was deafening. The hunter was nowhere to be seen. Had the strange force sent them over the edge? I hurried out of my hiding place and dashed down the walkway. A flurry of movement and white darted in and out of the corner of my eye.

I ran into the dark bay, barely slowing my steps and nearly falling into the abyss in my rush. I threw myself inside the capsule, slammed the door behind me, and dashed to the console.

"Take off!" I shouted, thrusting my hand into the green gel.

No response.

"Take off!" I cried desperately. "E-V! Take off!"

A whirring sound in the walls, but once again no response. The hairs on my neck stood up. Any moment now, I was certain, I would hear fists pounding on the door, and my strange journey would end in this dark room, trapped in this metal coffin.

"Fly!" I screamed, thinking of any word that could shake E-V into action. "Online! Talk! Move! Connect!"

"E-V?"

A new voice. One of the screens flickered and a face appeared, grainy and unclear. It appeared to be Fiinian in shape—a woman? As I tried to decide how to react, she spoke again.

"I-I don't understand," I stammered. "I don't understand you."

She didn't respond. The lower half of her face was covered so that I couldn't make out her expression. I waved my hand in front of the screen, uncertain if she could see me at all.

"Help me!" I shouted. "Please!"

Still, she said nothing. I was certain all was lost when she raised her voice and issued a loud command.

The capsule shuddered, shook, and began to move. I let out a breath of relief as it rose and began to drift forward. As it veered to the right, I saw a square opening not far in the distance, with the light of a million stars beyond it.

"Thank you," I said, leaning heavily against the console. "Thank you."

But she was already gone. Soon the darkness was behind us. The capsule veered again, finding its direction, and the perspective of the front window shifted. I gaped.

It looked just like the one on Fiina, but much larger, at least three times as large across.

And it was silver.

The square hatch where we exited slowly closed. I watched it, mesmerized, as the capsule eased its way back into the depths of space.

CHAPTER 9

WHEN THE SILVER ORB DISAPPEARED FROM SIGHT, I FINALLY allowed my trembling legs to buckle. On the cold floor, I struggled to decide whether to laugh or cry and settled for a short, sad chuckle.

But my relief didn't last long.

The shuffling in the hall was easy to dismiss as someone moving about until I remembered I should be alone. My breath caught in my throat as a pair of blue eyes peered around the corner. I scrambled to my feet and instinctively looked around for something to protect myself with, but the only thing nearby was the blanket I had retrieved from the bedroom cabinet. I didn't know what good it would do, but I grabbed it anyway.

It cautiously set foot into the control room, crawling like an animal and hobbling on its remaining arm. I moved away from it, keeping the control console between us. Its skin was flawlessly white, like a polished vase. Thin, shallow grooves met at perpendicular angles all over its body like a roadmap. The black patch on its chest had an oily appearance, glistening in the light as it moved. Though it was vaguely Fiinian shaped, its torso was disproportionately thin and its legs too long. The one remaining hand had three fingers that splayed wide and long when it walked, then retracted into short nubs when lifted. The arm severed by the hunter leaked a transparent fluid, dripping onto the floor in a slow trickle.

"H-hello?" I said shakily.

It tilted its head, responding to my voice. Then, with some struggle, it shifted into a bipedal stance, balancing carefully on its legs. It took a few steps toward me, but I moved again, shifting in a semicircle until the hallway was to my back, keeping the creature across the room. Silhouetted against the dark of space outside the window, its stark whiteness was eerie and unsettling.

It tilted its head again. To the left, then to the right. Its body wobbled, parts of its torso and limbs breaking, then reforming in a manner that reminded me of the flickers on Rosi's broken pixel screen. As it shuffled along, little ripples of white trailed behind it, wavering in the air, then pulling back into its body. Something about its movement reminded me of the relics on Meli's shelf and the microscopic cubes that held them together. Blue eyes blinked independently of each other. I took a step back. My foot bumped against the wall. The thing stopped shifting at the sound, eyes fixed on me.

It let out a sharp shriek and lunged at me. I screamed and ran. Slippery fingers grabbed at my ankle. I spun around and without thinking whipped the blanket in my hand at it. It pulled back and I took the chance to run inside the bedroom and slam the door shut.

It thumped against the door. I pressed my entire weight against it on the other side. Thankfully there was a lock. I slid it shut but kept my weight against the door's surface, fearing the thing could break down the only barrier between us if I did.

The thumping subsided. A scraping came from below and I looked down just in time to see thin white tentacles feeling their way inside from the tiny gap under the door. I let out a shriek and jumped away. They extended inside toward me, examining the surfaces they encountered along the way. I pushed myself against the farthest corner I could manage, holding my breath, terrified they could somehow sense me. Thankfully, they appeared to meet their limit halfway across the room and extended no farther. After what felt like an eternity, they retracted underneath the door.

I SAT in the corner of the bedroom, the blanket wrapped tightly around me. I had no idea how much time had passed since I had last moved.

The thing passed in front of the door again. Left to right. Right to left. I could see its shadow move by the shifting light seeping in under the door. Once in a while it tried to poke its way inside, and every time it did, I tensed in fear that it would finally reach me. It never did.

I dozed off sitting up, then woke up to the sound of slithering tentacles, just in time to see them retreat.

When had I last eaten? It would've been my wedding banquet. At the time I'd nibbled the food in front of me dutifully while maintaining my practiced smile. Though there had been many of my favorite dishes and cakes, I couldn't remember tasting any of them. Now, I would give anything to have a glass of fruit wine and a plate of cream cakes topped with sour berries. My mouth was dry as sand and my stomach was trying to eat itself.

The white thing outside moved past the door. Hunger, thirst, and fear wrestled each other inside me.

It paused momentarily, then moved on. I heard it clatter around the capsule, then return to the door again. I wet my lips, or tried to with my dry tongue, and stood.

I had no idea if there was food or water anywhere else in the capsule, but there was certainly none in this room. If I was going to have a chance against that thing, I had to do it before I completely ran out of energy. I looked around the room for anything that might help, then double-checked the locker just in case. Unfortunately there wasn't much to be found. I reached up and half-heartedly poked around the top surface of the locker.

Something struck my finger and clattered to the ground. It was a flat, round disc about the size and thickness of my palm. It flickered on as it struck the floor and a holographic image sprang to life. A woman smiled at me. She looked to be roughly my age or a little older, and though she was close enough to Fiinian in appearance, I could tell she was of another world. Her skin was a tan color unnatural to Fiina natives, and her hair, smooth and straight and cut into uneven layers, was so dark it was nearly black. I had never seen anyone without the natural white—or rare red—hair all Fiinians possessed. As I studied this woman, she tilted her head slightly, as if posing. The image was shown from the waist up, her arms folded as if leaning on a table. She winked, chuckled, and looked away, then flickered back to her original pose—an endless video loop.

I picked up the black disc and examined it. Aside from a button in the middle that replayed the hologram, it appeared utterly useless. Sighing, I tucked it into the pocket of the gray uniform.

There was nothing else of interest in the room. I held the blanket in my hands. It wasn't much to work with, but it would have to do. Fortunately, the creature was smaller than me. If I could catch it in the blanket, I reasoned, maybe I could throw it into the room and lock it in, then find some way to barricade the door. I had no idea if the door could be locked from the outside, but I would have to figure it out as I went. And if it didn't work . . .

Well, at least I wouldn't have to waste time starving to death.

I held the blanket tightly, gritted my teeth, and flung the door open.

It came at me, but I was ready. I held up the blanket between us and it dove headfirst into it. I wrapped both arms around it, fighting to get ahold of it as it struggled furiously. I flung it as far as I could manage into the room and threw myself through the door. For a single victorious moment, it seemed like I had won.

As soon as I turned to close the door, it barreled into me full force. My back struck the wall. My feet tangled. I could see nothing but a flurry of white. I reached out for support and found nothing but air. My body fell heavily to the floor. I turned onto my back and kicked at the creature relentlessly clawing at me. It was much stronger than it looked. I scooted myself into the nearest open space—the tiny common room—and tried to find a place to hide, or at least something to put between us. But the white creature pounced on me and pushed me down onto the ground.

The entirety of its weight was on my chest. I could barely breathe, much less struggle. Its body was still shifting and pixelating in an unsettling manner. Blue eyes disappeared and reappeared, staring at my face with intense concentration. It drew close, until those eerie eyes were less than a finger's length from my own. I closed my eyes and hoped death would be swift and painless.

Something touched my forehead.

I didn't dare look. It was smooth and surprisingly warm. The weight holding down my body shifted. The pressure on my chest eased as well.

I opened one eye, then the other.

A child looked back at me.

I blinked. They straightened and climbed off me. Slowly, nervously, I sat up.

Aside from the milky white skin covered in grooves and unnatural blue eyes, they looked exactly like a prepubescent Fiinian child. White hair cut in a round bob framed their round face. Slender arms ended in long, thin fingers. One of their legs ended just above the knee. No matter how they changed their body, they seemed unable to compensate for the missing limb.

Settled into this form, their aggression appeared to have disappeared as well. We regarded each other for a long time.

"Hello," I ventured.

They blinked.

"Hello?" I said again.

They tilted their head, as if trying to parse the word.

I lifted one hand and put it on my chest.

"Kova," I said, nodding. "I'm Kova."

They mimicked my motion, then nodded as well.

"Do you understand me?"

They opened their mouth, but nothing came out. I watched them focus and struggle. The expression of concentration on their face was so soft and innocent that I almost forgot they had been attacking me just a moment ago.

"Ko. Va." I said slowly.

They mouthed the sounds but did not speak.

"I'm from Fiina," I said, patting my chest and enunciating as clearly as I could. "Fii. Na."

They looked at me.

"Na," they said with a voice soft as baby bird's. "Fii. Na."

I couldn't help smiling, and they smiled back, pleased at their own effort.

"Where are you from?" I ventured, though I wasn't sure they were able to answer. "Where's your home?"

"Ho—" they began, then frowned, and tried again. "Hom. Om." They patted their own chest in the same manner as me, where the black patch had formed into a perfect circle. "Om."

OM KNEW MORE about the capsule than I did.

Despite having boarded the vessel just a day ago, they seemed to know exactly what they were looking for. After we'd adjusted to each other's presence, they rose with some difficulty to stand on their one remaining leg and hobbled toward the control room, gesturing for me to follow. Once there, I saw the source of the clattering sounds I'd heard from the bedroom. A box of what looked like first aid items had been pulled from a hidden compartment beneath one of the benches and pried open clumsily. Strips of what appeared to be bandages had been strewn everywhere. Om half sat, half fell onto the floor next to the open box and clumsily tried to bandage their leg. It was obvious that they'd attempted this more than once already without much success. I watched them attempt to wrap the wound again with all the concentration of a child trying to create their latest masterpiece with blunt pieces of chalk.

"Here," I said. "Let me."

Om held out the remaining bandage. I took it, sat them on the nearest bench, and wrapped the wound snugly. They mimed my motions, thin fingers mimicking my every move. When it was done, they folded their arms across themselves and shivered.

"Are you cold?"

They moved their mouth with some effort. "C-. Old."

I pulled the blue top off my torso and slid it over their head. It hung to just below their narrow hips. Om looked down at it, then looked up at me and smiled.

I sat down next to them. They regarded me cautiously for a moment, then leaned against my arm and let out a soft sigh, as if relieved. Gently, I reached out and brushed away strands of white hair from their blue eyes.

What an ordeal it must've been, to be so small and vulnerable, running for their life. My chest tightened at the thought of this little child, wounded and afraid, desperately trying to communicate and seek help from the only person to cross their path.

My stomach growled loudly. Om gave me a curious look.

"Sorry," I said. "Not much to eat here. I guess we'll be starving together."

Om thought about this.

"Eat," they said.

I mimed bringing my hand to my mouth. "Eat," I said. "Food. Hungry. Are you hungry?"

They nodded. "Eat," they repeated, and hobbled to stand.

I followed them. Much like the med kit, Om knew exactly where they were going. They led me to the common room and gestured at a rectangular cabinet that sat on a low counter.

"Eat," they said, pointing at it.

"There's nothing in there," I said, opening the door to show them it was empty inside. "See?"

Om gaped at me. "Eat," they said again, and pushed the cabinet door closed. They rooted around its sides, peering at each surface until they found a hole that I'd overlooked. It was just about three fingers wide. Looking closely, I saw that it appeared to be filled with the same green substance as the control console.

Om held out one finger and inserted it into the green goop. For a few long moments nothing happened. Then they pulled their finger out and looked at me.

"Eat," they said again, and opened the cabinet door.

A pile of what looked like transparent gelatin sat in the middle of the cabinet. I leaned in and tried to figure out where it came from but couldn't find anything that could've produced it. Om reached inside, grabbed a handful of the slippery jelly, and held it out to me. It was colorless and wiggled like a half-dead sea creature. Bits and pieces dribbled between their fingers. To say it looked unappetizing would be an extreme understatement.

Om pointed to the jiggly mass with their other hand, then mimed putting it to their mouth. "Eat."

"Eat," I repeated doubtfully. "Are you sure?"

Om looked at me, then at the mass in their hand. They pushed it toward me. When I didn't take it, they opened their mouth and pushed the jelly inside, shoving every last bit between their lips and licking off their fingers. They chewed a few times, swallowed, then grabbed the rest of the gelatin and ate that as well.

"Eat," they said, sounding almost happy. Seeing my hesitation, they reached out, grabbed my hand, and pushed it toward the hole in the cabinet. My fingertip touched the green goop inside.

A ripple of strange sensations coursed through my body and suddenly my mouth was filled with the taste of sour berries. Berries picked fresh from the hills, covered in silky cream, sitting atop warm cakes. The subtle sweetness and sharp sour juices burst on my tongue and then went away just as quickly. My teeth could almost feel the spongy texture of the cakes. It all came and went in a blink's time and before I could hold on to it, it was gone. I pulled my finger out of the hole, disoriented.

Om opened the cabinet. Inside was another pile of gelatin, just like the first batch but reddish in color—the color of wild sour berries. I reached out and pinched a small chunk between my fingers. It was unpleasant to look at and even worse to touch.

And yet, I could smell the berries.

I brought it to my nose and sniffed. It was all there. The sour berries. The fresh cream. The sweet cake. In that one whiff, my body ached for it. I pushed the gelatin into my mouth.

Perhaps it was my extreme hunger, or maybe it was the excitement of eating something so new and foreign, but the taste of the substance was incredible. While the flavors themselves were faint, the gelatin was much denser than it looked, and its texture varied despite its appearance. I could taste the berries, cream, and cake in the same bite, even at times sensing my teeth piercing the skin of a berry. Despite being bland, it was filling and satisfying, and melted in my mouth to quench my thirst as well. I grabbed another handful and devoured it, my body craving it after being without sustenance for so long. Om watched me with a pleased look on their face.

We spent a long time in the common room, taking turns making food with the strange machine. We ate with our hands, gigging at each other as the jelly slipped and slid between our fingers.

After we ate our fill, Om hobbled to the bedroom, where they lay down on the bed and looked up at me with tired, wide blue eyes. I fetched the quilted blanket and draped it over the both of us. Om huddled against me, a welcome warmth in the cold darkness of space.

CHAPTER 10

"You're far from home, aren't you?"

Om looked up at me, then frowned in an almost adorable expression of concentration. "Far," they said. "Far. From home. Om."

I chuckled and turned back to the control console. Om stuck close, carefully hopping on their one good leg, and peered at the green goop.

With a lot of time to kill and not a lot to do, I did my best to familiarize myself with the features of the capsule. E-V's helpfulness was limited. Half the time she didn't respond when I called, and when she did, she lost words often and sometimes used words in languages that I couldn't understand. Om appeared familiar with the basic survival features of the capsule, but the central console did not recognize them as a viable pilot—when their hand went in, no responses came. In the end, it was up to me to explore on my own.

After some trial and error, I was able to get E-V to display a clock that counted Fiinian time on one of the display screens. But I had little faith in its accuracy, as it randomly stopped and sped up. I had made my way up the ladder to the crawl space where there was room to sit up but not quite enough to stand. There was a window big enough to make the space feel less suffocating and a portable pixel screen that no longer worked. I imagined being a traveler among the stars who slept in this space, waking each day to suns and galaxies drifting by.

Mother and Meli had surely noticed I was gone by now. By my estimate, it had been at least five days.

Om nuzzled against my hand as we sat watching the stars go by in the control room. I patted their head gently, a motion they appeared to enjoy, and glanced at the clock. Not knowing how long our journey was going to be, having a way to track time, even an inaccurate one, was a small comfort.

"I had a sister." Om looked up. I hadn't talked about Rosi in so long. Thinking about her still made me nervous, as if I was going to get in trouble being caught doing something I shouldn't. Om gazed up at me with wide, curious eyes. I didn't know how much they understood, but it was nice to be able to break up the silence to attentive ears.

"Sis. Ter," they said thoughtfully.

"Do you know what that is?" Om seemed to mull this over. "Her name was Rosi. She was . . ."

I paused.

What was the best way to describe Rosi to someone who had never met her? My first instinct was to justify the fact that she was born gendered, something I'd had to do often as a child. But Om knew nothing about Fiina and its prejudices.

"She was always moving," I said. "She loved to try new things. She used to rearrange her room over and over just to see how it looks. And she loved animals." I laughed at the memories. "She used to get in trouble for bringing them home. But she just had to show me. It was her favorite thing to do. Everything was fascinating to her, and she just wanted to show it all to me, even if it got her in trouble."

"Trouble," Om said, maneuvering the word in their mouth. "Rosi. Trouble."

"That's the right word for her," I said. "It was like she was happy to be in trouble."

"Happy," Om said, then smiled to show they understood the word. "Rosi. Happy."

"That's right. Rosi was always happy."

Om opened their mouth, then closed it again. They frowned, then chewed on their tongue, something that they did often when trying to form words. I waited patiently. After a long moment, they lifted a hand and laid it on my chest.

"Rosi," they said slowly. "Kova. Happy?"

I gaped in amazement. It was the first time Om had managed to form a question.

"Yes," I nodded. "Rosi made me very happy."

Om grinned, as if glad for having received that answer. They thought a moment longer, then said with equal effort, "Where. Rosi?"

That question tugged at my heart unexpectedly. Sadness welled up in me suddenly and Om must've been able to tell, because their face fell. They put their hands on my arm and leaned against me.

"I don't know," I said. It was something I had never said out loud before. "She's gone. The black orb took her, but the black orb is still on Fiina and she isn't." Or maybe she was. Among the bodies they had supposedly found when it opened, had there been a young girl with a messy nest of white hair? To admit the possibility would somehow make it real, so I didn't. "The last thing she said was she wanted to show me something, and I still haven't figured out what that is."

"Find?"

I looked down at Om. "What?"

They chewed on their tongue again. "Find," they said with some difficulty. "Find. Rosi."

"Find Rosi?" I repeated numbly. "I'm not sure we can do that."

Om tilted their head quizzically, as if asking why.

"Because I don't know where she is." I pointed at the

capsule walls around us. "I don't even know where we're headed."

Om gave a shrug. It was so careless and nonchalant that I couldn't help but smile. "Find," they said again. "Kova. Find. See."

"I would love to find what she wants me to see," I said. "She wanted to show me so badly."

Om bounced up and down, suddenly excited. "Find!" they exclaimed. "See! Rosi!"

I patted their head. "So you're going to help me?" I teased.

Om nodded vigorously. "Help!" they said with all the innocence of a child. "Om help. Find."

Laughter escaped me. How long had it been since I had last laughed? "Alright," I said. "You're going to help me. You promise?"

"Pro. Mis?"

"It means you say you will definitely do something, and then you do it."

I wasn't sure Om understood at first, but they nodded again, this time with a serious expression.

"Om. Promise," they said. "Find. See. Promise. Om help."

I leaned down and kissed them lightly on the forehead. They cringed at the sensation but smiled broadly.

"And I'll help you," I said. "I promise. Wherever you're going, I will help you, too."

Om laid their head down in my lap. I stroked their back and hair.

Maybe what I was looking for was right in front of me, I thought. E-V had brought me to the silver orb, and to Om. Was Om what Rosi wanted to show me? I could believe that easily. She would have loved Om, a creature so kind, loving, and unique in their beauty. She would have pulled me by the hand to show them to me, shouting *Look, Kova! Look how amazing they are!*

I sighed. Om's optimism was infectious, and for a brief

second, I allowed myself to imagine Rosi. Was she really at the end of this journey, waiting for me? I pictured opening the capsule door to her smiling her crooked smile as she greeted me, somehow looking exactly the same as the last time I saw her, or perhaps older and wiser but still full of vibrant, untamable energy. She would take my hand and lead me out of the cramped space into something big, something amazing. Something worth the wait and the danger and the risk. I couldn't begin to fathom what it was.

And I couldn't wait to find out.

"Kova."

I blinked. There was nothing around me but white.

"Kova."

The voice was distant, but clear and incredibly familiar. I looked down and saw nothing. I had no body. There was only white below me and white above. The voice echoed from all directions.

I opened my mouth but nothing came out. The white abruptly vanished and became a deep, endless black. I sat up and gasped for breath. In the darkness, Om shifted next to me.

"E-V!" I shouted. "Lights!"

The bedroom lights turned on. I blinked against the sudden brightness. Soft hands felt along my arm.

"Kova?" I heard Om say in a small, concerned voice.

"I'm fine," I said. "I'm okay. I just . . ."

I just what?

Sounds and images cycled rapidly from my mind. I couldn't stop them.

Did I really hear her voice?

Om touched my face and shoulders in a series of frantic motions.

"Kova?"

My breath caught in my throat. Each one felt harder to push out. I felt like I was going crazy.

"Kova."

I stumbled out of bed, nearly falling. The motion made me dizzy. Om regarded me with concern.

Everything came at me at once. That night. The dream. The voice that echoed in my head. It all spun faster and faster, like a video stuck in a loop. I tried to think back to the cheery optimism I had felt just a few hours ago, but the noise and panic had me in its grip.

"Kova?"

"I'm fine," I said, though my chest was constricting painfully. I paced the common room. Were the walls humming? When did it become so loud? My head pounded. I struggled to breath. The dream and its endless field of white filled my mind, pushing against the walls of my skull. Rosi's voice echoed. Was it real? Was it a dream? Was this all a dream? I was falling. Falling into endless black then endless white then endless black again. Om followed me, grabbing at my hands, but I couldn't stand to be touched.

"I'm fine," I said again. My own voice sounded far away. The pressure inside me was building.

"I'm—"

My chest was inflating, pressing outward painfully.

"I—"

It exploded from me. A shockwave that burst from my body. Like the force that saved me in the silver orb but magnified a hundred times. It struck the walls around me with a deafening *BOOM* and I collapsed, striking my head against the nearest wall as I went down. Om cried out in alarm.

The world swam back and fear overtook me as I thought for a moment that I'd gone blind.

"Kova?"

I blinked.

My vision was fine. The capsule had gone pitch black. In front of me, I could barely make out Om's shape.

"E-V?" I called. *"E-V!"*

"Peripheral fun-tion. Offline."

"What does that mean?" I scrambled to my feet and felt around the darkness to the hallway. The glow of the control console and the wide window offered a modicum of light. I went toward it. All of the screens were off.

A whirring sound. I'd come to think of it as the gears turning in E-V's metaphorical mind.

"Essential f-functions. Only."

"What does that *mean*?" I asked again, though in the back of my mind, I already knew. By the eerie glow of the console, a white puff of air floated from my lips as I spoke. The temperature inside the capsule was dropping rapidly. "E-V?"

"Reducing—"

"Reducing what?" I shouted, shivering. The cold was intense, even beyond the protection offered by the gray uniform. Chilly air seeped through the seams, underneath my skin.

"Function." The volume of E-V's voice was decreasing. **"Reducing. Function. Peripherals off. Essential only. To. Destinat—"**

"E-V?"

The humming had stopped. The capsule was silent as a tomb.

"E-V!"

No response came. My feet lifted off the ground. I twisted and turned, trying to grab hold of something as my entire body floated weightlessly upward. Om let out a fearful cry. I heard little feet scraping against the metal floor, then losing grip as well.

Peripheral functions, as it turned out, included gravity.

. . .

WHEN IT CAME to the seasons, Rosi and I were often opposites. She adored the heat of summer and loved to spend warm evenings splashing in Radley Cove, swimming until her fingers and toes wrinkled like dried fruits. I was not nearly as fond of the sticky heat and preferred to be bundled up in layers, running in the chilly wind and buying fried dough from street stalls, so fresh and hot that it burned the roof of my mouth. Despite Mother's repeated nagging that I was to stay away from the grungy street vendors, I simply couldn't help myself once the air turned cool. I used to tell Rosi, as we took off our shoes and dared each other to stick our feet into the freezing ripples of the cove, that if given a choice I would always live somewhere cold, where I could wear a warm coat, feel the cold breeze on my face, and puff out clouds of white when I walked on the street. I lived for the cold.

But that was before I knew what it truly meant to be *cold*.

The capsule, when lit, was a tight, narrow dwelling made for function over comfort. Now, drenched in darkness and without gravity's restraint, I navigated the space like swimming through deep, murky waters. I lost direction of up and down, and aside from the control room, I could only find my way through by touch. The tiny hallway and rooms stretched on and on like an endless maze. Thankfully, I remembered the disc in my pocket. It flickered on when I pressed the button in its center, and the holographic image of the dark-haired woman sprang to life, offering just enough light to find my way around.

The food machine had shut down, but the sink in the washroom still provided water, freezing as it was. If E-V had really shut down all peripheral functions, then the only thing left to keep Om and me alive was water.

How many days were left? I'd heard that dying of thirst was far worse than dying of starvation. Whether that was true, I hoped not to find out.

Om shouted for me in the dark.

"It's alright," I called. "I'm here."

I grabbed whatever surface I could around me and carefully propelled myself across the hall, guided by the smiling face of the hologram. In the bedroom, I retrieved the patchwork blanket and the sheet from the bed and dragged them behind me to the control room. They would have to do.

"Come here, Om," I cooed into the darkness. "Come here."

The slender form wiggled its way toward me. I pulled Om in, curled myself around their body, and wrapped the blanket and sheet around both of us.

Then, I waited.

The cold was unlike anything I'd experienced before. It wasn't the bright, crisp chill of Radley. This was a different kind of cold. It was cutting, raw, and bitter. My arms and legs turned stiff. I lost feeling in my fingers. Though I did my best to keep Om warm, I doubted I was making much of a difference. The cold seeped through every layer of fabric and prodded my body with its frigid fingers.

"Cold," Om whispered, shivering. "Kova. Cold?"

"Yes," I said through chattering teeth. "Cold. But don't worry. It'll be alright."

"Alright," Om repeated, and embraced me. "All. Right."

I DRIFTED between waking and sleeping for an unending day. When hunger came, I fetched water from the sink. Drinking it was like ingesting ice. But I forced both of us to drink.

At times I couldn't tell if I was dreaming, thinking, or hallucinating. As the days wore on, I became convinced at different times that I was back home on Fiina, sometimes in my marriage bed and sometimes in Rosi's room. I bumped against various surfaces around me but couldn't distinguish the ceiling from the floor. Om shifted against me every now and then, and I curled myself tighter, preserving what little warmth we had between us.

"It's okay," I muttered whenever I felt movement against my chest. "I've got you."

The pain of starvation kept me from staying unconscious for too long. I bore it in silence, as it grew with every hour that passed. I had no idea how many more days of it I had to bear, but time might as well have stopped.

I chuckled to myself. This was the reward for my optimism.

I OPENED MY EYES.

My body was still drifting, weightless. I couldn't locate my extremities and could only assume—or hope—that they were still there.

The console's green glow illuminated the faint silhouette before me. Warm skin pressed against my side. I hadn't felt heat in what seemed like an eternity, and the sensation was indescribable, like another kind of hunger. My body, stiff as a puppet's, drew it in greedily, soaking up the warmth like a sponge, gravitating toward it like metal toward a magnet. A hand reached over me and pulled the blanket over us both, wrapping our bodies together tightly. I sighed.

Two long arms around me. My face pressed against a warm surface. Supple, but firm. Strong legs tangled in mine. My muddled mind tried to make sense of the sensations, but I was so very tired. All I knew was that I was a little less cold and I wanted to stay that way.

Darkness was everywhere. But the cold was a little further away. In the vast space, my world was inside this blanket.

"Alright," a voice said as I shifted my body. It was familiar, but different. "I got you."

CHAPTER 11

I BLINKED.

The ceiling had gotten taller. Rubbing the sleep from my eyes, I sat up. My surroundings were chilly, but nowhere near the deathly frigidity of the capsule. The feeling in my hands and feet slowly returned as I flexed them. I was lying on a hard, flat bed in a room with brown-gray metal walls. A pair of small screens sat on the nearest wall, though they were off at the moment. I looked down at myself and with a start saw that an intravenous tube had been connected to the back of my hand. Panic welled up in me and I frantically tore at the tape holding it in place.

"Don't touch that."

I jumped at the sound of the voice. Unfortunately, its owner's appearance did nothing to alleviate my worries.

"We had to give you a glucose infusion. You were in bad shape."

I said nothing. I didn't know where to begin. Instead, I held my breath as the newcomer came closer.

Their body was entirely metallic, delicate limbs and joints moving with alien grace, though that bothered me a lot less than the fact that they were headless. They spoke, though I couldn't figure out where the voice was coming from. They stopped in front of me, and a spray of blue light appeared out of their neckhole. I watched in equal horror and fascination as a holographic face appeared—two dots for eyes and a curved line for a smile.

But even more strangely, they were speaking East Fiinian dialect. Or rather, one of their voices was. Was there another voice underneath? I couldn't quite tell.

"You're lucky I still remember how to make these," they said, tapping the bag of liquid making its way into my veins.

I opened my mouth to speak, but all that came out was a dry cough.

"Questions?" the robot said with a hint of teasing in their synthesized voice, then let out a sound that I supposed passed for a laugh for a machine. "Oh, I'm sure you have plenty."

I tried to speak again but my sandy tongue refused to cooperate. I hacked painfully. The robot made a sound like a tongue clicking.

"I'll get you something to drink," they said. "Didn't think of it at first. Been a while since I had a drink, you know." They flicked their metal chest with one finger. "Don't go anywhere. The arena master's coming to talk to you after she checks out E-V."

I rubbed my face as they walked out of the room without another word. My head swam as I struggled to remember how I wound up here. I could remember the capsule, and the cold darkness of space, broken up by strange dreams as we . . .

My eyes popped open.

Om.

I looked around frantically, expecting to find Om on a nearby bed, connected to a tube just like me, their limp, skinny body lying . . .

I rubbed my face.

Another image came to me. Long arms wrapped around me. Strong legs tangled in mine, keeping me warm in the darkness. Had it been a hallucination? I couldn't tell. It didn't matter. Either way, Om was nowhere to be seen. I swung my feet over the side of the metal bed and stood, wobbling on my weak legs. I had to find Om. Just as I started to try to disconnect the tube in my hand again, another figure appeared at the door.

It was the woman I had seen briefly on E-V's screen. I recognized her immediately. The lower half of her face was still covered, as it had been when we had spoken through the screens on the capsule. The boots she sported were the same kind I wore, but over her gray suit she wore a short jacket that hugged her shoulders and ended just above her waist. Close up, I saw that she was a little smaller than me, though definitely older.

Even though her frame resembled that of an average Fiinian, her alienness was more apparent in person. Her hair was long and straight, transparent and shimmery like glass, draping over her shoulders. Her skin was tan and her fingers thin. And when our gazes met, I saw her eyebrows were silver and her pupils were two different colors—one was near black and the other a glassy gray, quite different from the rounded eyes and light brown pupils of Fiinians. Still, after the robot, the black hunter, and even Om, I found myself relieved to finally see someone shaped like a Fiinian. Whoever she was, she was the one who had helped me off the silver orb. She might even know something about Rosi.

The woman eyed the tube in my hand. I quickly stopped fiddling with it, like a child caught with their hand in the candy jar.

"Welcome," she said flatly. "I am—" She said a word, but the sound was strange. Just like the robot, I was hearing two versions of her voice, one layered over the other. Whatever she spoke naturally was buried under a copied voice that spoke in Fiinian. "Viva, enable phonetic naming."

"Yes," said a melodic voice. Much like E-V, "Viva" projected her voice from the walls themselves. "Phonetic naming enabled. Translation will be applied only where necessary."

"Let's try this again," the woman said. "I am Astra Ching, the master of this arena."

I opened my mouth but still couldn't produce a sound. I gestured at my throat, and she nodded.

"You were severely dehydrated when we found you," said the woman named Astra. "Seems E-V had malfunctioned and could only maintain a minimally survivable environment. Considering the circumstances, you did quite well. Once you're recovered, I'd very much like to hear how you came about E-V."

"Direct and to the point as usual."

I looked up as the robot returned. They handed me a cup of water. As I drank gratefully, I realized it was made of the same strange gray metal in Meli's collection. All too soon it was gone. I cleared my throat.

"Thanks," I said hoarsely.

"What's your name?" asked Astra. There was something about the way she studied me that made me uneasy, as if I were a box to be pried open to reveal secrets inside.

"Kova," I said, then coughed and held out the cup. "Can I have more?"

"Where did you come from?"

The robot took the cup from me. "Give the poor thing a moment," they said. "You can grill her after she's recovered. It's not like she's going anywhere. Besides—" They paused and gestured toward the screens on the wall. One of them flickered on, showing what appeared to be a hallway. "Your favorite minion just got back. I figured you'd want to talk to him."

Every muscle in my body tightened as a familiar black-clad figure stepped into view. I'd thought I'd left him behind in the silver orb. He walked down the hall, heavy boots rattling the metal floor beneath him. In one hand, he held the neck of a small, limp figure. A figure pure white with slender limbs.

"Fine," Astra said. I fought to keep my face straight as my eyes darted between her and the screen. The relief I had felt just a moment before at the sight of her completely evaporated. "Please go tend to E-V. She needs maintenance."

The robot made another clicking sound. "She needs the scrap heap."

"Two."

"Alright, alright." The robot—Two, apparently—turned on their heels and strolled out of the room with a sarcastic wave. "But she's only got so many reboots left. Don't blame me if the next one fries her circuits."

The woman watched Two go. I tried to calm myself. Om. He had Om. I glanced at Astra, the "master of the arena." She was the one who had ordered him to hunt Om. And now she had them. What was she going to do to Om, a poor, defenseless child?

And after she was done, what was she going to do to me?

I swallowed thickly. She had turned back to me.

"You should rest," she said to me, and started to walk away. "I have some things to tend to. I'm sure we have much to talk about later."

"No!" I exclaimed, followed by a fit of dry cough. Astra stopped and gave me a hard look.

"I mean," I stammered. I didn't know what to do, only that I couldn't let her go to Om now. Not without me. Even if I wasn't exactly in any shape to protect them, I couldn't leave them alone like this. "Let me come. Please. I just . . . I'd like to see where I am."

For a moment I thought she might say no. But she gave a small shrug and began to remove the tube from my hand. Even through her gloves, her hands were cold and hard, as if made of ice.

. . .

ASTRA WALKED QUICKLY and I struggled to keep up. We crossed wide domed spaces, and though they were not nearly as expansive as the interior of the silver orb, I still felt dazed looking up.

Being alone with her was unnerving. Ever since I had seen the black hunter on the screen, I hadn't been able to shake the feeling that I was in the wrong place at the wrong time. Whatever this place was, it wasn't where I was meant to be. I was supposed to be greeted by Rosi, with Om at my side, all of us smiling with relief that we'd survived the long ordeal and come out the other side together and reunited. Instead, I'd delivered Om right into the hands of those who hunted them.

The silence was unnerving. I cleared my throat.

"So what is this place?" I asked, trying to sound nonchalant.

"An orb arena."

"Arena?"

"You should save your energy."

I took the hint and said no more. After another series of narrow corridors, the path suddenly opened to a wobbly suspended walkway. Here a pocket of warmth cut into the chill. Another dark metal ceiling domed above us. Past the rusted metal railings, I saw lines and lines of black boxes. Most of them stood dark and silent, but a small cluster directly underneath us blinked irregular red and yellow lights. I thought I saw a single green light among the others, but Astra moved on before I could get a closer look.

The path we took ended in a dim room. Two figures were washed in blue-green light that emitted from a wall full of screens. The black hunter from the silver star met my gaze from behind his featureless mask.

I suppressed a shiver. My urge was to rush to Om's side the moment I saw them slumped against the wall, but I fought it. The hunter gave no sign of recognition when he saw me, and I let out a small breath of relief at that. Astra approached him.

"Solace," she said, gesturing at the white figure on the floor. "Took you a while. Is this it?"

"It's the one I could find," the hunter replied. His voice was layered, just like the woman's. Whatever this place was, it was translating their speech for my benefit. "There was another in a defunct holy ground. But I lost track of it."

"That's not acceptable. All Harbingers must be exterminated, especially if they saw one of us."

"It was able to manifest and caught me off guard."

Carefully, I edged closer to the white figure on the ground, nervous at what I was about to find.

It wasn't Om.

I let out the tiniest breath of relief. While they looked very similar, I could tell that this one was different. The grooves on their white skin were in a different pattern. After days in close quarters with Om, I'd learned that the grooves on their skin never changed from their basic pattern no matter how Om changed the rest of their body. This one also possessed dark green eyes instead of Om's crystal blue. Most importantly, they still had all of their limbs and were missing the black patch on Om's chest. As I stepped closer, they suddenly turned to look up at me. I started and stumbled back.

"Don't worry about that thing."

Astra was watching me. I took a few steps away from the white figure.

"It won't hurt you," she said. "It's broken."

Broken. I shivered. What a cold choice of words.

The black hunter named Solace zeroed in on me. "Where did *she* come from?"

"E-V's capsule." Astra motioned for me to come forward. I approached hesitantly, tense and guarded.

"H-hello," I said awkwardly. The hunter gave me a half-hearted nod.

"E-V is back?"

"Yes. And I think *she*"—Astra gestured at me—"just might be able to clue us in on—"

"Send her home."

An uncomfortable silence fell over the room.

"Excuse me?" Astra said. I could almost hear her teeth clench.

"Send her home," he said again. "She doesn't belong here."

"That *isn't* your call."

"You should have sent her home the moment you saw her," the hunter said. The displeasure in his voice was clear. Part of me was relieved that he only wanted me gone and not killed.

Astra cast a glance at me and I looked away awkwardly, occupying myself studying the room. Most of the wall space was covered with glowing screens. Several were broken. What looked like a black obelisk stood in the middle of the room. It was several heads taller than me and covered in wide cracks. A green substance similar to the one on the capsule's control console could be seen inside, emitting a strange glow.

"She doesn't need to be part of this mess," I heard the hunter say.

"We need to find out more," Astra retorted icily. Though significantly lesser than the hunter in stature, she was obviously the greater presence in the room. "And she might offer a clue."

"What could she *possibly* know? Having her here accomplishes nothing besides muddling things even m—"

"That's *enough*," Astra snapped, her voice rising. "We all have our jobs here. I am doing mine. Maybe you should do yours before you question *me*, starting with finding that Harbinger you lost."

I suppressed a flinch. The hunter said nothing else. Instead, he took a step back and gave a shallow bow that could only be described as sarcastic.

"Very well," he said, *"arena master."*

I stepped aside as he walked past us without another word and disappeared into the endless corridors. For a long moment no one said a thing.

Then, without warning, Astra struck out. In the split second she moved, I saw her hand and forearm transform into a crystal spike that drove straight through the forehead of the white form slumped on the floor. It gave a violent twitch and fell still.

Every hair on the back of my neck stood on end. Astra slowly retracted her spike. I was afraid to move. She glanced at me, as if just remembering I was there. The anger faded from her eyes as her hand returned to its normal shape.

"Sorry," she muttered, and began to walk out. "Come. We can talk somewhere else."

I waited for her to exit the room before allowing myself to look at the body on the ground, all too aware that it could easily have been Om lying there with a hole in their head.

CHAPTER 12

"CAN I RETRIEVE MY THINGS?"

Astra stopped. Even though most of her face was covered, I could tell she was agitated from the argument with the hunter named Solace. After seeing her lash out, I was even more fearful for Om's fate if they were left unattended.

"From the capsule," I stammered. "I just . . . I left some things there."

Astra tilted her head slightly. For a moment, I thought she might say no.

"Alright," she said. "Go ahead. Viva will guide you to the bay."

I nodded, trying hard to hide my relief, and headed off through the winding interior of the . . .

Arena?

That word meant nothing to me. It made me think of the televised sports that were so popular on Radley. Twice a cycle the people of East Fiina went mad for kobal, a rather silly sport in my opinion, involving oddly shaped bats and several types of balls. I couldn't begin to imagine any kind of game being played in this dreary place.

"Turn left," came Viva's voice.

I followed her instructions. The sooner I could make sure Om was okay, the better.

Then what?

I didn't dare—or didn't want to—think that far. As far as I could tell, E-V had not mentioned Om to Astra. For once, I was thankful for her unreliable functionality. I glanced at the walls uneasily. Would Viva say anything? And the robot named Two, hadn't Astra ordered them to perform maintenance on E-V? What if they'd already found Om?

Viva directed me to a wide bay. The floors, walls, and domed ceiling were all entirely made up of the same gray-brown metal. A row of capsules sat against a far wall, all similar in construction but slightly different. As I walked past it all, I couldn't help but wonder once again if this was what Rosi wanted me to see, but that didn't matter until I could be sure that Om was safe.

A pair of capsules twice the length of the one I had arrived in sat in disuse. Their side panels had been removed, showing their innards, which had been picked over for parts. Several others, roughly the same size as E-V's capsule, sat to the side. They were marked with symbols that I didn't recognize. E-V's capsule sat open across the bay. I hurried toward it, hoping Om was alive and had been smart enough to hide from Viva and Two.

I stepped inside. All of the capsule's lights were on, but Om was nowhere to be seen. The patchwork blanket sat in a pile on one of the benches in the control room. I pulled it aside in case Om was hiding underneath, but no luck.

Clank.

I froze.

The sound came from the bedroom. Someone else was in here. I opened my mouth to call for Om, but quickly closed it when I realized it could be Two going about their work. Carefully, I approached the bedroom and peered in.

The expressionless black mask turned, and I nearly screamed. The black hunter pulled his hand out of the metal locker. My nightgown and slippers, which I had placed in the locker, lay on the bed, the padding of which had been stripped and thrown aside. Whatever he was looking for, he hadn't found it. With a sigh, he pushed the locker door closed. I scrambled out of the way to give him a wide berth as he walked out of the room.

Leave. Just leave.

I held my breath as he approached the capsule door. He stopped before stepping out and looked back at me. I feared that he would question me, but thankfully, he said nothing and departed in silence.

Was he looking for Om? I hurried up the ladder as fast as my feet would carry me. The crawl space was empty. I descended the ladder and checked the common room, washroom, and storage. Still nothing. Though I was relieved not to find a white, lifeless body, the possibility that Om was now running loose in the arena brought on new worries. I retrieved my meager belongings, drank some water from the sink to further relieve my parched throat, and headed out of the capsule.

"Find what you need?"

I started. Two stepped inside, metallic feet clanking against the hard floor. Their holographic face flickered on. That lined smile, which I assumed was meant to be friendly, only unnerved me further.

"Yes," I said, showing them the bundle in my arms. "I did."

"Is that all?"

I couldn't tell if it was a result of their programming or the translation, but everything spoken out of Two's nonexistent mouth sounded vaguely sarcastic to my ears. I nodded.

"Here," they said, and handed me a cup filled with water. I had completely forgotten that I had asked for more water. Even though I had already quenched my thirst at the sink, I took the cup and emptied it. To refuse this small act of kindness seemed wrong, especially since this mechanical being was the only one who had presented me with *any* act of kindness after I'd woken up in this strange place.

As we exited the bay, I scanned the space around us as discreetly as I could, looking for a glimpse of white, maybe a small, slender form darting behind a sitting capsule.

Or someone taller. Larger.

I saw nothing.

"Did Eleven get into it with the arena master again?" Two said. The holographic face flickered and turned off, which I was grateful for. Having it looking back at me as they walked was unsettling. "I swear, it never ends with those two. Anyway, I've been instructed to get you settled."

"Eleven?"

Two paused, then snapped their metal fingers, which made an odd *ting* sound. "Solace, as he goes by now. I forget sometimes. Seems not that long ago we all went by our numbers. Some chose to reclaim their old names. A matter of pride, I suppose. Personally, I don't care either way."

I gripped the bundle in my arm tightly. I hadn't thought about it much until now, but a nightgown and some slippers were the only things still tying me to Fiina. I followed Two through the arena halls once more, through a different route this time. Without a guide, I would surely starve to death trying to find my way through these rust-colored corridors.

We arrived at a hall slightly wider than the others. Doors lined either side. Two went to one, opened it, and gestured for me to come forward. I approached hesitantly, afraid that they would shove me inside and bolt it shut.

The room was twice the size of the living quarters aboard the capsule, with the same rust-colored walls and a single round window that looked out into the dark of space. To the side there was a small washroom and a machine that I suspected produced the same gelatinous cubes. Aside from that, it was completely empty.

"W-what do I do in here?" I asked timidly.

"E-V didn't tell you about manifestation?" Two said, and I imagined them rolling their non-existent eyes. "Well, ask Viva to run some programs for you. If you're going to stay here, you'll have to get used to asking for her help."

Stay. I hadn't really accepted until now that this was where I was going to stay for the foreseeable future. I eyed the empty metal room with dismay.

"Get some proper rest while you can," Two said. "Your race sleeps, right? Actually, doesn't matter. Don't bore me with it. Just get comfortable. I have a feeling the arena master is going to keep you busy."

Busy with what?

I didn't ask. I didn't want to know. I couldn't stop remembering the white figure on the floor with a hole through their head. Two released the door and it hit my back, pushing me inside. Their metal footsteps disappeared down the hall outside. The door was left unlocked, but it didn't take away the uncomfortably prisonlike quality of this place. I stood there clutching my things, trying to wrap my mind around the fact that I was alone once more and so very, very far from home.

THANK GOODNESS FOR VIVA.

Navigating her was not too different from E-V in that she also required specific and detailed instructions to provide useful information. However, she was far more knowledgeable and useful. After a bit of trial and error, she created—"manifested," as Two put it—a bed in the empty room for me. I watched, mouth agape, as the shape of the entire structure grew seemingly out of nothing, one tiny block at a time. Even soft objects like sheets and pillows were pieced together by those same blocks. When Viva finished, I couldn't help touching every corner of the bed just to make sure what I saw was real. The half-formed baubles on Meli's shelf suddenly made sense.

Orb arena.

Was the orb on Fiina a place like this? Was this what Rosi wanted to show me? Too many questions with no answers.

I asked Viva about the time, and she gave me a response I didn't understand. I asked for time by Eastern Fiinian clock, and to my surprise she was able to give it to me. Early evening. I ought to be at dinner.

I made myself some gelatin cubes. Viva helped me manifest a plate and spoon so I didn't have to eat with my fingers. I ate them thinking of the food I would be eating if I hadn't stepped aboard the capsule. I'd had a place on Fiina and a role to play in my new family. I'd always known where to go and what to do and whom to smile for. Now, I was sitting in the middle of empty space, among beings whose ancestry I couldn't begin to place. I didn't know what was going to happen the next day, the next hour, or the next minute.

"Viva?" I called. I needed something to distract myself. Anything. Sitting in silence with my thoughts was unbearable.

"Yes?"

I gestured to the cubes. "What is this stuff?"

"An edible compound customized to each individual, based on flavor and texture preferences, as well as nutritional requirements to maximize health and efficient digestion."

I decided not to argue with the computer on the "flavor" of the vaguely fishy gelatin.

"What day is it on Fiina?"

"It is currently the Fiinian cycle 3102, the nineteenth day of the winter season."

I would not be there for the solstice this year.

"Where are we?"

She gave a string of coordinates and numbers, followed by

the name of what I assumed was a planet that we were in close proximity to. None of it made sense.

"Who is Astra?"

"Donna Astra Ching was the thirty-third champion of the game Headspace in the Galaxy of the Starry River, and the third master of this arena."

Headspace. Finally something familiar. Rosi and I had once spent many nights trying to decipher that word.

"What is Headspace?"

"Headspace is a game of competition and manifestation played throughout the known universe."

That told me very little.

"What is manifestation?"

"Manifestation is the act of creation. The arena and capsules utilize component cubes to recreate shapes and forms desired by the user. System intelligence can store frequently used manifestations in automated programs to be recalled as needed."

"What do you mean by user?"

"Anyone within the arena space can perform manifestation. Though certain high-level operations are reserved for the arena master only."

"Could . . ." I hesitated. "Could *I*?"

"Yes. You are currently an authorized user within the arena."

I set my plate aside and slid off the hard bed.

"So how do I do this?" I asked. "Manifestation, I mean. How does it work?"

"Object manifestation is the simplest," Viva said. "Imagine a simple object. Preferably one that fits in one hand. Larger objects may pose dangers to beginners who are not used to maintaining control."

A simple object. I thought of the cup on Meli's shelf. The arena hummed around me. I focused on the image in my mind. The sensation was strange, alien, and yet oddly natural at the same time. A ripple coursed through the air. I could feel motion around me.

The humming grew louder.

Something about this was familiar. I knew this sound, which seemed impossible, since I'd never once attempted this strange feat before. It reminded me of being inside the silver star, hiding from the hunter alongside Om.

The thought of Om brought a momentary pressure to my chest. The cup's image fell away, replaced by endless walkways and crumbling steps. Om was gone. My only ally, and I had no idea where they were. All at once, the fear of that moment came flooding back to me. Then, confusion. Om's innocent, childlike face, smiling up at me, followed by the undeniable sensation of being wrapped in the arms of someone different, someone tall and large and warm. But it was a delusion. A dream. A hallucination on the brink of death, however real it felt. But then Rosi's message. That had been a dream, too, had it not? My mind argued with itself, trying to untangle what was real and unreal. It overwhelmed me, filling me up like water in my lungs. I gasped, struggling to breathe, pushing the feeling away.

It exploded out of me. I stumbled back from the impact, like the kickback from a weapon firing, and fell heavily on my bottom. The surge struck the wall in front of me with a loud *BANG*, leaving a visible dent in the brown metal. I sat on the ground, shocked.

"Energy projection," Viva said calmly, "is a higher skill. Please refrain from conducting projection experiments outside the game floor, as damage may occur to infrastructure."

Carefully, I got to my feet, went to the wall, and examined the dent. I waited tensely for someone to come through the door and demand that I explain myself, then subsequently punish me in some horrifying and painful fashion for breaking E-V's capsule. But time ticked by and nothing happened.

"Would you like to try again?"

I shook my head. I'd had more than enough excitement for one lifetime. After splashing some cold water on my face to calm myself, I changed into my nightgown and lay down on the hard bed. The sheets carried an unpleasant smell—chilly, metallic, and like everything else, alien.

CHAPTER 13

DESPITE MY EXHAUSTION, MY SLEEP WAS FITFUL. I TWISTED AND turned, drifting in and out. Every time I woke blearily, I thought I was in a different place. My family home, Meli's bed, the cold capsule. In between, I couldn't keep my mind off Om.

Eventually, I had to admit that sleep wasn't going to get better and sat up. Without a sunrise, estimating the time of day was impossible. I inquired with Viva and according to her, morning had arrived in the technical sense. I couldn't recall ever rising this early in my life, but I was doing an awful lot of things for the first time lately.

My hair was a matted mess. After a few attempts and missteps, I managed to ask Viva to heat the water in the washroom to the right temperature for a proper washing. Manifestation was the last thing I wanted to attempt, but thankfully, Viva's auto manifestation provided me with a scratchy towel to dry off, a large comb, and a mirror. I did my best to sort out my countless tangles without much success. In the end, I asked for a band to tie it into a messy bun. When I pulled my hair back tight, the bald spot on the side of my scalp was clear and visible. Not long ago, Mother and Daris would've had a conniption fit if I let that spot show. But that was an entire lifetime and another world ago.

A knock came on the door just as I finished breakfast—gelatin that almost tasted like sweet porridge but not quite. I opened the door to find Two standing there, their smiling face flickering.

"Viva informed me that you were awake," they said.

I cringed inwardly at the thought of being watched.

"The arena master is waiting for you on the arena floor." One of their eyes winked ominously. "Are you ready?"

Was I? Did it matter?

We navigated the narrow corridors and I once again found myself on the suspended walkway over the blinking lights. I slowed over the railing and searched for the mysterious green light. Noticing my interest, Two stopped.

"This is the computing room," they said. "Used to be a lot hotter in here. It's where the materials used for manifestations are produced and recycled. In its heyday, all the machines here used to be active, and the arena could create entire fields, landscapes, cities, anything the imagination could hold. It could even generate illusions that led the contestants to believe they were in far greater spaces than they actually were. It was practically magic. But these days, its functions are a little more limited."

A series of soft clanking came from below. I looked down. A single green light pointed toward me.

"Hey, Nix," Two called.

The green light moved. I squinted. Using the lights from the nearby consoles, I could just make out the figure making its way through the rows of machines. It looked to be entirely mechanical, like Two, but while Two moved with smooth, organic motions, this thing was large, bulky, and lumbered with a jerky, awkward motion as it dragged itself through the space between the consoles. One of its legs seemed unable to bend. It scraped against the floor, bringing with it a grating, screeching sound almost like a dying animal. Its left arm hung by a thread, and I could see that it had once had two green eyes, but now only one remained. Where the other used to be was an empty, jagged socket.

"I know he looks a mess," Two said with a shrug, "but we can't fix him anymore. The arena masters prefer to keep him tucked here where he won't offend guests. Not that we have many guests, mind you."

I watched the thing—*robot? Being? Man? Other?*—reach up with his remaining hand and try to connect a loose wire on one of the consoles. It slipped out of his grasp multiple times, but Nix tried, again and again, infinitely patient, until he finally managed to connect it where it needed to be. Then, he dropped his arm and made a shuddering movement, like an old man rattling his weary bones with a heavy sigh.

"Can you at least attach his arm back?"

"That's not how things work here. Limited resources. Can't spare any parts or blocks. The arena master decides what's worth fixing and what's not. Besides, his body is operated through his own manifestation. These days he's mostly assisted by Viva. Without her, I'm not sure he even has the will to hold his body together."

Nix's green eye flickered, then lowered. The lights around him blinked. Some rhythmically, some out of phase, like a light show fighting to stay on at the very end of a long night.

"Can he see us?"

"Maybe. I don't know. Can't remember the last time he left this room."

Two was already moving on and I hurried after, casting one last glance at the pitiful metal creature and hoping dearly that this desolate place wasn't what Rosi wanted me to see.

I HAD no idea what to expect of the arena floor, but as I drew near it, I knew it had once been a marvel to behold. The domed space was enormous. Looking up at the arched ceiling nearly gave me a sense of vertigo. Tiny movements in the air caught the corners of my eyes, though I could never quite seem to catch them. The walls were covered in dents and discolored in patches. The marks of age and wear were everywhere. Here, the humming was loudest, though when I listened closely, a grinding noise accompanied it. It came and went at odd intervals, like an old engine struggling to continue its chugging against the wheels of time. Every part of this place was painfully, undeniably, exhaustingly *old*.

"What makes you think she'll tell you anything?"

I stopped just short of the entrance. From where I stood in the hall, I could just see two familiar figures standing together, their backs to me.

"She has no reason to hold back."

That was Astra's voice. I quieted my steps and did not make my presence known.

"She's scared," the first voice said. Solace. The black hunter.

"All the more reason she'll tell us what we need to find out."

"*If* she knows it."

"She got here with E-V. She knows *something*."

"And if she won't talk? What will you do to her?"

"Take next steps."

"Which is what?"

"It's not your business."

"It used to be." I heard the edge in Solace's tone. "You can't keep leaving me out of your plans and sending me on these pointless chases."

"They are *not* pointless," Astra said. I could hear anger bubbling in her. The calm in her voice was thin as spring ice in Radley Cove. "Either we figure out what they're doing, or we kill them all and it won't matter."

"You think that's the solution?"

"It might be the only one. And frankly, the easier one."

The chill of fear coursed through me. All at once I was watching Astra drive her spike through the white being's head once again. I nearly turned and ran before I remembered there was nowhere for me to go. Stepping out into the arena floor was the last thing I wanted to do, but Astra was expecting me, and to catch her bad side might mean a spike through my own head.

I stepped out of the hall and cleared my throat gently. The two on the floor turned.

"You can go," Astra said to Solace.

He said nothing. As he walked past me, he gave me a shallow nod and disappeared down the hall I had just emerged from.

Astra stood in the middle of the wide-open space. Several holographic displays glowed around her, bathing her in blue-green light. She turned back to them and didn't look up when I approached.

"Sleep well?"

I nodded nervously, though she didn't see. That inquiry appeared to be all the interest she had in pleasantries. I shifted back and forth on my feet, and something rubbed against my leg inside my pocket. I'd completely forgotten about the holographic disc that I'd used as a makeshift light in the dark capsule. This whole time I'd never taken it out. I removed it.

"Where did you get that?"

"I-it was in the capsule." I held it out to her. She took it without a word and tucked it into an inside pocket on her jacket, then waved one hand in the air. The displays disappeared.

"You are from Fiina."

I swallowed. "Y-yes."

"Which region?"

"East."

She waved her hand again. A holographic map appeared—the jagged shape of East Fiina. "So this is where she's been all this time," she said, half to herself.

I didn't know what to say, so I nodded again. Try as I might, I couldn't quell the unease inside me.

"There was an orb?"

"Yes."

"Show me where it landed."

I squinted at the map and pointed to a peninsula sticking out the north end. "Right here."

The map zoomed in. I pointed to Radley Cove, and it zoomed in again, displaying a clear image of the town. For a moment I felt a twinge of homesickness.

"This is an old map," Astra said. "I've spent some time on Fiina. Though that was quite a while ago. A planet with two cold suns and one hot was a novelty. Though you are quite the novel race as well."

"We are?"

Astra made a gesture to a different screen. "Viva, pull up the Fiinian racial profile."

A list of characters I couldn't read appeared on the screen next to the map. Astra scanned it.

"You are born hermaphroditic and genderless, and at puberty you develop masculine or feminine features, though as a society, you are given a choice to select one or the other through surgical means. Is this correct?"

"Well, yes," I said awkwardly. Hearing my entire race reduced to one single biological trait was strange.

"It's a unique characteristic shared by no other race I've seen. The majority of seed races are born with either a gender attributed to their biology or remain ungendered their whole lives."

"Oh," I said, unsure of what to do with this information.

"You possess homogenous appearances as well. Same hair, skin tone, and eye colors across the globe, with very little regional variation. A rare genetic mutation results in red hair, but that's the only difference."

"Is that not normal?"

"Not on most planets. Physical characteristics tend to vary

along a spectrum due to environmental differences in most worlds."

My mind spun. I couldn't stop looking at Astra and her glassy hair. Did she mean there were versions of beings like her with blue or green hair? Or skin red as summer rosalits? I couldn't begin to picture it.

"Viva," Astra said. "Show game records for Fiina."

"No such records exist," replied Viva.

"I didn't think so." Astra turned to me. "Headspace was never sanctioned for Fiina."

I stared at her blankly.

"How exactly did you end up on E-V's capsule?"

I'd been anxiously awaiting this question since setting foot inside the arena. I had gone over the answer in my head many times, and it was different each time. With every moment I spent in this place, I grew more apprehensive of its inhabitants. I couldn't shake the feeling that I needed to guard myself and my secrets. The less Astra knew, the better.

"A black orb came to Fiina," I said, carefully planning each word. "It sent a video to the entire world."

"A video welcoming you to Headspace."

"Yes."

"Were there any survivors?"

"I-I don't know."

"You don't know?"

"People disappeared. I hear they were found later when the orb opened."

Astra's eyes narrowed. "The orb opened?"

I nodded uneasily. "They found bodies. I don't know. I was young. Then people carved it apart and studied it."

"It didn't leave?"

"No. Was it supposed to?"

"And there was no broadcast of the games?"

"Games?"

She shook her head. "Never mind. What happened after that?"

"Not very much. People moved on. I didn't know much until I met someone who collected items that were found within the orb. They had the capsule in their possession. I was . . . curious."

"How did you activate it?"

"It was an accident."

I held my breath, waiting for her to ask more. How did I know the door code? How did I know how to operate the console? I'd thought up plausible lies for whatever she might ask, though I wasn't sure how convincing I was going to be. She waved a hand and brought up the map of Fiina again. I waited for her to ask me something else, but she only studied the map in silence.

"You can go."

I blinked. "What?"

"Go back to your room. Or take a walk. Whatever you like," Astra said without sparing me a look. "I need to think. I'll have Two fetch you if I need you."

"Oh," I said awkwardly, but Astra appeared to have already lost interest in me. I backed away from her and left the arena floor.

"WASTES NO WORDS, DOES SHE?"

I nearly missed the robot standing in the shadows of the nearest hallway. Their holographic smile flickered on as I approached.

"Yes," I said hesitantly. "She's very . . ."

Two let out a laugh. "You don't have to mince words," they said. "I've stood beside all three arena masters. I know exactly what they're like. Let's just say it takes a special kind of person to rise to that position."

I nodded and walked past them. They followed, metal feet clinking against the floor.

"I can get around on my own."

"I'm sure you can," Two replied. "But the arena master says keep an eye on the visitor. We've had some, shall we say, dramatics around here. Trust isn't her strong suit."

We walked through the halls in silence, and I found myself gravitating to the computing room, where I stopped and stood on the suspended walkway, leaning against the wobbly railing. The rhythmic, blinking lights calmed my noisy mind. I watched Nix drag his hulking figure through the rows of machines. He looked up occasionally, not at me but past me. Two stood behind me, leaning casually against the opposite railing, nonchalantly manifesting tiny geometric shapes the way a bored pedestrian might flip a coin in and out of their hands.

"Have you tried manifesting yet?" they asked as they noticed me watching the shapes—cubes at the moment—fly around their hands.

I nodded. Though I was impressed at their dexterity, attempting manifestation again was the last thing I wanted to do. "Can everyone manifest here?"

"It's a default feature, though the arena master possesses far greater control over manifestation than the rest of us." Two nodded toward Nix. "Although it was a little easier back when some of us had skin."

"Skin?" I repeated, uncomfortable at the implications.

"Didn't tell you that part, eh?" The cubes disintegrated, replaced by a trio of silver spheres circling each other in a complicated pattern. "Disrespect, I tell you. I was a champion before she was even an undivided cell."

Champion. I supposed it was a word that made sense if there was some sort of game involved.

"You weren't always . . . like this?"

"Not a fan of the metal?" The spheres broke up into nine

smaller ones and flew around Two like tiny insects. "I don't blame you. Most seed races haven't perfected artificial bodies, so they tend to be uncomfortable around mechanical beings. But I'm not sure you would've liked me more when I had skin. You people don't tend to respond kindly to people who look different from you. And by 'you people' I do mean anyone and everyone."

The question was on the tip of my tongue, but I couldn't bring myself to ask it for fear of offending them. Two seemed to read my mind.

"Wondering how I ended up like this?" I nodded. The holographic face winked. "Let's just say you should never fail an arena master. They get creative with the punishments."

I shuddered.

"Oh, don't look like that. It's not so bad." They flicked their metal torso with two fingers. "Solid and easy to maintain. Not to mention I don't have to choke down those awful jelly cubes."

"Does it . . . bother you?" I asked hesitantly.

"What, not having skin? Not eating? Playing errand drone to the arena master? Not especially. There are worse jobs around here." They pointed past me. "You see one right there."

I looked down, and it took a moment for reality to dawn on me. "Nix? He's also—"

"Flesh in metal? Yes." The spheres in the air vanished. "The arena masters find a way to use every last scrap of you. Efficient lot, they are. I mean, you saw the basements, right?"

I hadn't, but Two took my silence as affirmative.

"Heck, the basements were the pride and joy of the past arena masters. Delicate operation, that." A pair of tiny cones appeared. They orbited Two's fingers, then collided and fell away into puffs of "dust." "If you're bored, we can head back down there. I'll show you how the brains of the operation work."

"Yes," I said. "Let's do that."

. . .

THE ELEVATOR to the basement was narrow and the ride down was long. Two said nothing during the ride, and I couldn't help wondering if I was being lured into some sort of trap. If Two noticed my anxious fidgeting, they gave no sign. The light from their holographic face bathed the rust-colored walls around us.

The "basement" looked quite a lot like the rest of the orb. I was both relieved and disappointed not to have exited the elevator to something grand and terrifying. We were greeted with another hallway made of the same grayish brown metal. The walls were lined with doors on both sides. As we walked past them, Two leading, I nudged one with two fingers. It didn't budge. The next one didn't either. Neither did the third. Though every door hummed the same way the walls of the capsule did.

"Here we are."

I yanked my hand off the door, hoping Two hadn't noticed my curiosity. They had come to a stop at a door a few steps away.

"This is the only door I have access to," Two said. They lifted one metal hand and pushed. The door opened easily with a soft creaking. They stepped aside and I peered in.

My initial thought was that it was a child.

Two gestured with one metal hand for me to step inside. I did, walking carefully so as not to disturb the form in front of me, though I had great doubts that she had any idea I was there.

Now that I had a better view of her face, I saw that the figure was far from a child. Her stature was small, with arms and legs short even for her size. Her torso and hips were round and curvy. Beneath a head of long, black hair was a face that looked almost like a Fiinian, but distorted in a manner different from Astra's. Her forehead was larger, her nose was wider, and what I initially took to be eyebrows turned out to be a second pair of eyes. She hung there, face eye level to me but feet far off the ground. All four of her eyes were closed and she was smiling. She looked so peaceful that I could almost overlook what was behind her.

The back of her head was gone. Where her skull ought to have been was a neat crescent shape, as if her brain had been scooped out with a spoon. Circling to the side, I saw that she was also missing quite a bit of skin. The gray suit she wore had been split here and there, revealing thousands of silver threads that reached into her exposed muscle fibers. It was these threads that bore her weight, and as they left her body, they wound themselves into thicker wires that fed into the surfaces of the room.

"Who is she?" I asked, shuddering a little as I returned to the center of the room. From the front, the atrocities of what had been done to this poor woman were fully hidden, but I couldn't unsee what was behind her.

"Viva."

"The AI?"

"The real Viva." Two stroked the small woman's face with unexpected tenderness. "Or at least, what's left of her."

"How?" was all I could muster.

"She's working. She works every moment of every day for the good of the arena."

"Is she . . ."

"Alive? Very much so." They slid a finger through what was left of Viva's dark hair. "You see, the 'artificial intelligence' isn't actually artificial. This place looks like nothing but metal—and heck, I know that better than anyone. But underneath, it's alive."

I leaned a little closer to Viva. At first, I thought I was imagining it, but as the distance between us grew smaller, I realized it was coming from all around us. The walls, the floors. It was beneath the humming of the arena, but once I heard it, I couldn't unhear it. It permeated the atmosphere, entwined with the air itself.

"Is that her job, too?" I asked.

"What?"

"The music." Viva's faint, melodic voice wafted over me. "She's singing."

The holographic face turned off. When not washed in the flickering blue light, the age of the metal body was far more apparent.

"In a way."

Something about their tone told me they weren't interested in answering further questions. I watched them caress Viva's cheek and tried to imagine a person—an alien, but a living being every bit like a Fiinian underneath. Someone who had laughed and lived before being forced inside a cold shell. Someone who had once had dreams and desires that didn't involve layers of metal prisons.

"You know," Two said. Their tone was even and flat, but I heard something underneath. "I can't remember what having a living body feels like."

"What happened?"

"I told you," Two said, a hint of teasing in their voice. "I had a run-in with an arena master. You cannot cross the arena masters. They will do what they need—what they *want*—to keep this arena running. At the end of the day, the survivors of Headspace serve the arena. This is our role. Be it as operators or showrunners." A pause. "Or batteries."

Beneath that metal was someone who *loved*.

"There used to be so many of us," Two went on slowly. "Nearly a hundred. We were brought together under undesirable circumstances, but we still had each other. We were a family." They sighed, a heartbreakingly sad sound I hadn't thought they were capable of making. "That was many lifetimes ago. Now there are so few of us left."

I RETURNED TO MY ROOM. My mind and body were numb.

"Viva?"

"Yes?"

A chill coursed through me as I remembered her body—her real self—hanging in the basement.

"What . . . happened to you?"

There was a long pause.

"Glory be."

"What does that mean?"

No response. She didn't want to answer me, I supposed. Being aware that she was a living thing made me even more uneasy to be watched by her. Was E-V alive, too?

The more my discomfort grew, the more I could hear the humming of the arena. Energy built up inside me, just like it did in the silver orb and the capsule. I went to the sink and splashed water on my face until the humming receded.

Not long ago, I had been a perfectly primped bride. The tired woman in the mirror with her back to a rusty-colored wall looked like a different person. That red hair, once washed and oiled twice a day, touched and laid by my mother's careful hands, was now a knotted mess. I tried to use the comb Viva provided but could barely move it a finger's length without the teeth getting caught.

Why am I combing it?

I yanked the comb out. At least a dozen hairs came with it. I had spent so much of my life being told I was at my most beautiful with my hair as long as it could grow. I had sat through countless hours as other people ran their fingers all over my head, washing, pulling, and styling it. It was the mark of my beauty, a beauty I was told to maintain because it made me special. What did it matter now? Who was going to look at me and judge me for my hair on this desolate island in space?

Anger and frustration welled up in me.

"Viva," I said. "I need scissors."

A pair of large kitchen shears appeared. I grabbed them and began cutting with seething determination. Long strands, nearly half the length of my body, fell at my feet. I didn't look up at the mirror again until I was finished.

Red hair piled around me on the floor. The person in the mirror looked back at me with shaky but resolute eyes. Her hair was lopsided, longer on one side than the other, jutting out in all different directions. I did my best to even out the strands. My barbering skills were pathetic at best, and I could only hope that no one here knew Fiinian styles well enough to judge. And if they did, well, frankly that was the least of my worries.

I tossed the scissors aside, went to the bed, and lay staring up at the ceiling, listening to the arena's faint humming song and wondering if it was Rosi's intention to show me that the rest of the universe was as lonely and suffocating as the four walls surrounding my life on Fiina.

CHAPTER 14

DAYS IN THE ARENA PASSED SLOWLY.

After being enlightened to the reality of my surroundings, I initially became hesitant to engage with Viva. But lacking better things to do, I ended up conversing with her anyway. She possessed a vast amount of information. Information that I was not privy to.

"Glory be," she said when I asked about the details of the Headspace games.

"Glory be," she said when I inquired about the details of what had happened to Two and Nix.

"Glory be," she said, rather emphatically, when I tried to ask for something, anything, about the arena masters.

It was a brush off for when she couldn't answer my questions. No matter how hard I tried, phrasing my questions to get around her logic, she stonewalled me. There was much that I was ignorant of, and it was obvious that the arena master had no interest in granting me any answers.

I'd been summoned to Astra's side a few more times. She spent each one grilling me about the orb on Fiina and the order of events regarding my arrival, as if trying to catch me in a lie. I feared her, but more terrifying was the idea that every little thing she found out from me somehow contributed to her plans to "kill them all." While I didn't know who *they* were, I was quite certain it included Om. The fact that she barely looked me in the face didn't help. Every time she dismissed me, I was relieved to have avoided her wrath yet again.

I walked around the arena often, keeping an eye out for Om even though I never had any luck. I watched Nix work and kept company with Two as they went about maintaining various parts of the orb. They frequently attempted to entertain me by performing little tricks through manifestation. I appreciated this gesture at hospitality, small as it was. The irony that the one I found most alien in the orb was the only one who treated me like a person was not lost on me.

"You shouldn't be so afraid of manifestation," Two said as we made one of our many circuits through the winding hallways.

"I'm not afraid," I said, a little offended.

"Yes, you are."

I didn't argue. They were annoyingly astute. How many days had I passed in their company? Ten? Twenty? The longer I stayed in this place, the more I noticed the signs of age in its walls, floors, and inhabitants. I couldn't imagine how long they'd lived this way, nothing changing except the surfaces around them garnering yet another little scratch or scrape, day after day after day.

We passed the capsule bay. I hadn't intended to enter, but I veered on my heels and headed inside as we passed the door. Two paused, then followed, their metal heels clicking behind me. I'd been through the bay many times since my arrival. I always seemed to end up here, and aside from my weak hope that Om would magically appear, I knew it was because I had another reason.

The only way off this island was the capsules.

Two said nothing as I paced between the capsules, studying them. Most of them were very obviously out of commission, but a few, including E-V, were still functional. Being around them brought up unpleasant memories of being trapped in deep, cold space, but I couldn't help seeing them as life rafts, the only escape route I had if things went sour.

E-V's door was open. I peered inside. The lights were off. The control console glowed eerily in the dark.

"Must've been lonely," Two said, startling me out of my thoughts. "All that time by yourself in that thing."

I wasn't alone.

"Yeah," I replied. "A bit."

"I used to travel all the time. I liked doing it solo, but most people preferred to have a partner. You get on each other's nerves, but most of the time it's nice having someone to talk to besides the AI."

"Did you?" I eyed the console. The whole time I'd been aboard E-V, I'd had very little success in manipulating her controls. She flew as she saw fit and functioned when she felt like it. But then, I'd never had any instructions, had I?

Suddenly I was very aware of Two standing behind me, a veteran of this place with a wealth of knowledge. Knowledge I couldn't extract from Astra or Viva or E-V.

I stepped into the capsule. The lights flickered on. I went to the control room and glanced at the screens nonchalantly. As I expected, Two followed.

"Most of these didn't work," I said.

"They're old and not worth fixing," Two spun a trio of tiny silver cubes around their fingers. "All you really need is one. Two if you want to monitor a planet and communicate at the same time, but really, no one's forcing you to multitask."

I glanced at the control console, feigning boredom, though my heart was racing. "So how does she know where to go?"

"She has the galaxy mapped in her memory. We update it periodically, but not often. It's not like new planets spring up every other day."

"So she knows where to go if you tell her?"

"Usually, yes. Unless you want to take a scenic route."

She knows where Fiina is.

I didn't dare let myself follow this train of thought, but to know that E-V contained all the directions I needed was enough for hope to bubble up.

"I couldn't get her to fly right," I said, cautiously leaving out the part about my frantic attempt to escape the silver orb. "She doesn't listen to me."

"That's because you don't know how to talk to her." Two stepped forward and hovered their metal hand over the green goo. It rippled, responding to their presence. "You can't fight her. You have to listen and sync your body and thoughts with her. It's the same as manifestation."

Great, I grumbled inwardly. But then, how was it different from the mantras of my entire life? *Watch. Follow. Listen.* Over and over.

"If someone can't do that," I said carefully, hoping I wasn't being too obvious. "How can they fly it?"

Two turned to me. Their holographic face flickered. I couldn't tell what they were thinking, but after a moment, they pulled their hand away from the console and leaned against the nearest wall.

"The capsule can be operated entirely on verbal commands," they said. "By issuing the exact phrasing and wording needed to be understood by the AI, the pilot can do anything they need without directly using the console. Faulty as she is, E-V still possesses the basic functions of piloting and maintaining the capsule on her own. If she didn't, you wouldn't have made it here alive. If you can give her an exact destination and a location to orbit or land, she will get you where you need to be. You will have to tell her to engage in the optimally safe route, avoid the orbit of planets with established space programs, and steer clear of asteroid fields, but otherwise take the route of minimal distance. She should have more than enough provisions to get you wherever you need to go in this galaxy, but if you venture beyond that, it might get a little iffy."

They waved their hand. A black ball the size of their palm appeared. They tossed it into the air and caught it without looking. "But none of that is going to do you any good."

I started. "I-I'm just curious."

"Sure you are." Two tossed the ball again. "And I'm just talking for my health. It's not going to do you any good because first of all, you're not an authorized pilot. E-V got you here probably because her security features are lacking. But since you've been here, you've been specifically blacklisted as an unauthorized pilot. I told you, trust isn't the arena master's strong suit." They tossed the ball to me. I fumbled and dropped it. It crumbled back into blocks before it hit the floor. "Second, piloting the capsules is a skill. The AI isn't infallible. There are times when you will have to take over manually in an emergency. In space, there are no second chances. No new champion travels alone for that reason. The veterans accompany them until they get the hang of things. Long-distance solo piloting takes time. You already lucked out once. Think it'll happen twice?"

I swallowed thickly.

"You're not the first to want to escape this place," Two went on. "Heck, you might not be the last, even with how few of us are left. But trust me, this is not the way to go. You won't make it far out there alone, and you won't think the stars are so pretty in that final moment before your lungs pop like balloons."

I shivered and walked out of the capsule. Two followed. Neither of us said anything as I returned to my room. The space, both within the metal walls and outside them, felt vast and endless. I lay down in bed, pulled a blanket over my head, and wished I had a dark closet to hide in.

THE DAYS EKED BY. All I could do to keep from giving in to fear, paranoia, and the constant sensation of being trapped was to focus on what was in front of me, counting the steps as I walked through the winding metal corridors and watching the stars pass by outside. Viva still refused to answer my questions, and after my stint in the capsule bay with Two, I entertained no more delusions of escape. I was just beginning to think I was going to spend the rest of my days in this metal tomb when a new face crossed my path.

"Whoa."

A strong hand reached out and steadied me as I ran into them face first stepping out of my room. I lifted my gaze to mutter a thanks.

"Are you alright?"

Fiinian dialect?

The voice was familiar, but I was too distracted by the crescent of iridescent scales cupping the socket of his left eye to place it. Though they resembled the popular fashion trend of Fiina, these were not jewels or gems stuck on with glue. They were complex, delicate, and organic. The speaker was tall and his teal-green skin was hairless. His features were sharp and angular in a terribly flattering way.

He looked down at me. I was gawking like an idiot. His eyes were gold rimmed around a deep blue iris. The splash of scales along the side of his head and neck shimmered as he moved, as if underwater.

"Um," I said. "Yes. Sorry."

He nodded half-heartedly. I cleared my throat and felt very stupid.

"I-I'm Kova," I said, trying to sound casual. "You are . . ."

"Solace."

My blood ran cold as I suddenly noticed what he was wearing. The black armor sent chills down my spine. In his right hand was the featureless black mask.

The expression on my face must have changed, because I could see a shift in Solace's eyes. Concern? Suspicion? Om's severed limb flashed through my mind and I quickly forced a smile, perhaps a little too widely.

"Right," I said. "I just . . . I . . ."

"Kova."

Astra's voice made me jump. Solace slipped the mask over his face and stepped aside. Astra didn't spare him a glance.

"We are arriving at our destination," she said to me.

I hadn't realized we were headed somewhere. I wasn't brave enough to question her, but thankfully Solace beat me to it.

"Destination where?"

His language had switched. His voice was now layered with translation. Had I imagined that he spoke Fiinian?

She turned to him as if daring him to question her. "The Pinnacle."

"What for?" The edge in his voice struck fear in me. All at once I was back in the silver orb, cowering and terrified for my life.

"You know what for."

"You said you would send her home."

"As soon as possible, once what needs to be done is done. I need you to accompany her once we arrive."

I tensed at the suggestion.

"No."

Astra's eyes narrowed slightly. "This is our best chance to—"

"I have no intention of being around *her*."

Did he mean me?

Even with her face covered, I could tell Astra's teeth were gritted. "You are being childish," she said.

"Am I? I'm not the one who calls her 'Mother.'"

I held my breath, waiting for either of them to say something, but they didn't. Without another word, Solace walked away. I watched him leave. Astra didn't.

"Come," she said simply, beckoning me with a gesture like tugging on a pet's leash.

. . .

Two leaned against the wall of a capsule in the docking bay, playing with their manifested trinkets as usual. Their face flickered on as we entered.

"Please accompany Kova to the Pinnacle," Astra said, right to the point as always.

"Me?" Two asked, a pair of six-pointed shapes flying around one hand. "You're not going? I would think you'd want to oversee this personally. Mother dearest would surely be disappointed to miss the chance to see her favorite daughter."

"Stop running your mouth and do it."

The smiling hologram didn't change, but I thought I could detect a smirk in Two's voice. "Eleven got to you again, eh?"

I watched Astra carefully but audibly crack one knuckle before walking away. I allowed myself a small breath of relief at not having to spend much more time in her company.

"Oh, those two," Two said almost wistfully. They turned, opened the capsule door next to them, and held it open for me. I took a moment to scan the area for any sign of Om, though it proved fruitless once again. The capsule was a little different from E-V's. It was wider, but shorter. The interior was a little more spacious, but with smaller sleeping quarters that contained no furnishing. Two went to the central console and hovered their palm over it. It quivered and the capsule door locked.

"Short trip," they told me. "Much less exciting than your last one."

Whatever I had expected, the sight that greeted me from the window in the console room wasn't it. I stood before the glass, watching with mouth agape as the capsule drifted slowly out of the opening in the wall of the bay.

Everywhere I looked, there were orbs. Solid black orbs just like the one on Fiina, suspended in space. How many were there? Hundreds? Thousands? More? They extended in every direction. Soon I could see very few stars in the sky, as the orbs blocked them from sight. Compared to them, the capsule was a tiny minnow, adrift in a sea full of huge, silent predators.

"What is this place?"

"A graveyard," Two replied. The capsule shifted and I saw the glistening surface of the black orb we had exited from.

"Graveyard?" I pressed my face to the window, watching orb after enormous orb pass by. "Are all of these . . . dead?"

"All living things must die. The arenas are the same. The Pinnacle is a code name for the last functioning holy ground in this galaxy, and we've hidden it here."

I watched the sea of orbs drift by. Never in my life had I felt so small.

A silver orb appeared in the distance after an hour of threading between the dead arenas. We entered a completely black bay, just like the orb where I found Om. Though there appeared to be no AI assisting, Two knew exactly where they were going. When we stopped, they turned to me.

"Watch where you step," they said, and opened the capsule door.

We stepped out onto the hovering platform. I looked around. It looked exactly like the first holy ground, with a lit doorway in the distance but no platforms or steps.

"Care to try manifesting?"

I shook my head.

"I thought so. Follow behind me. Stay close."

Two made a wide gesture in the air. A series of small platforms appeared. They stepped on, heading toward the doorway. I hurried after them. The steps behind me collapsed as I stepped off each one. Had I not already done this once, my knees might've knocked harder as we moved over the bottomless abyss below.

We emerged on the lit walkway on the other side. This holy ground was vastly different from the one E-V had taken me to. The walkways crisscrossing above and below us were whole, uninterrupted, extending from the edges of the orb to its center, where a massive white column stood. Though it was in far better shape, I could still see signs of age and wear. I was still taking it all in when a large, heavyset form came barreling down the walkway toward us. I took several steps back in alarm as it grabbed Two with both hands, lifting them into the air as if they weighed nothing.

"Two!" it roared and spun Two around twice, holding them by the waist like a puppet. I feared that we had encountered some sort of hostile security measure guarding the holy ground when I realized the sounds it was making were not threatening growls.

It was laughing.

"That's enough, Mod," Two said patiently. The thing called Mod set them down. I blinked and a sleek black shape pounced on me. I let out a cry of surprise and shielded my face with my arms as it knocked me over. It perched on my chest, letting out an eerie chitter. I couldn't make out a single distinguishing feature on its body, the entirety of which was slick as if covered in oil. It pushed its featureless face toward me, let out a hiss, and the black substance began to peel back from its face.

"Whoa!" Two snapped their fingers. "Down, girl."

The thing whipped around and dashed off my chest. I sat up, relieved not to have been subjected to whatever horror show lay underneath its oily shell. Scrambling to my feet, I hid behind Two, who chuckled.

"This is Mod," they said. "The eighth champion of the Galaxy of the Starry River. I suppose you can call him the groundskeeper of the Pinnacle." They pointed at the oily creature, who was shaped like a young Fiinian child but sat like a feline. "And this is Sweetly, the ninth champion. Mod, this is Kova. She's our guest."

Mod stepped close to me. I was taken aback by his appearance. Up until now, everyone I'd encountered did not stray significantly from what I'd become accustomed to as "normal" Fiinian anatomy. Even Solace, with his exotic skin color and beautiful scales, or Two, with their metal casing, were within the shape and scale of that norm. But Mod was completely different. For one, he was huge. I found myself looking upward at him with my neck craned. His gray skin was textured like stone, but when I took the hand he offered, I found it was smooth to the touch. His eyes were small and round, like marbles embedded in his face, and his mouth lipless and wide as it smiled. Mod was unlike anything I'd ever seen before. A true "alien."

"I. Mod," he said, and the holy ground translated as the arena did. "You. Champion?"

"Kova is a *special* guest," Two said. "We don't run games anymore, remember?"

Sweetly wound herself around Two's metal legs, walking on all fours. Despite her unsettling appearance, there was a strange beauty to her. She moved with effortless grace and as I calmed down, I realized her chitters reminded me of the migrating birds on Fiina.

"By the way," Two said with a wink as they scratched Sweetly's chin. "I was joking when I called Astra the favorite. Mother's most beloved son and daughter are right here."

"Welcome," Mod said, grinning. He had large, flat teeth. "Welcome. To Pinnacle."

CHAPTER 15

TWO AND I FOLLOWED THE GUARDIANS OF THE PINNACLE DOWN the long walkway. Even ignoring their unusual appearances, Sweetly and Mod were completely different from the other inhabitants of the orbs. They walked with a certain lightness and flair, with Sweetly bounding next to Mod, occasionally nipping at his hand playfully, and him laughing and pushing her away gently.

Mod and Sweetly were *happy*.

We approached the enormous column at the center of the holy ground. Even though I'd been inside a holy ground before, looking up toward its top made me dizzy. "Speaking with Mother may be a little strange at first," Two said. "But don't let it bother you too much. Just relax."

They stopped. I did the same. Now that we were up close, I saw that what I initially took to be stone or marble was moving like a dense fog.

"Two?"

"Yes?"

"Who is *Mother*?"

"There's no short answer to that question." Two shrugged nonchalantly. "And frankly, I don't feel like explaining it, so I'll let her answer that herself. Go on in. I'm sure she already knows you're coming."

I eyed the fog with apprehension. "Go in?"

"Just step." Two put a cold, firm hand on my back, pushing me forward. I resisted.

"What happens after I go in?" The dense fog was a finger's length from my face.

"Relax," I heard Two say, which wasn't terribly reassuring, but the fog had already swallowed me.

It happened all at once. One moment I could see Mod to my side; then I blinked and he was gone. I spun around, expecting to find the walkway behind me, but that was gone as well. I turned around again, wondering if I should go forward, and suddenly realized I didn't know where "forward" was. I picked a direction, took a step, followed by another, and another.

The fog gathered around me, bumping against me like bundles of soft cloth, and yet when I tried to run my hand over it, it scattered. It swallowed all sounds, even my footsteps. I pushed my way through, blind and lost, hoping I was heading in the right direction.

"Blow."

I stopped. That was a voice.

"What?" I called. "What do you mean?"

"Put your lips together. And blow."

I drew a deep breath, pressed my lips together with a small gap in between, and blew out. A stream of air flowed from my mouth, more than my body ought to be able to hold. It parted the fog, splitting it like a knife, and it dissipated right before my eyes. I found myself standing in a small clearing. The fog circled me like a moving wall.

"You're quite the interesting visitor," the voice said. It came at me from every direction.

"Hi," I said awkwardly. "I-I'm Kova."

"I know who you are."

Though the fog had cleared the area around me, its heaviness lingered. Tendrils of it pried into me, trying to get under my skin. I instinctively batted at it, but my hands hit nothing.

"Are you . . . Mother?"

"I've had many names." The voice moved. It was now coming from behind me. "But that was when I had flesh to go along with my memories."

I didn't understand.

"You don't have to understand."

Can she hear my thoughts?

"And your memories as well. It used to be a privilege reserved for the gods."

The invisible fog was prying at me more aggressively now, pushing its way into my nose, ears, and mouth. I coughed and gagged, but it couldn't relieve the worst sensation of all—tiny, unseen fingers probing my brain.

"Stop," I said around a mouthful of fog. It felt like someone forcing wads of soft fabric down my throat.

"Relax." Now it was in front of me, right by my face. I could almost feel another person's breath on my cheek. "This is easier and quicker if you don't fight it."

"No," I said, stumbling and spitting, struggling against the invasive sensation. "Stop it."

"Just let go."

"Stop!"

All at once the fog was gone. My nose and throat cleared. My eyes watered as I drew deep, grateful breaths and coughed.

A single beam of white light descended from above. It pulsated back and forth rapidly as it hit the ground. I watched with equal horror and fascination as a figure began to appear, one speck of color and flesh at a time.

Mother faced me.

She was young. If I had to guess, I would say she had only just invigorated, if that. Then I remembered what Astra had said about invigoration being a rare occurrence. Just like Rosi, this was a child born female. She had dark, almost brown skin, black hair, and bright, violet eyes.

"The gods wouldn't have cared if you resisted," she said. "But I am kinder. If you'd rather speak with words, we can do that."

There was something about the way she spoke. She held herself with confidence, the kind that came only with time, experience, and knowing that you knew more than everyone else. A regard for others as lovable but lesser than. She smiled at me not like a host welcoming a guest, but like a collector regarding a rare and valuable find.

She reminded me of Meli.

"Trying to decide if you should be afraid?" She chuckled at my dismayed expression. "Don't worry; I can't read your thoughts anymore. I just know that look. They all give me the same look when they meet me for the first time."

I wrung my hands.

"You can speak," she said. "There's no need to be nervous."

I eyed her apprehensively. "I'm not sure what I'm doing here," I said at last.

"You're here because Stars sent you here."

"Stars?"

"Is she still insisting on the old phonetics from her world?" she shook her head. "That girl. She's had many names, too. Donna Ching. Thirty-three. Her own people called her Diamond Donna, a moniker referencing a gemstone native to their planet. Many of the orb's residents adapted their former names using their translated meaning after they abandoned their numbers. But she insists on Astra. Can't seem to let it go."

I didn't know what to do with that information.

"But you don't care about that." She lifted a hand and snapped her fingers in a manner similar to Two. "You're here because you know something the rest of us don't." The fog melted away into greens and browns and I suddenly found myself standing on a gentle, familiar slope. The green sea of

Fiina crashed against the coastline and a chilly breeze caressed my cheek. I couldn't stifle my shock as I saw the unmistakable shape of Radley Cove, complete with the black orb that rested in its center. Behind me, my family house stood with its thatched roof and gray brick walls.

"How . . ." I couldn't finish my thought.

"A moment in the mind reveals a thousand secrets," said the child called Mother. "I thought you'd appreciate a setting you know. Come, let's take a walk."

"I HAVEN'T PERSONALLY BEEN to Fiina," said Mother. "It looks lovely. But then, every seed race possesses a planet lovely in its own way." She walked next to me as we strolled the beaches of Radley Cove. Though the imagery around us was flawless at a glance, I was already beginning to notice that it was not a perfect reproduction. The pebbles under our feet were all the same size, color, and shape, and though I could hear crashing waves, the water was perfectly still. The hills surrounding the cove were in familiar but incorrect shapes and patterns. And the orb in the center of the water simply looked wrong even though I couldn't quite pinpoint why. This was not Fiina, nor Radley, but a construct created based on my own hazy memory.

"This is very weird," I muttered, then quickly hushed myself, fearing I would cause offense. But Mother only laughed.

"I have forgotten how strange the manifested worlds are to newcomers," she said. "I haven't forgotten many things thanks to the Pinnacle, but even before it became my home, I had not encountered a newcomer to our midst for a long time. Not after the games stopped." She gestured around her. "There used to be no building blocks in this space. It was reserved for the gods."

"Gods?"

"She didn't give you a proper orientation, did she?" Mother shook her head. "Stars was never a fan of orientation. But I suppose it doesn't matter. Tell me, how do your people view 'gods'?"

"They are fiction," I replied hesitantly, wary of offending her. She was, after all, someone Astra called "Mother," and after being in Astra's company, I worried what this strange little woman was capable of underneath that friendly exterior. "Invisible beings that grant wishes to children."

"An atheistic society. Good. That should make this a little easier for you. This part was always more traumatic for those from theistic worlds." Mother gestured with her hand and the clear sky above became deep dark space, dotted with stars. "It's not uncommon for planets with seed races to become increasingly atheistic over time, as they develop and grow themselves around the principles of science and technology. The fact is, the concept of 'gods' is a theoretical one, and given our limited understanding of the First Beings, theoretical is the best we're ever going to get. More recently, we referred to them as producers, though now that the game—Headspace—has ended, the old word has crept back in."

A myriad of black orbs appeared among the stars, drifting about like bubbles. Here and there, I spotted clusters of silver ones.

"The gods created this universe and everything in it. They had infinite patience and spent eons moving the pieces and shaping the environments, experimenting and testing to make the perfect seed races. For one purpose only—entertainment."

"Entertainment?"

"You don't have to believe me. But you will. We were all created flawed. Perfectly flawed in a way that makes us entertaining to the gods. We are seeds, planted by the First Beings. Then, they created the orbs. And the demigods."

Five figures, all different in shapes and sizes, appeared in front of me, startling me as I initially mistook them for living beings. One was small and neckless, with eyes that hovered over a rotund, ball-like body. Another was thin and scaly with joints like a segmented insect. A short, furry one with four arms smiled broadly. A tall one extended their long arms, but what came out of their sleeves appeared to be tendrils of smoke, the same smoke that emitted from their neck hole and supported what resembled a lump of crystal in place of a head.

And the last one.

I tensed. There was no mistaking that silhouette. In the video, white light obscured their features, but now I could see it clearly. Long and slender, with deep green, pupil-less eyes. Their skin was a warm gray, with a flat, slitted nose and thin, lipless mouth.

The figures vanished before I could get a closer look.

"The demigods are a very different type of being," Mother said. "No two are alike. Each one is designed specifically for the galaxy they watched over, meant to look harmless, unassuming, and based on the aesthetic preferences of the general populace. They are dedicated, loyal, and single-minded. They have one purpose and one purpose only—to harvest the seed races for their masters using the orbs."

Harvest. The word sounded terribly sinister.

The orbs vanished, as did Radley Cove. White walls shot up around us. The sound of screams filled my ears. I spun around just in time to see a person—an alien—crushed beneath an enormous metal ball. I screamed in terror as the ball came barreling down toward me, but it rolled harmlessly past, as if made of smoke.

"This is the game orchestrated by the demigods," Mother's voice said. I turned and turned but couldn't find her in the gruesome scene. "It varied from planet to planet, exploiting the skills of each race in search of a single champion from every world. Contestants were selected, then forced to play or die, depending on their skill in manifestation. If a planet could not produce a champion, it was deemed unworthy and destroyed.

The name of the game was Headspace, and the demigods lived and died by it. They cannot survive without it. It consumed them and was their only purpose. They're so focused on it that even though their fate depended on their ability to discover new champions, they cannot bear to run an unfair game. It is their pride and their obsession."

The terrifying sight disappeared. The fog walls returned, and Mother reappeared before me.

"We stand now in the holy ground. One of many," she said. "Those who survived the games and were deemed 'worthy' of the gods came to worship here, bringing with them their memories and emotions to feed to the gods. This is what the gods craved, and what they had an endless hunger for. In return for what we provided them, the orb kept us alive, gave us a home, healed us, and even kept us from aging. Aside from the demigods, every living being inside the orbs is a survivor of Headspace." She gestured around her at the fog. "Of course, none of that really matters anymore. You see, the gods are long gone."

"The gods," I said carefully, keenly aware of how strange those words still sounded. Radley Cove returned around us, like a picture exiting shadows. "They're . . . gone?"

Mother nodded. "They disappeared. There was no warning, no ceremony, not a peep. One day they were there; the next the holy grounds were empty. Every single one."

"Where did they go?"

She shrugged nonchalantly. "Who knows? It sent the demigods into quite a tizzy. They have no other purpose, you see. They were created with one purpose and one purpose only—to serve Headspace. My theory is that they lost interest in us, simple as that. We mean nothing to them. We are less than insects, less than dirt beneath their metaphorical feet. They gathered all they cared to from us; then they simply left.

All entertainment runs its course. Eventually it becomes boring. No matter how much the arena masters tried to spice up the games, they couldn't hold the audience's interest forever."

She watched me with an observant expression as she said this, as if curious what my reaction would be. I did my best to keep my expression neutral. After a moment, she bent down and picked up a pebble from the beach.

"So," she said, tossing it up and down in her hand, "an orb came to your world. I imagine it caused quite an uproar."

I nodded. "It did."

"There was no game on Fiina." Mother nodded toward the orb in the cove. "At least none sanctioned by me, and I ran nearly all the games in this galaxy. So if someone brought Headspace to you, it was done behind my back. Did they send a broadcast?"

"Yes," I said, relieved that she appeared to have extracted very little from my mind.

"Who was the narrator?"

I bit my lip. "I don't know," I lied. "It was just a blob. A shadow."

"And the capsule? They're usually coded or locked in some way. Astra kept E-V secured at all times. How did you get her to open?"

"She was faulty. I was looking around the capsule and it opened by itself."

"And she managed to find her way back to Astra?"

"Yes. I . . . I guess she just knew the way."

Mother's violet eyes flickered. My heart pounded. She took a small step toward me and tossed the pebble into the still water. One of her hands reached out and rested on my arm. Fog swirled around us.

"You're lying," she said, smiling gently.

My entire body went cold. "What are you doing?" I said, suddenly alarmed. The fog grew heavier on my body.

"What Astra sent you here for. Don't fight it. This will only take a moment."

The fog pried into me. Into my mouth and nose and ears. It seeped inside me and drilled deeper and deeper. I tried to scream but nothing came out. Mother's hands held me in place, violet eyes unblinking. I was suffocating. Her tendrils pulled apart my thoughts and memories, trying to get at the buried secrets.

No.

She pushed past the surface, past the cove and the orb.

No.

She broke down my walls, squinting at what I kept hidden.

Om.

Did she see them? I couldn't let her. I had to keep them safe.

Stop.

She pushed harder, reaching deep into my mind.

STOP!

A wave of energy burst from me. The tendrils disappeared. Mother's grip loosened and I stumbled backwards, falling gracelessly on my rear. She lifted her hands to her face. Her fingers disintegrated into tiny cubes, fading away into the air. She looked down at me, violet eyes burning. All traces of warmth disappeared from her face.

"Impressive," she said. "But it won't do you any good. I don't know what you're trying to keep from us, but there are no gentler methods than this. If you choose to reject our kindness, I'm sure my daughter has plenty of other methods to get the truth out of you."

I STUMBLED out of the fog like a fish thrown out of water. Two sat on the floor with Mod and Sweetly, their long metal legs crossed.

"Look who it is," they said, standing. "How was your conversation with Mother? Enlightening?"

The way they spoke was almost like an inside joke, but I was too frazzled to comprehend the punchline. Mother's bitterness lingered on me like an oil slick.

"I'm not sure," I muttered, rubbing my temples.

"Well, let's head back," Two said. "You can rest on the way."

A lump formed in my throat. I had forgotten for a moment that I had to return to Astra's orb. Astra, who was going to do who knew what to me to get the truth from me. The truth about Om. And the orb on Fiina. And the so-called demigod. I couldn't stop thinking about her words on the arena floor.

Take next steps.

Was bringing me to Mother the next step? What came after that? What was she going to do to me to get me to talk? What was she going to do to Om?

"Something wrong?"

"I—" I couldn't meet Two's gaze. "No. It's fine. I'm fine."

Though their holographic smile didn't waver, I had a feeling they didn't believe me. They led me over the walkway, bid goodbye to Mod and Sweetly, and manifested steps that took us to the capsule. Once inside, I sat heavily down on the benches in the control room and buried my face in my hands. Two steered the capsule out of the bay and back into the graveyard of dead orbs.

What do I do now?

Every passing second brought me closer to panic. Restless energy stirred in my chest, growing and pushing against bone and flesh. I bent over, put my head between my knees, and drew deep breaths, trying to calm the pounding in my chest. If I let it out, I might be looking at a repeat of the episode in E-V's capsule, and the last thing I wanted to do was drift through cold space again. Though was that really worse than what awaited me?

A metal hand rested on my back. I hadn't realized until that moment that I was rocking back and forth.

"Hey now," Two said. "No need to do that. I know Mother can be a little abrasive. Happens to the best of us. Even I'm not a fan of getting too close to her, and I knew her when she was still a shaky little seedling."

Tears rolled down my cheeks. Two patted my back as I hunched over, sobbing.

"Come on," they pleaded. "Don't do this. I'm terrible at this." They tapped their fingers on my back. "I really wish One was still here. She was so much better with people. Even if she *was* a devious . . ." They trailed off. "Well, doesn't matter. Look, I don't know what Mother said to you, but I'm sure she didn't mean to upset you. She's just on edge ever since Rosi."

My head snapped up. I raised my tear-filled eyes to Two.

"Rosi?" I asked shakily, unsure I'd heard right.

"That word Astra stumbled on," Two said, leaning back against the wall.

I stared at them, my entire body tense with anticipation.

"I guess Astra doesn't like to talk about it. She couldn't make sense of it though. None of us could. All it's done is drive everyone crazy. How long ago was that?" Two lifted one hand and appeared to count. "Well, I lost track. After we lost track of E-V, I think. Useless bit of information, if you ask me. Don't even know what language it is."

"It's Fiinian."

There was a long pause, and I suddenly realized what I'd said. Fear took over me as Two regarded me in silence.

"What?"

"It . . ." It was too late to pretend I hadn't said anything. "It's Fiinian."

Two sat up, mulled this over, and to my surprise, laughed. "Well look at that," they said between chortles. "You do know something after all." They paused. "Wait, Mother didn't ask you about that?"

I pursed my lips. "No."

"We should go back. I'm sure she'd be thrilled."

"No!" I cried. Two started a little. I was certain they saw the fear on my face. I expected them to tell me I shouldn't be afraid, or scold me, or turn the capsule around and demand that I tell Mother what I knew. But they stayed silent. I watched them tap their fingertips together thoughtfully, then let out a sigh.

"Look," they said slowly. "I get it. Mother is not a person to be trifled with when she has her mind set on something. And little miss arena master, well, let's just say I've seen what she's capable of. I don't blame you for not trusting them." A pause. "But you do realize that if you stick around them, you won't be able to keep what you know from them forever."

I nodded ruefully. "I'm scared," I admitted.

"Lots to be scared of out here. Everyone is scared when they first realize their world isn't as small as they thought."

"I'm scared that I don't know what's going to happen." I suppressed a shudder. "I can't trust anyone. I don't want to go back. Mother was angry that I wouldn't tell her what I knew. She said Astra will find a way to get it out of me." I wrapped my arms around myself tightly. "What's she going to do to me?"

Two said nothing. The silence was worse than any answer they could've given me.

"There is another way," they said after a long moment. "But if I show you my secret, you have to tell me yours."

I bit my lip. Could I trust them? I was so confused, so uncertain. All I wanted was someone to guide me. I looked at Two. Not long ago I couldn't even fathom their sentience, but here they were, watching me with as much concern as a face made with three lines could muster. I thought of the way they had looked at Viva, the way they had tended to me after my arrival and kept me company during those lonely days, and the way they tried to comfort me even now. In this strange and desolate existence, how odd it was that the one who lacked an organic body was the one who cared the most.

"Yes," I nodded. "I will. Please, just tell me what else I can do."

Two seemed to consider. I waited with bated breath. Then, their holographic smile flickered.

"Alright then," they said, and stood. They went to the console and hovered their hand over it. The capsule shuddered, stopped, then began to move again. But, I noticed, it wasn't going forward. It was turning toward a different direction.

I looked at them incredulously. "I thought you said I couldn't escape."

"Not alone." Two winked. "But you're not alone, are you?"

The capsule jerked forward and I nearly tumbled out of my seat. We sped through the graveyard at full speed.

"Where are we going?"

"Taking a scenic route. I can't tell you whom to trust, but there are other places to go for help. This is the only chance you've got. If you change your mind, we can still turn around. If we leave the graveyard, we'll have earned the arena master's wrath and there is no going back."

My hands tightened until they trembled.

"Let's go," I said.

CHAPTER 16

THE SEA OF ORBS PASSED BY OUTSIDE THE WINDOW. EVENTUALLY their numbers dwindled, replaced by stars once more. I watched them meld into the dark of space, expecting to see one of them break away to give chase as Astra realized we were leaving the dictated path. But none of them moved, and soon they were out of sight.

"Relax," Two said from the control console. "It will be a while before we're missed. The arena master is a busy person."

Though I believed them, I couldn't stop myself from nervously looking out the window. Even outside the graveyard, there were pieces of debris drifting in the space around us. The half-rotten husk of a black orb floated lazily by, its innards exposed like the remains of a predator's meal. A chunk of silver metal twice the size of our capsule, the wall of an old holy ground, sat tiredly among asteroids. Several smaller shapes hovered listlessly around it.

"Are those capsules?"

"Probably," Two said without turning. "Plenty of dead capsules around the graveyard."

A question sat on the tip of my tongue, but I did not ask it. It was pointless to ask whether any of the capsules had died with their occupants still inside, possibly still kept alive the way

E-V had kept Om and me alive, just barely on the edge of eternal sleep.

"You should rest."

I looked at Two. Rest? I couldn't imagine resting right now. My heart was pounding and my legs were jittering restlessly, the way Rosi's used to at the dinner table. How could they be so calm when we were in the middle of a daring escape?

And yet, despite my apprehension, I realized I was exhausted. My mind and body both ached. Though I tried hard to keep my eyes focused outside the window, keeping watch for pursuers, my eyelids grew heavy. As they closed, I thought I saw movement through my bleary gaze.

I STARTED out of an incoherent dream full of floating orbs and tall white figures and for a moment couldn't remember where I was. I didn't know how long I'd slept, but it couldn't have been very long because I felt barely rested. My back was stiff from lying on the hard bench and my joints creaked as I sat up. The window on the front wall was blacked out and the capsule appeared to have stopped moving. A heavy, scratchy blanket fell off my torso. I couldn't have manifested such a thing, so someone else must have put it on me.

Two.

I looked around, rubbing my eyes. The last thing I remembered was speeding out of the graveyard.

Did I see another capsule move? It didn't matter anymore.

Two was nowhere to be found and suddenly I was afraid I had lost another companion, the same way I lost Om. I pushed the blanket onto the floor and stood. The capsule door was open. Through it, I could hear voices.

"Hello?" I called.

The voices stopped. I went to the open door carefully and peered out.

"You're awake."

The voice was unfamiliar, but the surface beneath me wasn't. I regarded the greenish metal floor with dread.

Was I back in the arena?

I stepped out. Two figures greeted me. One was Two, smiling their usual holographic smile. The other looked at me with an amused expression, or at least what I interpreted to be amusement.

"Two was just telling me about you," he said. "Welcome. It's been a long time since I met a Fiinian."

He was lean and sinewy, with warm red skin and flat features. Thick, long black hair grew from his scalp and down the back of his neck, almost like a mane. Over his gray uniform, he wore a stylish collared coat. As he studied me, he smiled, and a vertical slit opened briefly on his forehead—a third eye.

"A little different than what you're used to?" he asked, noticing my shock. "It's quite alright. We are all aliens to each other, after all. I prefer to focus on the similarities." He raised both hands and waved them in an almost comical fashion. "Same number of limbs, better than nothing, right?"

I chuckled despite myself.

"I am the tenth champion of this galaxy," he said. "And the master of this arena." He paused. "Does that sound as pretentious to you as it does to me? It's just a word for whoever wields administrative functions of this thing. You can call me Able."

I nodded. "Kova."

"I know." He tilted his head toward Two. "Our mutual acquaintance here has been filling me in. Speaking of which," he reached over and tapped his finger against Two's chest. "How hard did you freak out when you first met this one? I thought I was going crazy or having a fever dream or something."

Two batted his hand away. "As if you're a prize," they said. "Look at her. Her people would probably mistake you for some kind of holiday decoration."

Able grinned and approached me. There was something

very disarming about him despite his exotic appearance. But then, I quickly reminded myself, I had initially taken Astra to be a friendly presence as well. And how wrong I had turned out to be.

"I'm sure you have a lot of questions," Able said. I had a feeling he noticed the uncertainty on my face. "You came from Astra's orb, right? Not that you would, but don't tell her about this place." He held a finger in front of his mouth. "It's a secret."

I looked around the bay. It was almost identical to the one in Astra's arena. "Is this an arena, too?"

"Oh, yes. There are plenty of these floating out there, as I'm sure you saw. Of course, most of them are in poor shape. This one's missing a few key functions, but at least the arena floor still works. It's taken a lot of work and a lot of time to maintain, especially while trying not to draw the attention of the favored arena master."

"Are you hiding from her?"

Able arched a brow. "Aren't *you*?"

I flushed and glanced at Two.

"Yes," I said softly. "I guess I am."

"Well, then there's no point pretending I'm not, right?" Able winked, then turned serious. "Don't get me wrong," he said. "Astra is a fine arena master. A savage one, but a fine one. She's done a lot of things to keep the demigods at bay for the rest of us, but that kind of thing changes a person, and over time, some of us have grown to disagree with her methods. Sometimes I wonder what she's willing to do and whom she'll sacrifice next to eliminate the demigods."

"Eliminate?" I echoed. It was such an eerie word. Astra's words echoed in my mind. *Kill them all.*

"I suppose you still have a lot to learn. Don't worry; we'll fill you in."

Two nudged Able.

"She's seen the basements."

"Then she knows." He shook his head. "The lengths she's

willing to go to . . . it's not that I don't admire it. I simply believe there are other ways. *Kinder* ways."

I nodded.

"But hey," he continued. "You shouldn't trust *my* word. Not yet, anyway. We've only just met. There's plenty of time to get acquainted. But before we do that, I need to thank you."

"Thank *me*?" I asked, confused.

"Yes, for rescuing our friend. Without you, he would've surely been lost. Astra's henchman is swift and merciless."

"He? Who is—"

The rest of the words caught in my throat as a figure appeared at the door of the bay.

Just like Rosi's message, he wasn't a dream.

WHEN STRADDLING the line between life and death, everything was an illusion. Those dark days in the capsule were little more than a jumble of images and sensations.

But now, as he approached me, I couldn't help but wonder if I was dreaming again. Logic dictated that he couldn't be real. And yet, there he was. My body still recalled the sensation of his warm chest and strong limbs pressed against me as we drifted slowly through the darkness together.

"I believe you gave him a name," Able said. "He isn't able to speak right now. We're still working on restoring some of his core functions, but he is able to communicate through other means. Sounds like you two had quite the adventure."

Him.

My mind chewed on this word. The pronoun for an adult, a grown man. I'd gotten so used to the infantile "them" that to hear Om referred to as "him" was almost strange. And yet, this person before me was definitely no longer the child who had lain giggling in my lap.

His body was the same flawless white. Thin grooves glistened in the light. He wore a uniform similar to the gray piece worn by Able and me, but it was white like the rest of him and almost appeared to be part of his body. Over his collar, I saw a peek of the black circle on his chest, which was now at my eye level. He looked very different, but his eyes, the same piercing blue as they always were, watched me patiently as I struggled to sort out this new shift in reality.

"Om?" I said uncertainly.

He smiled. Relief washed over me. I threw my arms around his neck and held him for a split second before realizing what I was doing. Embarrassment washed over me as I stepped back, though that seemed silly. After all, we had shared a bed and a blanket for many days and nights.

"I don't understand," I murmured. "I just . . . I don't even know where to start."

Able chuckled. He put a hand on the small of my back, guiding me toward the bay door. Om followed.

"Should I be calling him that?" I whispered to Able as we walked. "That's not really his name, is it?"

"We've never given him a name," he replied. "The seed races put much stock into what we are called, but names don't matter much to his kind. Still, he seems to have become fond of what you call him." He gave me a gentle, reassuring squeeze on the shoulder. "But there's plenty of time for that later. Come, you've had a very long trip."

THE ROOM Able showed me to was similar to the one provided to me in Astra's orb, but in stark contrast to her hospitality—or lack thereof—he went out of his way to check the facilities and ensure that I had running water and a working food machine, though just like on Astra's orb, there was not a single piece of furnishing.

"I apologize for the empty room," he said regretfully as I stood in the center of the small space. He thought for a moment, then made a gesture to Om, who nodded and walked out the door.

I looked around. "How long will I have to stay here?" I asked, then realized the question sounded rude. "Sorry, I just mean . . ."

Able waved me off. "Don't worry about it," he said. "I know you've been through a lot, and it's hard to feel safe right now."

I nodded. Despite the relief of having found Om, I couldn't help being on edge. There was still so much I didn't know, and being inside yet another black orb didn't exactly put me at ease.

"There's no AI here, unfortunately," Able went on. "Would you like to try manifesting?"

I shook my head. "No. I mean, I've tried. But . . ." I gave him a furtive look, hoping he wouldn't judge me for my incompetence. Thankfully, he only smiled.

"It's not a big deal," he said. "Some may tell you manifestation is the be-all and end-all in the orbs, but really it's just a matter of convenience. Tell you what, I'll go turn on the manual controls to maintain manifestation in this room, and we'll go from there."

He gave me a wave and walked out. I stood in the empty room and mused how strange my life had suddenly become. But I didn't have long to dwell, because a knock came on the door. Able was quick.

"Come in," I said.

The door opened and Om stepped inside. He handed me a gray bundle—Able must've instructed him to fetch me a change of clothing. He closed the door behind him and I suddenly realized I hadn't been alone with him since our reunion. Now that I could study him without distraction, I noticed that he looked sculpted instead of grown, every curve and detail molded with careful hands. His skin possessed a slight sheen, as if polished to perfection. His was hairless like Solace, but with softer, more symmetrical features and a rounder jawline. His blue eyes possessed an almost translucent quality, as if I could see through them to his mind. As my eyes traveled down his body, I realized that his damaged limb had been fixed as well.

An unexpected heat rose to my face and I cleared my throat awkwardly. Was it strange to look at Om this way, knowing that he was the same child who held my hand and curled beside me in the dark? Not that long ago, we had been huddled together in the capsule, limbs intertwined as we slept. They used to put their head in my lap and nuzzle my neck as we kept each other company. Back then I could think of nothing but protecting them—this vulnerable child alone in the universe. But this Om was not the one who needed to be protected. He was bigger, stronger, an entirely different being.

He was the one who had protected *me* when I toed the line between living and dying.

Om opened his mouth, struggled for a moment, then frowned and cleared his throat. He gave me a small, almost embarrassed smile, then lifted a hand and gestured in the air. A pixilated rectangle appeared in the air. He moved his fingers rapidly and a line of alien text emerged. They flickered, then changed into East Fiinian dialect.

ABLE SENT ME.

I nodded. The line of text disappeared. Om moved his fingers and a new line appeared.

I WILL SET UP YOUR ROOM.

I stepped aside as he walked to the center of the room beside me, where he lifted both hands like a conductor ready to direct an orchestra. His fingers danced in the air and objects began to take shape around the room. A bed with a thick pillow and blankets. A simple rectangular table and wooden chair. A mirror and modest dresser—not that I had much to put in it.

I'd seen this all done before in Astra's orb, but something about this was different. Everything created by Viva had a certain systematic, straightforwardness to it, like a program running one line of code at a time. Om's creations danced into existence, growing as if alive and organic. I couldn't stop watching his hands as they moved in the air.

Om turned to me as he finished manifesting the furniture in the room and I quickly pretended to study the bundle of clothing in my arms. Om gestured in the air and the blue screen returned.

CAN I HELP YOU WITH ANYTHING ELSE?

I started to shake my head, then stopped myself, suddenly worried that if I said no, he would leave.

"Are you okay?" I asked. "I was so worried about you."

His fingers moved in the air.

I AM WELL. BECAUSE OF YOU.

"I thought something bad happened to you. There was another one like you, and—" I stopped. Would it upset Om to know what had happened to one of his kin? I decided it wasn't worth mentioning at the moment. "I'm just glad you're okay." I glanced at the bed. "Do you want to sit?"

He nodded, but didn't move. It took me a moment to realize he was waiting for me. I went to the bed and sat on its edge. He did the same. For a moment it was almost like we were back in the capsule, with only each other for company. I told him all about my days in Astra's orb, my fears and worries, and how relieved I had been to find him again. He replied using the blue screen, and we laughed about our first meeting and the terrifying days I had spent hiding from him that now seemed so silly. His warmth filled the room and I noticed that no matter his form, his smile and the glimmer in his blue eyes remained the same. Om was still Om, and I was so very glad not to be alone.

A LOUD BANG shook the walls. I blinked and tried to decide if I was dreaming.

"Om?" I said sleepily. How long had I been out? The bed

was so much more comfortable than the bench in the capsule that I must've drifted off. Had he been lying with me?

Om turned to me, waved his hand, and the blue screen appeared.

HELP.

I blinked. "What?"

His fingers moved.

THEY NEED HELP.

I sat up, sleep giving way to alarm. "Who does? What's going on?"

But he was already out the door. I stumbled out of bed and followed him, my sleep-addled mind racing. I suddenly imagined Astra attacking Able's orb to hunt me down, being dragged back to Mother's temple and interrogated in an array of unimaginable torture. I hurried after Om through the winding hallways, terrified of what I would find at the destination.

"What's going on?" I asked again, but Om said nothing. I wondered frantically if I would be ready for a violent confrontation if the occasion called for it, but when we arrived at the capsule bay, I immediately saw that the help required was a very different sort.

A badly damaged capsule lay slanted in the center of the bay. Its hull was so severely warped that it looked almost deflated. Two and Able stood beside it. Seeing us approach, Able waved.

"Give us a hand!" he shouted. "Hurry!"

Om broke into a run and I followed. As we drew near the broken capsule, I saw that its door had been dented beyond recognition. Able pulled at the handle but it didn't budge.

"Grab hold," he said. "Hurry! She doesn't have much time."

Om grabbed the handle alongside Able and I took hold of his arm. Two dug their fingers into the side of the door. We all pulled together. I strained so hard that I thought my eyes might pop out of my sockets. Just as I thought we were doing no good, the stuck door opened with a pained groan. Able darted into the capsule without hesitation. A moment later he emerged, carrying in his arms a small, familiar white body.

"Move," he snapped as the rest of us scrambled out of the way. He laid the figure on the floor of the bay and tapped his fingers along the center of her chest. She was roughly the same size as Om in his child form, perhaps smaller. Her arms and legs were twig thin and her eyes, a pale seafoam green, were half open and listless. Long white hair tangled around her skinny neck.

"Is she alright?" I asked. As if hearing me, the girl shivered and her gaze rolled in my direction.

"She has multiple leaks in her core," Able said. He grabbed both my hands and pressed them firmly to the child's chest. "Hold your hands here. It'll keep her from leaking out while we find a way to help her. Can you do it?"

"I—" I stammered. Beneath my palms, I could feel a weak, uneven pulse, like blood struggling to flow through a vein.

"Push down!" Able snapped. I forced my hands down, pushing so hard my fingers grew numb. "Keep it that way," he said. "We're going to look through and see what we can use to salvage her core. We'll be as quick as possible, but you have to keep her alive, Kova."

"Alive?" I said. My arms were already trembling from the effort.

"Yes, alive." He gripped my shoulders. "You can do this. She's depending on you."

I nodded frantically, though I couldn't have had less confidence in myself at that moment. Something wet and sticky spread beneath my palms. Whatever passed for blood in the girl's body was leaking rapidly. Able gestured to Om, who knelt down beside me, laid his hands over mine, and pushed down. The flow of sticky liquid slowed.

"Stay like that," Able said. "We'll be back as soon as we can."

He stood, motioned for Two to follow. As they passed me, I suddenly remembered sitting on the bench in the capsule as Two had piloted away from the graveyard of black orbs. The dead capsules outside my window. One of them had moved. I glanced at the capsule we'd just pried open.

Was it this one? Could we have saved her earlier?

I had no time to dwell on that thought. I could feel the white-skinned girl bleeding out once more, so I hardened my focus and pushed down with all my might. Om did the same.

As their footsteps receded, silence overtook us. The only sound was blood pounding in my ears. I wished Om would say something to relieve the pressure of the moment, then remembered he couldn't speak with his hands occupied. His face was tightened in the grip of concentration. I had been so wrapped up in my own worries that I hadn't realized until now what an ordeal this must be for him, watching one of his own struggling to stay alive underneath his own hands.

"She's going to be okay," I said, and hoped I sounded reassuring. "We'll save her."

He didn't appear to hear me. His focused expression did not change.

"Hey," I said. He looked up. "I promise."

He nodded. The leakage beneath my hands was spreading despite our best efforts. The girl gave a weak shudder. Her green eyes fluttered and rolled back into her head. I listened desperately for footsteps outside the capsule bay, hoping against hope that Able and Two had returned with some miracle cure for this poor creature. But nothing came. Om's hands pressed down so hard on mine that my bones creaked, but I bit my lip and bore it. Time ticked by painfully, excruciatingly slowly. Drips of white substance snuck past my palms, gathering into a growing puddle. The girl turned her head slightly as she shivered again and fixed her gaze on me.

"You're going to be fine," I said, and tried to sound confident, but found it hard to do as I watched the light fade from those green eyes. Did she understand me? There was an upward twitch of her lip that was almost like an effort to smile or speak. But instead of words, what followed was a series of convulsions. She bucked hard and her skinny legs flailed like limp noodles. If Om's hands hadn't been on top of mine, I would've fallen backward from the force. But despite his efforts, I felt a hot gush of liquid flow forth underneath my palms.

Her body gave one last hard shudder. White liquid erupted from her lips in a fine spray, showering Om and me. She made a sound that I could only describe as a death rattle and fell still. My body turned cold as I watched her green eyes fade to black.

Om removed his hands from mine. I lifted my numb palms and tried to flex my fingers, only to find them covered in the dead girl's fluids. Though the liquid was white in color, a jagged black patch had formed on her chest, like a bruise spreading under the skin.

A hand touched my shoulder and I nearly jumped. I thought it was Om but turned to see Able standing behind me, holding a case of what I assumed were medical supplies—help that came too late.

"I . . ." I started. "I couldn't . . ."

He shook his head remorsefully, knelt down, and gently closed the girl's eyelids. Something about that gesture cut me to a depth that I hadn't known existed. Tears overflowed before I could stop them.

"I'm sorry," I said between choked sobs. "I'm so sorry. I tried, but she . . ."

"It wasn't your fault," Able said, but he didn't look at me. He put one hand under the girl's shoulders, another under her knees, and lifted her. "It was my mistake, putting this burden on you. She was in bad shape. I knew she wasn't going to make it, but thought I had to try. The result wouldn't have been any different no matter who was here with her."

He stood, the limp body in his arms. She looked so small

against his chest. One white arm dropped lifelessly to her side. I stood as well. Now that the heat of the moment had passed, I finally had a good look at the wide gash across her chest, slicing through the center of the growing black patch.

"What happened to her?"

"Someone must've attacked her." Able nodded at the wound on her chest. "Looks like a knife wound." Solace's curved blade flashed through my mind. "She must've escaped, but with a wound this severe, her piloting was affected. She crashed into the side of the orb."

"Was she trying to come here?"

Able pursed his lips. "Could've been an accident; could've been her last desperate attempt to find help. We'll never know now. All we can do is give her a respectful place to rest."

"I saw her," I blurted out. "Or . . . I think I did. I thought I saw a capsule move on the way here. Maybe it was her. I should've said something. I should've—"

He gave me a sad, weak smile and shook his head. "Maybe it was her; maybe it wasn't. But don't beat yourself up for it. You couldn't have known. The truth is, we are at war, and this is only one of many casualties. So long as the conflict remains, there will always be innocent lives that suffer. It's just the reality of things."

I watched him carry her away, somber like a funeral procession. My face was wet with tears and white blood. I wiped them away angrily. My chest was tight and I couldn't decide whether to scream or collapse.

A movement to my right. Om had summoned his display panel.

ARE YOU ALRIGHT?

I swallowed a sob. "Are *you*?"

He thought for a moment, then typed again.

IT IS THE CASUALTY OF WAR.

I took Om's hands and gripped them tightly. My gaze raked over the black patch on his chest. What had *he* suffered to earn this mark? Had he also lain bleeding and bucking while someone pressed their hands over his chest, keeping him from bleeding out on a dirty floor?

"You said you wanted to help me," I said. "I want to help you, too. I don't know what you're going through, or what war you're trying to fight, but I'm going to do whatever I can to help you."

Om's grip around my hands tightened. Then he pulled away, cupped his palms around my face, and kissed me lightly on the forehead, the same way I had kissed him in the capsule, after we'd sealed our first promise to each other.

CHAPTER 17

Able's orb was, for all intents and purposes, identical to Astra's. And yet it felt very different. I hadn't realized until now just how very accustomed I'd become to hard benches, brown walls, cold water, and lukewarm gelatin cubes. I'd taken for granted that any sort of living outside of Fiina consisted of these drab, lifeless colors and flavors.

"Believe it or not, making these contraptions heat something up is a trick in itself," Able said, tapping the food machine. He slid a cup of steaming liquid in front of me as I took a seat. "Here. Drink this. You'll feel better."

I took the warm cup, wrapped my trembling fingers around it, and took a sip. It was slightly sour but had a nice, refreshing fragrance. I hadn't stopped shaking since leaving the capsule bay, but the drink helped a little.

The space we occupied was similar to the usual residential rooms, but it looked nothing like the cold, metal cells. Stepping into it had me doing a double take at the tan-colored walls, wooden furniture, and linen drapery hanging beside a wide, square window. If not for the stars outside and the strange array of beings sitting at the table with me, I could almost mistake myself for being back on Fiina again.

"Is it to your liking?" Able asked as he slid into the chair across from me. "Apologies I don't know the flavor preferences of your people."

I quickly nodded and took another sip, grateful for the heat flowing down my throat and chest. Able gave me a reassuring smile, and despite the tragedy I had just witnessed, I could feel what was left of my doubt about this new arrangement start to melt away along with the cold inside my body.

"It's wonderful," I said. "I didn't realize heating something was an option. Or even making drinks at all."

"Usually the nutrient cubes are designed to provide hydration as well as nutrition. So if you know how to produce the right flavors in the cubes, then melt them, it makes for a passable drink." Able took a sip out of his own cup. "It's not a terribly efficient process, but once in a while, it's nice to have a bit of the old normal, wouldn't you say?" He paused. "I'd hoped to be able to give you a little more time to rest before we got serious, but it seems time is not on our side. Still, if you'd like to take a little more time to yourself, you certainly deserve to."

I looked at Om. His expression was neutral despite having just witnessed one of his own die. I couldn't guess what he was thinking, and my heart ached for him.

"No," I said. "Let's talk. I don't want to wait anymore."

Able smiled grimly. "Alright," he said. "I think it's time you had a proper introduction." Able gestured toward Om. "Kova, what you see before you is a Harbinger. There aren't many of them left. Om here is one of the last, a bit of a novelty these days. But let me start at the beginning. Tell me, what do you know about Headspace?"

The memory of the brief glimpse in the silver orb made me shudder. "I heard it's a game," I said. "Played to entertain gods, or something like that. And . . . there are demigods. They ran the games."

Able nodded approvingly and motioned for me to go on.

"But they're gone now. The gods. And the games stopped."

"All of that is correct," Able said. "Do you know what happened after that?"

I shook my head.

"The gods leaving was only part of the story. Their departure was not what unsettled life as we knew it. It was what followed." Able took a long sip of his drink, his brow knitted as if traveling down a lane of memory he would rather forget. "You see, the demigods are fanatics. Without the games, they didn't know what to do with themselves. They reasoned that with the gods gone, they had no purpose left, and by extension, *we* had no purpose left. They began to kill us off. Many of us fell quickly because we were given implanted chips when we first joined."

He lifted a hand and pointed to the back of his neck. "The earlier champions were told they were emotional regulators, but in reality their main purpose was to allow the demigods to keep track of us—and when they saw fit, kill us. Not only that, they were implanted in a way that they could not be removed without causing massive damage. The demigods are not violent by nature. They simply saw themselves above us, and when they decided we were no longer needed, they thought they were being merciful by killing us quickly and neatly. The chip is how Seven ended up where she is."

"Seven?"

"The seventh champion, Nasmi Kol. Or as you know her, Mother. She elevated the status of the champions. We went from servants to leaders because of her. This naturally caused quite a bit of upset among the demigods. They tracked her when she was traveling between holy grounds, trying to find a way to contact the gods, and used the chip in her neck to destroy her body. It would've worked, except she is . . ." A secretive smile crept across his face. "Let's just say she is special. Her connection to the gods was different from the rest. As a result, her consciousness was preserved, suspended in the sacred space of the gods. Fortunately, or perhaps unfortunately, she had already made plans to pass the mantle."

"To Astra?"

"She desired power, even if she would never admit to it. It is where her talents lie, and really, where she could best put her ruthlessness to good use. And I will give credit where it's due—when she took over, the tides finally turned."

"What did she do?"

"Waged war."

I DRAINED MY CUP. Om rose and brought me another. His fingers brushed against mine as he handed it to me.

"The war has gone on for a long time. It will continue until either the champions or the demigods are completely destroyed. The demigods tend to shy away from physical conflict, but that doesn't mean they aren't able to use others to do the dirty work for them. That's how the Harbingers came about."

Able waved his hand. I nearly leaped to my feet as a white figure appeared next to me. Followed by another. And another. And another.

Dozens of white figures stood around me, each with thin grooves on their skin that varied in pattern. Their deep eyes carried a spectrum of colors and their other features were merely shallow indents. They looked like templates not yet started, clay waiting to be molded.

"Harbingers were originally created to run the orbs as a replacement for champions. The demigods started making them when they grew frustrated with the champions becoming more rebellious. The Harbingers were used as maintenance workers, scouts, and researchers at first. After Astra took over, the demigods repurposed them."

"To fight?"

"It was an ugly conflict." Able nodded ruefully. "Astra led us against the demigods and hunted them down one by one. We —Mother's children—do not possess the chips in our necks. This is yet another privilege she granted us. It is a freedom that most champions from other galaxies did not have. It gave us an advantage. By the time the demigods realized what Astra was doing, their numbers had greatly dwindled. To counter her, they used the Harbingers to fight back. The Harbingers followed orders and hunted us. We suffered many losses."

I looked at the white figures. Was this really what Om was? I couldn't believe that the sweet, soft-spoken child who had kept me company in the capsule could be capable of harming anyone. But save for missing the black patch on their chests, these Harbingers looked just like Om, and they were lined up like spears ready to be thrown at the nearest target.

"But that's not what the Harbingers were intended for. They were meant to be the first ones to set foot on new planets to analyze and assess them for the games, setting the path for the arenas to move forward. They can change their appearances to mimic the locals, pick up new languages within hours, and store vast amounts of data in their memories. Should they wind up in a situation where they must survive, they can switch to more energy-efficient forms and stay alive for far longer than a purely biological being could without needing to eat or drink."

"Are they machines?"

"Not quite. They are somewhere in between. Our understanding of the Harbingers is limited. But near as we can figure, they are made with a combination of organic tissue and the building blocks of the arena. All of us who occupy the arenas have been fused and healed by the building blocks to some level, but the Harbingers are a perfect blend of both down to the molecular level, which is what allows them to transform and change at will. Some of them, like Om here, do have preferred default forms, often based on the cultures and races they've studied or for ease of movement and travel."

I gazed at Om with amazement. Sculpted with care he certainly was.

"Their obedience made them effective soldiers," Able continued. "But ultimately, they were not made to fight. The demigods became complacent when they took out Mother, not anticipating that a more savage arena master would take up the mantle. By the time they finally took Astra seriously, it was too late. Under her orders, demigods and Harbingers were killed on sight."

Kill them all and it won't matter.

"Then why is he here?" I asked. It was difficult to imagine Om as any sort of warrior despite his stature. Even in this form, he appeared quiet and reserved. I thought of him running from Solace in the silver orb. Surely he could've taken this form and fought if he was willing?

"Well, that's where things become complicated." Able gestured at Om. "You see, the common belief about Harbingers is that they are mindlessly obedient to the demigods, tools for them to use, and therefore pose a danger to all champions. Obviously, you can see that's not true."

I nodded.

"There are a few of us—very few—who believe that there's more to the Harbingers. They were, after all, created to live and learn, and what defines an intelligent being but living and learning? We don't believe that the Harbingers are a danger by nature; only that they are taught to do as they are bid by their creators, but given a choice, they are only trying to survive like the rest of us. It isn't their fault that they were born to walk this path. With the gods gone and the games no longer serving a purpose, don't they deserve a chance to choose as well?"

Those words tugged at me and I struggled not to let it show. Instead, I took another sip of the warm, sour drink to calm myself.

"We encountered this fellow a while back," Two cut in. They had a drink in front of them. There was something endearing about the way they indulged in the rituals of socializing even though they couldn't truly participate. "Astra's orders were always absolute—all Harbingers must be eliminated. But we took a chance on him."

Able nodded. "She—and those who follow her—saw Harbingers as mindless threats. But he didn't seem to mean us any harm, so we kept him here. His capacity for learning and logical thinking are absolutely incredible. He's helped us harvest parts and restore the orb. It was on one of these harvesting trips that he had a run-in with someone you already know."

I tensed. Able noticed.

"Don't think ill of Solace," he said. "He is not a bad person, merely loyal to a fault. He has suffered more at the hands of the current arena master than anyone, and yet he refuses to walk away. He will stick by Astra until the end, and unfortunately, I think that end will be a tragic one."

"Well, we lucked out, didn't we?" Two said, grinning widely as they tried to lighten the mood. "Om certainly did."

"How did he get back here?" I asked.

Two winked. "I told you I had secrets."

"Luck was on our side," Able explained. "Two was the one who checked E-V's capsule and discovered our friend before anyone else did. I had thought he was lost to us forever. Imagine my surprise when Two contacted me to tell me he had survived. He was in quite bad shape when I picked him up. Expending as much energy as he did with no replenishment was quite a gamble."

"Energy?"

"Keeping you warm. He had been in conservation mode until then, and had he not made it back here when he did, he would've run out of all reserves and shut down completely, which would've made his recovery much more challenging."

The sensation of being wrapped in Om's embrace came flooding back.

"Do you see now?" Able said. He had an expression on his face that I could only describe as pride. It was the look of someone who had been proven right after a long debate. "The Harbingers are so much more than mindless followers of the demigods. Unfortunately, not everyone can see that. You've now seen firsthand how dangerous it is to be consumed with hatred and anger. It makes you miss out on what's right in front of you. There are other ways to end this war, and I've been trying to find them. Ways that don't involve more killing, hiding, or dying. It's too late to convince Astra of that, but I think—I *hope*—that if I succeed, she'll come around and we can find some peaceful common ground at last."

He took a long sip of his drink as I tried to process all of this. It was all so big, so much more than I could comprehend. I felt woefully unqualified to be here, to even sit in the presence of these beings.

"Now then," Able said. "Two tells me you have a few secrets of your own. Tell me about Rosi."

I swallowed. I'd guarded Rosi close to my heart. Until now, I'd been too afraid to tell anyone but Om about Rosi. But Om was here now, safe and sound, because Able had shown him the kindness he deserved. Om trusted Able, and I could think of no higher commendation than that right now.

And if telling him about Rosi could help Om, then that was good enough for me.

"Rosi is my sister."

Able's eyes widened slightly, then his brow furrowed. After a moment, he burst out laughing, surprising me. He slapped a hand on his knee.

"Unbelievable. Is she really?"

"She is."

Able leaned back in his seat. "You know," he said, "'Rosi' is the first and only clue we've gotten in the struggle against the demigods. I won't go into the sordid details of how Astra obtained it, but before then, we'd known that the demigods were up to something. They were ransacking abandoned orbs and holy grounds, then retreating into silence for long periods of time, only venturing out to repeat. They even stopped hunting the champions, at least for a while. It wasn't hard to guess that they were planning something, but we had no way of knowing what. Astra was getting increasingly impatient and desperate. I snuck out from under her thumb when I couldn't stomach watching her execute any more Harbingers. Since then, I've been hiding out here, trying to do my own investigations."

He gestured toward Two.

"Two here has kept me posted on what's gone on in Astra's orb. Just because I don't agree with her methods doesn't mean I wish her ill. I still want to know she's alright. And Om has been nothing but helpful."

Om looked toward me. My face flushed.

"He helped us conduct a little experiment of our own." Able said. "But we weren't making much progress because we didn't have a lot to go on."

"What is it?"

"It's a bit complicated." Able leaned in attentively. "Won't you tell me your story first?"

I told him everything.

I started at the orb on Fiina, then the video, then Rosi's message. I recounted my life without her, followed by my courtship with Meli and discovering E-V's capsule. I told him how I had found Om in the holy ground and came to share the capsule with him, keeping each other warm and alive after the accident. I told him about Astra's cold treatment of me, my fears of what she might do if she found out about Rosi, and Mother's threat. The words poured out of me like a waterfall. I hadn't realized how much I ached to confess to someone.

When I finished, I let out a breath of relief and sat back, feeling lighter than I'd felt in a long time.

Able listened without interruption. When I was done, he reached out and took my hand.

"You, Kova Onasi," he said, "are a very brave person."

Tears welled up in my eyes, but I thought that crying right now wouldn't be very becoming of a "very brave person."

"Mother is a difficult one," Able went on. "She led us to freedom from the demigods, but really, in her best of intentions, she became our enslaver in other ways."

I nodded solemnly.

He winked. "Well, no need to dwell," he said good-humoredly. "You've given me much to think about. I'm not entirely sure what Rosi being your sister means yet, but I think somehow, you were meant to be here. There's something bigger than all of us at play, and it might take time to figure things out. But you've helped greatly. We now have precious knowledge that just might take us forward and finally end this war."

A bloom of pride swelled in my chest.

"Now then, since we're now completely honest with each other, let me tell you about our experiments."

I nodded.

"There is a rumor that the gods left something behind. Everything they took from this universe, all the memories, emotions, knowledge, and experience, is stored somewhere. A data core, with information and history gathered from billions of civilizations. And not only that, it contains some of their secrets as well, such as the workings behind Headspace, the orbs, the holy grounds, even the demigods themselves. We believe the demigods are searching for the data core. But we can beat them to it."

"What will that do?"

"The information will give us an advantage in the conflict. Not only over the demigods, but over Astra as well. If we succeed, then there need be no more bloodshed, and no more

Harbingers"—he pointed to Om—"will suffer and die needlessly. All we have to do is find it."

"How will you find it?"

"If rumors are to be believed, the data core emits a signal that can be perceived by seed races, as it is primarily constructed of their thoughts and memories. Though some are thought to be more sensitive than others. We need to establish a link, but it must be done with someone who is sensitive to the core's signal."

I mulled this over.

"They took Rosi," I said slowly, hoping I didn't sound stupid. "If they took her, could it be for that reason?"

Able brightened. "Why yes," he said. "That's an excellent theory. If your sister was taken, there's a good chance the demigods have found her receptive to the data core's signals. They must be trying to use her to establish a signal to the data core."

"I'm her twin," I went on, suddenly excited. "If she can produce the signal, maybe I can, too!"

Able leaned forward. "Brilliant!" he exclaimed. "Of course! If she sent you a message, then there's a good chance she was in contact with the demigods' technology, which stands to reason someone found her useful, or at least interesting enough to allow her access to it. And you said she wanted to show you something, isn't that right?"

"Yes," I said eagerly.

"If we find her, we will surely find what she wanted to show you. And who knows, maybe what she wanted to show you is what we've been seeking all along."

I stood, unable to contain myself any longer. "Let's go! What do I have to do?"

Able grinned. "Let me show you."

. . .

STILL IMAGES and moving videos scrolled by me. I waved my hand the way Able taught me, watching with amazement the pictures and faces from worlds I'd never seen and could never have imagined. Lacking an AI, the controls in Able's arena had to be worked manually and precisely. I had to be careful and exact with my movements to reach the content I wanted, but the database of the arena offered endless wonders despite my clumsy navigation.

Yatam, Lynphix, Urso, Maeda, Aeffid, Earth . . .

I had never been allowed access to the database on Astra's orb. But here, Able gave me free rein and I gaped, slack-jawed, at the wonders of the universe. Jungles filled with red trees. Dancers wearing shoes that left red footprints in intricate patterns on white sand. Mountains that dwarfed the little hills of Radley like a common Fiinian standing over the little sand crawlers of the cove. Rain that fell not in drops of water but flakes of ice, striking the ground and shattering like broken gems.

But the database held more than that.

There were records on every person to ever set foot into the game of Headspace. Intricate details of their lives, languages spoken, personal relationships, the exact amount of time they lasted in the games, and their "expertise," whatever that meant. Extensive profiles were also kept of every champion to have come out of the game within the Star Net Galaxy—or, in their terms, the Galaxy of the Starry River. The arena floor displayed them, four or six to a screen, before me. They varied greatly in stature, age, size, and appearance.

Eleven.

His image was framed with a black border. Something about his game set him apart, I supposed.

I turned a few screens down.

Thirty-three.

Astra.

She looked different. Very different. I realized with a start that the face on the holographic disc from E-V's capsule was hers. Dark eyes, choppy hair, red lips. Was this how she had looked when she'd competed as a contestant of Headspace?

"You can watch recordings from their games," Able called to me. He was off working with Two and Om on a different portion of the arena floor. Unlike in Astra's orb, where the arena floor lay bare, the floor of this orb had been arranged into some sort of experimental laboratory. Wires, machinery, and parts whose functions I couldn't begin to comprehend covered the floor.

I moved my hand over Astra's image. Several lines of text appeared.

"What does this mean?" I asked. Translation on written text in this arena was spotty. I could only be grateful that the audio portion still worked enough to allow me to speak with Two and Able unhindered.

"The top one gives you a list of all rounds from their game. The next one is highlights," Able replied. "I'd go with highlights. The games are a pain to translate."

I chose the second option. A figure appeared. At first glance I thought there had been a mistake. The entire right side of its body was swollen and protruding in points. I watched in horror as it swung its fist and struck a smaller figure, smashing it into the ground. Its victim let out a pained shriek that chilled me to my core.

A child?

Protrusions grew on the creature's body, resembling clusters of crystal. There was a sickening sound, like wet fabric being torn. I stifled a gasp.

Sweetly.

I recognized her from the Pinnacle. She shrieked, scratching the ground around her with her remaining arm, as if trying to get away. There were others nearby, contestants from the planet Earth, all of whom were staring at the disturbing spectacle, a mixture of shock and disgust on their faces.

The dismembered arm was thrown aside. Bile retched up in my throat as the creature slashed at Sweetly with crystalized claws, tearing her to shreds.

The image froze.

Another hovering screen appeared. This time I could easily recognize Astra, with her dark hair and hard eyes. She was standing alone inside a circle marked on the arena floor. Also inside the circle was an enormous creature that looked like a crude amalgamation of several other animals. I hoped dearly that this thing wasn't native to her planet because any world that housed such a beast would simply be too horrifying to imagine.

But Astra wasn't moving. She stood in place, as if in a trance. I thought at first that she was paralyzed in fear, as I surely would be in her position. But as the camera zoomed in on her face, I saw that she wasn't scared at all. Instead, the expression on her face was relaxed, serene. She rotated her head slowly, as if stretching out her neck. There was a small, subtle smile on her face, as if she was lost in some old, pleasant memory.

The beast paced back and forth, looking at this little creature before it. Then, it charged. I gasped as it opened its massive maw to swallow her whole.

In a movement almost too fast for me to see, she threw one hand upward into its mouth. A burst of glimmering crystals sprayed from her arm into the animal's mouth. It stopped in its tracks, looking confused, but that moment of hesitation was enough for the crystals to grow into its flesh, hooking it in place. It tugged, trying to pull away, but Astra was somehow holding her own against it, despite being a mere fraction of its size.

Spikes of crystals pierced its skin, sticking through its eyes, ears, and skull. Its tail—which bore what looked like the head of an enormous reptile—reared up to strike, only to fall a split second later, its head sliced neatly in half. Had I blinked, I would've missed the crystal blade that formed on Astra's free arm.

More crystals emerged from the beast's body. It pulled, struggled. Its other heads howled weakly until it fell heavily onto its side.

The crystals crumbled from Astra's body, detaching her from the animal. She took a step back.

The image froze again. Another appeared.

A shadowy figure, standing in what looked like a long-abandoned garden under a dark sky. The image blinked, as if something had been adjusted, and Astra appeared in the shadow's place. At the center of the garden stood a stone statue. It was shaped like a Fiinian—or more likely, shaped like whatever Astra's race was called—but with wings, which was a strange combination. Certain factions of her race must've been born with them. Where its face once had been, however, was a cluster of familiar-looking crystals.

Beneath its pedestal were more crystals, a huge cluster of them, taller than Astra herself. Splayed atop it was a body—a fellow contestant from Earth. I couldn't distinguish their age or gender, only that they were bent and folded into unnatural angles. Astra looked at the body for a moment, looked to another area of the garden as if checking to see if anyone was there, then hurried away.

The image froze.

I looked back to the first one—the crystalized monster, tearing apart poor Sweetly.

Is this her, too?

One more screen flickered on. Astra was kneeling, covered in . . . I squinted. Covered in what? It was dark blue, and everywhere, all over her hands, legs, and clothing, puddled on the floor. As I tried to identify the substance, the camera shifted, and another figure lying on its back appeared.

Solace.

For a moment I thought he was dead. It was illogical, as I

had just met him, alive and well, but so much of the substance —blood—was coming from him. How any being could lose that much blood and still be alive was difficult to imagine. I watched as he shuddered, then rolled onto his side. Days worth of gelatin threatened to make a reappearance when I saw that he had been gored. One of his trembling hands was pressed against his abdomen and I loathed to think what would come tumbling out if he moved it. And his other hand . . .

"I think that's enough of that."

I shook myself out of my trance. I hadn't even noticed Able coming up behind me. He waved a hand and the screens disappeared.

"You're looking a little pale," he said, steering me away from the screens. "The games are not for the faint of heart. You should take it easy with those clips."

My mind was numb. The images were seared into my eyes even as I walked away from them.

"What happened to him?"

Able shook his head. "I told you, Solace has suffered more than anyone. It's not something you should dwell on. If we succeed, tragedy like that will never have to be repeated again."

He led me to the machinery Two and Om were working on. They stepped aside as we approached.

"This is our pride and joy," he said, gesturing at what looked like a haphazard pile of gears and wires. I couldn't make heads or tails of it, but there was a long reclining seat covered in worn fabric in the middle of it. Maybe it was the pointy-looking machinery and metal bits around it, but I couldn't shake the feeling that it looked awfully sinister.

"How does this work?" I asked, eyeing the straps hanging from the armrests.

"It's much easier to show you than explain."

I stared at the contraption. My resolve to help end this war sounded a lot grander in my head. Now, in front of this pile of metal and wires, I wavered. Able didn't rush me. Neither did Two. They stood patiently by.

"Is this going to hurt?" I asked at last, feeling like a coward but needing to know what to expect.

"Only a little," Able said softly. "And only at first. No more than a pinprick." My fear must've been obvious, because he added, "You don't have to do this. We can find other ways."

"No," I said quickly. "I want to."

"You're certain?"

I nodded, hoping he would hurry before I changed my mind. He helped me into the chair and leaned it backwards until I was almost lying down. Om stood beside me and took one of my hands in his. It was comforting to know he was nearby, but the relief did not last when he released me and began to fasten the straps on the armrests around my wrist.

"What are you doing?" I said, slightly alarmed as Two began to fasten the other.

"It's for your own safety," Able said. "You might jerk around when it kicks in. Wouldn't want you to punch yourself in the face or fall out, would we?"

As I debated whether I should protest, I felt something cold and sticky being stuck to my temples. Behind me, Able said, "Turn it on."

There was a series of clicks and a whirring sound.

"We can stop at any time if it becomes too much for you," he said. "Your safety and comfort are our absolute priority."

"I'll be fine," I replied, though it felt like a lie.

"Good luck," I heard Two say. Somehow their sincerity unnerved me more than their usual sarcasm. Then, the hum of the arena was in my head. But it had a different rhythm, one that somehow matched the beat of my pulse. I started to become dizzy. Dots appeared in my vision, spinning and multiplying rapidly. I struggled to stay focused as they moved faster and faster. Just as I thought I was going to be sick from the motion, they disappeared, and I saw only one thing.

A door.

"Do you see it?" Able said.

"Yes," I replied. Both of our voices sounded terribly far away. "What do I do?"

"It's simple." I could hear him but I couldn't see him.. The door opened a crack. A breeze blew through it, carrying with it the scent of the salty sea. "You only need to do what comes naturally. Om will guide you."

CHAPTER 18

THE BREEZE OF THE SEA CARESSED ME. PEBBLES CRUNCHED beneath my feet. This was different from Mother's recreation, which was a pantomime at best. This was real, or at least as real as my senses could convince me it was. I took a deep breath, relishing the cold salty air as it entered my lungs.

The chair was gone. So were the wires and the arena's metal walls. The clear waters of Radley Cove rippled under the gentle sea breeze. There was no orb here, only the green waters and white pebble beach. The hills surrounding the cove were rife with rosalit flowers. Once every ten to fifteen cycles, there came a season when the rosalits bloomed white and in such abundance that the hills became completely covered. The last time this had happened was . . .

A shrill laugh caught my ear. I turned just in time to see two children running toward me. Their faces became clearer as they drew near, and I gasped as they ran into me. And through me. They ran to the side of the water, trouncing and splashing with their boots.

Then, they stopped. Like a video being paused.

I started to walk toward them, only to be pulled back. My heart gave a little jolt when I realized Om was holding my hand. He cleared his throat.

"This," he said with obvious difficulty, gesturing at our surroundings.

"You speak Fiinian?"

He gestured at his mouth and throat. "Many. I learned. Many languages." He gestured at the environment again. "Your. Memory."

"My memory," I echoed. By the water, Rosi and I, barely ten cycles old, stood with frozen smiles on our faces. Droplets of cold water hung in the air around us. A few hours later, we would be back home, with Mother shouting at Rosi for getting both of our winter clothes dirty.

"Remember?" Om asked. I nodded.

"I never got in trouble," I said. "Mother always blamed Rosi for everything. We both became ill for several days after. Running around in the winter with wet clothing. It was only natural. But we had no regrets. We never did."

The scene before me started moving again. The younger version of me jumped into knee-deep water with both feet. I felt the cold water seep through her clothing even though my own body was dry. Rosi laughed, bent down, scooped up handfuls of water, and flung it toward the younger me, who returned it, shouting and shrieking.

"We always did this," I told Om. "Every winter since we could walk. We went to the cove and splashed in the cold water, no matter how much our parents forbade us." The mirage of our younger selves reached down elbow deep into the water. "We dug around for shells and pebbles until we couldn't feel our fingers." The child version of me stood, shaking a wet, wriggling thing in their hand. "Sometimes we found mud eels. Rosi always tried to take them back, claiming she could keep them in a tub of water. Mother always threw them right back out."

"Your world," Om said. His voice was sounding a little smoother. The longer he stayed next to me, the more his speech seemed to recover. "It's beautiful."

"I'm sure you've seen many beautiful worlds."

"Some," he replied thoughtfully. "It is my job. To travel. And see. And learn." He paused. "I did not see yours."

I breathed in the sea air deeply. "Honestly, I didn't either. I lived in Radley all my life, within sight of this cove. I never set foot outside the town. Rosi and I have been down every street and been in every shop. This was my whole world."

"LOOK!"

I turned and a splash of wet mud hit my face. Rosi's laughter filled my ears.

I looked down. Mud and salty water dripped from my fingers. How long had I been digging? I couldn't remember when I'd started to dig, but I must have. That's what we always did in the winter.

Rosi squatted next to me, messy white hair congealed in clumps with mud. Mother would have a fit later and order Kit to scrub her clean before she was allowed at the dinner table. Rosi hated being scrubbed, but that never stopped her from getting dirty. Her pants and shoes were already soaked up to her knees, though the frigid cold didn't seem to bother her in the least as she held up her latest prize.

"Check it out!" she shouted excitedly, waving the slippery gray mud eel she'd just pulled out of the mud. "It's got red eyes. Only the gray ones have red eyes. The black ones have black eyes. See it?"

Wiping mud off my face with my sleeve, I squinted at the wriggling eel. Its eyes were indeed red, and it looked quite unhappy to be handled so roughly. It swung its tail hard, slipped out of Rosi's hand, and immediately burrowed itself into the mud before she could grab it again.

Rosi scrunched up her face in disappointment. "Aw, and I was going to show you how it had a split tail," she said with a pout. "Did you know only the ones that lay eggs have split tails?

And it only splits in the winter when they get ready to lay eggs, and then it grows back together in the spring. Isn't that amazing?"

Most school children learned about the anatomy of mud eels in primary education by the time they were aged eight cycles. I would hardly call it an "amazing" fact. But I grinned at Rosi nonetheless. All the kids in Radley knew about mud eels and their split tails, but Rosi was the only one who knelt in frigid mud just so we could both see proof with our own eyes.

"Maybe we'll find another one," I said, and thrust both hands into the mud. "A black one this time. They get split tails, too, right?"

"Yeah!" Rosi exclaimed, brightening. She dragged her wet shoes through the mud, but one of her feet caught. She tumbled toward me. I opened my arms to catch her, already knowing that I wouldn't be able to bear her weight and that we were both about to fall into the cold, salty water, drenching ourselves from head to toe. We would choke and sputter, then laugh as we dragged our filthy selves back to the house. We would both be roughly scrubbed down and Mother would punish Rosi once again, but whatever she did wouldn't be enough to wipe the triumph off Rosi's face at having finally seen a mud eel with red eyes and split tail. For days after we would both have runny noses and warm cheeks and a perpetual chill from the exposure, but we would not regret a moment of it. We would spend our days recovering from the illness huddled together under warm blankets, sneaking treats from the pantry, and laughing, always laughing. In that brief moment as she fell into my arms, I saw all those things clear as day, though I didn't know how. I closed my eyes expecting to be momentarily drowned in the murky water.

But it didn't come.

I opened my eyes again. Rosi's surprised eyes were in front of mine, unblinking. My arms were lifted, waiting to receive her, but she had stopped in the air, her white hair billowing behind her, frozen in time.

"Rosi?"

"Kova."

That voice wasn't hers. It was someone else's. Someone was calling me.

"Kova."

"Leave me alone," I said, though I wasn't sure who I was talking to. All I wanted was for time to move again, to start up so I could carry on with life, back when it was simple and easy and I was never alone.

"This isn't real."

Yes, it is, I wanted to say. *She's right here. This is my life, and it's real.*

"It's time to go."

A hand on my shoulder. I pulled against it, pushing myself forward to wrap my arms around Rosi. But I caught only empty air.

I OPENED MY EYES.

For a moment the smell of the sea stayed with me and I felt cold, wet clothing clinging to my skin even though I saw the rust-brown dome above me.

"You did wonderfully," a voice said.

I blinked. A hand rested on my back and helped me sit up.

"When did I . . ." I couldn't quite finish the sentence. A sharp pain struck my temples and made me wince. It subsided to a dull ache as I massaged it and tried to clear the stars in front of my eyes.

How much time had passed?

I tried to think back. For what had felt like most of a day, I had walked that pebble-covered beach, with Om's hand in mine. We had watched the children—Rosi and me—run and shout and laugh. Every now and then, they had stopped mid-motion. In these moments in between time, I'd spoken to Om. I'd described the gray winter skies and the frigid waters, and how much I'd loved the salty smell of the sea as a child and the sensation of mud sliding from my hands.

And then . . .

And then I'd been back. Back in my life. Back in my childhood. I'd been back in the cove with mud on my legs and Rosi by my side. It was real, and more importantly, it was *right*.

"How long was that?" I heard someone ask—Able. I looked up to see him standing with Two, reading a series of incomprehensible codes on a blue-green screen.

"Four minutes," Two replied. "And thirty-two seconds."

They couldn't be talking about the time I'd spent inside that strange door?

"This must seem very confusing," Able said.

I nodded. My head swam.

"What you just experienced was an elevated state, also called a dream state by some. It's a little difficult to explain if you're not used to the functions of the orb. But for the most part, it is a more immersive version of the games. Rather than simply replicating a physical environment, the arena immerses the participant on both a physical and mental level, making use of their memories, sensory data, and thought processes to create an entire other world. Within the mind, even time itself can be changed and manipulated, which is why a few minutes can feel like a day."

I stared at him blankly. Able chuckled.

"Are you a little lost?"

Lost? Perhaps that was one way to describe it. I rubbed my eyes with both hands. Rosi's presence lingered as if she was standing right in front of me. It was less like waking from a dream than stepping out of another life.

"The dream state is seductive," I heard Able say. "It convinces you everything is right and wants you to stay."

"It was real," I muttered.

"It only feels that way, and that's what you have to remember to keep from getting lost in it. Om here did his job keeping you from sinking too far."

A warm hand on my shoulder. I laid my hand over Om's as he sat next to me.

"Thanks," I said quietly, though I almost didn't mean it. My heart ached for the dream that still lingered in every fiber of my being. I wanted to laugh and cry at the same time, so I settled for a tired sigh. "Is it done? Did it work? Did you find the data core?"

Able chuckled. "I wish it were that simple, but we've made an excellent start. The signal you generated was strong and clear. In fact, it seems to be the strongest when you focus on memories of your sister." He gave me a bashful grin. "I must admit I had my doubts, but it seems I've underestimated you."

I was too tired to show my pride, so I simply smiled.

"We'll continue tomorrow," Able said. "I think this is the closest we've ever come to our goal. All you have to do is focus on Rosi. Soon, this conflict will end and all of us, including the Harbingers, will be free."

CHAPTER 19

EARTH.

Its waters were blue and its seas were vast. The people came in a spectrum, from those dark as night to those even paler than Fiinians. Their hair came in a vast variety of colors and textures. I marveled at a child with a headful of gorgeous, soft black curls that sprouted like a tight bundle of blooming flowers.

"I spent a long period of time here," Om told me. His speech was much improved. Must like in the capsule, he seemed to learn from me through our interactions.

"Were you fond of it?" I asked, watching as a trio of farmers draped in long tunics and broad hats tended to a small field of crops. Another child ran by me, a much younger one, barely able to stand on their chubby legs. They stumbled and fell into the mud. The older child quickly doubled back and helped them up.

"It is not my job to be fond of things or not," Om said as we watched the kids run off together. "But as with every planet, there was much to learn." He took my hand as he spoke, an act that never failed to send a tingle through my body. "This world suffered a major climate crisis. Many died, but not all. Those that remained learned to start over and live in harmony with the natural world around them." A woman with sun-kissed skin passed us, a large basket of red fruit balanced on her head. She wore large, shiny hoops through her ears and many bangles on her wrists that clinked against each other as she walked, like notes of music. She joined a circle of others sitting around a fire, and they welcomed her joyfully and shared the fruit she brought. "They had grown solitary in the height of their prosperity, but having to readapt has humbled them. They have rediscovered family and community. It is the nature of seed races to change and grow."

I watched the group around the fire laugh amongst themselves. They possessed very little, but they were full of joy. The children soon joined them and were showered with hugs and kisses from every adult in the group. I couldn't determine who was their mother or father, but it didn't matter. They were loved.

"It's funny you say that," I said slowly.

"Is it?"

"I am one of them. A seed race. Aren't I?"

"You are."

"I don't remember 'growing' much." Another woman exited a nearby hut and joined the group at the fire. She was visibly, glowingly pregnant. A new life brewing, soon to join this loving family. "I lived a lot of the same days, with the same people, being told the same things."

"That might be," Om said as we walked alongside the field of crops bathed in golden sunlight, "but it does not preclude your potential to do so."

LYNPHIX.

Fiina had its share of oceans and lakes. Having grown up by the seaside, I had always looked to the sea beyond Radley Cove and thought there was nothing more endless and infinite. But the bright blue water of Lynphix gave a whole new definition to infinity.

Everywhere I looked, there was water. The horizon was uninterrupted by dry land in any direction. Sparkling structures could be spotted here and there, blending into the glistening waves.

"Is there no land anywhere?" I asked, admiring the half-submerged buildings, the majority of which appeared to be made of transparent glass and crystals.

"Almost all of the planet's surface is underwater," Om said. "There used to be small islands present in certain regions, but as civilization advanced, they were razed to make way for development."

"So they never come out of the water?"

"The people of Lynphix are amphibious, though they prefer to be submerged as their bodies and skin are more adapted for living underwater. Most of their cities and towns have components above and beneath the surface, though they travel faster in the water due to their physiology, so even the aboveground areas are often connected by water tunnels. Major facilities also possess the ability to lower beneath the surface to minimize damage from inclement weather."

We stood on the water. Waves lapped at my feet, and though I felt them, my shoes stayed dry. Om squeezed my hand. I gasped and clung to him as the "ground" below me gave out and we fell beneath the surface. Being underwater was disorienting, and sensing my apprehension, Om wrapped both arms around my shoulders as he held me steady, waiting patiently for me to adjust. In his embrace, I slowly relaxed, just in time to see a Lynphixian, a vision of sleek limbs and translucent violet-blue skin, swim past. Sunlight breaking through the water's surface struck their side and I saw delicate gills open and close. They cut through the water as if dancing to the flow of the current and receded into the distance toward a large, transparent structure shaped like a series of enormous, interconnected bubbles.

A group of smaller figures exited the same door—children. They glided through the water. One was bright yellow with a pair of black spots on their back. Another was a fiery orange with white stripes across their entire body. A bright green one with an intricate brown pattern swam in tight loops.

"They're so beautiful," I breathed. "I've only seen those colors in aquarium fish." I paused. "Is that a bad thing to say? I shouldn't compare them to fish in a tank, should I?"

"It is only natural," Om said, "to draw comparison to what is familiar to you."

"Rosi loved aquariums," I said, watching the Lynphixian children. "When we were little, there was only a small one in Radley, with a few large tanks. Looking back on it, it was hardly a worthwhile attraction, but Rosi was obsessed. She said the ocean was like another world. They built a much bigger one later, but she never got to see it."

"And what did you think?"

I thought for a moment. "I was always told to focus on what was in front of me. I had a tutor. She taught me the names of the fish and made me memorize them." The children swam by us, close enough for me to feel the ripple stirred by the delicate fins on their legs.

"They are blood family. Siblings or cousins."

"How can you tell?"

"They have similar facial structure. Complexion varies vastly in this race, but familial facial traits are generally passed along consistently. They have a strict caste system and tend to partner and mate one-on-one within their own caste. This also results in certain features being passed along more often in some groups than others. These all children carry features common to the mid-tier caste."

"Caste?"

"It refers to different levels of social classes, usually based on heritage and wealth."

"I know. I just . . . I guess I just thought that wouldn't exist outside of Fiina."

"Nearly all advanced civilizations in the galaxy possess some manner of caste system."

I found this a depressing notion, but I didn't say it. Instead, I allowed myself to enjoy the beauty in front of me. Om's arms were still around me. I put my hands over his forearms where they crossed in front of my chest, tracing my fingertips over the lines of his bones and muscles, and there we stayed, watching the glory of the vast universe, shrunk down to the inside of the single door.

"You must've seen thousands of worlds."

"I have lost count."

"Are they all as beautiful as this?"

"Beauty is a subjective concept."

"You've never thought about whether something is beautiful?"

Om mulled this over. I'd learned that whenever he was lost in thought, he looked into the distance, and his grip around me loosened slightly.

"I did encounter a small planet," he said slowly. "It was new, and unnamed. I'd seen so many civilizations, but this world was untouched. Its seed race still was in its infancy, leading slow, uncomplicated lives."

"Have you been back?"

"That world is no longer alive." Om paused. "But there must be something to that untouched nature. For the first time, on that world, I thought about the fact that seed races are beautiful."

FIINA, once more.

I watched myself walk, before friends and family, to the

altar. Om showed me the universe. Injecting variety into my sights and thoughts, Able had said, would prevent me from sinking too far into the comfort of my memories. But in the end, we always returned to the familiar, where I was drawn to, where the signal was the strongest.

It was supposed to be an important day, an exciting one. My coming of age, the day I declared my intention for how I intended to carry on with my life into adulthood. It was an emotional day, and I was emotional indeed, but for all the wrong reasons.

"Rosi was taken by the orb before this," I told Om. "She didn't get to be there for my ceremony."

The me at the altar, draped with seasonal greens and pink rosalits, looked up at my Mother. The ceremony was to be short and brief, and there was to be a celebration after. Mother nudged me, urging me to smile, but I couldn't. I still recalled the feeling of trying to force my lips to curve upward and failing. In all the pictures from my invigoration day, I wore either a blank look or an awkward half grin.

"Coming of age ceremonies are common," Om said. "In fact, most civilizations have them, though their markers for maturity are different."

The younger me turned to face the gathered crowd. Despite all of Mother's efforts to throw me this celebration, there was no cheer in my heart. I only wanted it over with so I could return to my room and hide.

"Do you have a name for this ceremony?"

"Yes," I said. "It's Invigoration Day. It's the day we announce whether we want to enter adulthood as male or female."

Mother was beaming. She stepped forward. She was excited to announce that I was going to be her son from this day forward.

"I changed the plan last minute," I said. "I cut her off and told everyone I wanted to invigorate as a female."

"Is that what you had always wanted?"

"Honestly, I didn't care either way. But when I stood here, all I could think about was Rosi."

"You chose to be like her."

"Yes."

I would always remember Mother's shocked face on that day. I had interrupted her plans and taken her off guard. She felt I betrayed her by not telling her earlier, but I hadn't understood my own desire until that moment. I watched her falter, then recover, then change her announcement as if it was the plan all along.

"What happens when you invigorate?"

"Nothing if you want to stick with what you were growing into. For others, it's a simple medical procedure. At least, it's simple when done during puberty. There are plenty who choose to invigorate later in life to change their established sex, but it's a more difficult procedure then."

"If she hadn't been taken, would you have chosen to stay male?"

My younger self was now being paraded before visitors. They told me I was going to be a beautiful woman when I grew up, and I forced myself to smile. I smiled so much that day my face hurt by the end.

"I don't know."

Om said nothing more. We stood, side by side, hands entwined, my head resting against his shoulder, watching the younger me twist her face into yet another joyless grin.

Stay, the dream state beckoned to me. Om squeezed my hand and we moved on.

THE SPRAWLING CITY before me was unlike anything I'd ever seen before. I craned my neck to look up at the tower before me stretching to dizzying heights. Behind me, people gathered around an enormous fountain where sprays of water danced to music being played from every direction. Layers upon layers of silver and blue buildings stretched into the distance.

"I've never seen buildings so tall," I said, breathless at the sight. "Everything is flat on Fiina. I never thought buildings could be built so high."

"This world prides itself in high structures," Om said. "This is the tallest man-made structure on its entire surface."

"What's it used for?"

"Commerce and private residence."

The idea of living so high off the ground sent chills down my back. "Is it safe to live there?"

"The natives consider it to be. Many seed races possess a desire for reaching great heights. There are different reasons for it, but primarily, it seems that achieving great height is viewed as a manner of achieving greatness, as well as dominance over others."

"Everyone wants to be better, I guess," I said. "I always thought other worlds would be so different from what I knew, but somehow they're all like Fiina in their own way."

The tower and fountain faded, replaced by the familiar shore of Radley Cove. The hill appeared, then streets and shops. The town of Radley painted itself into existence before us. The old bookshop came into view, along with the spice cart that was always set up by the curb in front of it. The vendor, a middle-aged woman with a broad smile and a large mole on her neck, bid us good morning as we passed. A man holding a bucket of yellow rosalits offered one to us. A winter gift for young lovers, he said. I waved him off and he walked on to find the next potential customer.

"He was not there last time," Om said.

"He was there for most of my childhood. I just forgot."

We followed the bustling street, walking under tall metal poles holding street lanterns by the pair. This time, I remembered that in the winter, the city adorned the poles with green and white ribbons in the winter months, an old cold weather tradition that fell away when the town began to expand.

Every time we returned to Radley, I remembered a little more. An extra moment. Another detail. Despite knowing this was only an illusion constructed by the arena, and though my most recent memories of it were filled with frustration and confusion, I was still most at ease walking by the cove, smelling the salty air and hearing the voices of pedestrians and the folk songs of buskers holding old string instruments.

This was the Fiina from my childhood. The Fiina filled with thatched roof houses and little street stands selling grilled fish and fresh flowers. The Fiina before the orb came, before the money poured in, before the worn brick walls were torn down to make way for shiny new shops filled with wide-eyed tourists.

This was the Fiina where life was simple, when it was just me, Rosi, cold winters, and guileless laughter. It was also here that the draw was the strongest. Radley beckoned me like a long-lost friend, whispering in my ear that this was home, this was where I belonged, that I ought to let go of the hand that held mine and fall into that peaceful feeling forever.

Come home, the town around me whispered, and my mind and body longed to drift after it like leaves carried in the breeze.

"Focus," Om said gently next to me, and I was grounded again. A chilly breeze caught me from behind. I shivered and a memory came to me. A shop appeared to my right, with a glass storefront filled with thick, patterned scarves. I stopped in front of it. Om looked at me quizzically but did the same. I touched the glass gently and admired the display inside.

"This shop isn't there anymore," I said to Om. A wide red knitted scarf appeared around my neck. "Mother used to send Kit to buy all the children scarves in the winter. I lost many of them running around town, but I always remember this one.

It's extra warm and I loved the color. It's the only one I shed a tear over when it went missing."

Om ran a curious hand over the scarf. "How interesting," he said. "Clothing and fashion vary so much from world to world, even between region, culture, and age group."

I looked him over, then lifted a hand and touched his neck gently. A scarf appeared, wide and patterned in shades of dark green, wrapped loosely and draped over his shoulders. I chuckled.

"Something amusing?"

"Green and white." I adjusted the scarf around his neck, eyeing the ribbons around the lantern poles. "You fit right in."

Om touched the scarf and looked down the street. The lanterns flickered to life, illuminating the path on both sides and bathing us in their glow. I imagined myself standing there all night, watching the light reflected in his blue eyes.

"GOOD WORK."

I opened my eyes. The rust brown of the arena dome greeted me.

"How do you feel?"

I blinked. The straps around my wrists had already been loosened. I slowly sat up. As usual, Om was there next to me. The sensation of the sea breeze was still on my skin and I nearly expected to see the scarf around his neck.

"Fine," I said hazily.

"We've made a lot of progress in the last two days," Able said.

Two days.

I'd lost track of the hours long ago. Time spent within the floating door was a mystery. I'd gone through days and nights at varying intervals, on many worlds, watching suns and moons rise and set.

Able and Two were fiddling around the machinery as

always, whispering about data and signals and other things I didn't understand. I had been curious at first, but as time wore on—at least for me—I'd found I didn't care.

"You did very well," Able told me cheerfully. "Better than we could've ever hoped." I was pleased at his compliment. Able's positivity was infectious.

The black ones. They create worlds.

Was this what Rosi wanted to show me? I breathed deeply. The exotic worlds Om showed me spun before my eyes, blocking out all other sights and thoughts. For the first time since embarking on this strange journey, I entertained the thought that I was close to the answer. Black orbs that create worlds. I was here, wasn't I? Did Rosi experience this as well? I envisioned her giggling as they attached the sticky leads to her temples, then laughing with joy as she ran through one world after another.

Om helped me up. I got to my feet but kept my hand in his. His hand had become almost a natural extension of my own body.

"Get some sleep," Able said. "You should eat, too. We're done for the day."

"Alright," I said blearily. How much time had passed since I'd last slept? The last time I'd returned to my quarters was seven planets ago. I could barely remember where the room was.

Two and Able walked away, talking between themselves. I watched them go. Om stood by me, waiting patiently as he always did. I let out a sigh.

"Are you alright?" Om asked.

I turned to him. Had I known him for a few days or many seasons?

"Can you turn it back on?" I asked when Two and Able were safely out of earshot.

He glanced at the machinery. "Yes, I can."

"Turn it on. I want to show you something."

He took care to strap me back into the seat, then waded through the jumble of wires and glided his hand over the controls. A moment later, the hovering door appeared before me. As we stepped through, I took his hand in mine, purposefully wrapping my fingers around his rather than the other way around.

The winter streets of Radley reappeared, right where we'd left off. I closed my eyes for a moment, took a deep breath, and allowed the memories to come back. The colors and smells and sounds flowed through my mind, and when I opened my eyes, the scene had changed.

Rows of colorful flags hung from rooftops, forming a vibrant cover over the streets below. The lanterns burned brightly with blue flames, a spectacle reserved only for this special season. Pots of rosalits adorned every doorstep and window. Silver lights covered bare-branched trees and doorframes. Mounds of snow carved into a variety of shapes and forms lined both sides of the street. Vendors selling decorative hats and scarves, festive toys, and steaming treats called out to crowds of pedestrians from their booths, each lit brighter than the next, vying for the attention of passersby. Music played and I tapped my foot to the familiar beat.

Om looked down at himself, a mixture of fascination and confusion in his eyes. I had dressed us both in the common cold weather garb of the sea regions—dark-colored coats with waterproof outer layers, long scarves, warm slacks, and brown boots that crunched in the thick snow.

"This is the annual winter festival," I said as a gaggle of children ran by us. Fiinian children with pale skin and white hair. "When we were little, these were the best days of the cycle for Rosi and me."

Two small figures brushed past us, one wearing a thick, dark red scarf. I gave Om's hand a gentle pull and he followed me as we kept in pace with the younger versions of Rosi and me.

"Is this a fond memory for you?" he asked. A few paces in front of us, Rosi and I stopped to admire a booth filled with tiny paper wheels that spun on sticks when the wind hit them.

"It is," I said. "But I'd forgotten about it until recently." The toys quickly lost their novelty. Rosi pulled my sleeve and led me to another booth. "My mentor, she taught me how to block out things that were unpleasant or distracting. I used to have to do daily exercises that trained my mind to focus on certain things and not others. It was confusing, but effective."

"Why did you need such exercises?"

"My mother didn't want me to think about Rosi. It distracted me and made me moody."

The vendor at the second booth fanned the flames of his grill. Whole skewered mud eels glistened in the fire, covered with fragrant sauce. He handed over two skewers of grilled eel to Rosi and me. We bit into them eagerly. The hot, salty, slightly smoky taste filled my mouth. I remembered this flavor, this feeling of being excited to try something different, anxious about being caught, and the thrill of breaking the rules. I could fall headfirst into this sensation and never come out, but I focused on Om standing next to me instead. The eel meat was dry and tough, and tiny crunchy bones tickled my throat, but I ate as quickly as I could even though Mother was not around to catch me.

"Rosi could always convince me to do things. If not for her, I probably would've spent most of my childhood inside, being taught how to be prim and proper." I watched the two children run across the street, ogling at a series of snow sculptures shaped like a school of swimming fish with patterned scales. We followed them to the end of the street, where an enormous pile of snow had been shaped into a smooth slide. Children and adolescents ran up one side and slid down the other. When I was a child, that slide had seemed so tall and steep. "Here's where she convinces me to go down that slide with her.

I slip halfway down and we both end up landing on our faces and nearly break our noses."

We stood to the side, watching Rosi and me scale the mound of snow, then come tumbling down. My body felt the impact of the ground and the cold, wet snow on my face as we struck the bottom. I remembered pain, then I remembered laughter.

"This was my favorite memory." I shook my head. "Before I really understood the differences between Rosi and me. This Radley doesn't exist anymore. It's gone. The town looks different now. The festival no longer allows unlicensed street vendors, and the street lanterns have been replaced with programmable lights."

"Seems it's still very much alive in your memory."

Rosi and I dusted ourselves off, laughing. The sounds around us slowly faded. Shopfronts and snow sculptures disintegrated. My memory was growing vague.

"I think that's enough of my rambling," I said, suddenly self-conscious. "What about you? There must be a favorite memory of yours. You've seen so much. I can't even imagine."

"Favorite?" Om said slowly. "I haven't thought about it. What qualifies as favorite?"

I mulled this over. Never had I had to explain the idea of "favorite" to someone. It seemed such a natural thing—everyone had a favorite something or other. But then, Om wasn't "everyone."

"Something you think back on fondly," I said, choosing my words carefully.

"I don't look back often. Harbingers are only meant to hold information long enough to be transferred to our masters. Old memories are erased for new ones. It is how we are designed to function."

I brushed this aside. "It's how we function, too. The 'seed races.' We don't remember everything either. New stuff in, old stuff out. But the important stuff stays."

"I have never deemed one piece of information to be more important than the rest."

"You remember that planet. The new one that was untouched."

He thought for a moment. "I do. That world was different."

"Then it's your favorite," I persisted. "Or maybe it's not. It could be an experience. It doesn't even have to be a good experience. Sometimes it's bittersweet."

"Bittersweet?"

"Something both good and bad." I saw the confusion on his face. "Something that wasn't great when it was happening, but you kind of look back on it and it makes you feel . . ." I put a hand over my chest. "Warm."

"I see," Om said slowly.

Suddenly, darkness took over. I started and felt around blindly. Om's arm wrapped around my shoulders.

"What's happening?"

"A memory," I heard him say, though I could not see his face. As my eyes adjusted, I recognized the scene. By the glow of the green console, I saw the hazy form floating in space, two bodies intertwined, a blanket wrapped around them like a cocoon, turning slowly, weightlessly in midair. Outside the wide window of the control room, countless stars and planets drifted by.

"Is that us?"

"As you said," he replied. "A memory better thought back on than lived in the moment."

Everything felt hot, from my face to my chest to the pit of my stomach. Like the snow of Radley, I could feel the sensations of this moment as well—the blanket stretched tightly against my shoulders, his body around mine. I could touch both of him at the same time—the one in the moment, and the one in the memory.

"Thank you," I said quietly. "For that. I would've died if it weren't for you."

"As I would have," he said matter-of-factly, "if you hadn't come along in the silver orb."

"Was it dangerous? Able said you had very little energy to spare. What if . . . you ran out?"

"That was a possibility. But a risk worth taking."

I reached up and followed his chest and shoulders to his neck and face. I touched the ridges of his features and the delicate grooves on his skin. I pulled him down and without seeing, found his lips and brought them to mine. I drank him in.

A flash of white light seared my eyes.

I blacked out for a moment and a pair of hands caught me. I exited and entered consciousness multiple times in what felt like a single moment. When the stars before my eyes finally cleared, I found myself half sitting up on the chair with Om supporting me.

"W-what happened?" I asked blearily.

"The simulation ended abruptly." I tried to focus on Om's voice. He was undoing the straps around my wrists. My ears were ringing. "I apologize. I usually try to ensure the exit from the simulated space is gentler."

I shook my head. My brain rattled in my skull. When the rust-brown dome finally swam into focus, I rubbed my flushed face.

"I'm sorry," I said, too self-conscious to meet his eyes.

"It's my fault," he said. "I lost grasp on the simulation environment."

"Because of me," I said. My face burned. "I shouldn't have done that . . . in there."

"Yes," he said. "But we are outside it now."

As part of me had already started to plot my escape from the embarrassment, his words took a moment to sink in. I looked up at him as he cupped my face in his hands. I shivered as his lips found mine this time and lingered. Blood pounded in my ears, drowning out the hum of the machinery all around me.

"Was that correct?" he asked as he pulled away.

I took his hands, intending to move them away, but found I couldn't. Instead, I pulled him close and kissed him again. His world was terrifyingly, inexplicably bigger than mine. I was treading a road I'd never walked before, and all I wanted was to keep going.

"Come on," I said, and took his hand.

If we had run into Able or Two in the halls, I might've lost my nerve. My heart was beating so quickly that I wasn't sure my resolve could've survived a single curious glance.

I took him to the little room where I slept, to the bed he had manifested for me. He lay down next to me, just as he had during those cold nights in the capsule, and kept me warm.

CHAPTER 20

I LAY AWAKE IN THE DARKNESS.

A heavy arm was draped over my waist. Om's chest rose and fell. His breath tickled my neck. If he wasn't organic, he certainly felt like it. I laid a hand over his shoulder gently. I knew the rhythm of his breathing well, whether he was lying next to me, curled in my lap, or wrapped around me in the dark. In every form, his breathing kept the same rhythm.

I could stay like this forever.

A scraping sound caught my attention before sleep could overtake me. I craned my neck to see movement in the hall. The light seeping in from underneath the room door was being broken up by a moving form. Someone was outside. I debated waiting until they went away, but they appeared to be pacing back and forth.

I sat up, careful not to disturb Om's sleeping form. I felt around in the dark, found my clothes, and put them on. Two or Able must have noticed that Om was missing and become worried. I might be in for a bit of an awkward explanation. Quietly, I pushed the door open.

No one was there. I stepped out, peering to the left. Before I could check the right, a hand slipped around my face and pressed against my mouth. Another grabbed me around the waist, pinning my arms to my sides tightly. I let out a shout of surprise that came out a muffled croak.

"Don't panic," said a familiar voice in Fiinian dialect.

I bucked hard. The attacker released me. I spun around, facing the armor-clad figure.

"Sorry," Solace said, peering down both directions of the hall, then holding up a finger to where his mouth would be under his helmet. "I had to keep you quiet." Seeing no one was coming, he grabbed my arm. "Come on."

I shook out of his grasp, trying to wrap my mind around his sudden appearance. I had hoped I would never see him again.

"You shouldn't be here," he said, and started to grab my arm again. I pulled out of his reach.

"Don't touch me."

He took a step forward. "I need to get you out of here."

"Why?"

"Y—"

He stopped midsentence. His gaze went past me and I followed it. Om stood behind me. My blood went cold as I saw the curved blade appear in Solace's hand.

"No!" I exclaimed, shielding Om with one hand and pushing him back into the room.

"Step away from it," Solace said. His voice had taken on a lower, darker tone.

"Get away from me!" I shouted. "I'm not coming with you!"

"You don't know what that thing is." Solace took a step forward, but I refused to move.

"Yes, I do," I said firmly. "He's a Harbinger. And he's not dangerous."

The blade spun in Solace's hand. "Whoever told you that," he said, "is lying to you."

Something struck him from behind. He stumbled and fell to one knee. I gasped at the sight of the blade sticking out of his back. It disintegrated and dark blue blood seeped from the wound. His own weapon disintegrated as well.

"Hey, Eleven. Long time." Able smirked. "Miss me?"

Solace sprang to his feet and struck out, hitting Able's head, chest, and stomach in a series of movements I could blink and miss. Able took the blows and stepped back with each one, but none of the blows quite landed. They seemed to stop a hair's length from making contact. With a sneer, Able struck back and with a single blow knocked Solace clear across my line of sight. He landed on his back heavily and tried to sit up. Able waved his hand and something shifted in the air. Solace fell back, held down by the sudden change in gravity. Able walked up, unhurried, and drove one foot into his stomach. Solace let out a pained groan.

"That old wound still gets to you, doesn't it?" Able said. His cheery, friendly demeanor was gone, replaced by a chill that matched the arena's cold air. "All this time, it's never healed completely. You pushed yourself beyond what the arena could repair, and for what? That little woman? Look what you are to her now—just another pawn in this war."

"You filthy traitor," Solace hissed through gritted teeth. "I should have known it was you."

"Were you surprised?" Able pushed his foot down further, pressing his heel into Solace's belly. "You know, it wasn't a hard decision to make. Faking death is pretty easy in the middle of a war." He sighed wistfully. "All that time groveling at Mother's heel, only for her to pass the mantle to that brat. I had no future there, so I had to make my own."

"By betraying the rest of us."

Able shrugged. "Sure, if you want to call it that. It's really just a bonus." He leaned down over Solace. "You were always a tough one in the arena. But even in this pathetic landfill, administrative function will always trump."

Solace struggled, but Able only pushed down harder, pinning him in place. He nodded toward me.

"Tell me, how did you find her here?"

Solace didn't answer. I heard his pained breath as he tried to free himself.

"She's chipped, isn't she?"

I felt around my neck frantically, hoping he was joking. Able smiled under unsmiling eyes.

"I'm guessing she doesn't know."

My fingers touched something on the back of my neck, just under my scalp. A scar the length of my finger, protruding above the skin.

Solace's fingers turned. Another blade appeared in the blink of an eye and sank into Able's calf. Able let out a surprised yell and stumbled back, but even before he steadied himself the wound was healed. Solace scrambled to his feet.

"Just let her go home," he said. "She's not part of this."

"Isn't she?" Able smirked. "I'm not the one who chipped her. But I should thank you. Saves me the trouble of chipping her myself, not that she's going anywhere." He nodded toward me. "Actually, let's make sure of that."

He raised a hand and snapped his fingers in my direction. I gasped as my arms were suddenly bent backward painfully.

"Om?" I tried to pull out of his grasp, but he only held tighter. There was something terrifying about the blank look in his blue eyes. "What are you doing?"

"Following orders," Able said. "It's what he's made to do. Harbingers follow the commands of demigods. Failing that, they default to arena masters." He let out a cruel laugh. "Honestly, you're so easy. All I had to do was parade that pretty toy in front of you and you fell right in line. If Astra were half as easy to distract, I wouldn't have had to go to all this trouble." He turned to Solace. "Now then, what to do with you? Do you want to crawl back to your mistress like a good boy, or do I have to send you back in pieces?"

Solace spun the blade in his hand. Om's grip on me was painful and every time I wriggled, he held me tighter.

"Let her go," Solace said. "You can do whatever you want to me. She doesn't belong here."

"Oh, she very much does," Able said. "But it hardly matters at this point. We've gotten exactly what we needed."

A slender metal hand reached over Solace's shoulder to his temple and I let out a surprised yelp as a hot bright spark shot from its fingertip. I hadn't even seen Two approach. They stepped over Solace's unconscious body to Able.

"Well," they said. "If I didn't choose a side before, I suppose I certainly have now."

"Don't think I didn't appreciate it," Able replied, kicking Solace's weapon out of his hand. It struck a wall and disintegrated. "Stubborn to the end, this one." He turned to me and smiled that same friendly, disarming smile that had welcomed me into his arena. "Well, no more secrets between friends, I suppose."

I couldn't comprehend what was happening. Just a few minutes before I had been lying blissfully in Om's arms. Now everything had gone horribly awry.

"I imagine you have some questions," Able said. "Unfortunately, we are on a tight schedule, so we'll have to stash you away for the moment. Don't worry; if you get bored, we'll send the Harbinger in to entertain you." He winked and I felt sick to my stomach. "You've found out by now that it's very good at doing exactly as it's told."

OM—THE Harbinger, whatever he was—held my arm as we shuffled after Two and Able. His grip was cold, unyielding. Even through my clothing I could tell that something about him had changed, as if he had somehow become less alive, more mechanical. There was no warmth to his skin, no expression on his face, and I had a feeling that if I were to put a hand on his chest right now, I would find no heartbeat.

"I don't understand," I said, trying to keep my shaky voice steady and failing.

No one acknowledged me. Om's blue eyes, once inquisitive and deep, now looked like glass. He dragged me along as if I were no more than a piece of luggage.

"You're hurting me, Om," I said. He didn't respond.

"You're wasting your breath," Able said with a hint of amusement. "That thing doesn't recognize names. It goes by a code and a serial number."

"That's not true!" I said heatedly. "I gave him this name. He knows it."

"Really?" Able said without turning around. "Harbinger, what is your moniker?"

Without hesitation, Om rattled off a list of numbers and letters, some of which could not be translated by the orb, punctuating each sound with the finality of a finger striking a board of buttons and keys. Able chuckled.

"Do you see?" he said. "The name means nothing to him. He—*it*—connected with you aboard the capsule and used your memories to build itself into a working condition. You are nothing to it but data. If I wanted to, I could order it to wipe its memories of you and it would do it before you could take a breath."

I glanced at Two, hoping to see something in their body language to refute this terrifying suggestion, but received nothing in return.

"Where do you want to put her?" they asked. Able shrugged, his eyes full of derision.

"Anywhere. She's only a Fiinian."

I bristled. "What does that mean?"

"It means," Able said unhurriedly, "that Fiinians are garbage. Do you know what kinds of animals change their biological gender the way you people do? Worms. Fish. Soft, slippery amphibians that squirt out their guts when you step on them. You're a planet full of lower life forms pretending to be people."

I spat at him. My spit landed on his arm. He flicked it away in annoyance and gave Om a nod. Without warning, Om grabbed me by the back of the neck and slammed me against the wall of the hallway. My bones rattled from the impact.

"Ease up now," Two said. Their holographic face turned from its default smile to an uneasy expression with a flat line for a mouth. "We're not done with her yet. And by the way, what do you want to do with the other one? Should we send him to drift in a capsule?"

They were talking about Solace. I struggled to focus as Om pulled me along again.

"You're still too squeamish to off a fellow champion?" Able teased. "If I recall correctly, that was once your specialty."

"Don't," Two snapped. For the first time since meeting them, I heard their cheery tone falter. "You know precisely why I did what I did for H'otto. Besides," they gestured at me, "I only agreed to help you get her here. I have no interest in provoking Astra further."

"Don't worry about her," Able said. "As for him . . ." He sneered. "I know exactly what to do with him."

I KNEW THESE ROOMS.

The moment I saw the hall of closely spaced doors, panic welled up in me. Images of Viva's body, hanging by wires threaded in and out of her limbs and exposed brain, came flooding to mind. I yanked against Om's grasp.

"No," I begged, my feet fighting against the metal floor as he dragged me, one difficult step at a time. "Not here. Don't lock me in here."

Om's vise grip didn't loosen. Energy welled up in my chest and threatened to burst forth, but I forced it down, fearing that letting it out could result in more harm to me than the others. It escaped me anyway, but only in a weak push.

"Was that a ripple projectile?" Able said to Two, who shrugged nonchalantly. "Seems she's still got a little too much fire in her." He gestured to Om. "Just for that, you'll have to watch as I do this, Fiinian."

He motioned for Om to come forward. My entire body tightened.

"No," I begged. "Don't."

"Harbinger," Able said, loud and clear to Om's face, "administrative reset. Full memory wipe. Retain essential functions only."

"No!"

Om's blue eyes lit up bright, then began to flash rapidly. He still maintained his grip on me, and it didn't loosen even as I screamed his name and hammered on his chest. The days and nights we'd spent together, curled up in the capsule, holding each other in the frigid darkness, walking one planet after another hand in hand, bodies entangled in the throes of passion, all burned away like embers. A broken croak escaped me as his eyes went dark, then slowly lit up again.

"Reset complete," Om said woodenly. "Awaiting instructions, arena master."

Able's face spread slowly into a smug grin. "Sedate her," he said.

Om lifted his free hand and placed it on the back of my neck. I nearly fooled myself into thinking I saw affection in his eyes until something jabbed me between the shoulder blades and everything began to spin. I heard the sound of a door opening, then metal floors came rushing up at me. I went sprawling. The door behind me began to swing shut and I lurched at it, blocking it with an outstretched arm. It struck my forearm, and I cried out in pain as the bones in my arms cracked and shattered.

"Oh, for gods' sakes," I heard Able say. My head swam but I

clenched my teeth and refused to move out of the doorway. "Give her another dose."

"Let's not."

I glanced up to see Two standing over me. They gestured to Able and Om. "You two go on. I'll fix her up."

Able rolled his eyes. "Fine."

Footsteps receded from me. A metal hand slid under me and pushed me away from the door. I muttered a protest but was too weak to resist. Two sat me up against the wall of the tiny room and examined my broken arm.

"You could make this a lot easier on yourself," they said, tracing a finger over my skin. A strange tingle coursed through my muscles and broken bones. I twitched. "Don't move. This is easier if you stay still."

I swung out with my other hand and only managed a weak swat. Two brushed me off.

"He wiped him," I said. My tongue felt large, like it was swelling and filling my entire mouth. "Why?"

"Because that's who Able is." I hissed as my bones knitted themselves back together. "He doesn't care about anyone or anything besides what he's got his sights on, and he'll always be several steps ahead of you."

I tried to speak, but my mouth was numb. I wriggled and stretched it, trying to loosen the muscles.

"Did you really think you came up with the idea to test the signal by yourself?" Two went on. "He led you from the moment you arrived. Made it seem like it was your idea. If you hadn't come up with it on your own, he would've found some other way to get you there. Able doesn't like to force people to do things. He always says you get better results if you can get the pieces to move on their own." They tapped my forehead. "But really, you're too easy. You even fell for that little show with the broken doll."

"Doll?" I croaked.

"That one he dug out of the basement to put on that little show for you."

I coughed, trying to will my mouth to move. "That was fake? She . . . she was . . ."

"That thing's been sitting around here for a while. He just dug it out and turned it on. You needed a little push, and he gave it to you."

"He cut her?" I asked with a shudder. "To convince me?"

"Oh, no. He didn't cut it." Two paused. "Told it to cut itself. He doesn't like getting his hands dirty."

"Did . . ." I didn't want to ask this question, but couldn't stop myself. "Did she feel pain?"

Two said nothing. The world was fading out around me.

"I trusted you," I muttered.

"Yeah, you did." There was amusement in Two's voice. "Silly thing to do, really. Why did you do that?"

Because I thought you cared, I tried to say, but couldn't get the words out. Two released my arm and I slumped to the floor. The holographic face flickered off.

"I don't owe you an explanation," they said, then flicked my nose with their metal finger. Their motion left trails in front of my eyes. "But I will say I didn't mean for any of this to cause you harm. It's not personal. It was never about you."

"Then what?" I gasped, struggling to keep my eyes open.

"Nothing," they said, and walked out. As the door closed, I heard them say, "It's not about any of you."

CHAPTER 21

"Kova."

"Rosi?" I couldn't feel my mouth move. I looked down and saw I had no body. "Rosi!" I shouted, though my words were silent and weightless. I could almost see them floating in the air as they left my mouth.

I listened. Nothing.

"Rosi?"

There was a whisper in the air. It reminded me of when Mother tried to invade my mind at the silver orb. But it wasn't the same. Not entirely. There was also a strange warmth, like I was surrounded by water being slowly heated. I struggled to breathe, but the heat only suffocated me further.

"Rosi!"

The whisper grew louder, then quieter, then vanished.

I WOKE UP.

A metal tray sat in the corner of the room. I sat up, grabbed the glass of water sitting on the tray, and chugged it. My throat burned like a dry fire.

With the water gone, I turned to the plate. The gelatin cubes weren't terribly flavorful, but at least they were familiar. I ate them, carefully picking up each one with my fingertips. I was starving, and I had no idea how long I'd spent drifting in and out of strange dreams and hallucinations.

As I shoved each gelatinous cube into my mouth, I tried to sort out how I'd ended up here. The memories of Fiina, Meli, my wedding, and the cove were incredibly far away and long ago. I had lost track of how many days had passed since I'd left Fiina.

I finished the last bite, chewing thoroughly and almost resentfully.

How long had I been in this room?

I'd lost track of that, too. I was provided a meal of gelatinous cubes every few hours, enough to keep from going hungry for too long, and I'd eaten at least ten of these tasteless meals. The sedation they put me under left me in a drowsy stupor, which I'd spent alternately staring into space and dreaming. It also must have left me itchy, as I often woke with welts up and down my arms, though I couldn't remember scratching them.

I threw the plate across the tiny room. It clattered against the wall and spun awkwardly on the floor. My anger bubbled and seethed. I'd fallen for his charm hook, line, and sinker, just because he'd offered me a smile and a hot drink at the right time.

And Om.

The thought of Om made me wish I had a few more plates to throw. My hands tightened into fists. Om was gone. Wiped, like the machine he was. In the end, there truly was nothing more to him than data and machinery. How stupid I had been, thinking he was more.

If I somehow got out of here, I promised myself, I was done with this. Done being used. Done with all of them. I would find a capsule and take off, no matter where to.

Whatever Rosi wanted me to see, this couldn't be it.

. . .

"KOVA."

I was back in the white room again.

"Kova."

Loud and clear. She was closer this time. So close I could almost feel her breath. I looked down and once again, saw no body. I was a floating head. Or perhaps just a pair of floating eyes.

"Rosi?"

Silence.

"Rosi! Where are you?"

No answer. I listened, seeking the voice that radiated from the white walls around me.

"Rosi, please help me." My words hung in the air as if they had weight. They made the air heavier, thicker. The more I spoke, the thicker it became, like hot steam filling the space all around me.

"I don't know what to do. Please."

Heat. Pressure. It had been hot last time, too. But now it was boiling.

"I'm so lost. I don't know where to go. Please show me."

Was there a valve on this room? Could it open, or was I going to be cooked alive here?

"Rosi?"

The more I panicked, the hotter it became. It grew and grew but I couldn't stop.

"Rosi!"

The hot air contracted like air being sucked out of a lung and then burst all at once. I screamed, but no sound came out. The world around me shook like a planet being split and the air roared with invisible fire.

Then, darkness.

I ROLLED ONTO MY BACK. My head pounded. Something was wedged uncomfortably under my waist. I reached and moved the empty plate out of the way.

At first, I thought my eyes were having trouble focusing, but as the walls and ceiling slowly drifted into view, I took a breath, sat up, and coughed. My head hurt like I'd just hit it on something. Had I fallen? Was I even standing? Or was I dreaming again?

Everything was a haze and whatever I'd seen and heard in my sleep was already faded and gone. I cursed myself, the room, and everyone I'd encountered since Radley had vanished beneath the clouds, then wondered if I ought to lie back down when my gaze landed on the cell door.

It had split, lying open and splayed in pieces as if it was made of paper. I stared at it for a long moment. When the scene didn't change, I got to my feet.

The walls around the door were dented as if something had struck them full force. Now that I was seeing clearly, I saw that the dent extended all the way around the room, roughly at my eye level, like something had exploded from where I stood.

My heart lurched. I stumbled toward the door, running my hands along the jagged edges, making sure it wasn't a hallucination. My mind battled with itself. Escape hadn't seemed remotely possible, and I still couldn't understand what happened. Was it a trap? A trick? Before I could decide, my body was already moving on its own. The space left by the torn halves was a tight squeeze, but if I sucked my stomach in, I could just about climb through. I ended up with two long scratches on my calf, but a few tense moments later, I was alone in the hallway.

Stars danced before my eyes. I shook them away.

I was free.

Holding my breath, I waited for someone or something to barrel down on me and catch me unawares. No one came. The metal hallways echoed their silence all around me.

I had to go. The direction didn't seem to matter. I only knew I had to get away from *here*. Picking the nearest hall, I hurried down it.

I found the elevator up, then spent what felt like forever

wandering the corridors and peeking around corners. Without an AI's guidance, I had a hard time finding my way around the maze of hallways, though I knew that it was probably the lack of an AI that was allowing me to go around undetected. I went over a familiar walkway suspended over a computing farm. But unlike the one in Astra's orb, where a small section still flickered with light, this one was almost all dark. Many of the machines and boxes below had fallen into disarray, piled on top of each other, with the occasional blinking lights here and there.

If I could just find my way to the capsule bay, I told myself, I could find a way out of here. What came after that, I would have to play by ear.

Voices.

I pressed myself against the nearest wall, paranoid I'd been seen. But no one appeared. Carefully, I made my way through the halls. The voices came from the end of one hall that ended at what looked like a balcony overlooking an open space—the arena floor. Whoever was speaking sounded like they were too preoccupied to come after me.

"Give him back to me, and I'll let you retain most of your limbs."

I knew that voice. I took a few steps toward the balcony, then dropped to my stomach and crawled, trying to stay out of the sightline of those below me.

"Always so quick to violence." That was Able. I could just barely see the top of his head from where I was. The other person I had a better view of. I could see her glassy hair and the familiar covering over her face. "Solace wouldn't approve. Wasn't that one of your favorite things to fight about? How you're always so quick to cut."

"Shut up," Astra snapped. She hadn't raised her voice, but the hairs on the back of my neck stood up when she spoke.

"I couldn't give him back if I wanted," Able said with a

nonchalant shrug. "You're a little too late. If you're lucky, there will be something left for you to remember him by."

Astra bristled. I could see her seething anger from the balcony. "Where is he?"

"Two didn't tell you? You didn't open up their chest and cut their brain into slices one at a time until they gave up all their secrets? Seems like your style."

"I will do exactly that. And then I will do the same to you."

Able laughed. I knew I should go, but I couldn't turn away.

"Need I remind you whose arena you are currently in," he said.

"Arena?" Astra tossed a derisive look at the pile of wires and machinery. "Just like you to build yourself a throne in a trash heap so you can play king. This place is beyond defunct. It's a shell. You can barely even call it an arena." She paused. "Though I *am* curious who is helping you run it."

"Are you implying something?"

"You have no AI. So where are they?"

"Who?"

"The demigod piloting this thing. I highly doubt you took a chance out here in a defunct orb alone. And an orb without an AI can only be manually piloted to this capacity by a demigod." She narrowed her eyes. "Bring them out and I'll kill you both mercifully."

I could hear the uncaring amusement in Able's voice. "So cocky," he said. "You've always been a wild one, even when you were just a meek little contestant. Remember those days, Astra? Such fun. Such hubbub, all for 'Diamond Donna.'" His voice lowered. "Ever wonder if all those people were right about you?"

I didn't see Astra start moving, but I saw where she ended. One moment she was across the room and the next she was in front of Able. Her right arm had changed to the shape of a long spike, translucent and cloudy like it was made of crystals, almost identical to when she'd stabbed the Harbinger through their head. Its tip was a hair's width from Able's face, where he had stopped it with one arm. A metal plate had sprouted from his forearm and caught the blow just in time.

Astra pulled back immediately and came again. Able caught each blow effortlessly and parried it aside. I flinched at every clash. Astra was fast. She drove Able back with each strike and her speed only increased with each hit.

And yet, there was not a hint of worry on Able's face, and even from where I was, I could see that she was not gaining ground through her power—Able was allowing her to do so. He blocked her with a thin smile on his face as if playing a game, the same smile he'd worn when he drove his heel into Solace's stomach and watched him squirm in pain, like a cruel child torturing a bug.

Astra's movement slowed for a fraction of a second and Able took it. With a single blow he knocked her across the room. She struck the floor heavily and I thought I heard her spine crack against a piece of the machinery she slid into. Without even a hiss of pain she was on her feet again, but it was already too late. I watched her attempt to take a step and fail. Something held her down—the metal surface itself had grown over her feet. Able's smile broadened. He approached her unhurriedly and struck out, the metal plate on his arm now shaped like a large blade. She blocked and the crystal spike connected to her arm shattered. I watched as what was left of it formed itself back to the shape of her hand, though her skin was still translucent and I could make out the shape of bones and joints underneath.

Able raised one hand and glided it through the air. I saw ripples moving in the space around them. They swirled about Astra and tightened around her in spinning circles, restraining her arms by her sides.

"Look at you," Able said. "Pathetic." The air currents tightened around Astra's head and neck. I heard her gasp as they restricted her airway. My breath caught as if I were the one being strangled. Could I really watch her die? Able pulled the cover from Astra's face and I saw her features clearly for the first time.

Her skin was translucent from the nose down. Not clear like glass or plastic, but cloudy like uncut crystal. Her lips were nearly white and I could vaguely see the forms of her jaw bones as she fought to breathe.

"I'll never understand why she chose you over me," Able said. He grabbed Astra's chin and turned her face this way and that roughly. "Even among us, the anomalies who don't even fit in with our own people, you're a freak. Maybe the real reason Eleven ditched you is because he can't stand to look at your disgusting, splintered face anymore." He brought his face close to hers. "Mother won't be happy to lose her protégé, but she'll forget all about it when she sees the gift *I'm* preparing for her. So, would you like your death to be quick or interesting? Either way, I'm going to enjoy this."

I couldn't watch this. I struggled briefly on whether I should run now and spare myself from having to watch her execution or do something to help her, which was a ridiculous thought, as there was no way I stood a chance against Able. My body tingled as I heard the hum of the arena. Could I manifest? Would it even do any good when I had only achieved a weak ripple before? But thankfully, I didn't have to make the decision.

The restraints around Astra's body suddenly dissipated. I thought it was Able's doing, but the look of surprise on his face told me otherwise. In the split second he took to contemplate the occurrence, Astra's arm formed into a bulky mallet-like shape and smashed against his face. He regained his composure quickly and manifested a shield to protect himself, but it shattered as soon as it was formed.

Astra's blow caught him square in the chest. There was an exclamation of surprise that was cut short as the wind was knocked out of him. She pinned him down on the floor, panting hard, trying to catch her breath. After a tense moment, Able laughed. It was not his usual smug chuckle, but a cold, dry laugh of resignation.

"What do you know," he said, looking up at the domed ceiling above. "Failed by my own arena. I suppose that's fate paying me back for reaching too high." He glanced at Astra, face split into a grin. "You win, Thirty-three. End me how you see fit."

Astra straightened. She shook her head. "I'm not done with you yet," she said, and lifted her gaze to the balcony.

"Meet me in the capsule bay next floor down," she said to me. "Unless you want to become a permanent resident."

CHAPTER 22

I STOOD AWKWARDLY IN THE CAPSULE BAY WATCHING ASTRA DRAG Able into E-V's capsule. He hadn't said much, but that thin smile stayed on his face as he passed me. It was the self-satisfied look of someone who was privy to secrets unbeknownst to everyone else in the room.

Astra hadn't spoken either since we'd left the arena floor. She'd made an attempt to restrain Able with whatever she could find in the mess of wires and machinery, but in the end gave up and broke both of his wrists instead. He didn't make any attempt to resist, probably because with his arena shut down and two useless hands, there was no point.

"Don't try anything," I heard her say as she pushed him into the sleeping quarters. "Manifestation in this capsule is limited to me only."

"Wouldn't think of it," Able replied. "Ol' faithful E-V. I'm surprised she's still functioning. Certainly more resilient than the original, isn't she?"

Astra's hand twitched. I thought she might have something to say, but she only shut the door to the room and locked it behind her. There was a heaviness to the way she moved, as if she dragged parts of her body along on frayed strings.

"Are you coming?" she said tiredly, and it took a moment to

realize she was talking to me. I quickly nodded and entered the capsule, only to stop in my tracks when I saw the pile of what I initially took to be scrap metal sitting in the control room.

"Kova!" came E-V's voice. She sounded genuinely happy to see me. I forced a smile, even though I had no idea if she could read my expressions.

"Hi, E-V," I said, unable to pry my eyes from Two's dismembered limbs. Leaning against the control console was their metal torso, completely encased in translucent crystal. The holographic face was turned off.

Without a word, Astra shut the capsule door and went to the console. She had covered her face and hands again, but knowing what was underneath the fabric, I couldn't help wondering exactly how far the mutation of her body went. If she noticed me staring, she gave no sign. The capsule slowly drifted out of the dead orb, leaving the empty husk to wander the silent space among others of its kind.

"Kova," E-V said. **"You. OK?"**

"Um," I stammered. Was I? "Yes, I'm OK."

"Astra. You. OK?"

Astra said nothing. She looked straight ahead out of the window to the dark of space.

"He OK?"

That twitch again.

"He OK?"

Her fist clenched. I heard the crinkling of crystals rubbing against each other.

"He OK?" E-V persisted. **"He. OK? He OK?"**

"Shut up!"

I jumped. Astra slammed a fist against the control console. I took a fearful step back as she turned and kicked Two's crystal-encased torso, sending it rolling against the benches.

"Shut up, E-V!" I flinched as one of her fists drove through the nearest screen, sending glass flying everywhere. "Shut up! *Just shut up!*"

I scrambled out of the way of her tirade, but the capsule was not exactly spacious. Astra pulled her hand out of the broken screen and her glove slid off. She straightened and seemed to suddenly remember I was there.

"Wondering about this?" she asked, holding up her crystalized fingers. The joints of bone were just visible underneath the surface, a truly unnerving sight. I shook my head quickly, but hiding the unease on my face was impossible.

"This is what happens to people who abuse the arena's powers," she said, waving her hand in front of me. "The arena giveth and the arena taketh away. Overuse it, and it will find its way inside you, take over your body until it becomes a part of you. When you cross that line, there's no going back. You take the arena with you even when you leave it. It's in your blood."

"He OK?"

Astra smashed a fist against the wall, leaving a sizable dent. "I said *shut up*, E-V! He's not OK! I *failed* him, just like I failed everyone. Shut up and leave me alone!"

I backed away, wondering how I was going to protect myself if she turned her anger on me, but thankfully she didn't, and E-V finally fell silent. I watched, terrified, as she unleashed her rage on the walls and flickering screens, hoping she wouldn't smash the window and leave us all to drift in the vacuum of space. When she was nearly out of screens to smash and walls to dent, she finally began to calm. I gave her space to collect herself. She slumped onto the bench next to Two's torso, buried her face in her hands, and stayed there for a long time.

I lingered in the hallway, uncertain what to do next. I was just debating if it would be rude to hide in the common room when she looked up.

"I'm taking you home," she said.

I was sure I'd misheard her. "What?"

"I'm taking you back to Fiina. It'll be a bit of a long trip, but the orb should be able to move faster than E-V." She sighed. "He was right. You don't belong here. This isn't your fight."

Her hands dropped away from her face and the mask did, too. She grabbed it and pulled it off from around her neck. The crystallization reached all the way down over her chin, neck, and into her collar. I had a feeling it extended well beyond that, too.

"I'm tired of wearing this," she said. "So you'll just have to get used to looking at me."

"No," I said quickly. "I, uh, it's not . . ." I cleared my throat. "I just thought . . ."

"What?"

"I thought . . ." I swallowed. "Mother said that you would . . . do something to me. To get information."

Astra arched a brow. "She said *what*?" She scoffed. "Typical. Making claims and expecting me to follow through." She eyed the worried expression on my face. "I'm not going to torture you, if that's what you're thinking."

It was exactly what I was thinking, but I didn't say it. She suddenly looked so much smaller than me, and so old despite her smooth face and youthful body. Her eyes were dark, and her shoulders drooped as if always bearing weights far too heavy for them. How long had she been like this, old and heavy beyond the age written on her face?

Quietly, gingerly, I stepped into the control room. The ground was littered with glass. I nudged Two's limbs out of the way and sat down on the bench next to Astra, keeping a respectful distance between us.

"I'm sorry," she said quietly.

I didn't know what to say, so I nodded.

"Mother was the one who taught me. I guess I took her lessons to heart more than I thought." Astra chuckled sadly. "She had so many rules and philosophies for how things should be done, how one ought to conduct themselves as a champion and as an arena master. I never really paid much attention when she went on about it. But then, I never pictured myself in her place back then. Then the war came, and we lost so many. I guess the more I lost, the more I hung on to her teachings. This mantle, the arena, and her lessons were all I had left."

"What did she teach you?" I asked carefully.

"Protect. Guide. Lead," Astra replied. The way she recited those words made me cringe. It was all too uncomfortably familiar. "That was the job of the arena master, she always told me. Protect the champions from anything that might threaten their wellbeing. Guide the newcomers so they know how to conduct themselves and work the functions of the arena to their own betterment. Lead them so they do not stray, because to stray is to run into danger." She took a deep breath and let it out. "And above all, accomplish these things no matter the cost, and no matter what others think of you."

"Is that what you did?"

"Yes, unfortunately." She gestured toward the bedroom. "Actually, I always thought she would put Able in charge, so it was quite a surprise when the mantle was handed down to me. I didn't want it."

This was different from what Able had told me, and I was beginning to doubt many things I'd heard from Able. "You couldn't give it to someone else?"

Astra pursed her lips. "Let's just say she made some very persuasive arguments. I did as she told me. Because despite our differences, she had protected all of us for so long. Protect, guide, lead. Take on the burdens, keep your secrets close, no one needs to know more than they have to for their own good. It was Mother's playbook. Look where it's gotten me now. Alone, and a failure."

I laughed. I hadn't intended to, and Astra gave me a confused look. I quieted myself before she could take offense.

"Sorry," I said, stifling my chortles. "It's just funny. I've never left Radley my whole life. When I came out here, I thought everything was so different. Turns out we're not different at all."

"Is that so?"

"Let's just say I'm familiar with following a mother's playbook."

Astra's white lips cracked into a smile. "How about that?" she said. "Different worlds, same blueprint. It never fails." She glanced out the front window. Able's orb had faded out of sight. "So, are you ready to go home?"

I thought for a moment. "Do you know how to make a hot drink?"

WE SAT TOGETHER in the common room, cups of hot, pungent liquid in front of us. Astra took a long sip, and I did the same. She tapped her fingers on the hot mug.

"I don't know where to start," she said.

I shrugged. "Start anywhere."

As she spoke, it occurred to me that I was hearing about the history of this universe for the third time and marveled at how the experience and perspective of each person living through this chaos varied so drastically. She told me about Earth. A world I'd never been to except in the simulation, but inexplicably familiar, just like every world Om had shown me inside the floating door. A world with blue seas and blue skies, billions of people and trillions of ideas. A world where a black orb appeared.

The orb brought with it a deadly game—Headspace. Its inhabitants were forced to play for the entertainment of the gods. The number of contestants dwindled after each round until a champion emerged.

"Her name was Evie." A wistfulness came over Astra's face as she spoke that name. "She was the true champion of Earth, the real Thirty-three. But she took pity on me at the last moment and sacrificed herself so I could live. I tried to strike bargains to save her, and the arena restored her. But the restoration was imperfect. She was remade, but asleep. I waited for her to wake up."

"Did she?"

"No. She never did. Seasons came and went. Our world went through turmoil and chaos trying to heal from the games during that time. Headspace leaves scars that run raw and deep. Ten cycles went by before her body finally broke down for good. I was the only family she had. So I stuck around long enough to bury her. Then, I left."

"Left?"

"To join the games."

"Why, if it was so traumatic for your world?"

"Because while I was waiting for Evie to wake up, there was a man who had been patiently waiting for *me*."

She told me about Solace—Eleven—and the real reason he had lain bleeding before her on the arena floor.

"I met him during my time in the game. He was already a veteran of the arena. We came to know each other through awful times, and when circumstances weren't in my favor, he stuck his neck out for me." She chuckled sadly. "Solace, always putting himself in danger for everyone else. It's hard not to love someone like that."

"So what happened?"

"The war happened. We've had to do things to survive. Difficult things. Here I thought fighting to live in the game was hard. But this, it's so much worse. It's long, never-ending, day and night. It wears on you, chipping your existence away a single moment at a time. When Mother was incapacitated, I took over the arena, which only made things between Solace and me worse."

I took a sip of the stuff in my cup. It was very different from the drinks Able made and had an odd, almost spicy taste to it. I wasn't too fond of the flavor, but it did bring a nice warmth to my body.

"Solace was kind. And when the universe was cruel, he stayed kind. I didn't. I didn't understand at the time why Mother handed the mantle to me. But now I do." I watched her tighten one of her fists then force it loose, as if trying to steady herself. "I'm just like her, trying to save everyone in all the wrong ways."

"He left you because you took over as the arena master?"

Astra shook her head. "Not quite. He stuck with me through it, even though I was awful to him at times. He stuck with me even as my body began to change to this, because I abused the limits of the arena to take on the demigods, again and again. But in the end, I did something even he could not forgive."

Dread came over me. "What did you do?"

"I burned a planet."

ASTRA GAVE me enough time to hide the shock and disgust on my face before she went on, and for that I was grateful.

"It was a small planet. The seed race had just begun to take hold. Their population was under a hundred thousand and they were still mostly agrarian. They were undeveloped, untouched by the demigods." Astra paused. "Listen to me, justifying it, as if the planet being young made it any better. They're gone now, all of them. And without the gods, they will never be restored."

Untouched. Hadn't Om mentioned a world like this? I remembered with a chill the last thing he'd said on the topic.

That world is no longer alive.

"Why did you do it?"

"At the time it was necessary. We had been tracking a demigod who we believed possessed information as to what the others were doing with the salvaged parts of the orbs. The demigods are usually a careless bunch, but this one had grown wise as the war went on. He evaded us for a long time, and we chased him from planet to planet, until we finally found him on this one." Astra tapped her fingers against her cup. "But finding him was the easy part. If we made any attempt to land on the planet, he would detect our presence and flee again, and we would have to start this chase all over. We had been at it for so long by then, and to lose him simply wasn't an option."

"So you . . ."

"I burned it. Turned it into a wasteland in a flash. Back when the games still ran, the arena masters used to burn planets that couldn't pass the games, sometimes quickly and sometimes slowly for a good show. I chose the most merciful way. Everything on its surface was dead before they knew what was happening." She turned to me. "That's how he looked at me, too."

I looked away. "Sorry, I just—"

"It's fine. I deserve it. It was a horrible, monstrous thing to do. But it seemed like the right choice at the time. We went down to the planet and found what was left of the demigod, and from his mind we were able to extract one word—Rosi. It was the only clue we'd received up to that point. I still remember that day. There was a very brief moment of relief, that it hadn't all been for nothing. And then Solace left."

"Left?"

"Took off without a word." Astra gestured at the space around us. "In this capsule, actually. I forget sometimes, but Evie was precious to him, too. Losing her was hard on both of us. This AI is a poor imitation, but we both still hung on to her. I didn't question it when he left. I thought if I just gave him space to cool off, he would come back to me like he always did. And he did come back. But when I greeted him, he looked at me like—" I heard her swallow thickly. "Like he didn't know who I was. After that, he started wearing that damned suit more and more. I rarely saw his face. It was like we were back to how we were when we first met—strangers tiptoeing around each other. Looking back on it, it was a long time coming. That planet was just the breaking point."

"Did you figure out what Rosi means?"

"No. The root language could be anything. We actually

considered one of the Fiinian dialects, but nothing's for certain. I'm not sure it's anything worth chasing at this point. Maybe it was all for naught."

I shook my head. "Rosi was my sister. When the orb came to Fiina, the video it played had a demigod in it. After the people stopped disappearing, Rosi sent me a message. It was the code to open this capsule."

Astra stared at me for a long time. Then, to my surprise, she began to laugh.

I TOLD HER EVERYTHING. From the arrival of the black orb to breaking out of the locked cell. No secrets left. While she listened, she got up and made us another serving of the warm, spicy drink. I wasn't sure if I was imagining it, but the more I drank, the more relaxed I felt.

"Is this . . ." I examined the cup's contents as she set it in front of me. "Wine?"

"Something like that. Whatever you'd consider wine on your world anyway. Nearly every seed race imbibes in some manner." Astra lifted her own cup. "I'm the one who figured out how to heat these things up, by the way. The champions tend to lead very minimalistic lives and give very little thought to creature comfort. Solace especially. But when I took up residence in the orb, I refused to give up what little comforts I had left, so I found a way to recreate whatever I could. Some of it caught on." She took a long sip. "I won't ask what Able told you about me. I'm sure it wasn't pleasant, and frankly I don't blame you for believing him."

I drummed my fingers on the cup. "Did you put a chip in my neck?"

Astra lowered her drink. "Yes," she said. "It was done when we recovered you from the capsule. The original intention wasn't for tracking. Its primary function is to act as a built-in mood stabilizer. This life is a lot to take, and having it went a long way toward keeping the champions, especially the newer ones, from losing their minds. I had it put in just in case you needed a little help adjusting to all this, but luckily, it hasn't been needed. To be honest, I'm surprised that thing can still send out a signal strong enough to track. Bit of a miracle, really, considering how old it is. We can take it out as soon as we get back if you want. The chips weren't so easy to remove back in the day, but these days they barely function, so it's a simple procedure. Still, you must admit it came in handy when we needed to find you."

"So that *is* how you found me." I reached back and felt the scar. "If you don't mind, I'd like it out."

Astra shrugged. "Sure. I'll make sure it's done before we get you to Fiina."

I rolled this idea in my head. I could go home now. Really go home. Back where it was safe and warm and smelled like the salty sea. I could pull out of this dangerous world and return to the four walls I'd once known.

But I hesitated.

I watched Astra over the top of my cup. She couldn't leave if she wanted to. Though I couldn't imagine myself being of any real use to her, leaving her when she was more alone than ever seemed wrong. Besides, I still hadn't found what Rosi wanted me to see, and I couldn't end this journey without at least trying a little harder. There was nothing waiting for me back home except a space on a shelf, and it could go on and wait a little longer.

"Actually," I said, "I thought I'd stick around a little longer."

Astra arched a brow. "Really?"

I nodded. "Yes. Rosi said she has something to show me, and it doesn't seem right until I find out what it is. So I'd like to stay on this ride a little longer, if you'll have me."

She gave me a small smile. "Good."

. . .

"ANOTHER DRINK?"

I shook my head. Everything was swimmy. "I think that's enough for me."

"Something else then."

She rose and filled our cups with a light, fragrant liquid. I sipped it gratefully, waiting for my head to clear.

"I still don't know what Able wants with you. I dug through his 'experiments,' but they didn't make much sense to me."

"What about all that stuff he said about the data core?"

"The data core is an unverified rumor. The demigods have made wild claims about its existence, but they are also fanatics who will twist the truth to fit anything they want to believe."

"So he's lying?"

"Not exactly." Astra glanced over her shoulder toward the door of the sleeping quarters. "Able's wily, but he's no fool. If he thinks there's something to all this, then maybe there is. It's also possible that he's told you a bunch of bunk for some other purpose entirely. He's not likely to enlighten us, of course." She turned back to me. "By the way, what happened to that Harbinger you mentioned?"

I shook my head. "I don't know."

"There's not many of those left." She met my eyes. "And yes, Solace would have killed—Om, was it?—if you hadn't interfered at the holy ground."

"I heard you talk about killing them all, and it just . . . it really got to me. I thought they were alive."

"You did, huh?" Astra leaned back in her seat. "I don't enjoy destroying those things, if that's what you're wondering. They aren't supposed to be alive, but they sure do look it. I've been playing this war game for so long, and if we can't figure out what the demigods are doing, then the only thing to do is to destroy them and their soldiers. It's the last option. Solace knows this as well, though he doesn't like to admit it."

"There's really no other way?"

"It's them or us." Her eyes were dark and serious. "Something you have to understand about demigods—they see us as lesser beings. In fact, they barely see us as sentient beings at all. They do not value us, or respect us, or even think we have a right to live if we do not serve as entertainment. We have no way to win them over, and no bargaining chips against them. The only thing they respect, outside of the gods, is the game. With the gods gone, Headspace reigns supreme. It is unfortunate that the Harbingers have become casualties of war, but you have seen now that they are also no more than tools for the demigods to use against us."

I thought of Om and the way he'd erased everything we had been through together in a blink, like a machine. "I feel so stupid."

"If it helps, deception and pretense are what Harbingers were made to do. It's not their fault that their entire existence is to fool others into thinking they're something that they're not. Without it, they would not be able to scout the seed planets nearly as effectively."

It didn't help, but I didn't say so.

"Was it good, at least?"

"What do you mean?"

"You know exactly what I mean," Astra said. "You don't have to be bashful." I blushed nonetheless. "We've all done it. Harbingers are made to be pleasing. They're beautiful, and they instinctively know how to take shapes that are attractive to others. They possess many features and skills that help them integrate into modern societies, and many of those skills are sexual in nature. Back before they were reprogrammed to target us, it wasn't uncommon for the champions to use them as an occasional stress reliever. For a quick romp, they're not bad."

She talked about them like objects. Things to be broken. Tools to be used. Toys to be played with. I wanted to be offended by this for Om's sake, but that urge quickly deflated as I recalled Om looking at me with his blank eyes just minutes after we'd lain together, rattling off a series of numbers and letters as he awaited instruction.

"I can tell you're bitter," Astra went on. "You can be bitter, but remember that you can't hate something for doing what it's made to do."

I couldn't argue.

"So, what do you think we should do now?"

I looked at her in surprise. It was not the question I expected to hear. "You're asking *me*?"

"I don't see anyone else here," Astra said, gesturing at the tiny common room. "Frankly, I'm tired and out of ideas. I thought I was doing the right things for so long as the arena master, and what has it gotten me? A lot of lost champions, betrayed by the only people I thought I could trust, an arena on its last leg." She sighed. "When I first met Solace, he referred to himself as a disgrace for being the only survivor of his kind. I didn't understand it then. I get it now. Mother left me her playbook and I've failed it. Completely and utterly."

That word scraped at my nerves.

"Aren't you tired of that?"

Astra's drink stopped halfway to her lips. "Of what?"

"Playbooks. Labels." I gestured at her. "You keep putting those labels on yourself. Arena master, champion. What does that even mean? I haven't been here very long and I'm sick of hearing it." The image of Uttam's back retreating among a field of rosalits came to mind. "Someone asked me that question a few cycles ago. I haven't seen him since, but I haven't stopped thinking about it."

Astra regarded me curiously. "And what happened to him?"

"He left. He wanted to do something different. Stepped out of the playbook, I guess." I laughed, though I didn't expect to. "I was so jealous. I couldn't admit it then, but I wished I could leave, too. Just walk out and do what I want." I paused. "What do *you* want?"

She said nothing. I could see her fighting herself. It was all too familiar.

"I want him back," she said. "It's ironic. I took on the gossiping voices of my entire world for trying to put me in a box, and here I am, sitting in another one."

"Just get out of it."

"Speaking from experience, are you?"

"Trying to." Perhaps it was the liquor, but I was feeling unusually brave. "Let's go do that. Get him back. Maybe I'll find what Rosi wants me to see along the way. Whatever else happens, happens."

"Alright," Astra said. "Let's do that." She raised her cup. I looked at it in confusion. "It's a common tradition on a lot of planets. Clinking cups together as a toast to new life decisions and friendships."

"Oh." I grabbed my cup, only to misjudge the distance and bang her cup far too hard, spilling most of both our drinks.

"I think you've definitely had enough," Astra said. I put down the cup sheepishly. "Now then, you've told me about Rosi, but that doesn't answer the big questions. We still don't know what exactly Able is planning, whether any of what he said about the data core is real, or what your sister really has to do with it. And if you're correct, then the demigod who appeared on the video in Fiina is already dead. We extracted Rosi's name from what was left of his brain. So, barring finding another demigod, Able might be the only one with any inkling of Rosi's significance." She thought for a moment. "Actually, there is another person, although they're not going to be any easier to break."

CHAPTER 23

TWO'S SMILING FACE FLICKERED ON AS SOON AS ASTRA RELEASED their torso from the crystal.

"Well, well," they said, sounding amused despite their situation. "Greetings, arena master."

Astra dealt a swift kick to their side and the metal torso fell over. Through the empty neck hole, I could see a jumble of wires and metal. Peeking out from between the gaps of electronics was what looked like a pulsating pink mass.

"Just give me a moment," Astra said to me. Her right arm was already elongating into the shape of a long spike. She raised it and brought it down on Two's chest with a loud *clang*.

"Hey!" Two exclaimed. "Watch it with that thing!"

"Tell me where Solace is."

Two laughed. It was a strangely sad sound. "The little arena master wants her toy back," they said in a sing-song voice. "What's wrong? Are you upset that someone else is playing with him?"

The spike came down on Two's chest again, leaving a sizable dent and making their entire body jerk.

"Be careful! My brain's in this thing."

"I'll pull it out through your neck hole and step on it if you don't tell me where he is," Astra said. She lifted the spike again.

I watched as it reshaped itself, becoming a long, thin blade. She turned it and pointed the tip at a narrow seam on Two' chest.

"That's not funny," Two said. I thought I detected a hint of apprehension for the first time.

"This is your last chance." Astra's tone was dark and solemn. "Tell me where Solace is and I might overlook you betraying me."

"Betraying you?" Two laughed dryly. "It's not about betraying you. None of this is about you. I have nothing to say to you. What are you going to do? Hook me up in the basement? I'm afraid there's not enough of me left to do any good."

Basement?

The blade went into the seam. The metal around it creaked painfully as she turned it.

"Hey! Stop that!" Two yelled. But Astra only pushed harder. The blade went in another finger's length. "Stop! Wait!"

"Stop!"

The cry came out of my mouth before I could stop it. Astra looked up at me in surprise. Two tried to wriggle away from the blade. A gash almost wide enough for me to stick a finger through was left where it went in. I grabbed Astra's arm and pulled her off. She looked from me to Two, then back again. Her arm slowly returned to normal. I approached Two.

It isn't about any of you.

"You said that before," I said to Two.

If Two's holographic face could roll its eyes, I was sure it would've done it then. "What?"

"That it's not about us." I glanced at Astra. "Any of us."

"So?"

"So it's about the one in the basement."

Astra gave me a surprised look. "Viva?"

A heavy silence fell over us. After a long moment, Two spoke up.

"How did you figure that out?"

"It's the only other time you talked like that," I said.

"Like what?"

"Like you cared about something."

The holographic smile flickered off. I knelt down next to them.

"Either you're very observant," Two said, "or I've become unsubtle in my old age."

"Viva can't be restored," Astra said, arms crossed. "You know that. Once someone undergoes conversion into the AI system, the process can't be completely reversed. Besides, she was severed." She turned to me. "There is no way to fix Viva; that's why she's in the basement in the first place. The first arena master broke her, and this is the closest she can get to living."

"Oh, I am perfectly aware," Two said. "I don't want her to live. I want to let her die."

It was not the answer I expected. "Die?" I stammered.

"Care to tell her about Axi, arena master?"

Astra's lips tightened. I rose from my kneeling position and sat down on the nearest bench. After a moment, Astra did the same.

"Axi was the previous AI core," she said. "She was the first AI plugged into the arena. Champion Five. For a very long time, she was the voice of the arena to all of us. Too long, I suppose."

"She broke?"

"She went insane," Two cut in from their spot on the floor.

"Living things degrade," Astra said. "The arena sustains us, but to exist in that unnatural state, it simply can't last forever. She started singing. Only here and there at first. We chalked it up to a quirk. But then she began to do it more and more. She sang in different languages, cycling through all that information stored in her head. We asked her to stop, since she liked to do it when most of us were asleep, and she did it through every channel in the orb. But she couldn't stop. She sang day and night. Then she started losing words, and when she couldn't find the words, she screamed."

"Screamed?"

"Screamed like she was in pain. At the end of each scream, she would make a sound, an inhale like she was choking and couldn't catch her breath, even though she had no lungs."

"That's a sound that stays with you," Two said. "You hear it, even after it stops. Even after they rip the wires out. Even after her voice no longer answers your questions. Even after they throw the rest of her into the nutrient pool." They paused. "I heard Viva sing."

Astra tensed visibly, though she kept her voice even. "Did you?"

"When I visit her, I hear it in the walls close to her. It's very soft, and nonsensical. She won't respond when I ask her about it. You heard it, too, didn't you?"

It took me a moment to realize they were talking to me. I nodded. "Yes, I did. It was . . ." *Eerie? Strange? Sad?* ". . . quiet."

Astra's expression was neutral, but I could see her lips tighten. "How long has this been going on?"

"Some time."

"You want her to die before she screams," Astra said.

"Yes. Able knew this. He made me a deal. Since only an arena master can unplug the AI core, if I were to help him keep tabs on you and occasionally source a few parts, he would unplug Viva after he, well, *displaced* you."

"Charming," Astra said with a scoff. She crossed her arms and closed her eyes. Neither Two nor I said anything as she took several deep breaths. Her teeth ground audibly.

"Okay."

Two's hologram flickered on. There was no smile this time, only a flat, shocked expression. "What?"

"I said okay."

Two stared at her—or whatever qualified for staring for them—for a long time.

"You're going to unplug Viva?"

"Do you want to question me until I change my mind?"

"No," Two said quickly.

Astra opened her eyes. I had a guess that she was as surprised by this decision as the rest of us. "Before I go through with it, can you actually take me to Solace?"

"No." Two's face vanished, replaced by a single glowing arrow, pointed toward me. "But she can."

STANDING in the control room of Astra's arena, I couldn't help but marvel at the fact that I was really back. I hadn't thought I would be, but then, I'd been wrong a lot lately.

Astra stood before the cracked black obelisk with Two next to her.

"You could've just asked me to release Viva," I heard her say. "And saved us all this trouble."

"Ask you?" Two replied. "Like how *he* asked you—*begged* you on his knees—not to burn that planet?"

Astra did not answer. She removed her gloves and laid both hands on the surface of the obelisk. The space between her palms began to rise as a strange white object emerged. It was vaguely in the shape of a face.

"You're sure about this?"

Astra arched her brow. "You're the one who wanted this."

"I suppose I didn't expect you to go through with it. You're leaving the orb without a pilot."

"I'll transfer controls to E-V."

Two let out a short laugh, but quickly stifled it when Astra gave them a hard glare. "Sorry. E-V is fine. I'm sure she'll do well."

Astra held the white, distorted face. She breathed in deep and let it out. Then, she placed her thumbs on its cheeks, just below the eyes.

"Administrator identified," Viva said. "Champion Thirty-three, Astra Ching. Loading privileged fun-tions. What is your o-der, aren- master?"

We all heard those lost syllables, but none of us commented on it.

"No orders," Astra said. She stroked Viva's face gently. "Good night, Viva. Sleep well."

"Good night, arena master."

A sound traveled through the arena, like a soft whoosh accompanied by a series of clicks. Mechanisms turning off, machines powering down. The room suddenly became eerily silent. I hadn't realized until now how ever-present the arena's hum was.

"Get to the basement," Astra said to Two. She stepped close to them and attached what looked like a small metal strip to their back.

"What's that?"

"A tracker. In case you decide to *wander off* again." Astra's dark eyes were hard. "Just because I'm doing this for you doesn't mean you have my trust back."

Two gave her a mock salute. "I expect no less, arena master."

"Now go. Lay her to rest. With dignity, like she deserves."

I WATCHED SILENTLY AS Two disconnected Viva's body from the wires that hooked her up to the arena. The majority of the lights were off when we arrived save for dim, yellow emergency lights. But as Two worked, some of the lights slowly came back on.

"E-V must be settling in." It took me a while to realize they were talking to me. Without the holographic head, it was difficult to tell where they directed their attention.

"I guess so," I said. "I'm sure she'll do fine. She's done fine for me."

"I mean no disrespect by this," Two said. "But E-V is an idiot."

"She's just a program, isn't she? She doesn't . . . have a body somewhere?"

"No." Two pulled a handful of wires from Viva's neck. "If we had her body here, she wouldn't be such an idiot. The real Evie was clever. But this one is only a mimic, with faulty logic and terrible security. It's anyone's guess how long she'll last as the primary AI." They examined the remaining tissue inside Viva's skull and sighed. "Not that Viva would've hung on that much longer." They gestured to me. "Little help?"

I hurried forward and took Viva around the waist, holding her limp body up as Two continued to disconnect her, a challenging task with their somewhat sloppily reattached arms.

"I suppose I should apologize to Astra at some point."

I shifted Viva's weight. "You must be glad, right? You crossed an arena master and lived."

Two paused their work briefly. "I did say that, didn't I?" they said. "Well, I might as well say sorry to you, too. Most of what I told you was just to make sure you would step away from Astra without a fight. At the end of the day, I guess I'm more like Able than I care to admit."

"So it wasn't true?"

"Some of it was. An arena master broke me. The first one, before Seven. He was a demigod. Seven had her flaws, but without her, I would've been left strung up in this basement a long time ago. And Astra. Astra is brave. She pretends like she's tough, but inside, she's more scared than anyone. Doesn't stop her doing what she needs to though." I glanced at the tracker on their back. "This thing, by the way, is just a gesture. The trackers are junk. But she had to put on a show as the big, bad arena master, even if it's just for herself."

My arms grew sore under Viva's weight, but fortunately Two managed to finish their task quickly and I was able to set her down on the floor. I had no idea how long she'd been strung up, but she looked frightfully alive. Her cheeks were rosy, and her eyes gently closed. If I hadn't been looking into the gaping hole where her brain ought to be just a moment ago, I'd think she was sleeping. Those long lashes looked like they might start fluttering at any moment.

"Is she . . . alive?"

"For the moment," Two said. They knelt down next to Viva's body and brushed her dark hair out of her face. It was a terribly slow, sad gesture. Suddenly, without warning, Viva's eyes opened. I nearly jumped out of my skin as she drew a breath and uttered a single word.

"Beloved," she breathed, then closed her eyes again.

I stood to the side, tense and waiting for her to move again. But she didn't.

"What was that?" I said, my pulse still racing. "What did she say?"

"My name."

"What?"

"Beloved," Two said, their voice full of tears they could no longer shed. "It's the translation of my birth name. I only told her once. But after all this time, she still remembered."

THE THREE OF us stood on the arena floor. I said nothing as Astra tried to call up holographic images, which formed, then quickly dissipated. She tried an image of Fiina, then a projection of the galaxy. Both held together less than two seconds before scattering. Two, who usually had something to say about everything, stayed silent. I supposed that to make snarky comments about E-V would be rather unbecoming given what Astra had just done for them.

After several attempts, Astra gave up with a sigh. There was an awkward stutter to the arena's usually smooth hum. E-V was fighting to stay in control, but her limitations were obvious.

"Alright," Astra said. "Here's what we know." She pointed at me. "Kova. According to you, an orb came to Fiina and abducted many people after running a continuous initiation video featuring the demigod K'azen. None of them returned and they presumably died inside the orb, except for your sister Rosi, who was never found and managed to send you directions to unlock E-V's capsule."

I nodded.

"And Two. Able faked his own death and bribed you with the promise of freeing Viva to get you to keep tabs on me so he could stay hidden."

Two shrugged. "Well, when you say it like *that*, it just sounds sleazy."

"He was restoring a defunct orb. What was he doing with it?"

"He thinks the demigods found the data core. Or found something that could lead them to the data core."

"Do you believe him?"

"To be perfectly honest, I have no idea. You know what Able is like. He is very good at convincing you of anything he wants you to believe. They found *something*. I don't know if it's really what he claims it to be."

"You saw it?"

"Can't be certain. Whatever it is, he couldn't get close to it, but he had this belief that with the right signal, he could follow it."

"And then what?"

"Beats me. If he is to be believed, then the data core—or what he thought to be the data core—will actively connect to signals generated from the memories of seed races. He used the dream state games to produce the signals."

Astra's brow furrowed. "Dream state games only operate on very specific stored scenarios and are incredibly inefficient to run."

"He only needed to run enough scenarios to get this one's brain churning." They jabbed a thumb in my direction. "There were plenty of stored scenarios in the archives. They're just raw footage from scouting missions, but to someone who hasn't been off planet, it's more than enough. In fact, he started prepping it as soon as she appeared."

I arched a brow. "He knew about me?"

"I was keeping him updated, remember? Fiinian was one of the many languages that the word 'Rosi' could've stemmed from. I hadn't thought there was much connection. But he was convinced it wasn't a coincidence. Lo and behold, he was right on that one."

"What happens if it does connect to me?"

"Ah, more stuff I don't know. Like I said, I never quite believed what he was saying, and as long as he held up his end of the bargain, I didn't really care what he thought he was doing. He wanted me to bring you to him, preferably in a cooperative mood. Quite a coincidence that you bonded with the Harbinger. If I'd been aware of that from the get-go, I wouldn't have shipped him off to Ten while you were still passed out. Would've been fun watching you try to explain that to the arena master here."

"Say he finds this thing," Astra cut in. "What does he plan to do?"

"You think he shares his secrets with me? He didn't share with any of us."

"Us?"

"You didn't think I was the only one he tried to hook?"

Astra scowled. "Where's Solace? You said Kova can take us to him."

"Well, it's a theory," Two said, then quickly added as a cloud passed over Astra's face, "but it's a good one. Ten may not have been keen on sharing his secrets, but that didn't stop me from snooping. For all the lip he gave you about E-V, the security in his orb was practically nonexistent. He did encrypt most of his notes, but I was able to break enough of his code to get the gist of things."

"Aren't you the trustworthy one," Astra said, but the corner of her lips twitched upward.

"Just planning for contingencies. See, the data core, if that's what this thing is, has no distinguishable channel of communication. Either it has no communication functions or it was never turned on. Either way, every time it was within reach, the only way to connect to it was to board it."

"It can be boarded?"

"According to Ten's notes, at least. And as you can probably imagine, he was not about to take that risk himself. He convinced others to do it, and I believe there were some unwilling volunteers as well."

"What happened to them?"

"They didn't come back."

"None of them?"

"Not one. Based on his notes, that thing doesn't stick around long, so even if the scouts tried to come back, it ran off before they could get out, so no one was retrieved. I don't know exactly how many he sent, but I imagine he didn't explain to them what happened to the ones who went before, or he wouldn't have had so many volunteers. As far as I could tell, it produced no results whatsoever. Didn't stop him from sending them, though." Two paused. "We made contact briefly before you showed up. I believe he sent Eleven to it."

Astra drew a shuddering breath. I watched her try to decide between anger and despair. Luckily, she did not succumb to either.

"Is he alive?" she asked through gritted teeth.

"No clue."

Astra's knuckles cracked. The sound was like crystals being snapped in half. As she processed this, I spoke up.

"Did you see anything about Rosi?"

Two snapped their fingers. "I was waiting for you to ask that," they said. "The answer is yes, but that part was harder to crack than the rest. Whatever he knew about her, he *really* wanted to keep secret."

My chest tightened. "What did you find?"

"The little I was able to decipher pointed to a connection with the data core. As far I could tell, what he told you about her being receptive to its signal is true. Surprising, really, that he was forthcoming about that much. But then, he probably never meant for you to leave his orb alive, so it didn't matter."

"Is she alive?"

"No idea."

Astra cut in. "Was he working with a demigod?"

"It's entirely possible. Though if he was, I never saw them."

"So," Astra said, rubbing her temples. "To sum up, we still don't know what happened to Rosi. If Able is to be believed, she is connected to the data core or whatever it is, but we don't know where it is or what Able planned to do with it."

"Quite a conundrum, isn't it?" Two said. That sarcastic cheeriness was returning. I was quickly gaining respect for Astra not having ripped off their limbs earlier and in greater frequency. "So what's the plan, arena master? I doubt you'll be able to break Able."

"I won't have to," Astra said. "There's someone better suited for that."

CHAPTER 24

THE ORB SHUDDERED.

In the short time I'd resided in the arena, I had never once felt its movement. It simply glided along, smooth as a boat on undisturbed water, as if it was one of the stars. I had come to take this for granted, and judging by the look on Astra's face and Two's body language, they had, too.

I was not fond of the idea of being around Mother again, but Astra assured me that I was in no danger. Even though I wasn't fully convinced, I was far warier of the ride there.

The trip to the Pinnacle was supposed to take only two or three days, but with E-V at the helm, we had to travel much slower, extending the journey by nearly three times. Every few minutes, the orb let out a shudder like a vehicle driving over a bumpy road. Sometimes it was soft, barely noticeable; other times it rattled so hard that I wondered if it was about to break apart at the seams and leave all of us drifting through the vacuum of space.

To make things worse, E-V sang. Once in a while she would hum out a little tune, sometimes with intelligible words, sometimes all nonsense. She sang about rain in a place called "Spane." She sang about stars, and she sang about "rowing bows." She sang a song about how no one had told her that life would be this way, which I would've quite liked if not for the arena rattling about like a broken wind-up toy.

I tried to distract myself on the arena floor, but the open space felt terribly unsafe. So I found my way to the control room, where I watched Astra attempting to query the database, only to find out that E-V could not pilot the arena and operate the database at the same time. Every time she tried, the orb jerked to a stop. She sighed heavily but said nothing. I eventually wandered to the computing room, where I peered down at the blinking boxes under the suspended walkway. There were very few lit now, and the silent giant Nix had stopped moving. He stood, metal jaw agape, looking up at the ceiling and awaiting instructions from an AI that had no resources to spare him. One green eye blinked at irregular intervals. Two accompanied me there and attempted to make a joke to lighten the mood, but the arena shook, and we both gripped the railings to remain standing as Nix tumbled sideways into the nearest machine. After that, they didn't have much to say.

To conserve processing resources, Astra began to shut down the orb piece by piece. The arena floor went first, then the lights in the basement, then heating and air circulation in unoccupied rooms. She even shut down all the food production machines except one. The areas available to roam grew smaller and smaller, as if the darkness was creeping in on us, driving us into a corner.

Silence had an echo.

I'd never noticed this before in the cramped capsule. Though the chill and quiet were equally eerie in the orb, its size lent an extra layer of ghostliness to our surroundings. The silence expanded and filled every nook and crevice, and it grew with every additional function turned off. As the humming decreased, the silence swelled like a bloated beast. I kept to the lit rooms, leery of peering down the dark, endless halls.

"Stay in the control room," Astra told me as I followed her through the computing room. "You'll be warmer." I watched as she shut off the lights one by one, though she left the last one on for Nix, a single bright spot next to where he stood motionless. I couldn't tell whether he could see or hear anything, but Astra still took care to make sure he was not left in complete darkness.

The control room was the last place with any decent amount of warmth left. With Astra and Two rushing around the orb, frantically trying to compensate for E-V's uneven piloting, I dreaded being left on my own. It was all too easy to believe I was completely alone, surrounded by never-ending darkness and silence that extended far into the empty space. But in the end, the cold made me give in.

On my way there, I tried to manifest a blanket for myself, but the sensation of the act plus the dreary surroundings evoked uncomfortable memories, and I had no success. Besides, I wasn't certain the arena could sustain any decent manifestation anyway. Though I understood Two's desire to free Viva from her fate, I wished we could've stayed warm just a little longer.

Viva.

I shuddered. I was going to be alone with the obelisk. Though her face had disappeared off it after she was unplugged, it still reminded me far too much of a tombstone.

I stepped into the control room.

I saw the obelisk, but it was the least of my concerns.

Before I could decide whether to be relieved, terrified, or worried, he turned to me and smiled.

"Looks great, doesn't it?"

I snapped myself out of my daze as Two approached from behind. They walked by and casually flicked the Harbinger on the side of the head. He didn't flinch.

"We don't usually have active Harbingers around," Two said as they went to the wall of screens. A few of them were flickering. Two turned each one off before looking toward me with their holographic face, once again smiling its default smile. "Not safe. Never know if it's still programmed to serve some other master. But we needed the extra hands. Luckily, this thing was easy to fix." They gestured toward the Harbinger with a hint of pride. "Good as new. Never say I don't know how to tinker."

I couldn't tear my eyes away from the man—*Harbinger? Thing? Tool?*—in front of me. Despite what everyone else said and the proof I'd seen with my own eyes, I had trouble thinking of him as anything but a living being. I had mistaken him for Om at first glance since he had almost the same build and facial structure, but now that I took a closer look, he was actually quite different. His eyes were a light green that reminded me uncomfortably of the Harbinger that had died in Able's orb. He smiled broadly, showing his white, even teeth, a contrast to Om's reserved smiles. His face was rounder and his shoulders broader. The pattern of the grooves on his skin was different as well, and he lacked the black patch on his chest.

This was the Harbinger Solace brought back.

He regarded me for a moment. Then his body began to change. His white skin gained a more natural tint. Smooth white hair sprouted from his head. His body shortened and curved. Colors began to appear in patches and formed into clothing—a dark red tunic similar to those popular in East Fiinian fashions. His features took on a more feminine shape, pale full lips and round eyes.

"Well, look at that," Two said with mild interest. "I wondered if that feature was still working."

The Harbinger blinked. Bright brown eyes shimmered from behind long strands of silky white hair. Something about the way she moved her mouth reminded me of the girl in Daris's etiquette class who had taught me the right way to put my lips on hers.

"It's a very useful thing," Two said, "to be able to look like an attractive member of the nearest seed race. No chameleon suit or makeup needed." They laughed at the shocked look on my face. "Guess you haven't seen this little trick before. Able's pet was too broken to shift out of default state, but this one's still mostly intact. It must be picking up your preferences since mine are harder to read."

The Harbinger brushed a strand of hair out of her face. There was a very shallow groove left where Astra's spike had gone through, but if I hadn't looked for it, I wouldn't have noticed.

"Patched it up well, didn't I?" Two asked. I cleared my throat.

"Yes," I said. "What's she doing here?"

"Keeping an eye on the processing loads for us. Can't trust it to wander around where we can't see it." Two tapped one last screen. It flickered on, then off again. "Looks like we're good here. Everything nonessential is off now." They started to leave. "You staying here?"

"I— Astra told me to come here."

Two snapped their fingers. "Ah, right, cold out there, isn't it? I forget sometimes. Advantage of being all metal." They looked at my shivering form. "I'd make you something thicker to wear, but this place probably won't hold it. If you need it, though, cozy up to that." They pointed at the Harbinger. "It generates pretty good heat in a pinch. You know that already."

Was that a jab? It didn't sound like it. I turned to watch them saunter away. Even they didn't see this being as anything more than a space heater, despite being mostly machine themselves.

Then, I was alone with the Harbinger.

I SAT ON THE FLOOR. There used to be a bench here, but it had disappeared, probably because it was a manifested structure. It was indeed warmer here, but still just a hair below the level needed for comfort. I wrapped my arms around my knees and kept out of the way as the Harbinger paced back and forth, occasionally turning on the displays to check one of many graphs and images I didn't understand.

I watched her. She was breathtaking. Astra had told me Harbingers could take on shapes pleasing to others, but I'd never imagined it to this degree. It was as if she had shaped herself to everything I desired, both consciously and subconsciously.

"Would you like me to join you?"

I blinked. She was talking to me. Her voice was clear and crisp, like a songbird.

I started to say no, but curiosity won over. "Sure," I said, and nodded to the spot next to me.

She sat down. Warm she certainly was. A faint heat radiated off her. It was pleasant and my cold skin welcomed it. But there was something superficial about it, like the heat of a churning engine.

"Is there something I can do for you?" she asked me.

I regarded her curiously. She ought to be identical to Om—attractive, intelligent, and made to serve. While I didn't want to be reminded of Om, I couldn't deny my wandering mind.

Would this Harbinger also keep me company, listen to me, pleasure me, then betray me if she were instructed to do so?

"Tell me about yourself," I said.

"I am not terribly interesting," she said. "I would much rather hear about you."

I thought for a moment. "I came from Fiina. From a place called Radley. It's small and smells like fish."

She smiled. Actually, that smile never left her face. It simply broadened or diminished. "That sounds fascinating," she said.

"Not especially. I'm sure you've been to many more interesting places."

"It is only my duty. I would much rather hear about you."

I frowned.

"How many planets have you been to?" I pushed. "A number. Please."

Something on her face changed. Her smile froze. At first, I thought she was becoming upset at the question, but then I realized she was thinking. Not the way a person contemplated, but like she was running a calculator in her mind.

"Three hundred and ninety-six," she said. The way she said that number was wooden, like it was recited by the voice of a computer.

"Which one is your favorite?"

That frozen look went away. The smile was back. "They were all equally lovely," she said. "Tell me about your world."

She was talking in a loop, as if there was a script to be followed and it always led back to me talking about myself.

"I lived on a hill covered in rosalit flowers," I said, watching her face carefully.

"What are rosalit flowers? They sound lovely."

"They're flowers that grow all over Fiina. They're very adaptive and usually considered a weed, but many people like them. They bloom differently depending on the local climate. We used them as decoration at winter festivals, or sometimes lovers presented them as gifts to each other."

"How nice. What takes place at the winter festivals?"

"It's a little different every cycle. Most of the time there are games and food. Children run around in the snow. The shops set up booths in the streets."

"That sounds terribly fun. What sort of games did the children play?"

She wasn't conversing with me—she was pumping me for information. With every new thing I said, she paid me a compliment and invited me to tell her more. In a random encounter, it could be construed as friendly curiosity. I imagined her on any planet, engaging with the locals and filing away the tidbits in her mind. Her speech pattern was formulaic, but who was going to notice during a short conversation with an attractive stranger?

"How do you see me?"

That glazed look again. Something was computing in her mind.

"You're a lovely person," she said.

"How do you know that? You barely know me."

"I am an excellent judge of character."

"What do you think of Astra?"

"The arena master is a lovely person."

"Because you are an excellent judge of character?"

She paused. Confusion. Struggle. Then she brightened again.

"Tell me more about the festival."

Her smile was beginning to irritate me. I stood. She did the same. Her body language said she was being attentive, but I had a feeling she was just taking cues from me. She observed me, followed my lead, and took whatever information she could from me that would be useful to her prime directive.

Watch. Follow. Listen.

I put a hand on her arm. Her warmth wasn't unpleasant, but it also wasn't real.

For a quick romp, they're not bad.

Astra had said that. I reached behind her neck and pulled her in.

Her lips were warm, but I felt that quick pause again, as if she was analyzing me. It lasted only a moment; then she put her hands on me. First on my waist, then on the small of my back. Under normal circumstances, I wouldn't have thought anything of it, but now I couldn't help but think that she was following a sequence of commands in her head. She wasn't exploring my body, but touching me in select, specific places in an order intended to trigger pleasure. Was there an index of popular Fiinian sexual practices in her head? Did she have a list of common erogenous zones she was ticking off?

I pulled away and pushed her hands off me. "That's enough," I said.

"Certainly," she said, still smiling.

I sat back down, and she sat as well. I moved a little farther from her, just enough to benefit from her warmth. She smiled at me for a while, and when I didn't engage her in conversation, said nothing. After a while, she got up to check the screens, then obediently returned to my side. If I ordered her away, I was sure she would find herself another corner to sit or stand in, and when I changed my mind, she would return at my beckoning.

A perfect, obedient tool.

"Go disable circulation in the capsule bay."

At first, I thought the command was directed at me. I was about to say I didn't know how to do that when the Harbinger next to me stood and walked out. Astra sat down next to me. Wrapped around her was the colorful quilt from E-V's capsule. She held out half to me.

"Want to share?"

I nodded. The room had grown colder with the rest of the orb shut down, especially without the Harbinger's heat. Though a little snug, there was enough room under the quilt for both of us.

"This was mine," Astra said. "I brought it from my home planet. I even went to the trouble of infusing it with building blocks to keep it from falling apart. I couldn't stand how drab everything looked in the orb and the capsules, so I added some color."

I looked down at the quilt. How ironic that I was once again wrapped in this thing, huddled against someone, in a cold, silent vessel.

In fact, it felt just like the capsule, I realized. My arm was pressed against Astra's. She was warm, a living being. Her heat reminded me of Om's, far more so than the nameless Harbinger's.

"The Harbingers," I ventured.

"Yes?"

"Are they really not . . . alive?" I hesitated. "I know they're not supposed to be. But . . ."

"That's a difficult question," she replied. "The concept of 'living' as understood by the seed races is rigid. Beating heart, circulating blood, and such. Or consumption of energy and growth, in terms of plants. But the reality is there are more complex beings in existence. The demigods, for example. They live as some sort of extension of the gods, almost parasitic, and become lost without their host. To this day, I don't fully understand their existence and connection to the gods."

"And the Harbingers?"

"They're somewhere in between. If being alive means consuming energy, circulating blood, and producing living tissue, then yes, they are alive. But if it means growing and changing, then no, they are not."

"What do you mean?"

Astra leaned back against the wall. I did the same, pulling the quilt tightly around my body. "I used to wonder why the gods were so fascinated by us," she said. "We must seem so simple, so dull and stupid compared to them. We can't even fathom how they live. But as time went on, I understood that it is because we change."

"Change?"

"We are not simply the way we are. We are, each one of us, the product of billions of cycles of evolution. We change with each generation. We adapt and grow and become new versions of those who come before us. We build on what we learn. Even within a single lifetime, we are continuously changing. It is as they named us—we are seeds, meant to grow." She extended one hand out of the quilt. A small shape began to form in her hand, possibly a plant of some sort to illustrate her point. But it quickly dissipated.

"I see," I said slowly. "And the Harbingers are not made to change?"

"They were created with both organic matter and the materials of the orb. They are able to consume energy and in turn use it to move and live and heal, the same as us. But they do not learn and reason. Their minds are made for storage, not experience and logic. For all intents and purposes, they are containers to carry information and to be emptied out at the convenience of their masters."

I bit my lip. "Do you think some of them could be different?"

Astra glanced at me. "You're thinking about the one in Able's orb." I nodded. "Didn't he erase you from his mind at a single order from his master?" She must've seen the pain on my face, because her expression softened in sympathy. "Tell you what, when we get to the Pinnacle, if we are able to extract something useful from Able—that's a big if—and *if* we still have resources left after we take care of whatever it is he's involved in, I'll take a shot at helping you find that Harbinger. I know what it's like to want closure."

"I appreciate that," I said, though I had no idea if that was what I wanted.

In the chilly silence, we sat together. Astra soon fell asleep, her head resting on my shoulder. She looked so tired, and so small. But then, we were all tiny in this vast universe, and I had never felt it as deeply and intensely as I did in that moment. I was so very, very far from the walls of my little life on Fiina.

CHAPTER 25

THE ORB GAVE A RATTLE SO VIOLENT THAT I INSTINCTIVELY reached out to grasp something, rubbing my eyes blearily. The quilt was wrapped around me. Astra stood in front of one of the display screens.

"We're here," she said as I joined her. "We'll have to feel our way to the bay. Gravity will be a little spotty as well, so stick close to me. Yell if you start drifting."

I swallowed nervously. "You're sure that Mother . . ."

"Won't torture you for information?" Astra said nonchalantly. "She was just trying to scare you, hoping I'd come up with something. Besides, we know who has the real information now. Too bad her tactics won't work as well on him." Seeing the apprehension on my face, she gave me a thin smile. "Relax, Kova. Most of us aren't as horrid as we seem."

I nodded uncertainly and followed her.

Lights flickered on as we approached, then flickered off as we departed each area. Staying within the pockets of illumination was unnerving and I couldn't stop picturing a myriad of awful things reaching out at me from the darkness. Astra seemed completely unfazed. After what I'd seen of the Headspace games, this must be little more than a morning stroll for her.

Walking through the halls turned out to be more challenging than anticipated as well. When Astra said gravity was spotty, I expected to find pockets of space where I floated into the air, but as it turned out, the gravity varied from step to step, and often shifted midstep as well. I stumbled, trying to keep my feet on the ground and adjust how far and hard to take each step.

"Well, well."

I tensed.

"How's life treating you, Fiinian?"

I wanted to say something as I laid eyes on Able standing with Two at the entrance to the computing room. Something about being betrayed and used and a number of words not appropriate for polite company, but nothing came out. His arms dangled awkwardly at his side, still broken, which was probably the only reason they had not bothered to restrain him.

"Please prep the capsule," Astra said to Two. "You'll be able to navigate the halls faster alone."

"And leave you alone with this one?" Two asked. "Sure you'll get him there alive?"

"Just go."

Two seemed about to say something else but decided against it. I watched them vanish down the dark hall.

"Tight ship you're running," Able said to Astra. The shadows falling over his eyes made me shiver. The welcoming warmth he'd possessed when we'd first met seemed like a strange dream.

"Just keep walking," Astra said, pushing him along.

"Here I thought this was the orb that would withstand the test of time. Suppose that's too much to ask for."

"Walk."

She shoved him on. I followed meekly behind.

"Bit dark in here," Able commented as we drew close to the suspended walkway. Below us was a graveyard of dead machinery. "Barely any blocks, too. I assume E-V isn't running the security functions so well either, is she?"

No one responded.

"Are there even blocks on the game floor? That's probably too much to ask."

Astra stayed silent. I did the same.

"She never was good for much, was she? The—" Here Able said a word that seemed to fail translation. I didn't make out what it was, but Astra certainly did. I heard the sound of his head hitting the side railing. Before I even processed what had happened, Astra seized a handful of black mane and smashed his mouth against the rusty metal. He came away bloodied and collapsed to the floor.

"Oh, little Astra," he said around a mouthful of blood. "Always so predictable."

"Get up," Astra said. Her voice was surprisingly even.

"Give me a moment, would you?" He turned and spat out a tooth, then grinned at me. I tensed at the sight of dark blood dripping along his chin. "Is she always such a slave driver? You can tell me."

I looked away from him, trying my best not to engage.

"Don't you miss the better days?" he asked. I squirmed under his leering gaze. "Living your best memories, seeing new worlds. Let's go back to that, what do you say? You can have your doll back, too. It won't remember you, but it'll still do for recreational activities."

I flushed in embarrassment. Astra stepped between us, blocking me from his sight.

"Get *up*," she said again.

Able chuckled. "Don't get huffy. I was just asking her a question."

"There's nothing you need to say to her."

"On the contrary," Able said. He maneuvered himself against the railings, tried to stand, and failed. "There is plenty for me to say to her. She and I had some good times, you know.

We've got a lot left to accomplish." He struggled against the railing again. Astra crossed her arms and waited. "There're good things waiting for her. Exciting things." He got to his feet and rested his weight against the railing. "Or maybe you're right. Maybe I have nothing useful to say to her. Not useful to *you*, anyway. But I was right about something."

"What's that?"

"Well, two things. One, there really aren't many blocks left in this place."

"And?"

"And that useless AI of yours isn't limiting access to them."

I let out a startled cry as Able swung an arm—now fully healed—and caught Astra across the face. She staggered to the side, and he wrapped his arms around her neck from behind, lifting her off the ground. She kicked and he wobbled. They both stumbled against the railing, their weight rattling the entire walkway.

Astra transformed her arm, but Able was faster. A thin blade appeared in his hand and plunged into her side. She screamed in pain as he pulled it out and stabbed her again, this time below the ribs. Her manifestation broke apart and her hand shrank back to its original form.

I jumped on Able and tried to make a grab for his arm. The three of us tumbled to the floor. His elbow struck me in the face and my teeth rattled. I grabbed the hand that held the knife, but he was stronger than me and jerked away easily. I saw as if in slow motion as he lifted it again, his eyes zeroed in on Astra's neck.

Do something. Do something.

The hum of the arena sang in my head. Images and sounds cycled rapidly in my head, too quick to follow. Then all at once it stopped and a single picture filled my mind.

I lunged forward and my fingers, now curved into the pointed talons of a pebble lizard, raked across Able's face. He let out a cry that was more surprise than pain. His weapon scattered into blocks and for a split second none of us moved as we stared at my mutated hand, pointed claw tips covered in dark, sticky substance.

"I—" I started, but it didn't matter. Every fiber of my being froze at the realization that I had drawn blood. I knew I needed to take advantage of this moment, but couldn't bring myself to. The sensation of breaking flesh drove a chill through me, and the manifestation crumbled almost immediately.

Able recovered first. He grabbed Astra by the arms and rolled under the railing, off the side of the walkway, plunging into the darkness below. I crawled to the edge and leaned over the side as far as I dared, straining to make out their shapes in the darkness. Nix was nearby, but the bright spot Astra had left him did not lend nearly enough light.

Voices. The sound of a struggle. I squinted as hard as I could, calling Astra's name but not expecting a response. I heard Astra shout, then immediately be cut off. There were a few seconds of alarming silence. Then, Able spoke.

"This is why you were never fit to be arena master," he said. "You are predictable. It makes you weak. All I had to do was say a few words about that cripple and you lose your focus every time."

I searched frantically for a way down, but the only ladder leading downward was broken, and to jump from this height would surely break multiple bones.

Astra was silent. Whatever was happening, Able had the upper hand.

"You keep holding on to these worthless beings around you, hoping saving them is going to make a difference. It won't. The new era is coming, but *you* won't be around to see it."

I shouted down to them, but once again received no response.

Manifest. Do something.

But the moment had passed. My hand had already returned to its normal state. If not for the blood under my nails, I would have thought I'd imagined the whole thing. I tried to prompt the images in my head again, to reach out for the hum of the arena, but the memory of raking through another person's skin stifled me.

Bang.

Every light in the computing room turned on, brighter than I'd ever seen them. I nearly went blind from the sudden assault of light from all directions. I covered my face with both hands. From beneath came a series of heavy thumping.

Squinting against the bright lights, I peered down just in time to see Nix pull Able off Astra. I heard Able exclaim in surprise before being lifted off the ground. Nix took a shaky step backward, his torso twisted in a strained angle, enormous hands wrapped around Able's forearms. Astra coughed and sat up on the floor. I gasped at the sight of her bloodied scalp.

Able swore and fought, but Nix held tight, taking another stiff step back before freezing in place. The last flicker of green light in his eye went out. He stopped, arms raised with Able trapped tightly in his hands, like a statue.

The lights turned off as suddenly as they'd come on. I found myself plunged into darkness. I grasped the nearest railing and tried to regain my bearings.

"Astra?" I called.

A tiny light flickered on, no more than a candle's worth. I saw Astra below me, the weak light in her hand as she approached Nix, Able still trapped in his arms. He was saying something, curses that couldn't be translated. But Astra ignored him. She lifted a hand and stroked Nix's dead eyes gently.

"Brave Evie," I heard her say. "How am I ever going to make it without you looking out for me at every turn?"

THE DEATH of any sentient being was a funny thing.

Not funny like a joke, but funny like the kind of laugh one

might let out if they didn't know what else to do. Death was not simply the stopping of breathing lungs and beating hearts. It was the end of every thought, every experience, and every emotion ever felt by that being. Some believed that on one's deathbed, their entire life played before their eyes, and in that way, they got to live all over again.

Being the sheltered child I was, I had little experience with death. Mother had always taken care to keep me away from difficult, unpleasant things. And so, until the Harbinger in Able's orb, death had remained an abstract thing. Much like air, its existence was known but never seen or heard. Though occasionally I did sit and wonder what it might feel like, with the same curiosity of any adolescent. What was it like to one moment be alive, with thoughts, emotions, opinions, and dreams, and the next to simply stop? To go from a person to a body, suddenly cut off from all the senses that connected you to the world. Did the mind go before the body, or did the body go before the mind? I would never find out, I supposed, until it was my turn to go. A tapestry of life burnt to dust in one moment.

All that to say, I never expected to experience death from inside the dying.

"Evie."

I shuddered from head to toe. The voices coursed through me, vibrating through the walls and floors, rattling my bones.

"Evie."

Getting Able out of Nix's death grip wasn't easy and getting back onto the walkway less so. Astra forced Able to ascend before her on a ladder that flickered in and out of existence in pieces. Whether they managed the climb through pure luck or sheer determination, it was hard to say. They reached the walkway just before the lower half of the ladder crumbled, and Astra immediately struck Able on the back of the head. He fell to the ground, dazed, just as the walls began to speak.

"Good job, Evie."

I looked toward Astra, but she didn't meet my eyes. Instead, she slowly dropped to her knees and covered her ears with both hands.

"You're OK."

That voice coming at us, bouncing off every surface with such force I could almost feel it hit my skin, was hers.

"Do you understand what's going on?"

Was that Able's voice?

"She can hear you just fine."

Astra's voice again.

"I can't swim either. Just think hard. Think of something that can swim."

This was different from the Harbinger. I'd been merely a spectator then, watching a life leave its body from the outside. I was inside now, intimately aware of a consciousness dimming as it snuffed out its last ember.

"Evie and I have decided this is our favorite headline."

"You think that looks good? It's not even the right colors. Why didn't you ask for a normal tree?"

"Yes, he's hot. Why are you making me say it?"

These were her memories, playing now as the last of her artificial life flickered out. The lights around us blinked, but fewer came back on each time. The chill was quickly becoming a paralyzing cold. I hugged myself as white puffs of air escaped my nose and mouth.

"Don't do this! You're supposed to win!"

Were these the memories of the real Evie or the AI?

"Let's explore. Make the best of it, right?"

"That planet he showed me. You'll love it."

"Just like cats, but bigger. What do you think, Evie?"

"Evie."

"Evie."

Astra's voice dominated the recordings. Every now then someone else cut in, but it always returned to her. The sounds began to play faster and faster, until it became little more than gibberish. The lights dimmed. I huddled next to Astra and put an arm around her. She was shaking. I couldn't imagine what it felt like, to experience the death of a dear friend from the inside and hear their memories of you from several lifetimes play out as their light and warmth seeped out like water from a leaky cup.

We stayed for a long time in the shaking lights, frigid cold, and haunting voices. Until suddenly, they stopped. Our surroundings plunged into complete darkness.

"Brave Evie." The recorded voice slowed to a crawl. Then, the voice I recognized returned. **"Good. Night."**

Astra stood. I heard her shuffle, and a soft green light lit her face. She held one of Nix's mechanical eyes in her palm.

"Good night, E-V," she said softly.

THE PATH to the capsule bay was far from easy. Our only source of light was Nix's eye, which Astra had taken after the ordeal in the computing room. Without E-V, the gravity in the orb was even less reliable. Even Able, unpredictable as he was, appeared to acknowledge the danger of the situation and did not make any further attempts to rebel. The fact that Astra kept her crystal spike pointed at the back of his head probably also contributed to that.

I was initially worried about the stab wounds on her side, but she assured me she was alright. When I wasn't convinced, she lifted her shirt tail to show me the gaps in her crystalized torso left by Able's blade. They were split like dry earth, bloodless seams that reached deep into her body.

"The advantage of being me," she said almost cheerily. I decided not to ask if they hurt.

The bay, thankfully, had a modicum of light. Two had lit

three of the sitting capsules for illumination when we approached. Astra pushed Able into one of them and gestured for me to board after her. Two leaned against the doorway, arms crossed.

"So," they said. "What's the plan?"

"The only option we have," Astra replied, locking the door to the room where she'd just shoved Able. "The orb can't run in any functional way without a demigod pilot or an AI core. Unless we plug someone else in, we'll have to take refuge at the Pinnacle."

"Then?"

"I don't know." Astra paused. "I guess this is it."

"Oh, come now." Two's holographic smile glowed against the capsule wall. "You're not going to get sentimental on me, are you? It's not like we started on such a great note."

"No," Astra said with a small smile. "But you don't exactly start on a good note with anyone."

"True enough."

"Doesn't mean I won't miss you. Time made a fool of all of us equally, after all."

"Wait," I interrupted. "What do you mean? They're not coming?"

"Tsk. You didn't explain it to the newbie?" Two lifted a hand and flicked their metal torso. "Not enough blocks in the holy grounds to move me. The demigods don't like building blocks in the gods' temples, being that it's a place reserved for the holy ones. I can last a while if I stick close to the center core, but eventually they'll start breaking down and there's not enough computing power there to generate more, especially since we have to keep the stairs in place in the bay. Once they run out, I'll be a useless pile on the floor."

"So you're staying here?" I looked past them at the orb's cold, dark interior. "By yourself?"

"Nix is here," Two said brightly. I started to explain what had happened in the computing room, but Astra stopped me with a hand on my arm—it didn't matter. "There's no AI, but the residual power can keep producing new blocks for a long time, even if it's just in small amounts." They paused. "Besides, it doesn't feel right to leave her alone."

I didn't need to ask whom they meant.

"Take care of yourself," Astra said.

"You, too, arena master." Two winked at me. "See you around, Kova. It's been a heck of a ride."

"Good luck," I said, unable to think of anything else to say. Those words felt woefully inadequate as they pushed off the capsule and walked away. The holographic smile flickered, then turned off as the rest of their body was swallowed by darkness. Astra closed the capsule door. The sound of it slamming shut was heavy with finality.

"Let's go," she said as the window in the control room began to grow clear. The graveyard of black orbs peered back at us, welcoming its newest member.

CHAPTER 26

There was something unexpectedly comforting about seeing Mod and Sweetly again. Instead of being alarmed at Mod's enormous frame barreling down on us, I found myself smiling as he picked me up and swung me around. Sweetly chirped and attempted to leap into my lap, knocking me down in the process. I patted her on the head and she nuzzled me. After the miserable trip, it was nice to be around happy faces.

However, Mod's smile faded when he saw Astra dragging Able out of the dark bay, both of his arms completely encased in crystal, so heavy that he could barely lift them enough to walk.

"Hey, Mod," Astra said. She pushed Able aside and embraced Mod briefly.

Mod looked from her to Able, then at me. I could almost see the gears turn in his head. "Solace?" he asked, his large tongue struggling against the delicate sounds of the name.

Astra shook her head. "He couldn't come."

"Oh," Mod said, obviously disappointed. "Like Solace."

"I know you like Solace."

"Two?"

She shook her head again. "No."

I expected Mod to ask more, but he appeared to accept this

simple answer. He turned his attention to Able, looking quizzically at his crystal shackles.

"Able got into a bit of trouble," Astra said.

"Trouble?"

"Nothing for you to worry about."

Sweetly hopped out of my lap. She sidled to Able's side and appeared to sniff the crystals. He regarded her with annoyance.

"Get lost, freak," he snapped.

Sweetly didn't move away. Instead, she circled him. Once. Twice. On the third time around, she stopped in front of him. The black substance on her face peeled back, like the tide receding. Underneath was an unexpected familiar face.

"You may know how to play the arena," she said in Mother's voice, "but you will never be fit to run it."

Able swung his heavily weighted arms toward Sweetly, narrowly missing as she leapt out of the way. She dashed behind Mod, who held an arm out in front of her protectively. Astra pushed Able down the walkway away from the pair. I quickly followed.

"Mother always say," Mod muttered as we made our way toward the center of the orb.

"Say?" I asked. "Say what?"

"Able. All smart. But no trust." He shook his head almost remorsefully. "No trust at all. No one trust Able."

Even though I knew what to expect this time, entering the wall of fog was still a discomforting experience. I lost track of both Astra and Able quickly and had to fumble my way around alone, unable to hear their voices or footsteps. But when the fog suddenly parted and I found myself once again standing in the clearing, I realized they were only a few paces to my right.

"Hey!" Astra called, shoving Able along. "Seven!"

No sound. No response.

"Nasmi!" she called again. Able rolled his eyes. Astra scowled in frustration.

"Mother," she finally said through gritted teeth.

"I do love hearing you call me that."

I jumped. Mother stepped next to me and winked, as if she'd been there all along.

"She's always been stubborn," she said, leaning toward me as if sharing an inside joke. "She's willing to use that title to the others, but to call me that to my face, she could almost never do."

I stared at her, my entire body stiffening in fear.

"That's quite a look you're giving me," she said.

"You threatened to have me torture her," Astra said, annoyed. "Started a hell of a lot of trouble for me." She gave Able a shove forward. Mother raked her gaze over him.

"I see that," she said. "Now what exactly happened here?"

I waited for Astra to explain, but Mother approached her instead and the air shifted. I shivered at the memory of her invisible tendrils trying to drill themselves into my mind, but Astra didn't flinch.

"I see," Mother said after a moment. Her face grew solemn. "There's no way back, then."

"Unless we could repurpose another orb," Astra said in a tone that told me this was a near impossible task, "we have no other options."

"So that's it. End of the line."

Astra nodded. "Nowhere else to go."

"That's because you're useless."

Able's voice was almost jarring. All eyes turned to him. He winked at Mother and nodded toward the crystals around his arms. She snapped her fingers and they dissipated. Able let out a relieved groan and rubbed his wrists. He stretched his arms, went to Mother, took one of her hands, and kissed it. Mother gave him a measured smile.

"Able, Able," she said. "Faking your death. Fighting with your siblings. Again. It never ends with you, does it?"

I saw Astra struggle to keep her face straight.

"He has betrayed the rest of us," she said, an edge in her voice. "I believe he has been working with the demigods, and if you can extract the information we n—"

"She doesn't need to *extract* anything from me," Able said, cutting her off. He took both of Mother's hands and looked down into her eyes. "I will gladly give it to her. I just didn't want to hand it over to *you*, little sister, because it is a gift for Mother, and for her only."

Astra began to speak, but Mother raised a hand to silence her. The way she was looking at Able suddenly made me very afraid.

Something was about to go very wrong.

"Speak," she said. "I'm listening."

Able's smile broadened.

"The gods are gone," he said.

"Obviously."

"There is a void in this universe. It needs a new god."

"And how do you imagine that happening?"

"It can't," Astra cut in. Mother raised her hand again, but she didn't stop. "You know better than anyone that we do not function at the same level as the so-called gods. And there is no way to reach the gods where they are."

"No, there's not," Able said dismissively. "But we can create one. We've never been under any delusion of what we are to the gods. But even though they've lost interest in us, they've left behind a gift."

"The data core is rumor," Astra seethed. "There is no proof it exists."

"Patience, little sister," Able said mockingly. "The adults are talking."

Astra opened her mouth to speak again, but no sound came

out. I saw confusion, frustration, and anger play on her face, then realization dawn—Mother had silenced her.

"We have made a grave mistake going against the demigods," Able continued. Mother's attention was on him, undivided. "It is their mistake, too. This conflict has benefited no one. But it's not too late to remedy that. While the others have been occupied fighting a war, I have opened communication with the other side. It took a demigod named K'azen to show me the true opportunities that exist in the universe." He sighed and shook his head. "It is unfortunate that he is not around anymore. Your favorite daughter burned him to a crisp, along with an entire planet of innocents."

If Mother weren't around, I was sure his skull would be skewered on Astra's spike by now.

"This new god," Mother said slowly, "how do you propose we create them?"

"That honor is reserved for the most deserving of us." Able arched a brow.

"Me? That's quite a tall order."

"I can think of no one more suited." He enclosed one of her hands in both of his. "You do not have to be the god of the old ways. We own this universe now. There are newer and better ways to be a god."

"And what do you mean by that?"

"The data core. It's been found."

There was a moment of thick silence. I wondered if Mother believed him, but her face was impossible to read.

"It was a tricky task," Able went on. "But once we realized what we were doing wrong, the rest was easy. The data core could not be hunted. It was not a mere object, waiting to be unlocked. The demigods sought it for ages, thinking it could be dug up like buried treasure. But they were going about it all wrong. The data core cannot be pursued. It can only be called."

A hint of surprise finally overcame Mother. "Called?"

"Yes." Able's voice was even, but his excitement was obvious. "The demigods never fully tapped into the potential of the orbs. There are far greater ways to conduct the games. However, the first to discover those secrets was our dear Astra."

The look on Astra's face was indescribable. She struggled for a moment, as if trying to figure out the meaning of Able's words. Mother waved her hand and Astra cleared her throat.

"I did no such thing," she said after a moment, her voice restored.

"Oh, but you did." Able looked over his shoulder with the expression of someone who knew they had all their game pieces in the right place. "Were you not the first one to test the elevated stage in your game?"

"Elevated—" Astra paused. "The bonus round?"

"It was an experiment that we feared testing for a long time. Think about it—a dream state game with freely manipulatable time and space, no longer limited to the constraints of the physical arena. The possibilities would've been endless. Didn't you ever wonder why we never used it again?"

"Because no one after me asked for a bonus round, and the dream state games are extremely resource intensive and inefficient."

Able shrugged. "Sure. That's part of it. But the real reason was your little bonus round showed us exactly how risky it was. The minds of seed races are not made to endure such long, extended purgatories. Boredom sets in, then frustration, then fear, then madness. You were certainly resilient. Sixty cycles walking a dead planet. Impressive. Perhaps having lived through the arena prior had given you a leg up. But the average being would not survive such a long, arduous task without losing at least some of their sanity. And that's just a simple round. Toss in something more difficult, turn that purgatory into hell, and they'll wear out even faster." He shook his head. "Oh, I'm sure Solace is having a heck of a time right now."

"What does that mean?"

Able only smirked. Astra struck out at him, but Mother was

faster. Her fist stopped a hair's distance from Able's face, and he didn't flinch. I felt the fog move and the next thing I knew, Astra was sliding across the white floor on her back. Mother lifted a finger to her lips to shush her, then motioned for Able to go on. He took Mother's shoulders and looked into her eyes.

"I've discovered something," he said earnestly, excitement sparkling in his eyes. "What the data core is truly meant for. It's not just storage. It's an arena. One unlike anything we've seen before. With it, we can run the games on a grand scale. Every world. Every being in this universe can become a contestant of Headspace, simultaneously."

I opened my mouth, but no sound came out. I coughed, still silent. I turned to see Astra attempting the same. Mother had silenced us both as she listened, entranced, to Able. I started to take a step toward them, but my feet stayed in place, and I fell face first, catching myself just in time before breaking my nose on the hard floor.

"Just let me finish what was started," Able was saying. "With the data core, this is all possible. It can change everything. Don't you want to be the new god of this universe? The one that receives the endless dreams, knowledge, and experiences it has to offer? No more defects, no more errors, no more scouting one planet at a time. Every planet in this universe will achieve its full potential as an eternal arena."

Fear coursed through me. I met Astra's eyes and saw the same horror on her face. But there was nothing we could do except watch as Mother reached up and lovingly took Able's face in her hands.

"Oh, Able," she said, pulling him close. "I always had a special place in my heart for you."

He smiled, confident that he had won.

"But after all this time, you never understood me once."

She brought his lips to hers. For one moment nothing happened. Then, he struggled, followed by muffled screaming as black sludge began to leak from his eyes.

CHAPTER 27

I SAT ON THE FLOOR. MY MIND WAS A JUMBLE AS I TRIED TO MAKE sense of what had just happened. I couldn't take my eyes off Able, or rather what was left of him. Lying in a puddle of black sludge was what looked like a sack made of skin and hair. I gagged and was thankful there was nothing in my stomach. If I started vomiting, I might not be able to stop.

Astra looked less disturbed than me, though just as surprised. She paced carefully around the puddle, nudging the lifeless extremities with her foot. The sight of the skin sac quivering like a deflated balloon finally proved to be too much and I had to look away. I stood and sidled to her side.

"Stop looking at it," she said as she saw my expression.

I pulled my eyes away from the shapeless form on the floor. "It's just . . . we still don't know. He didn't tell us very much . . ."

"It's fine," Astra cut in. "Whatever the truth is, Mother got it."

I thought about asking how but decided I didn't care to know. Mother approached Astra. Watching the two of them standing together, I suddenly had the feeling that they'd stood like this many times in the past, face to face, a million words unspoken between them.

"So," Mother said, "you finally let her go."

Astra opened her mouth to speak, but nothing came out. For a moment I thought Mother had silenced her again, but she let out a choked sob and tears rolled down her face. Mother reached out and embraced her and for a moment I thought she might pull away, but she didn't. I went back to my spot on the floor and sat with a sigh.

How did I get here?

I remembered getting ready for my wedding. I'd escaped that day because I couldn't handle the thought of being married. I'd thought I had to find some sort of closure before setting the rest of my life in stone, that I had some unsolved mystery to hunt down, that I could still find some miracle Rosi left for me and magically everything would be different, and better.

Well, this is certainly different.

I ran a hand through my hair and felt a moment of surprise when it ended before I expected it to. Right—I'd cut it off. In a fit of frustration, I'd thought I could take control of the only thing at hand, so I'd chopped off my hair like a child breaking a toy.

I thought back to home. To Radley Cove. The peaceful waters and the smell of the sea. The hills covered with rosalit flowers, the sounds of the festivals. I imagined myself running up and down those hills with Rosi at my side. I pictured myself as I was now, grown up, walking those streets, watching the new generation of children shouting and playing.

With Meli at my side. I would be married to her. That was my reality.

I pictured myself sitting in Meli's house, having breakfast served to me by Galen. Meli delighted in hosting gatherings. I would doubtlessly be the centerpiece at each one, at least for a while, so her friends and business associates could coo and dote on the fact that she'd married such a rarity, a real beacon with hair as red as the day was long. I would be dressed in the finest fabrics, my hair cleaned, oiled, and styled. At night, I would sit in front of the mirror in Meli's bedroom—*our* bedroom, run a comb through my long hair, and listen to Meli talk about her latest business venture or some interesting bauble she'd acquired. She would probably bring me home something when she traveled. Little toys and treats to keep me smiling. And I *would* smile. I'd had lots of practice smiling. I was prepared for a life with lots of smiling. I saw myself sitting in front of that mirror and smiling.

Day after day.

After day after day after day.

I shuddered and opened my eyes. The fog swam into focus.

I ran my hand through my hair again, and this time felt an unexpected sensation as I found it short.

Relief.

I lifted my head and shook it hard.

I was so utterly, incredibly relieved.

I could fool myself into thinking I wished I hadn't left, but that was a lie. If I hadn't left with E-V, I would've left some other way. Left like Uttam did, seeking freedom outside the playbooks, and the price of leaving might have been greater when I finally did. Would I have left behind children? Would I have left in old age, regretting my life every step of the way? I had been so afraid without Rosi around, for so long, but strangely, that fear had slowly subsided with each day outside of Fiina, ebbing away like a drying brook.

I didn't regret any of it. Even if I returned now, my old life was surely no longer waiting for me. It ought to be a sad thought, but somehow it filled me with hope. I hopped to my feet.

"Hey," I said to Mother and Astra. "I have an idea."

. . .

"INTERESTING," Mother said slowly. I could see—and feel by the quiver in the air—that she wasn't convinced.

"It's our only shot," I said, looking to Astra for support. Unfortunately, she looked dubious as well.

"The conversion to an AI core is permanent," she said. "Once converted, there is no going back."

"I know," I said. I had forgotten, but I wanted to sound confident. "But it's the only way we'll get around. Do you really want to sit here and do nothing?"

"You're suggesting we plug her in." Astra nodded toward Mother. "It would be a one-way trip. There's no way to get her back out again without killing her or letting her deteriorate. We would lose the safe haven of this orb, not to mention her ability to extract information from anyone else we might need."

"What safe haven?" I could see the surprise on Astra's face. "This is a prison. What's going to happen if someone—I don't know, another demigod—finds us here? And if we stay here, who are we ever going to need to extract information from? If we leave, we *might* find some answers. If we stay here, we're definitely *not* going to find them. And we're definitely *not* going to find Solace."

Astra's expression changed. A sliver of hope peeked through, then quickly disappeared. I didn't blame her, but I was beyond doubt. I turned to Mother.

"I ran out on a wedding," I said. She arched a brow at that. "*My* wedding."

"You don't wish for it to be in vain, then," Mother said. "Having left the person you loved, you wish to see this to some sort of end to make it worthwhile?"

I scoffed. "No. I'm glad I left. I didn't want to get married. She was going to put me on a shelf like a trophy. I spent every day of my life smiling and nodding while my mother prepared me for that wedding, and then I was going to spend every day of the rest of my life smiling and nodding to my wife. At least none of *you* are making me smile and nod."

A small grin crept to Astra's lips.

"My point is, I sat around a lot while everyone moved around me," I went on. "And I'm done doing that. I'm sure you're done doing that. Aren't you bored sitting here, waiting for your children to come to you? Don't you want to take a risk, for their sakes?" I gestured around at the fog around us, pointedly overlooking Able's remains. "Don't you want to protect them and help them instead of looking at *this* all day?"

Mother looked at me, then at Astra. Neither of them said anything and I wondered if I'd gone too far. My heart pounded loudly.

"I let myself be trapped in a box all my life," I said. "Don't make the same mistake."

Mother laughed. I flinched, fearing I'd said something wrong. But she reached out and took my hand in both of hers.

"How strangely the universe works," she said. "Seems like just yesterday I stood before the gods, a foolish little child, pleading with them to just take a risk."

Piping Mother into the orb turned out to be a bit of a technical challenge, but Astra managed to make it work. She connected E-V's old capsule to the silver orb, then after a lot of maneuvering and cursing in exotic languages, neither of which I understood much of, Mother's voice spoke out from the speakers of the capsule. The process was then repeated aboard the orb, along with quite a lot more cursing.

"Would you look at that," Two said, twirling a pair of tiny floating spheres around their fingers as Astra busied herself with the configurations. The holographic smile glowed from their neck hole. "Little Nasmi, back on board. Just like the old days, eh?"

"And you are still as pleasant as ever," Mother retorted, though she sounded rather cheerful, which I hadn't expected. "Truly nothing has changed."

"Gotta keep the spirits up somehow." Two manifested several more shapes and orbited them around their hand, then transferred them from one hand to the other. Even though they hadn't admitted it, I could tell that they were thrilled—and relieved—not to be abandoned to rot with the orb. "This will be fun. I imagine you'll be far more adept at operating the arena than the previous cores. After all, no one knows this orb better than Mother dearest."

"Was that a jab, or have you finally changed your mind about that title?"

Two snickered. "Not a chance. The rest of these kids may call you Mother, but I've still been around longer than you have. You'll always be little Seven to me, cowering and crying in the capsule because she's afraid of the big, dark space." The spinning shapes vanished. Their tone suddenly became serious. The smiling mouth turned into a flat line. "You *do* realize this is a one-time thing, don't you?"

"Of course I do," Mother replied easily.

"Just checking." Two clapped their hands together and slung an arm around my shoulders. "We should celebrate."

Astra looked up briefly from her work. "Celebrate? Never pegged you for the celebratory type."

"Don't sound so gloomy. It's been a long time since we've all been in the same place. Calls at least for a toast, right? Heck, I'd even throw a cup of something down my neck hole if it wouldn't short circuit me. I'll go yank Mod and Sweetly off the arena floor. They're going to dent the walls even more with all their tumbling around."

With that they dragged me away. I looked back at Astra, who shrugged. Helpless, I followed.

THE SCENE before me was surreal.

Save for the few drinks I'd shared here or there in the

company of the others, meals had been mostly solitary until now. I had forgotten what it was like to sit at a full table surrounded by faces and voices. Even on Fiina, meals with my family were usually quiet, formal affairs. Once or twice, I'd been invited into the homes of friends—usually friends Mother disapproved of—and found myself shocked at their loud, chatty mealtimes. I'd spent much of my childhood wondering if my upbringing was the abnormal one and missing, in the back of my mind, the chance to sit at one of those noisy tables again.

In this orb, surrounded by aliens from worlds whose names I could barely pronounce, was not how I'd imagined revisiting that experience.

I sat at the rectangular table Mother created on the arena floor. Sweetly rubbed her face against my ankle, then rested her chin on my lap. I petted her sleek head and neck. Across from me, Mod chatted at me brightly. I couldn't understand most of what he was saying, either from his clumsy pronunciation or due to my own lack of knowledge on the topics, but his enthusiasm was infectious. I smiled and nodded along as he talked animatedly about "crying mountains" and "cats," the latter of which he seemed quite enamored with.

Two brought several plates to the table and appeared quite pleased with their culinary skills despite possessing no mouth or tongue. I hadn't thought that "cooking" with those funny little boxes meant anything besides producing flavorless cubes and the occasional drink, but their concoction was quite impressive. Every dish looked the same save for slight variations in color and transparency, but their flavors and textures varied greatly. I was surprised to find one light and crispy with a sweet taste, and another dense and savory. They also melted several cubes into drinks—some bubbly and fruity, some smooth and mild, and more than one that made my head swim.

"That's Astra's favorite," Two whispered as I swallowed a

mouthful of brown liquid that burned pleasantly on its way down.

I sampled the food and tried to keep to myself initially. I was, after all, the outsider in this little family that had just reunited. But with Sweetly refusing to budge from my lap, Mod and Two chattering loudly, and the fact that my drink cup never seemed to run empty, I soon found myself joining the festivities, unable to contain my laughter as Mod got up from the table, tipsy from the drinks, and made an awkward attempt to dance. Mother played music from the walls and Two laughed and clapped along. Even Astra cracked a smile at the sight. Sweetly nudged me from my seat as the scene around us changed to one of celebration. Hundreds of figures appeared around us—dancers in long white robes, spinning in synchronized circles as clouds of red and pink blossoms flew from their billowing sleeves. Mod spun with them, then took my hands and spun me as well. I danced until I was dizzy and had to release his hands. I stumbled back to the table as Mod dragged Two away.

Astra was nursing a drink and watching the scene. I slid into the seat next to her.

"Having fun?" she asked, her gaze fixated on the arena floor, where Mod, Sweetly, and Two were weaving in and out of the mirage of dancers.

I nodded. "I am. Which is weird, after . . . everything."

"It wasn't all bad," Astra said slowly. "We've had some good times. At the end of the day, we are a family."

"I didn't know Two could cook."

"Well, sometimes there's not a lot to do. You learn whatever you can to keep yourself occupied and find joy wherever it can be found." She tapped a finger on her cup. "We knew what we had to do, going from world to world, spreading chaos and death. But it was survival for us, and as bad as it sounds, we all got used to it at some point. We were all outcasts of our own worlds, seeking refuge and companionship inside the orb. We shared our culture and knowledge and taught each other about our home worlds. It was never an easy life, but sometimes we were almost happy."

I looked toward Two. "Is that why you forgave them? After what happened with Able?"

"I get why they did what they did. They're not like Able, and I understand how they felt—and still feel—about Viva. In their shoes, I would've done the same."

I wanted to say something more reassuring, but anything I could say would sound like empty promises. "Two seems happy," I said instead, "to have Mother back."

Astra took a long drink and shook her head. "No. I know my sibling. They're just looking for distractions. Mother can operate the orb at full capacity, but how long it can run that way without coming apart at the seams is questionable. From here on out, every stop could be our last."

I HAD no idea how long the festivities lasted, but eventually the noise died down, the plates were cleared, and the scene around us changed to a peaceful night. Mod and Sweetly huddled together and drifted off on the sandy beach. I sat at the edge of the water, pant legs rolled up to my knees, letting the warm waves lap at my feet.

"It's amazing what the arena can do with a powerful AI core," Astra said as she settled beside me. She lifted a hand and a crowd of glowing insects danced around her fingers. "I'd almost forgotten what it was like."

"It's incredible," I agreed, looking up at the star-filled sky that was far too real. "I've never imagined anything like this. It's like a whole world contained inside a terrarium."

"That's not too far from the truth." Astra dipped her finger into the edge of the water. A series of tiny paper boats, each carrying a lit candle, appeared and drifted into the waves. Astra picked up one and held it out to me. As my fingers touched it, it exploded into a shower of sparkles. "Want to try?"

"Try?"

"Manifesting. You managed it when we were tussling with Able, and now's as good a time as any—the arena hasn't been able to support this level of manifestation in a long time." Astra cupped her hands together, then opened them. A flock of white birds flew from between her fingers. "It may look like party tricks, but manifestation means survival for us long-term residents. Come on, give it a proper shot."

She stood and gestured for me to do the same. I hesitated but did as she bid. She moved behind me, took my right hand in hers, and lifted it, like a painter showing a student how to create their first brushstroke. Her fingers were cold and hard, but they moved dexterously around my own.

"Picture something," she said. "Not just how it looks, but its parts and components. A knife is not just a knife. It has a blade and hilt and weight. A cup is not just a cup. It is made of ceramic or wood or glass, and each one of those things will feel different to your skin."

I drew a blank. Funny that my mind always seemed to be full, and yet, when told to think of something simple, it completely cleared itself. Astra saw my empty stare and gave my hand a gentle squeeze.

"Let's try a ball," she said. "A glass ball. It's transparent, and it's heavy. It's the size of your palm." She turned my arm so that my hand faced up. "Do you feel the glass?"

I did. I held the image in my head. It wasn't quite as clear as the pebble lizard's talons, but I could feel it pulling into existence, like a tiny void on the surface of my skin, drawing in surrounding matter from the air. I held my breath, worried that even a small puff of air from my lungs would break the moment. The glass ball came together in my hand like a mirage, gradually at first, then all at once.

"Good," Astra said in my ear. "Now hold it."

"Hold it?"

She moved my fingers until they were cupped around the ball's clear, smooth surface. My mind struggled to wrap around the fact that I had just created something out of thin air. That moment of doubt, unfortunately, broke my focus and the ball crumbled between my fingers.

"I can't do this," I said, and tried to drop my hand, but she gripped my wrist and held me up.

"You're thinking too much. In the heat of the moment, during a game, you learn fast and rely on instinct. That's why you managed it when Able attacked me. It's like looking at an optical illusion—it works better when you relax and let your senses take over. Let's try something else."

The swarm of insects reappeared, each lit up like a tiny lantern. They danced in front of me in loose, lazy circles.

"Move them," Astra instructed.

"Move them?"

She released my hand and extended her own fingers. A dozen lantern bugs broke from the swarm and came toward her. They circled her fingers in a manner that reminded me of Two fidgeting with their own manifestation. She curled and bent her fingers and the bugs followed. When she extended them again, the bugs departed to rejoin the swarm.

"Like that," she said. "Reach out, connect with them, and call them."

I extended my own fingers and tried to reach out to the bugs with my mind. I could sense them, like tiny little vibrating points in the air. I tried to pull them toward me, but the swarm showed no sign of response. I tried harder. A few of the bugs drifted lazily toward me, then changed their minds and went off in another direction.

"Be firm," Astra said. "Know what you want them to do and picture it in your mind. They will move with certainty only if you do. It's less like issuing a verbal command and more like grabbing an object from a table—you don't consciously order your arm to move, but your body knows what to do."

Swallowing thickly, I braced myself, focused my attention on the lantern bugs, and pulled with all my might.

They flew at me like missiles. Astra shoved me out of the way. Two of them zipped past my cheek, cutting my skin with their thin, tiny wings. Astra blocked their assault with one arm and gestured with the other. The swarm flickered and disappeared.

Astra lowered her arm and examined her clothing. Her jacket was covered in dozens of tiny cuts. I touched my cheek and came away with a sliver of blood. She gave me a nonchalant shrug.

"That wasn't bad," she said. "Try again?"

I shook my head so hard my vision blurred. Memories of the dark capsule bubbled up and my chest tightened. There was no way I was going to risk damaging the orb when we finally seemed to be back on track. I was worried Astra would push me, but she only regarded me with concern.

"You're discouraged," she said. It wasn't a question.

"I'm not cut out for this," I said. "Every time I do it, something goes wrong. I almost killed both Om and me. I don't want to do that again. I can make do without it. I'm sure I can. I have so far."

Astra seemed to debate this. I worried she would brush aside my concern, but she didn't. Instead, she sat back down on the sand.

"I hope you're right," she said simply.

I lowered myself next to her. The silence was uncomfortable in the light of my failure, and I was desperate to change the subject. "Where's Two?"

"Finding something else to be distracted by. They're not much for heart-to-hearts. I think they'll be seeking out a lot of distractions for the foreseeable future." Astra picked up a pebble and threw it into the water. "They don't like to talk about it, but they're the only one left who has witnessed both Mother's rise to power, then eventual downfall when the gods left. To watch her locked into the AI core, doomed to one day die in rambling insanity, it's not easy for them."

"What about you?"

"Me?"

"How do you feel about it?"

"Right now, I just want to find Solace. Then, I want to see you home. After that, I don't know."

Home. The word felt incredibly strange.

"I can't imagine going back to Fiina," I said quietly, guilt welling up as soon as the words were out of my mouth. "I mean, it's not like I really want to stay here either, but . . ."

"But you don't know how to continue your old life now that you've seen what's out here."

I nodded.

"That's the curse of expanding your horizons—they can never retract again." Astra threw another pebble into the sea. "It's the same reason I ultimately ended up here as well. I can't say whether it was the right choice, only that it was a choice I made. I also can't tell you if you'll regret it if you don't choose to go back. I've made too many regrettable choices myself to give that advice."

"I'm just not sure what to do next. After we do whatever it is we're about to do."

"Well," Astra said, "maybe it's not about what, but who. Is there someone you'd like to go home to?"

I shook my head. "No one I can think of, really. What about you? If this orb stops functioning, where will you go? Home to your planet?"

"I have no home there. It stopped being my home even before I left." Astra looked up into the simulated sky. "For a very long time, home was wherever Solace and I both were. But I think I can't reclaim that home anymore."

"I'm sure we can find him," I said, though it sounded like a lie. "You'll have him back."

She shook her head. "I'm not going to have him back."

"You don't know that yet."

"I mean even when—*if*—I find him," she said, "I'm not going to have him back. He's been chained to me for too long. So fiercely loyal, he is. I loved him for that, but he deserves better than this. Better than *me*. If I find him, I'm going to let him go."

CHAPTER 28

THE CHAIR SAT ON THE PRISTINE WHITE ARENA FLOOR. MOTHER seemed to favor a clean, white design, though Astra looked somewhat put off by it, which was evident by her expression when she first set foot into it. I quickly stopped slip-sliding around the slippery surface with Mod and Sweetly.

Two tapped the armrest with their metal finger. "This was much easier to set up," they said. "Pretty sure the other cores couldn't have handled running Able's mishmash code to get this thing to work." They motioned for me to approach. "So, ready to meet your new partner?"

"New partner?"

A familiar figure entered the arena floor following Astra. I recognized the Harbinger from the control room immediately. She caught my eye and smiled her soft, winning smile. Her hair shimmered and changed from white to silvery crystal, like Astra's. I squirmed uncomfortably under her gaze.

"No," I said.

Two tilted their holographic head. "You don't like this one? Sorry, but it's all we've got."

"Can't I just go in alone?"

"Being inside a dream state is tricky. Staying focused enough to guide the simulation instead of letting it guide you is very difficult. The Harbingers keep you focused. Without one, you're liable to get very lost very quickly."

"Why does it have to be a Harbinger?"

"The dream state is tuned to accommodate one occupant at a time. Harbingers can compartmentalize their thought processes to avoid being affected by distractions or unintentionally altering the environment. In fact, the machine doesn't even recognize Harbingers as a living being. Two regular occupants with active minds would cause too much disruption."

"Is this really going to work?"

"Your guess is as good as mine, but it's the closest we could come to Able's setup, and at the very least, we should see if it turns on."

I eyed the Harbinger uneasily. Did she ever stop smiling?

"She's not like Om," I said. "I know you don't believe me, but he was different."

"Doesn't matter, does it?" Two replied in their trademark nonchalance. "Either you go in with her, or you don't go in at all. We can't risk you losing your mind in the dream state. Aside from the fact that we'd never figure out what Able was up to, we kind of like you."

I couldn't help chuckling. Astra laid a hand on my arm.

"If you're not ready," she started, but I shook my head before she could finish.

"I am," I said. I was not going to become any more ready than I already was, and she knew that, because she nodded and said nothing more.

I sat down in the chair. There were no straps on this one, which I was relieved by. I truly disliked the feeling of being tied down. Cold metal nodes were connected to my temples and the Harbinger took my hand.

"Last chance," Two said. "Want to back out?"

I shook my head. "No."

There was humming, then the door appeared.

"Focus on your own memories," I heard Astra say. "It's the best chance we have to replicate the signal."

I reached forward with all my senses and pulled it open.

The first thing that greeted me was a strange nothingness. For a moment I couldn't find my body in space. My stomach, which felt at least half a world away, did a flip-flop, and my hands pawed at the infinite black sky—or ground; it was hard to tell which. My entire body scattered like the pieces of a broken cracker and threatened to float out of my reach. My mind shattered into a hundred pieces, each grasping at a different memory. I struggled trying to hold on to a dozen thought processes at once.

Find one.

I grabbed onto the image of Rosi and followed it, feeling along it like a rope.

Rosi. Childhood. Winter.

Something gripped me, like a hook in the darkness. I held onto it for dear life as the world around me slowly solidified. Nothingness became black, then black became white. My feet found ground and pieces of my body pulled together like metal shavings toward a magnet. I drew a shuddering breath and blinked hard. The air smelled of chilly seas and roasting fish.

The winter festival swam into view.

It was the exact same scene I'd walked with Om. The greens and whites, noisy street vendors, and rosalit flowers. But every time I took my eyes off something, it began to fall apart into a series of tiny blocks just outside my peripheral vision. Everything was fragile and temporary, and the more I dwelled on it, the more unstable the diorama around me seemed.

"This is lovely."

The Harbinger girl stepped next to me. I half expected her to take my hand the way Om did, but she didn't. She stood next to me, smiling her cardboard smile and admiring our surroundings.

"Do you have a name?" I asked her.

She didn't look at me. Something about her smile looked different, as if she was struggling to maintain it. I snapped my fingers in front of her eyes.

"Hey!" I said. "Focus! I said, do you have a name?"

She blinked and turned to me, then rattled off a series of letters and numbers, most of which I could not understand, just like Om. I sighed in exasperation, which did not seem to faze her in the least.

"I'm going to call you Prin."

"Certainly," she said with a nod, then looked away again as if unable to help herself. Her smile faltered. I waved my hand in front of her face again and she turned back to me, the smile returning.

"Come on, Prin," I said with a sigh, wondering if she was really supposed to keep me focused or if it was going to be the other way around.

As we walked, it occurred to me why I wanted to call this Harbinger "Prin." She reminded me of my older sister in more ways than one—obedient, smiling, never contradicting a thing I said, just like the real Prin in front of our mother. But while the real Prin endlessly sought approval from her idolized parent, the Harbinger appeared to give no thought to whether I liked or disliked her. She simply followed along, stayed a step behind me, and kept smiling.

The winter festival went on around us, full of joy and vigor. I could smell dough being fried, sugar being spun, and nuts being toasted. A street vendor showed off a colorful, clam-shaped toy that made a crispy clacking sound when struck just right between the palms. A circle of kids surrounded him, clamoring to see it work. He moved his hands in a giddy rhythm, producing a happy, intoxicating tune with two clackers at the same time.

Clack. Clack clack. Clack.

It was almost like a song, a voice.

Clack clack.

Come home. Come home.

I reached out and gripped Prin's arm. Touching her grounded me back in reality a bit, but when I looked behind me, I saw her taking in the scenery with a strange expression on her face. Her smile was gone again.

"Prin?"

"This isn't home," she said, as if reciting a line handed to her on a script, but she wasn't even talking to me.

Clack clack.

I felt dizzy. Prin gave me a glazed look. Our surroundings abruptly shifted. I stumbled and nearly fell as night suddenly dropped over us like a half-ton weight. There was no fade from light to dark. One moment it was the middle of day; the next, the sky had gone black and the lanterns had been lit. Half the street vendors were wrapping up their booths and the streets had grown quiet save for the crunching of snow underfoot. I blinked and tried to get my bearings.

"Prin?" I called.

No response. Not even her wooden, scripted answer. I spun around and around again. She was nowhere to be seen.

"Prin!" I shouted.

Nothing. She was gone. I was completely and utterly alone.

I breathed deeply, in and out, trying to focus on the cold air, the snow crunching under my feet, anything to keep me from drifting off into the tantalizing oblivion. I walked, concentrating on what was in front of me rather than the voices whispering to me in the back of my mind.

"Kova!"

I started. The owner of the voice stepped into view.

I knew her. Of course I did. This was the winter festival from the cycle before she disappeared. She and I had snuck out of bed at night, hoping to catch the last of the night market, which Mother had forbidden us from attending because it was far too late and cold. We got out through the back door and ran, hand in hand, to Main Street, only to gasp in disappointment at the vendors putting away their fares.

"Maybe there's still something open," she said and took my hand. "Let's go look."

I followed her, like I always did.

A rotund man wearing an apron smudged with grease and a face wrinkled from many cycles of hearty smiles spotted us. He trudged through the snow, one lame leg dragging shallow trenches in the white powder, and held out a paper bag puffing white steam toward me.

"Here you go, little loveys," he said. "Last of the batch. All yours."

I remembered this. He'd been there that night, selling balls of golden fried dough packed with dark sweet jam. When he'd seen Rosi and me wandering the cold streets with crestfallen eyes, he had offered us the last of his treats.

"We don't have any money," I said.

A friendly smile stretched through every layer of winkles on his broad face. "Don't need any," he said. "I'll have to throw them away if no one took 'em. Don't need to pack on any more here, eh?" He patted his sizable waistline and pushed the bag at me. "Go ahead. On the house."

Rosi spoke. Except she wasn't really speaking. It was like a distant echo that reverberated in my own mind. But it was her voice. And it was real.

And everything felt right.

She said a cheery thank you to the vendor, and I did the same. We had to eat these quickly, because Mother always said such treats would rot our teeth, and she would be furious to know we were out here, far past our bedtime, stuffing our faces with fried dough and sugary jam. We scampered to the side of the street, brushed snow off an old, creaky metal bench, and huddled together. I reached into the bag, handed one piping hot sweet to Rosi, and grabbed a second on pointed fingertips.

The first bite was pure joy. Hot jam stuck to my gums and burned my tongue, but I didn't mind. I was too lost in that single spot of warmth on the cold night. When was the last time I'd tasted something so wonderful, so welcoming? It must've been . . .

Well, it must've been the last winter festival.

I looked up at Rosi. "At least we got this," I said around a mouthful of sweet dough. "We better get home. Mother will be mad."

Rosi nodded.

"Come home," she said.

I frowned. That didn't sound right. She was supposed to tell me it was fine, and that she wanted to show me how the snow slide looks with no one sliding down it.

"Mother will be mad," I said again.

"Nah," Rosi replied brightly. "She won't know. We'll get back in time. Come on, you have to see the snow slide. It looks so weird at night with nobody coming down it."

We finished our treats and I stood. Rosi grabbed my hand.

"Come home," she said again.

"What are you going on about?" I said. "Aren't we going to see the snow slide?"

"I—" she started but did not finish. The scene around us spun like paint caught in a whirlwind. I reeled and cried out as Rosi clung to my hand.

"Rosi!" I screamed. The world stretched into streaks of color and her grip on me began to loosen.

"Come home," she repeated. "Come home."

"I don't understand!" I shouted back, but she was distant, far away. I felt her fingertips glide against my wrist, then slide away.

"Rosi!"

COME HOME.

I rubbed my eyes. There was a familiar scent in the air.

Come home.

I knew this smell. It was Kit's breakfast porridge. As soon as I identified it, I heard it bubbling away in her favorite dark clay pot, the way it did every morning of my childhood. It enveloped me in its warm familiarity.

My feet struck the ground. Even though I couldn't see it, I knew it was the floor of the hall leading to Rosi's room. How many times had I walked down this hall, both morning and night, knowing she was waiting for me, giggling under her covers?

Everything was white, but everything was familiar. When I reached out, my fingers felt the pleasant chill of winter, my mouth was filled with the sweet taste of jam, and the smell of Kit's porridge and Mother's autumn potpourri filled my nostrils. A voice whispered in my ears. I couldn't place whose it was, but I knew it was someone I knew, perhaps everyone I knew, melted into one.

Come home.

I could stay here.

Come home.

Tantalizing, seductive. It beckoned me. If I sat, I had a feeling I would find my old bed under me, soft and comfortable, covered in the silky sheets Mother went out of her way to procure for me. I would hear Uttam thumping around in the next room, Prin singing for her weekend music tutor, and Father rearranging books in the study.

I'm so tired.

I hadn't noticed until now, but I was exhausted. I couldn't remember why. What had I been doing? Running around the cove? Staying up too late in Rosi's room? Rolling down the hill outside the house? It didn't matter. I was tired, and I just wanted to go home and rest. Everything else could wait.

I was still walking, my feet clacking against the hall floor.

I was going to my room. I couldn't see where I was going,

but something directed me. A second nature, like birds following the suns and sea waves. If I followed this hall, I would end up where I needed to be. Then I could rest for however long I wanted.

At home.

Someone called to me. A faint voice telling me this wasn't home. But it was so far away, so foreign, so unrecognizable. Whose voice was it anyway? I waved it away. It repeated itself, over and over, but fading a little more each time.

Come home.

I wanted to be home.

I wanted it more than anything I'd ever wanted. I wanted to go home and never leave, and why not? I was already there. I wanted to stay.

Forever.

Home.

Images floated before me like smoke. My room was so close now. Any moment, I would open that door, step through, and be where it was comfortable and warm. My life was there. My memories. Like the embrace of old friends. Like the beckoning of a warm lover. I hadn't felt this way in so long, though I wasn't sure why. After all, I hadn't gone anywhere. I was home all along. I was just tired. I just wanted to be warm again. I hadn't been warm since . . .

Since . . .

An image solidified. I followed it. It was dark, and it grew and swallowed me. I stopped walking.

I was warm.

He kept me warm.

The ground waved like water and suddenly I was falling. The white called to me, but the black pulled me back.

Come home. Come home.

Focus.

That voice was different. I held on to it for dear life. I knew that voice. That was the voice that had guided me through dozens of worlds. The owner of that voice kept me grounded by conversing with me, by holding my hand gently, by showing me new things to keep me alert and aware.

He showed me those things. Just like Rosi used to.

A cool breeze caught my cheek. My entire being turned toward that chill and I willed myself to dive toward it as if entering the surface of a freezing lake. I reached out, not just with my hands but with my mind and senses. Something wrapped around me.

Strings?

The sensation was difficult to articulate, and familiar in a way I couldn't describe. I had felt this before. In the silver star, in the capsule, in the black orb as Astra guided me with her fingers around mine. But this was different as well. In my moment of dazed confusion, I didn't fight it, instead allowing it to guide and move me. The invisible strings wrapped around my fingers, and though I couldn't tell if I was the puppet or the puppeteer, I relaxed and flowed with it.

Was this what manifestation was supposed to feel like?

My feet found ground and pieces of my body pulled together like threads being shortened. I blinked hard. The strings were gone. The air smelled of chilly seas and roasting fish. The seductive call of home faded away, at least for now, and the winter festival swam into view.

It was the exact same scene I'd walked with Om. The greens and whites, noisy street vendors, and rosalit flowers. But every time I took my eyes off something, it began to fall apart into a series of tiny blocks just outside my peripheral vision. Everything was fragile and temporary, and the more I dwelled on it, the more unstable the diorama around me seemed.

Focus.

I forced myself to remember the winter festival. The smell of the food from the stalls, the chill of the wind on my face and weight of the winter clothes on my body, the sound of laughing children. The spell of the dream state was broken, at least for the moment. I was in control though I didn't know for how long. I searched for the strings but they were beyond my grasp once more. The environment around me threatened to collapse. I had never realized how often my mind wandered, skipping from one thought to the next. Staying laser focused on one memory was nearly impossible. I pinched my arm and clapped my hands. I needed something to ground me and keep me in the present, anything to prevent my mind from wandering. It was so much easier with Om around.

Om.

I took a deep breath and let it out slowly. I thought about Om, recalling the sound of his footsteps as he walked next to me, and his hand around mine. A shape appeared next to me, transparent and blurry at first, but slowly refining itself. I searched my memories for the warmth of his skin and the texture of the scarf I'd laid around his neck. The shape became opaque, though it stayed ever so slightly rough around the edges. A phantom of a memory within a memory, solid and real so long as I didn't look at it directly. I took his hand. My body remembered every detail of him even if my mind didn't. With his fingers around mine, I began to walk.

Everything was just as before—the noisy vendors, the running children, and the childhood selves of Rosi and me. I followed them, trying to recall the details of that day, constructing the scene as I went. I had no idea if this was doing what it needed to do, but I was doing the only thing I knew how—remembering.

The child versions of Rosi and me tumbled down the snowy slope at the end of the street. A few older children threw snowballs at us. We returned a few, then moved on, veering away from the main street. I followed.

"There used to be a bread shop here," I said to the phantom Om next to me, pointing to the street corner. He didn't answer, but speaking to him kept me in the moment. "They did good business until the town began to expand. Then suddenly no one was interested in traditional recipes anymore. The old couple who owned it sold it. It was prime real estate, and they made a great profit, but I still hated to see it go."

Rosi and I disappeared into the doors. I stood before the shop's glass window. At first, there was nothing inside, but as the memories returned, shapes and figures appeared like water vapor disappearing off a mirror. I watched the two bent old men who owned the shop coo at us and hand over free sweet buns, piping hot from the ovens.

"This was always our last stop at the festival. It capped off our day. A festival never felt complete without a visit to Mik's Baked Treats." I smiled at the memory. The phantom Om's fingers tightened around mine—not of his own will, but of mine. The images of Rosi and me ran past us out of the door.

"It's funny," I said to the phantom. "Every day that passes, life seems a little more complicated. There were a lot of things I don't miss about Fiina, but the simpler days, I'll always miss those. I—"

The words caught in my throat as I spotted the couple walking past us. I did a double take and the environment around me quivered and changed.

Well, not quite changed.

Rewound.

I looked behind me. I was no longer standing next to Mik's Baked Treats. Instead, I was standing in the middle of Main Street, among the street vendors. The phantom of Om next to me vanished. The images of Rosi and me ran past, toward the nearest stall. The couple followed them, passing by me less than two steps away.

"This shop isn't there anymore," the other me said to Om—the real Om, or rather a version of Om far closer to the real thing. A wide red knitted scarf appeared around my—the other me's—neck. "Mother used to send Kit to buy all the children scarves in the winter. I lost many of them running around town, but I always remember this one. It's extra warm and I loved the color. It's the only one I shed a tear over when it went missing."

Om ran a curious hand over the scarf. "How interesting," he said.

I spun around, taking in my surroundings. They were the same, yet different. Solid. I let my mind drift to thoughts of the orb and the beach Astra and I sat on the night before, but the street scene stayed. Nothing changed.

The other me and Om were getting farther away. I hurried after them, staying a step behind. They didn't notice me.

"Something amusing?"

"Green and white. You fit right in."

They were not my memories. I stepped a little closer and reached out. My hand phased through their bodies like they were nothing but holograms. This street was not of my construct. Someone else was moving this scene.

Om touched the scarf I created for him and I felt the sensation of fingers sliding across thick fabric. His hand holding mine tightened ever so slightly and I felt that as well, not as the hand being held but the hand wrapped around mine.

This is Om's memory.

How was this possible? I followed them, the phantoms of Om and me, the sensation of his memory growing stronger by the moment. How could I be present inside his memory? I'd watched Able reset him, deleting everything. Was this scene stored inside the orb? Or inside the data core? It didn't matter. His memories wrapped around me, tightening around my senses. I could almost touch the strings holding this scene together. I grasped those strings and pulled. That sense of control returned, but only for a moment. Then they pulled back, yanking me out of the diorama of Radley into oblivion.

DOZENS OF WORLDS and hundreds of faces flew before my eyes in a flash. I lost my bearings and there was no up or down, only sounds and images. It was like watching a hundred films at once, gleaning bits and pieces as they flew by.

Faces, voices. The memories of others flooded my mind. I saw dozens of games of Headspace played, solemn-faced champions crowned, lives lived, loved ones lost, worlds left behind. And emotions. So many emotions. These were not dull, gray memories of the dead, but the dreams of the living. The minds that carried them were still very much alive, searching for their purpose in these endless illusions.

Dizzy and nauseous, I grabbed the first image that looked familiar and focused on it. The world around me screeched to a stop. My brain and stomach lurched as I landed heavily.

THE SKY above me was bright blue with a hint of violet. Lush blue-green grass covered the ground beneath my feet. I took a step and nearly stumbled over a short cliff. Below me was a large body of water that glistened so brightly I had to shield my eyes. At its shore, I spotted a familiar shape with gray, rock-like skin. Like Mod but smaller and rounder—a child.

"It's really made of crystals?"

A figure appeared next to me. She looked exactly like she did projected from the little holographic disc. Her dark hair was short and sleek, hanging in an uneven bob that framed her round face. Her skin was a soft tan color that glowed in the sun. She looked younger, and it wasn't just the fact that her body had not yet been overtaken by cloudy crystals.

"It has a similar cellular structure to crystals on your world, which makes it a hazard for almost all organic forms. Except, of course, its native inhabitants."

This voice I knew as well. The younger version of Astra smiled in my direction. I hadn't imagined she was even capable of such an expression—open, clear, and happy. But she wasn't smiling at me. Solace stepped forward. His body phased through mine as he rested a hand on Astra's waist. She leaned against him. I felt her warmth and my heart—his heart—skipped a beat.

"I never thought something like this could exist," she said, and I noticed every detail as she moved and spoke—because in his memory, he saw it all. She was wearing a blue top—the same one I found in E-V's capsule—that hung loosely off one shoulder over black leggings and ankle boots. She stood not with militant straightness but with relaxed curves. There was a brightness about her that had long since faded.

This was not the Astra I knew—Astra the arena master, Astra the favored daughter, Astra who'd burned a world without batting an eye. This was the Astra *he* remembered. The one who looked at him with adoring eyes, whose face brightened whenever he entered the room, and who fit her body into his like a puzzle piece.

She slipped both arms around his waist and squeezed playfully. "Take me somewhere else," she said, grinning.

"Somewhere else?"

"Another planet. Another country. Anywhere. I want to see everything."

Solace didn't speak. I felt him struggle as Astra gazed up at him expectantly.

"I think I should take you home."

Astra's face fell. "Home? Why? You're not bored of me already?" she asked teasingly, then a sliver of worry slipped in. "You're not, are you?"

He leaned down and kissed her forehead. "No, of course not," he said. "But you've already been away for a long time. Don't you think it's time you return?"

"Return to what?" she asked, an edge creeping into her voice. "The whole world gossiping about me? Not being able to go out without a hundred cameras pointed at me? Having my house pelted with shit by Crish's worship cult? Getting pawed at by every man that crosses my path, hoping he can score with 'the chick who saved the world'?" She pressed her cheek against his chest. "I just want to stay with you. I'm so tired of the noise."

The struggle again. I heard it loud and clear. His desire to keep her close and safe versus doing what he thought was right.

"I know it's not all pleasant," he said, "but there will be plenty of time to see the universe in the future. You still have a home to go back to, and you should return while you still can. The longer you spend away from Earth, the more difficult it will be to connect with your own kind."

"Maybe I don't want to connect with my own kind anymore."

"Not even Evie?"

"That's not fair."

He ran a hand through her hair. There was something soothing about the way it slid between his fingers.

"It's easy to say you want to disconnect when it's still just an option. Every world has its good and bad, but it's where you came from. Don't be in such a rush to disconnect from your roots."

Astra didn't argue, but I could see that while she agreed with him, she wasn't in a rush to admit it. They stood at the edge of the cliff, arms around each other.

"If I go back," she said, "will you take me on a proper honeymoon next time?"

He smiled. "Yes."

"Not just a pit stop. I want to see at least five planets." She thought for a moment. "Maybe ten. And I want to come back here."

"Of course."

She stood on tiptoes and kissed him. Her lips were warm and soft.

"I can't do what you do."

He gave her a puzzled look. "What do you mean?"

"You forgive everyone. My people were even less kind to

you than they were to me, but you still push me to go back to them. I can't do that. Sometimes I feel like I can't ever let those things go and that's just who I am. You've gone through stuff like this so many times. I don't understand how you're able to keep going on and let everything slide off."

"Does that bother you?"

She shook her head. "No. Understanding you will never be easy. I can accept that. But loving you has never been hard."

"Kova."

I spun around. Everything was white. The cliff and lake were gone.

"Kova."

I tried to reach out, but I had no hands.

"Rosi?"

"Kova!"

My eyes snapped open. At first, I thought my body was covered with heavy weights, but as I blinked away the haze, I saw Astra on top of me. Her hair was a mess and her face covering hung lopsided from her neck. The expression on her face could only be described as a frightful panic. She held one of my wrists in each of her hands, pressing them painfully against the armrests.

"Kova!" she shouted again. I flinched.

"I'm here," I said. "I'm awake. What are you . . ."

I tried to move and found I couldn't. Astra held me down with almost the entirety of her weight. I struggled but she pushed me back down. Two stood next to us. Their holographic face was off, but they were leaning over me as well.

"Let go," I said, struggling.

She looked at me hesitantly, then slowly eased off me, looking strangely paranoid as if expecting me to bolt up and escape like a convict running from the law. I flexed my fingers, numb from her death grip.

"Why are y—" I started, but the rest of my words vanished as I lifted one arm.

My skin was covered in deep, bloody scratches. I hadn't noticed when I woke up, but now that I saw them, the sting of pain settled in. My forearms and the backs of my hands looked like someone had taken a metal rake to them. Something trickled down my cheek. I touched my face gingerly and my fingertips came away with more blood. My cheeks, neck, and chest all stung. I looked down. The chair was covered with smears of blood.

"I—" I stammered, suppressing the scream of horror that threatened to escape me. "Wh—"

"Don't move," Two snapped as I tried to sit up.

"What happened?" I finally managed to say, unable to tear my eyes away from the ghastly wounds that covered me. Everywhere I looked, there was more blood. I didn't want to imagine what my face looked like.

Two didn't answer. Instead, they made a gesture in the air.

"Seven," they said. "Need a little patch work over here."

I hissed as my skin burned. The sensation was like being poked with the pointy legs of a thousand insects. The wounds on my arms and face began to knit themselves together. I lifted a hand but Two pushed it down.

"Don't scratch," they said. "Let her work."

"What happened?" I asked again, wincing at the almost unbearable itch.

"I'm sorry," Two said. "This is on me."

I blinked in confusion. "What do you mean?"

There was silence. I scanned the room. Astra had removed her face covering and was using it to wipe streaks of blood from her hands. In the corner, I saw Mod and Sweetly huddled together. Their faces were stripped of their usual cheery demeanors as they peered at me with a mixture of fear and apprehension.

"I always thought Able was overly paranoid," Two said after a long moment. "Strapping people down. Seemed like such overkill."

I swallowed and looked at my arms again. The bleeding was slowing, and the fresh wounds were becoming angry-looking welts. Flakes of red stained the space under my fingernails.

"I did this to myself?" I asked incredulously.

"We stopped you before you could get to your eyes."

I shuddered at the thought. "I didn't feel it."

"You'll be fine," Two said. Despite having no face to speak of, I could tell they were unsettled by the sight of my body. Astra, Mod, and Sweetly all appeared to be avoiding my gaze. What did they see? As I'd walked down the chilly streets of Radley, had they been screaming my name and fighting to keep me from destroying myself?

"Where's . . ." I nearly said "Prin," then remembered only I knew her by that name. "The Harbinger, where is she?"

"That thing?" Astra said, a hint of disgust creeping into her voice. "I sent her away. She overloaded almost immediately. Too much sensory input. To be expected, I guess. Most of this is uncharted territory, not to mention largely untested. She was either faulty or the amount of information generated by the dream state was too much for Harbingers. I don't know how Able was able to make it work, but he must've been exceedingly lucky not to overload that Harbinger."

Or he was different, I thought but did not say, my mind drifting back to the scene in Om's memory that I had just walked through. My wounds were mostly healed now, though the scars looked like they might last a while. I ran a finger over the pink welts gingerly.

"Did it work?" I asked. The thought of doing this again frightened me.

Astra shook her head ruefully. "I don't know. I don't even

know what 'working' means for this mess. Maybe this was a mistake. We can't put you through that again. We—"

"Incoming entity."

Astra stopped. We looked at each other, then at Two, who gave a small shrug.

"Incoming entity," Mother repeated from overhead. The dome above us began to turn transparent. The dark of space appeared above us, and there it was, like a white sun, growing and expanding against the black backdrop.

CHAPTER 29

THE WHITE ORB MEDITATED AMONGST THE STARS.

Astra, Two, and I stood, head craned up and arms crossed, as we studied the mysterious sphere. It was small, at best a third the size of the black orbs, but something about it was incredibly *dense*, and foreboding, like the difference between looking at a wad of fabric versus a ball of steel dangling just above one's face. It was completely unreflective and there was not a single mark, opening, or flaw on its surface.

"It won't come any closer?" Astra asked.

"Correct," came Mother's voice. "When I try to move closer, it moves away. This is as close as we can get."

"Is it really the data core?"

"I cannot confirm that."

"Can you scan it?"

"Scans return no results."

I couldn't take my eyes off the white orb. Somehow, I couldn't shake the feeling that it was looking back at me.

"Are you ready?" Astra asked.

"I don't know," I said, and it was the truth.

Mod and Sweetly were nearby, but they weren't terribly interested in the white orb after the initial novelty wore off. Astra went to each of them in turn and gave them a tight embrace. Sweetly looked confused, but welcomed the attention. Mod's big arms were around my torso before I could protest, crushing the air out of me.

"Whoa, Mod," I said. Sweetly hopped up and rammed her head against my face. I relented and let them have their way. Astra approached Two.

"If you've got something clever to say," she said, "do it now."

Two winked. "I'll save it for when you get back."

"Mother," Astra said. "Transfer administrative rights to Mod."

"Alright."

She doesn't think she's coming back.

Mod set me down. I suddenly felt emotional as well.

Am I *coming back?*

"Let's go."

I nodded. Astra gave Mod one last hug.

"You are the last arena master of this orb," she said to him. "I'm sure whatever you do, you'll make us proud."

Mod grinned. "Be safe," he said to us, working his thick tongue around the word. "Kova. Too. Be safe. You are. Family."

THE WHITE ORB wasn't cold.

The sensation of being somewhere warm enough to be comfortable was strange after spending time in Astra's and Ten's arenas. Though it appeared to be structured much like the other orbs, complete with a bay for the capsule to dock, it was different in very significant ways. For one, entering it was strange. I had thought we would need to search for an entry point, but as we approached it, an invisible force simply guided us, gently but forcefully, toward a particular point on the surface. After a tense moment of thinking we were going to crash, we entered the bay seamlessly, not too unlike entering the foggy center of the Pinnacle.

The capsule bay was completely white. The floors, the

domed ceiling, even the railings and doors. All perfectly, flawlessly white. And something told me that nothing was painted. If someone took a knife to this place and sliced off a cross section, every exposed surface would be totally, completely white.

All in all, it was not what I expected a data storage facility to look like.

Astra stepped off the capsule on high alert. I could see her arm twitch as our feet hit the white ground. If someone jumped us at that moment, I had no doubt her blade would be in their neck in half a blink's time. She insisted on getting out first to scope out the area, even though we both saw that the bay was empty when we pulled in.

"What are we looking for?" I asked apprehensively.

"Not sure," Astra said. She reached up and scratched at her face, then her arms. "This place is messing with me."

"Messing with you?"

"It's trying to do something to me." She lifted her shirttail. On her side, just below the ribs, were the gaps left by Able's knife. As I watched, they began to knit together rapidly, until there wasn't a sign of the wounds left at all. Astra pointed to her cheek and nodded at me. "You, too."

Now that she mentioned it, I sensed it, too. The wounds on my face were tingling. It wasn't the unbearable itch from the black orb, but a soft, almost pleasant sensation. I raised my arms and marveled as the pink welts I'd left there earlier disappeared completely, leaving my skin clear and unblemished. It even removed the cuts and scrapes from the last few days and a mole I'd had since childhood.

"Wow," I breathed.

Astra scratched her face again. "It's trying to decide what to do with my skin," she said. "I can feel it. Like it doesn't know if I should be flesh or crystal."

"You're both, aren't you?" I said hesitantly. She stopped scratching and gave me a strange look.

"It stopped."

"Stopped?"

"When you said I was both, it stopped."

"What does that mean?"

She gave me a long look. "I'm not sure," she said, and started toward the bay's exit. "Let's go. Be ready to defend yourself."

I wanted to ask her how I was supposed to do that, but I already knew the answer. Having zero confidence in my ability to manifest anything, I could only hope that something would work out in a pinch.

The smooth, flawless hallways were at least twice as wide as the halls of the black orb, and so white that corners and edges blended into each other. The floor was completely white as well, and instead of connecting to the walls at a seam, simply curved from horizontal to vertical. The entire place looked like it was grown organically rather than built. I couldn't spot turns until we were almost close enough to miss them and my eyes watered from the glaring white that assaulted me from all directions.

Astra hadn't said much since we left the bay, but the longer we spent wandering the hallways, the more I could sense her agitation. That was yet another bizarre feature of this orb—my senses were enhanced. It was as if my pores had been opened and information was pouring in. I could feel Astra's fingertips sliding against the smooth walls, her boots striking the ground, and the growing unease that gnawed at her. I felt her senses as if they were my own, as if I was in two places at once, just like being inside the simulations.

After about half an hour of aimless wandering, we saw the first one.

Astra spotted the figure first, standing slack-jawed against the white wall. She reached out a hand and stopped me, her other hand already starting to change shape. But it quickly reverted when we drew close.

"Leeds!" she exclaimed, and before I could figure out what was going on, she had broken into a run. I hurried after her as she went to the figure and grabbed them by the shoulders.

The alien had light pink skin patterned like a pebble-paved road. Two sharp skull ridges rose from just above their brow to the back of their head, where the tips met at the base of their skull. Their mouth opened slightly and I saw two rows of flat teeth as they appeared to attempt speaking. Astra snapped her fingers in front of their dull brown eyes, which didn't blink once.

"She can't see me," Astra muttered. "This is Leeds. She was the thirty-first champion of this galaxy. She went missing a long time ago. I thought she fell to the demigods."

She peered into Leeds's eyes, which wasn't easy since the alien's head was bobbing around like a drooping balloon. Just as she tried to talk to her friend again, Leeds suddenly shuddered and I gasped in horror as she lifted both hands and raked her own cheeks with her hard, claw-like nails, pulling the skin like it was made of rubber. Her eyes rolled back as rivers of pink, milky blood flowed over her face and neck.

"No!" Astra gasped and grabbed both Leeds's hands, pulling them away from her face.

Leeds shuddered again, a movement almost like a seizure, and fell limply onto her side. The moment Astra released her, she grabbed her own shoulders as if hugging herself and dug her nails deep into her skin. Her eyes were empty, unfeeling, betraying no pain or even awareness of the damage she was doing to herself.

Was this what I had looked like?

"Stop!" Astra exclaimed. She grabbed Leeds's arms again and tried to restrain her. "Leeds! Stop it!" She pushed her friend onto her back and straddled her, straining to immobilize her hands. "I can't leave her like this. We have to take her back!"

I looked past her down the long, white hall. "What about the rest of them?"

Astra looked behind her and her eyes widened. Along the slippery walls, at least twenty figures lingered. Some leaned against the wall; some sat and stared into space. Two or three paced slowly. No two were alike, though they all wore the same listless expression on their faces—or what I presumed to be faces on some of them.

And all of them were biting or scratching themselves.

"No," Astra muttered. She was shaking. "Stop them. I have to stop them!"

I knelt. Leeds stared blankly up at me, through me. Something was happening to her face. Her skin was moving, like marching insects. Astra turned back and I knew she saw what I was seeing, too.

Wounds closed. The trickling blood stopped, dried, and disappeared. Within moments, her damaged flesh was repaired good as new.

"It's fixing them," I said.

Astra nodded. Tentatively, she released her grip. Leeds immediately brought her wrist back to her face and sank her teeth into her own skin. Astra pulled her hand away, but the teeth marks were already disappearing. The white orb worked fast.

"Why are they doing this?" Astra asked no one in particular. She stood and reluctantly left Leeds to her ghastly task. She scanned the others, who were all doing the same—scratching, biting, bleeding, and healing.

"They're dreaming."

"What?"

I stood. I hadn't been certain in the dream state, but now that I was here, I knew. I had seen what was going through their heads. Each and every one of them. They were alive and dreaming—if what they were doing could be called living—and fighting it every step of the way.

"I saw their dreams. All of them."

"Which means what?"

"I'm not sure," I said hesitantly. A terrible thought occurred to me and I shivered. Ten cycles ago I had lain in bed, dreaming of Rosi and the message she'd brought me. And again, lying in Able's cell, listening to Rosi's voice and waking to welts on my arms. If I hadn't been woken quickly enough during those times, would I have kept on scratching myself until I was bloody and raw? Would I have gouged out my eyes without even realizing?

Without the orb to heal them, would they continue until there was nothing left?

"Do you know them all?"

Astra pursed her lips. "Some of them. I thought they were dead."

"Are they all champions?"

"I assume so. Some of them are from other galaxies." Astra gestured toward a segmented being with no arms but at least four pairs of legs that ended in sharp, dangerous-looking points. "Different blueprints. I've never encountered champions from other galaxies before. I don't even know if the orb's translations will work for them." She shook her head in frustration.

Something clicked in my mind. "We're being translated."

Astra gave me a look. "What?"

"We're being translated right now. This orb, the data core or whatever it is, is translating us. We don't speak the same language, right?"

Astra thought about this. "Whoever is running this place, they want us to be able to communicate."

And are probably watching us.

We moved on, though I could tell leaving her friends behind was difficult for Astra. We weaved our way through one white hallway after another. Sometimes we found a door, which we went through, having no real sense of direction. We came across other occupants, all of whom were wandering mindlessly about.

"We've gone in a circle."

I slowed my steps. Astra had stopped. I did the same, though I could see nothing of interest besides white and more white. I started to ask how she could tell when I saw the reason.

There, about fifty paces in front of us, sitting with her mouth open, was Leeds. She was staring at the ceiling now, gnawing on bloody fingers, and tapping the floor with her foot to the beat of a tune only she could hear.

"Is this a maze?"

"It's trying to be." Astra pointed to the door at the end of the hall. "They've been directing us. We follow doors that open, and it leads us in a loop." She placed both hands against the wall and closed her eyes for a moment. It took me a second to realize she was listening for the orb's hum. I waited, afraid to disturb her.

After a long moment, she opened her eyes and stepped back. "It won't sing for me," she said. "I've noticed it since we got here. It's blocking me, the same way an arena master can set the orb to limit manifestation for everyone but themselves." She glanced at me. "Wild guess, it's not blocking *you*, is it?"

"I . . ." I swallowed, suddenly nervous. "No. It's not."

She looked around us at the white walls. "I don't think it wants me here," she said. "This thing came because it responded to *you*, not me. When you told it I was both flesh and crystal, it stopped trying to fix me. It only wants you."

"But why?"

"Beats me." Astra looked me up and down. "But I have a theory."

"What is it?"

She took a step toward me and cradled my cheek in her hand. My heart skipped a beat as I thought she might kiss me. My face flushed with heat. Her fingers moved up to my head.

"I'm sorry," she said.

Without warning, she grabbed me by the hair and slammed my face against the nearest wall. In an instant, the humming boomed through me, as if I was standing far too close to a thumping speaker pumping out heavy bass. Astra held my head tightly and wouldn't allow me to pull back. My inner ear vibrated and I had trouble breathing.

"I know you can hear me, Rosi," I heard her say. "Give me my husband or I'll cave your sister's head in against this wall."

The shuffling footsteps around us stopped. My line of vision was limited, but I could sense the change. Hostility. Alarm. Leeds, the only figure I could see, had turned toward us. Though her eyes were no more focused than before, she pressed her back against the white wall and used it as support to get to her feet. She walked toward us in an awkward shamble, as if pulled by strings. Others followed. Astra's fingers wound tighter in my hair.

"I'm not joking, Rosi," she said. "I won't leave here without him. How fast can your puppets tear me apart? I bet it won't be faster than me splitting her skull."

They stopped. The other figures formed a loose circle, as if trying to decide on a course of action.

Was Rosi really here?

"Now."

The figures surrounding us collapsed like cloth dolls. They lay staring emptily in various directions, as if the strings holding them up had been cut. A door opened. Astra pulled me away from the wall as a familiar figure stepped through.

Unlike the others, he didn't shamble or hang his limbs like empty sacks. If his eyes were empty and staring past us, I couldn't tell behind the black mask. For a moment I was taken back to our very first encounter, when I'd hidden from him in the silver orb, holding my breath for fear of being seen. He didn't say a word. Neither did she. He led out one hand and the building blocks responded to his call. The curved blade appeared in his hand. He spun it around his finger.

Astra wavered. We both saw the neat cuts in the folds of fabric at his wrists and joints, between the harder parts of his armor. The teal skin underneath had healed completely, but it was obvious that the sweet, nostalgic dream he lived in did not keep him from taking his blade to himself.

"So that's how it is," Astra said, releasing me.

"What are you doing?"

She gave me a nudge. "Sorry, but you're on your own from here."

I looked at the door Solace came through and stepped into it, but couldn't bring myself to walk all the way through. "What are you going to do?" I asked, looking back.

Astra shrugged. "I'm going to take him back with me." She looked at the blade in Solace's hand. "Or I'll die trying. Either one is fine."

"Please don't say that."

She smiled. It was the same smile I'd seen in Solace's memory—open, clear, and truly happy. Then, she pulled the covering around her neck up over the lower half of her face.

"Good luck," she said, then added, "Be brave. Keep yourself safe."

I knew what she meant by that, but there was no time to argue about my pathetic manifestation. Solace shoved me roughly through the door and by the time I steadied myself, the door had closed. The seam around it disappeared as if it had never been there in the first place.

The hall was silent and empty. I was alone.

A sliding sound behind me. I turned around. Another door had opened. Followed by another, and another, a series of openings leading directly to the heart of the orb.

Nowhere to go but forward.

CHAPTER 30

EVERY DOOR CLOSED BEHIND ME AS SOON AS I STEPPED THROUGH. With each step, the silence seemed to grow. Even my footsteps were being swallowed. I saw a few more of the alien occupants, all of whom were lying on their sides or backs, staring. The halls I crossed became shorter and shorter. Soon I could see their dead ends on either side.

The last hall was little more than a square room. I took a moment to collect myself in front of the final door—the only one that didn't open automatically.

What was behind it?

Part of me wanted to run—a useless thought, as the door I'd come through had already closed and disappeared like the others. I had nowhere to go, and I had left behind my only companion.

Had Rosi been waiting here, all this time, to show this place to me?

The door opened and I stepped through.

The structure of the wide room was familiar. The ceiling was domed and there were no doors in sight save for the one I'd just stepped through. But what caught my attention was the air. It was dense with movement that I could sense more than see—building blocks, billions of them. I'd known they were there in the other orbs, but never to this capacity. This place was so densely packed that I almost felt like I was underwater.

Though the room itself was much smaller than the ones on the black orbs, I knew that it was an arena floor. It was brightly lit, though I could find no light source. Like the holy grounds, the light seemed to be coming from the walls themselves.

"So you finally made it."

I didn't notice him initially. His white skin and clothing blended into the white of the room almost seamlessly. Only his piercing blue eyes stood out. His name was on the tip of my tongue, but I stopped just short of speaking it. He circled me slowly and I fought not to squirm under his steady gaze.

"All this time spent waiting for you," he said, an oily intrigue in his voice. He wasn't being translated—every word out of his mouth was East Fiinian dialect. But it wasn't the voice I'd grown accustomed to hearing as I'd held his hand while we'd walked between illusions inside the floating door.

"So many people," he went on. "So many bodies and minds, all fallen to the dream state within a day of setting foot in here." He paused. "Well, except that last one. He lasted almost twice as long as the rest, the stubborn child."

I felt my innards tighten. "They're hurting themselves," I said in a small voice.

He waved me off nonchalantly. "All part of the process. Dream states are unnatural, after all. The body rebels. But it's alright. I'll fix that part once I get this thing under control."

I said nothing else. Truthfully, I couldn't think of anything to say. I was terrified of this stranger looking at me through Om's eyes.

"Do you recognize me?"

I shook my head.

"You should." He looked down at himself. "Granted, I look a little different now. But I would think my voice left a decent dent in your memories."

It had, though I was reluctant to admit it.

"You were in the video."

"Correct."

"You brought the orb to Radley Cove."

"Correct again."

I swallowed thickly. "You're K'azen."

He clapped Om's hands together. Twice. The sound echoed off the smooth white walls around us.

"Wonderful. You're not as dull as I expected. Seed races. Can never tell quite how smart you all are. You're really just one tier up from the primitives you evolved from." He looked me up and down as if appraising me for sale. "Which one are you? Mammal or reptile? Oh, it doesn't matter. You lower life forms are all the same."

I tried to keep my back straight and my face stoic. "You died," I said. He let out a dry laugh.

"Did that little girl you came with tell you that? Well, you'll have to forgive her for being mistaken."

"I don't understand."

"Then let me show you." He put a hand—Om's hand—on my shoulder and I suppressed a flinch. "After all, that's what you're here for, isn't it? We've got plenty of time to kill and frankly I've missed having the chance to enlighten the lesser creatures since the games stopped." The light dimmed and stars appeared above. "In the beginning, there were gods. Until there weren't."

K'azen loved to hear himself talk.

I watched him move around the room. He was inside Om's body, a body I knew too well, and he spoke of gods and games, which were stories I'd partially heard before. But he was different from everyone I'd met since departing Fiina. Even Able, who'd carried a similar air of arrogance and oily charm, wasn't quite the same as this man—being, creature, demigod, whatever he was.

"Surely your new acquaintances have taught you about the games by now."

I nodded.

"The games were glorious," he said, almost wistfully. "Truly a masterpiece. Some say that life in this universe was the greatest creation of the gods, but that's just a delusion. We all exist because of the games."

Above us was endless space. But it was different from the projections inside the black orbs. The sensation was difficult to describe. I could feel the weightlessness and the presence of the planets, even though my feet were still firmly planted on the ground. The white orb offered far more than a cosmetic difference from the other orbs. It was a different entity entirely.

"The gods left, you see, because we could not live up to the games. After all this time, we were still just dull little creatures failing to fully use what the gods gave us. To some degree, the demigods were to blame. We were supposed to be the masters of the games, and yet, some of us somehow let a *seed* outdo us." He shook his head. "That short one with the purple eyes. I have to give credit where it's due. But it isn't her job to step up, do you understand?" He looked at me intensely.

"I . . ." I stammered. I had no idea what to do. Everything was terribly confusing. I wished Astra were here. She would've demanded answers instead of standing and listening to his prattling. But she wasn't, and I wasn't brave.

"It is *our* job." He gestured at himself. "It was the job of the demigods to serve the gods. To entertain them. To feed them. To harvest for them."

K'azen waved his hand toward the dark of space and another white orb appeared, followed by four black ones that orbited it. He gave me a look and I realized he was proud. He was thrilled to be showing all this to me and to have an audience for the first time in who knew how long. He craved what little attention I gave him.

"The greatest gift from the gods," he said. "The data core.

Every bit of information since the beginning of time from this universe, stored within this marvelous white orb. Every story, every piece of history, both recorded and unrecorded, are here. Every memory and every dream ever offered to the gods, right here. Finding it was far from easy, but then, it's only to be expected. It wouldn't be a treasure of the gods if it weren't reserved for those who prove themselves worthy of it."

The black orbs stopped circling. They arranged themselves into a perfect square below the white one. For a moment, nothing happened. Then, four beams of light, so thin I could barely make them out, shot out from the white orb to the black ones, like an insect catching its prey with silver thread. The black orbs began to turn white, starting where the light struck, spreading until they had all become completely white.

K'azen winked at me. "Amazing, isn't it? A hidden feature of the data core. It was a surprise to me, too, finding that little secret. We thought the data core would lead us to the way to find the gods again, but as it turns out, the gods meant for us to find our own way by creating a new order using their gift. The games run by this miraculous orb will be unlike any other."

"That's what Able said," I murmured.

"Able?" K'azen appeared confused for a moment, then brightened. "Ah yes, Able. I remember him now." He shook his head. "Poor little gullible seed."

"I thought he was your partner."

"Partner?" K'azen scoffed. "With a seed? I'm sure he would've liked to believe that. The seed races always fancied themselves above their station. He was amusing, I'll give you that. And helpful when he thought there was something to gain. Tell me, where is he now?"

"He's dead."

"Really? Just as well, I suppose. He wouldn't have liked it when I tossed him into the games with the rest of the riffraff. But let's move on."

The stars above began to rearrange themselves. Several—

sixteen if I counted correctly—planets began to move toward the orbs. They arranged themselves as well, into four squares, each under the four new white orbs. The silver light strings extended, this time leading from the orbs to the planets.

My body went cold at the sight. K'azen stepped close to me. I fought not to shrink away from him. "Did you know that's what they were made for?" he said. "Every planet in this universe possesses the potential to become an arena. Haven't you ever wondered why every intelligent race in this universe desires to create information networks?"

I shook my head numbly. K'azen walked a circle around me, relishing being able to put on this show, loving my reaction.

"It's because they want to be connected. And they want to dream. It never fails. We steer technological advancement, but they set their own goals. Every single time, they strive for connection, for virtual worlds, digital realities. It's because they are programmed with the desire to get lost in their own heads. This goes back so much deeper than just the arena. The orbs are just stages. The real game was always intended to be played on a much higher level."

"I don't understand."

K'azen laughed and flicked my nose. "Of course you don't. It's ironic, the part *you* end up playing in this whole thing, being the insignificant little thing that you are. Let me put it in the simplest of terms for you—the seed races were made for entertainment and entertainment only. You are programmed to get lost in dreams and imaginations, never realizing that your own minds were always meant to be the ultimate arena. In the mind, time is but a concept. Contestants can live a thousand lifetimes in a matter of minutes. They can generate infinitely more content than the archaic games."

"That sounds . . ." I grimaced. "Horrible."

Anger.

I felt it even though K'azen's smile didn't falter. He rolled

Om's eyes. "What do you know," he said dismissively. "A seed could never understand the grand plan of the gods."

And yet you're here telling me about it.

I watched the orbs above me, but kept my eyes on him out of my peripheral vision. I had wounded his pride. Once upon a time, when he had an audience of billions, he probably wouldn't have cared about my opinion at all. But right now, he had only me.

They have one purpose and one purpose only—to harvest the seed races for their masters using the orbs.

"What does any of this have to do with me?"

K'azen spread his arms. "Why, everything. At least, it has everything to do with Rosi."

I started. "Rosi?"

"The data core was beyond our understanding. It needed a translator. We needed the data core to understand us the way we understand each other. Someone needed to tap into it and speak to it. But that is no small task. It is not receptive to our kind, since it was built to connect to the seed races. But the seed races are fragile. We went planet to planet, seeking potential candidates. So many broke in the process."

The bodies. They'd found them in the black orb on Fiina.

"The champions, they're more resilient. But even then, they couldn't last very long. They survived, but they fell under its spell, trapped in their own dream loops, unable to open her up. It takes a special mind, one that is strong, durable, and inventive. It must create worlds and inspire others to do the same."

"And that's Rosi?"

K'azen smiled. "Ah, Rosi. What a mind. What a gem. I was beginning to give up hope when I came to Fiina. So many candidates. So little success. And that pesky black-eyed Earthling on my tail this whole way, making everything harder. Then, the perfect one. A mind built for dreaming." He sighed. "But, alas, the dreamers are the hardest ones to tame. She didn't like being told what to do. Ran off with the data core. Made me chase her in circles around the galaxy—*me*, the one who gave her all those wonderful dreams. Can you imagine?" He pointed at me. "But I don't need to do that anymore. Because soon this orb will have its first proper master."

"I-is Rosi here?" I asked.

"In a manner of speaking."

"What does that mean?"

"It means there's enough of her here to operate the orb."

Images of Rosi strung up with silvery strings to white walls flashed through my mind. Was there a basement here as well? Had Rosi been hanging like Viva for the last ten cycles, the back of her head cracked open like a ripe melon? Dread lodged itself in my throat.

K'azen circled me again, looking at me like I was a fish to be filleted. "You are a gift. All that happened to bring you here, in this moment. It's truly miraculous. The blessings of the gods have truly smiled upon me." He tapped his front, at the center of the black patch on Om's chest. "Just like with this fellow, who just happened to be on a planet that was being burned. Sturdy, these Harbingers. He was the only thing that survived—except me, of course."

"So you took over his body?" My insides crawled at the thought of K'azen being present at all the intimate moments I'd shared with Om.

"Oh, nothing quite so barbaric. Let's just say I'm hitching a ride. There I was, practically dead, and a voice spoke to me. The voice of the gods. It told me I could use this Harbinger as my body. I should have died, but I lived. The gods willed it, just like it is their will that you be here. They have guided us, every step of the way. And it is their will that *I* become the master of the ultimate arena."

"Sure," I mumbled.

"And now, my little Fiinian," he said, "we move on to the final phase of the plan. You. With you here, I can finally begin to change the universe into what it should've been in the first place."

"Then what?"

"Then, a new universe. But nothing for you to worry about. All *you* have to do is talk to Rosi."

"Me?" Panic was welled up inside me. I imagined planets full of people, biting and scratching themselves without the orb to heal them. "Why me?"

"I already told you, dimwit," K'azen said impatiently. "She won't listen to me." He leaned close to me. "I've heard her whispers," he said in a voice that was almost seductive. "She won't talk to me, but I can hear her sometimes. She wanted you here. She wants you to see what she does. She wants so badly to show *you*."

Those words sent a chill down my spine.

"*This* is what she wants to show me?"

"That's right." K'azen's fingers snaked their way to my chin. "It's your destiny to be here."

"That can't be it," I said. My body trembled. All I could think about was Leeds sinking her sharp nails into her own flesh. "This can't be what she wants to show me. I don't want to see this. I want no part of this."

Silence. I waited for his wrath. Would he threaten me? Torture me? Make me scream until I gave in? But K'azen did none of those. To my surprise, he smiled.

"I don't *have* to physically harm you," he said lightly. "Tell me, how old are you?"

"I-I'm . . ." I couldn't tell where he was going with this. "Twenty-two cycles."

He looked at me blankly, then let out a short laugh. "Oh, I have no idea how long that is. Every planet's different, you know? Hard to keep track. But judging by your complexion and physical maturity, I'm guessing you haven't been alive all that long. Nothing but a blink's worth of time, if that. You can't even comprehend how long I've been alive. Heck, I bet even those children out there in the halls seem old to you. Tell me, do you know what eternity feels like?"

I shook my head wearily.

"You will." He gestured at the white walls. "I can be very patient. I can close my eyes and doze while empires rise and fall around me. I can stare at these walls and live in my mind while generations live and die. I can wait. Can *you*?"

I glanced around nervously. "Can I what?"

"Sit in utter silence, completely alone, in this room. I can't control the orb fully, but I can run its basic functions. I can work the arena floor, manifest rooms and lock doors. Can you imagine it? Day after day, for one lifetime after another? How long do you imagine you'll last before you succumb to madness and beg for death?" He rubbed his chin as if lost in thought. "Well, that wouldn't be so easy either. Nothing to off yourself with here. I imagine sister dearest would want to keep you alive, so even taking your own life would be challenging, especially with only your bare hands to work with."

Fear crept through me. I knew he could see it.

"So," he said. "What'll it be? Shall I step out? Come back in ten—what did you call it—cycles? And see how you feel? How about a hundred? How will you feel then? Maybe you'll be more cooperative when you've picked most of your skin off from the sheer, utter, crushing boredom."

He lifted a hand, a strangely ominous gesture.

"You have five seconds to decide," he said. "Talk to Rosi, get her to open up and acknowledge me as arena master, or spend eternity sitting in here wishing for death." He began to fold his fingers down one at a time. "Five."

My heart raced.

"Four."

Sweat beaded on my forehead.

"Three."

They do not value us, or respect us, or even think we have a right to live if we do not serve as entertainment.

"Two."

We have no way to win them over, and no bargaining chip against them.

"O—"

"Wait!"

He stopped. That last finger had not yet touched his palm. "Yes?"

"Let's play."

K'azen's face twitched. "What?"

"You want me to talk to her, right?" My brain was barely a step ahead of my mouth as it churned rapidly. "You said you can work the arena floor, right? Let's play for it. If you win, I'll talk to her. And tell her to do what you want."

The only thing they respect, outside of the gods, is the game.

"Why would I do that?" he said. "It would be far easier to leave you in here for a few lifetimes until you decide to be more obedient."

"Unless I go too far out of my mind to talk to her," I said. I sounded far braver than I felt. I had to keep him here. I had to keep talking. "You don't want that to happen, especially if I'm the only one she'll listen to. Besides, don't you want to try out these new games of yours?"

He cracked a smile at that. "So, you are willing to attempt the dream state games, just for a one in a million chance to win against me?"

"I think my chances are better than one in a million," I said huffily, though inwardly I thought they might not be better by much.

K'azen thought for a long moment. I tried to keep myself steady, though I was on the verge of collapsing from nerves. Finally, he spoke. "Alright," he said. "I'll humor you. Let's play. Shall we define the stakes? If I win, you tell the white orb to relinquish administrative functions to me."

"What if I win? What promise do I have that this game will be fair?"

K'azen scoffed. "Just like a seed. I am not like the pretenders. I am the genuine article. No game from me would ever be unfair."

Could I trust him? I had no choice. Whatever he had in store for me, it couldn't be worse than slowly waiting for madness in a white room.

"Okay," I said. "If I win, you let me talk to Rosi of my own accord."

"And what will you do?"

"I don't know yet." It was the truth.

"You're delaying the inevitable. Your kind was made to live in dreams. Even if you don't allow the orb to do her work, you will still one day find your own way into dream states and virtual realities. It was always the plan. Why let it go to waste?"

"I'm not a big fan of plans."

K'azen appeared outwardly calm, but I knew he was excited. The orb sent his excitement coursing through me as if it was my own. He craved this. He needed it. Like an addict he desired the game that he had been deprived of for so long.

"Well then, contestant from Fiina," he said with a wry smile. "Let's play Headspace."

CHAPTER 31

"FIVE ROUNDS."

"Why five?"

"You wouldn't know this," K'azen said. He waved a hand and the dark of space faded away, replaced by the white domed ceiling. "But in its prime, Headspace started with five rounds. It allowed the contestants a chance to figure out the game without severe consequences—well, aside from losing their lives, but that's just part of the game. In honor of the heydays, five seems like the right number." He paused and gave me a disparaging glance. "Unless you don't think you can survive five rounds?"

"Of course I can," I lied. "How many do I need to win? Three out of five?"

"In the old days, you would have to survive each round to move on." He shrugged. "But tell you what, if you can make it through three of the five, I'll call it a win. I'll even be extra generous and give you this." With a turn of the wrist an object appeared in his hand. He handed it to me. It was a gold, round token just a little smaller than my palm.

"What's this?"

"A free exit."

"From what?"

"A round of your choosing. It can only be used once, and you'd have to take a loss, but if you want a round to end before the time has run out, you use that."

I turned the strange object over in my hand. "Why would you give me this?"

K'azen smiled. The joyful anticipation radiating from him chilled me to my core. "Because," he said, "it wouldn't be much fun if you were to lose your mind before the rounds are up, would it?"

"Okay," I muttered, and slid it into my pocket. He was toying with me to make the game more fun for himself. I didn't need the orb's signals to know that if he thought I could win for a second, he would not be agreeing to this deal. He had every advantage and I had none. My only comfort was that he couldn't mangle me so badly that I couldn't communicate with Rosi afterwards.

"And by the way," he said. "You're not as subtle as you think."

I flinched inwardly. "What do you mean?"

"I see you looking at this." He gestured at Om's body. "Sorry to disappoint, but this one isn't available for you to play with anymore." He tapped Om's temple. "Full reset. Clean erasure. Nothing but a shell for me to ride in."

"Oh," was all I said.

"But if you're good and do as you're told, I'll find you another one. There's no shortage of these things in the dead orbs." He raised one of Om's hands and studied it. "Still, maybe it's good for something. Tell you what, I'll let you play with it a little longer. We used to use these things as hosts of the games. Much more efficient than the seed racers who claim themselves to be arena masters. I'll step out. Let this thing take you through the games. A full Headspace experience. What do you say?"

"I—" I began, but it was already too late. The world around me liquified and the ground fell out below.

. . .

A WOODEN SURFACE rushed up at my face and I struck it full force. My nose gushed blood. The surface beneath me was unstable and I reached out to steady myself on the nearest surface, only to receive a splinter in my finger. I hissed in pain and pulled it away. The ground wouldn't stop rocking and I could feel the sticky blood flowing down over my mouth and chin. The air smelled like salt.

I was in Radley Cove.

Or rather, a version of Radley Cove. I was beginning to lose track of how many versions of Radley Cove I'd seen up to now. This one was big, at least three times as wide as the cove back home. The hills that surrounded the water had become towering peaks that loomed over me. The beach was far away and made of golden sand instead of white pebbles.

I was on a wobbly wooden boat pinned together with rusted nails and half-rotted wood. It was barely big enough for me to stretch out in if I lay flat on my back. The waves bobbed it up and down, and me along with it.

A small island sat in the middle of the cove. I was just close enough to make out the fierce blood-red eyes of its sole inhabitant, whose enormous gray body occupied nearly its entire surface. It was at least three times as long as I was tall. Three thick legs ended in claws as long as my hand, and one ended in a stump. A forked tongue snapped in and out of its jaw as it locked eyes with me.

Last time I'd seen it, it was crawling over Mother's meticulously arranged breakfast table.

There was nothing else of interest in the cove. The lizard hissed, showing rows of sharp teeth that would tear the flesh from my bones easier than shredding paper.

"Welcome, contestant."

I didn't even see when he appeared. He stood on the water as if it was a solid surface. K'azen's voice and smug expression were gone.

"The game will consist of five rounds," he said woodenly.

His demeanor reminded me uncomfortably of the Harbinger in Astra's orb—stiff, rehearsed, following an invisible script. "Each game will require completion of a different goal. Some will also include a time limit."

Om looked at me—or rather, past me, not a shred of emotion on his face. I studied his face, searching for some trace of recognition. I found none. He lifted a hand and pointed to the island. "Your target for this round is there."

"What am I supposed to do?"

"Remove the target from the island."

"What does that mean?"

He was already gone. Something wet struck my hand. I looked down to see the blood from my nose dripping liberally. I inhaled and tasted more blood.

Stay calm. Stay calm.

I touched my nose gingerly. It was definitely broken. Not five minutes after opening my big mouth to K'azen and I'd already gone and gotten hurt. The pain and blood were terribly distracting. I couldn't think straight. The lizard hissed again.

There was nothing I could do about my nose right now. I leaned over the side of the boat, scooped water into my hand, and cleaned my face, trying to keep my breathing even until the bleeding slowed. It would have to do for the moment. I could worry about fixing my nose after I survived this game.

The giant lizard on the island eyed me lazily, then lay down to sun itself—where was the sunlight even coming from? It shifted. Two legs and a stump moved. The last leg did not. I squinted. There was something near its foot, obscured by its thick tail. I needed to get closer.

How do I move?

My choices were limited. I stuck my hand back into the water and pushed it back like an oar. The bow of the boat shifted slightly. I sighed.

The journey to the island was painfully slow. K'azen must

be enjoying watching me struggle at a worm's pace. I alternated between the two sides of the tiny boat, pushing the water with my hands to move it forward a hair's distance at a time.

There had to be a better way. I lifted my hands out of the water. Astra shaped her arms and fingers at will. Could I do the same? I closed my eyes and concentrated.

My body shifted. The sensation was strange. My bones moved. I gasped at the odd feeling. It was like trying to hold multiple pieces of a puzzle in the air so they could be joined together all at once, forming the perfect picture. Except I had far more pieces than hands and the puzzle's solution was not quite in view. Adding to that was the foreign and incredibly uncomfortable sensation of rearranging my own body from the inside out. It wasn't so much pain as an unbearable, itchy grind that couldn't be relieved. The sensation was even worse than the energy projectiles. I opened my eyes and my bones snapped back into place. Gritting my teeth, I relented to my fate and continued my extremely slow push toward my destination.

My arms were sore by the time I was close enough to take a good look at the island. The lizard gave me a lazy look and went back to sunning itself. I steered the boat until I was looking at its scaly form from behind and tried not to think too hard about how easily those sharp claws could pierce my skin. As I rounded the far side of the island, I finally understood the game.

A thick chain wrapped around its left hind leg; one end was secured on a thick metal pike with a large metal lock. The lizard shifted and the short chain clanked but did not go very far. An almost comical-looking red arrow was painted on the lizard's flank, pointing at something shiny nestled against the crook of its tail—a box.

I assessed my options—there weren't many. I could paddle to the shore and see if anything useful could be found, but I could already see all around the cove from where I was and there was nothing of interest. In fact, the cove appeared to be enclosed. I hadn't noticed until now, but the mountains formed a full circle around the cove—really more of a lake. I had nothing at my disposal but the boat.

I could try to sneak onto the island, though there wasn't much space to sneak. I could attempt to throw a rope or hook to grab the box. That thought made me laugh, seeing how I probably couldn't even manifest a proper rope in the first place, much less throw it with any amount of accuracy.

The lizard's red eyes followed the movement of the boat. If it felt threatened, it wouldn't hesitate a moment to bite me in two.

If it felt threatened.

I moved the boat a little closer. The lizard pushed its front legs against the ground and lowered its head. If this was indeed meant to be the same animal constructed from my memory, then it was a pebble lizard no matter how big it was. And Rosi had shown me exactly what to do with an agitated pebble lizard.

I paddled the boat around the island until I could see the box clearly. The lizard's tongue flicked in and out of its mouth, a sign of unease.

I moved the boat in a zigzag pattern, approached the island slowly, and avoided direct eye contact with the lizard. It relaxed a little until the boat touched the land. Then, it stood and maneuvered its body to face me.

I didn't stand. Instead, I crawled out of the boat on all fours, keeping my head close to the ground. I moved slowly, inching forward, continuing in a wide zigzag, practically staying in place as I crawled back and forth. The lizard watched me, then looked away and lay down again.

It was working.

It hissed. I'd let down my guard and moved too quickly. I slowed my pace and kept my distance. This couldn't be rushed.

Sand and stones dug into my hands and knees, but I

couldn't move faster. I was already tired. Patience had never been my strong suit.

It took at least half a day. I got close to the lizard bit by bit. It alternated between being agitated and relaxing. The box was nearly within reach when it finally decided it had had enough.

It only took half a blink's time. One moment I was reaching toward the box, victory in sight; the next its teeth were buried in my calf. I bit back a scream as searing pain coursed through my body. I sank my teeth deep into my lower lip and tasted blood.

Don't scream.

I tightened my fists and fought against the pain. I had to stay calm. It was only biting for now. If I screamed, it might startle and pull.

"It's okay," I said, half to myself and half to the lizard. Its teeth were still in my leg. I could feel it piercing my muscles, sinking deeper. I laid a hand on its tail.

"It's okay," I said again through gritted teeth. "See? No harm done."

I slid my hand back and forth gently. The teeth in my leg loosened ever so slightly. I hummed. Softly at first, then louder as I rubbed its tail.

Slowly, gradually, the teeth pulled out of my leg. The lizard drew its head back and regarded me with curiosity. I didn't look up at it, but I smiled. The last time it had looked at me like this, I had just caught it after it took a nosedive off the dining table.

"Thanks," I said. Blood gushed out of the holes on my leg, but my fingertips touched the edge of the metal box. I pulled it close to me and opened it. Inside was a key. I dragged myself over to the metal pike, unlocked the large lock, and unwound the chain the best I could. When it was done, I finally looked up at the lizard.

"Well," I said tiredly. "There you go."

The lizard blinked. Then, slowly, it lifted itself onto its three legs and one stump. Its enormous tail swept across half the island as it dragged itself to the edge of the water, waded in, and swam away.

My leg bled. I maneuvered myself into a half-sitting position, hissing in pain. Two crescent rows of holes led nearly to my bone. The sight of it made me gag.

A single ring appeared on the little finger of my left hand. It was gold and embedded into the skin like a metallic tattoo. A mark for my victory? I didn't have the energy to think about it. Every movement was painful. I couldn't even stand. I willed the wounds to close. For a moment it seemed like it could almost work. The torn flesh constricted, pushing more blood out in the process. But the moment I relented my effort, it snapped back into place.

"You have completed the round successfully."

I looked up at Om's expressionless face in irritation. "Yes," I said. "I did."

"The second round will begin soon."

"You're going to have to give me a moment," I said, gesturing at my bloody leg. "I can't stand up."

"That is of no consequence."

"Easy for you to say," I replied. "There are holes in my leg. What do you expect me to do?"

"That is—"

He stopped. I regarded him curiously. He didn't just stop speaking—everything on him paused as if someone pressed a button. It only lasted a moment, but I saw it. When it passed, he knelt without a word and began to mime a strange motion around my wounded leg.

I held my breath and kept still. He repeated the motion a few times and appeared to be thinking. Then, he made a wide motion in the air with one hand and a white strip, as wide as his hand, appeared. He wrapped it around my leg. It tightened itself around my wounds as it was applied. The look of concentration on his face was too familiar.

The last time he'd made those motions, I was bandaging

his severed leg in the capsule as he looked on, still in the body of a child, copying my movements as I went.

Full reset. Complete erasure.

He wasn't supposed to remember.

"Om?"

He reached up and put a hand on my cheek. I gasped in pain and surprise as my nose snapped back into place. I drew a breath and felt the air rush in clean and clear. I moved my leg carefully. With the wound properly dressed, the pain lessened.

And he was gone. I had just enough time to feel my heart skip with hope when everything went black.

CHAPTER 32

"KOVA?"

A hand touched mine and I jerked away in alarm, only to go tumbling off a nearby ledge. My body struck the ground gracelessly and I heard someone gasp.

"Oh my! Are you alright?"

I sat up. Dim light seeped in from behind semitransparent curtains. A shuffle of feet and someone was in front of me, helping me up. I stood and my long red locks fell over my shoulders.

"That was quite a fall," said the person who helped me up. A hand slipped around my waist. Soft lips found mine. "Come back to bed."

I jerked my head around the dim room. As my eyes began to adjust to the darkness, I began to recognize the shapes. The bed, the dresser, the walls. My wedding gown was laid carefully on a chair in the corner. A quick look down revealed I was wearing not a form-fitting gray suit but a loose, flimsy nightdress.

Meli smiled and guided me back to bed. I sank down onto it heavily. She held my hand and gave me a concerned look.

"You look ill, love," she said. "What's on your mind?"

I touched the strands of hair hanging over my arms. It was

still long and luxurious, just like how it was on my wedding night—tonight. I looked toward the bedroom door. It was shut. Did I not sneak out there in the dead of night, dressed in next to nothing, and . . .

"Kova?"

Pictures. Sounds. Pain. Panic. They had been so vivid a moment ago. But now, sitting in my marriage bed, with Meli's hand around mine, the memories melted away. I tried holding on to them, but they slipped further out of my grasp with every passing moment.

"I was . . ." I muttered hesitantly. "I was dreaming."

"What about?"

A woman with a crystal face. A man with white skin.

I shook my head. The images faded. "Nothing. It's not important."

Meli pulled the blanket over both of us and draped an arm loosely over my waist. "Get some rest," she said, snuggling against me. "We have a busy day ahead of us."

I lay on my side, staring into the darkness and trying to recall the evening. We had gotten married. I'd snuck out into the garden shortly after Meli fell asleep and tried to access the egg.

Capsule.

But the code didn't work. Or the door was rusted shut. It never opened. I never managed to get inside.

Hi. I am E-V.

I'd had a small fit, but ultimately realized it was a foolish delusion. Did I really think that chasing a silly dream from my childhood was going to change everything? My world was small. It had been the walls of my mother's house, and now it was the walls of Meli's house.

I was where I was meant to be.

Home.

There was something else in the back of my mind. A voice that sounded almost like my own. It was shouting, but so very far away. I was tired. Somehow, I felt like it had been ages since I slept in a soft, warm bed.

I came home.

Despite my best efforts, I drifted off to sleep, dreaming of dark space and white orbs.

I WOKE up to sunlight streaming through the curtains. Meli was already gone. A maid entered with a silver tray and left before I could mutter a thanks. I sat up. My hair was a matted mess, and my back was stiff. I poured myself a cup of hot tea from the pot on the tray and took a careful sip. It was a little bitter, but the heat was welcoming.

If you melt them, they make for a passable drink.

I shook my head. After I'd failed to find my way into the metal egg, the rest of my night had been filled with strange, vivid dreams. I'd even fallen out of bed once. What would Mother say if she saw me act like such a fool on my wedding night?

I got out of bed. Another maid came and took the tray and teapot, then a third brought me the outfit that had been selected for the day. Everything in Meli's household ran like a well-oiled machine. I ought to get used to it. After all, it was my household now, too. I cleaned up, brushed oil into my hair, set it just how Mother liked it, and got dressed in the green gown Meli had custom fitted for me. The first maid returned to help me lay a crescent of gems around my eye. When it was all done, I looked at myself in the mirror.

I looked like a married woman, whatever that meant. But that was what Mother would say.

"Kova?"

Meli stood at the door. She looked radiant as usual. Every hair in place, silks and pearls draped in layers of tame luxury.

"Are you ready?" she asked, beaming. "Oh, don't you look

lovely. Come, the guests will be here very soon. I can't wait to show you off."

"Be there soon," I said. She disappeared out the door again.

Show me off.

Those words stirred something in me, but I brushed them off. I ran the brush through my long hair again.

In the light of day, the choice was clear. Last night was only a moment of madness. Wedding jitters. What did I think was going to happen if I managed to pry that rusted pile of junk open? I ought to be glad that no one had caught me. I wouldn't want my new wife to think I was snooping around on such an important night.

I was exactly where I was meant to be. I fit in here. This was where I was meant to live and stay.

Home.

THE HOUSE WAS FILLED with guests—yet another thing I would have to get used to, being a member of this household. Meli was a woman of society, and as her wife, I must present myself as the picture-perfect match to her. While Mother and Daris had trained me for this my entire life, taking lessons and stepping into the arena were two entirely different things.

Brunch had been laid out in the main hall. I sat to Meli's right at the long table. Mother beamed at me from the other end. Several other family members and important guests whose names I had yet to memorize joined us. Other guests toasted us from their own tables.

I kept a smile on my face. Smiling was expected.

"Here's to many cycles of joy for the new family," someone said. Others cheered.

I smiled. Everything was normal.

"What a wonderful addition to my collection," Meli joked. Or at least, I thought it was a joke.

I smiled. Everything was comfortable.

"I think the madame of the house has finally found her prize," shouted someone who sounded undeniably inebriated from the far end of the room.

I smiled. Everything was safe. And simple.

I ate my meal and joined in the toasts. I had never seen Mother look so happy or proud. Several guests approached us to present us with gifts, as was tradition at the wedding brunch. Meli went out of her way to call the attention of the room as she laid the gift she got me around my neck—a large pink pendant on a thin silver chain. It was very much not to my taste, but I knew the script for receiving gifts by heart, so I feigned surprise and gave a delighted cry of joy, then made an exaggerated show of kissing her.

I was where I was meant to be. I could play this part. I was home.

"Aren't you tired of that?"

Of what? I nearly said, then I realized the question had come out of my own mouth. Meli gave me a confused look.

"What did you say, love?"

I quickly smiled. My smile was my shield. "Nothing," I said. "I was just wondering if you're tired. It's been a busy few days."

"Oh, love." Meli gave my hand a squeeze. "It certainly has. How are you holding up?"

I nodded. "Fine. I just—"

Just what?

"I'm a little drowsy," I said. "I'll go freshen up a bit."

I stood. Mother stopped me to ask if I was alright, and I reassured her I was only going to use the washroom. Meli had turned her attention to her guests as I left the dining hall. Galen watched me go. I avoided meeting his gaze.

In the washroom, I splashed a bit of water on my cheeks, careful not to disturb the meticulously laid gems around my left eye. They were different from the ones I wore for the wedding, which were circular, broad, and bright. These were small, flat, and in more uneven shapes, with almost an iridescent sheen. They looked almost naturally grown in the right light.

Like scales.

I exhaled.

I was exhausted, and the day's festivities had barely begun. I felt as if I hadn't had a good night's sleep in ages, and all the noise around me came in chaotic layers that gave me a headache.

I'm home.

I shook my head. Why did I keep thinking that? Who was I trying to convince?

I exited the washroom, and instead of heading back to the dining hall, went the opposite direction toward the garden. I pulled up my hem as I stepped outside, careful not to get my dress dirty.

The chilly sea air hit my face and I breathed a sigh of relief. I walked the perimeter of the garden slowly, admiring the flowers and lovely little pond.

Home.

I shook my head again.

I want to be home.

My body itched, as if my flesh was uncomfortable in its own skin. I looked up and for a moment expected to see the world fade away. Why? This was real. This was where I wanted to be, secure within walls that protected me. Walls I never had to leave if I didn't want to.

I want to be here.

My head thumped, like the beating of a distant drum. There was a humming in the air. A humming I knew. A humming that had accompanied me for a long time. But how could that be? I had never heard it before. I pushed it away.

I want *to be here.*

My gaze landed on the small structure in the far corner of the garden. Just last night, I was inside it, prying my fingertips to the bone trying to get the egg open. It never did budge.

Calibrating. Language set.

I wouldn't have found anything inside it anyway.

Taking off.

I tore my eyes away from it.

I am E-V.

I sank to my knees. Suddenly, getting the dress dirty didn't seem so important. I forced myself to take deep breaths as the world swam around me.

What *would* have happened if I'd opened it? Would it have shut me inside and flown away? I tried to laugh at that thought but found that I couldn't. I pictured myself standing inside the egg, looking out through the front window at Radley growing smaller and smaller below me, knowing I might never return to it again. It was a scary scene to picture. So final. So alien.

And so absolutely beautiful.

My arm stung. I looked down to see I had sunk my nails into my skin. I forced my fingers to loosen.

I don't want that. I want to be here.

A light plinking sound caught my ears. I lifted my gaze and realized I was next to the fountain. The circle of large stones around it was splashed with water droplets. The fish inside the pond swam to the surface, as if expecting food, then swam away when they realized I had nothing to give.

Plink. Plink.

I tried to focus on the sound their tail fins made as they broke through the water.

Plink.

I leaned over the edge of the fountain. The fish swam in hypnotic circles. I watched them, trying to clear my head.

A shuffle from behind me. I spun around just as a pair of hands wrapped around my neck and pushed my head underwater. I gasped and water flowed into my mouth and nose. I struggled and the hands held tighter, forcing my face deeper and deeper down. Through the water's hazy surface, Galen's stoic face stared back at me, mouth pursed in concentration as if focusing on a stubborn stain or difficult recipe.

I fought and clawed at his wrists. Water filled my lungs. I struggled to hold on to consciousness but was losing the battle rapidly. My strength left me. I was drowning.

A tiny red fish swam near me and flicked its tail just inside my field of vision. A tidal wave of images flooded my mind, rippled from that tiny movement.

A watery planet. Beautiful amphibious natives. His hand around mine. White face, blue eyes. I saw it for only a split second, but it was enough. Memories and sensations filled my mind. Darkness. Cold. Huddled for warmth and hoping death did not find us too quickly. Fear and panic and . . .

And . . .

I felt them again. The strings. They were all around me. I reached out with my senses, grabbed them, and pulled with all my might.

A burst of energy exploded from me. Suddenly, Galen's weight was gone. I sat up, gasping for air and blinking the water out of my eyes. Galen sat on the ground, a few steps away from me, looking dazed.

I moved before I could overthink, diving on top of him. I held him down with my weight and tightened my hands around his throat, the same way he held his around mine. Water dripped over my face and my mind cleared all at once. The clouds that had been wafting over my mind blew away.

My fingers tightened around his neck. My strength was not my own. The strings of the arena made me strong.

"You filthy commoner," he choked out under my grip. "You are not worthy of her."

"No," I said, struggling to see through my wet hair. "You're right."

"You don't love her."

"No. But you do."

He said nothing else. He didn't have to. He wasn't real. No

more real than the visions of Radley in winter, or the waters of Lynphix, or the mountains of Earth.

"Kill him."

I didn't see Om appear, but there he was, right next to us.

"In order to win the round, you must kill him."

I swallowed. Blood pounded in my ears.

This isn't real.

But it felt real. His body was warm. His eyes were fearful, but the bitterness seeped through. I'd seen the way he'd looked at me every time I stood at Meli's side. If I had stayed on Fiina that day, was this what would've happened? Would he have waited for a moment alone with me and ended my life right then?

My fingers shook. My body trembled.

Killing was an easy thing to think about, but faced with a living, breathing person, even in a dream state, it was something else entirely. The thought of digging my fingers into living flesh and watching the life drain out of someone's eyes was more than I could handle. I had already experienced this once in Able's orb, when I'd watched the light go out of a Harbinger's eyes as her blood seeped through my fingers.

We stayed that way for a long time, my hands at his throat. Or perhaps it only felt like an eternity.

I released him.

"I can't do it," I said shakily. "I can't do this."

The garden faded, along with Galen, the house, and the fountain. The colors melting away, the smells dissipating, even the movement of the breeze became a cold stillness.

It wasn't real after all. None of it, despite how desperately part of me wanted to cling on to it. My head felt like it was clearing as my memories sorted themselves out. I had left home. I might never go back.

And I was relieved.

I turned to Om.

"Did I lose?"

"Yes," he said. "You lost. Your score is now one win and one loss."

"You were going to make me kill him. With my bare hands."

"You could have chosen any method."

I stood. "This isn't you," I said. "*You* wouldn't make me do that."

"The game will continue," he said flatly, and disappeared.

CHAPTER 33

Another ring, this time on the fourth finger. This one was black instead of gold. Two rounds down. One win, one loss.

I should've killed him.

I brushed the thought away. There was no point lying to myself. I couldn't do it. The sensation of sinking my fingers into Galen's flesh was far too real. Even given extra time, I couldn't really bring myself to kill someone with my own hands. And I hoped dearly that K'azen would stand by his claim of being fair and not force me to attempt it a second time.

Meli's house and garden were gone, replaced by a thick gray fog. The ground beneath me had changed from the lush garden lawn to a dry, cracked dirt surface.

My gray suit, the same one I'd worn since stepping aboard E-V, was back in its place. There was something comforting about the sight of it. The bandage around my leg was back as well. I ran a hand through my hair—coarse, choppy, and short. Just a moment ago, it had been hanging down close to my waist, brushed and oiled to perfection.

The previous round was fading. The sensation was like waking from a dream—ironic, since I'd entered it thinking this was the dream I was waking from. The difference between reality and illusion was becoming increasingly blurry. I still recalled the sheets on Meli's bed against my skin, the smell of the food in the dining hall, and the strain of my muscles as they pulled my face into stiff smile after stiff smile.

It was so real. When I was in it, there was nothing that could've convinced me otherwise. My mind and body alike had bought into the illusion, like my reality shifted at a whim and I was completely ready to accept it. Was this real? Or was I just waking up over and over through layers of dreams? I closed my eyes and shook my head.

It doesn't matter.

When I opened my eyes again; the fog had receded enough for me to make out the building in front of me. A little house with a familiar thatched roof. The ground behind me led to a slanting slope. I'd spent some of the best times of my childhood rolling down this hill and picking rosalit flowers.

Home.

But it wasn't quite the same. The ground beneath me, once filled with soft weeds and crawling, pill-shaped bugs, was dry and lifeless. There were no rosalits in sight. A breeze blew through, and I smelled salt. Radley Cove was still there, or rather I assumed it still was. Much of the area around me was still obscured by fog. What version of it was I going to see this time?

A rattling behind me. The wind had blown open the door to the house. Unable to stem my curiosity, I stuck my head through, wary of something leaping out at me. But nothing happened. I stepped inside. It was eerily quiet, though exactly how I remembered it. I crossed the living room to the kitchen, sliding my fingers along the surfaces I passed. It didn't look abandoned. Nothing was worn or dusty. If not for the strange fog and dead hill outside, I could almost convince myself it was real.

At the dining room I stopped.

Two people sat at the dining table. I recognized them even before seeing their faces. Four more chairs sat empty—Father's,

Uttam's, my seat at Mother's right hand, and one at the end of the table, for Rosi.

Neither of them turned to look at me. In fact, neither of them moved. They sat, stiff as boards. There was no food or drink on the table. As I drew closer, I spotted another person at the corner of the room. Kit, larger than life as always, stood in her usual spot as if waiting to serve, but there were no plates being laid out or meals being cooked. She simply stood in place, hands folded, eyes looking forward at nothing. I gave a wide berth to the people at the table and approached her. The sound of my own footsteps was far too loud against the floor, so I tiptoed. Kit didn't turn. Her face had a strange, grayish pallor to it.

I waved my hand in front of her face, but she didn't blink. I snapped my fingers next to her ear and she didn't flinch.

I went to the table.

There they sat. Mother at the head of the table, Prin at one of the middle seats. Uttam wasn't here. Of course he wasn't. He hadn't been home in several cycles. They sat with their backs straight, eyes forward. Prin was dressed to impress as always. My father wasn't in sight either. If I ventured down the hall, I might find him in the same room he'd spent the last few cycles in as his health deteriorated.

I circled the table. No one acknowledged me. Mother and Prin shared Kit's gray pallor and colorless lips. As I approached Prin, I cautiously held out a hand in front of her face.

"Prin?" I said. No response. I moved my hand closer, slightly fearful that she might lunge forward and bite me.

"Prin?" I said again. My fingers were right in front of her nose.

There was no breath coming out of her.

I shuddered. The room full of my dead relatives suddenly felt terribly constricting. I pulled my hand away from Prin and my finger brushed her cheek as I did.

Images and emotions exploded in my head. I reeled and

nearly passed out. Time pulled into itself like a contracting muscle, then sprang loose in every which direction, without logic and order.

I lived as Prin standing in front of the mirror naked, a child barely in their teens, searching for all the faults on their body, their heart wrought with self-loathing.

I lived as Prin, just having given birth to her first child, breathing a sigh of relief that they were born healthy and ungendered. I felt her fear, ever so slightly, at the thought of becoming a pariah in Mother's eyes for having a child with any flaw at all.

I lived as Prin, on the eve of my own first night home as an infant, themselves a mere child, confused and jealous, knowing they were never going to be first in Mother's eyes.

I lived as Prin, two bynights before her wedding, sneaking down to the cove to meet with a girl who worked selling dry goods on the docks. She had coarse hands but soft lips and warm thighs, both of which Prin savored for the last time with tears in her eyes.

I lived every moment of Prin's life. Every emotion she'd ever experienced flooded my senses. I felt every scene with painful intensity, and as soon as one lifted, I was thrust into another. It was all too fast and yet excruciatingly slow. I couldn't breathe or move. My mind was heaved around like a ragdoll in a whirlwind.

I dropped to the floor. Before I even hit the cold surface, Prin's life had faded. That fall lasted an entire lifetime. I sat there, dazed, feeling as if I'd just spent my whole life—or rather, Prin's whole life—walking through a tunnel and had just emerged on the other side. Even the air tasted different.

A creaking sound. I quickly scooted back as Prin's chair moved. But she didn't get up. She only turned slightly, pushing her chair just enough back to twist her torso. From where I sat on the floor, I watched her neck turn stiffly until she faced the dining room window, then stop.

I got to my feet, poised to defend myself. Prin didn't move. Her empty eyes continued to stare forward. Though wary of taking my eyes off her, I followed her gaze to the window.

Most of the fog outside had cleared, and I could see the hill leading down to Radley Cove. There wasn't a single blade of grass or one living tree in sight. The entire hillside was covered in dry, cracked dirt. Even the hills surrounding the cove were bare of life, and the cove itself was dry as well. From where I was, I could make out the inlet leading to the sea. It had been blocked by a pile of debris. All up and down the hill, standing with empty gazes, were people.

I left the house.

Some of the people I recognized; others I didn't. But for the most part, they were locals. Old man Neeli stood in the middle of the street in front of my house, gray-skinned and mouth agape. I approached him and waved a hand in front of his face. Unsurprisingly, he didn't respond. I braced myself and touched his cheek with my fingertip.

His memories assaulted me.

I felt the pain from when he broke his leg as a teen, climbing over a wall to escape the bandits who'd killed his parents. I clenched my teeth as he dragged himself over two hills on that shattered leg to get away.

I suffered the relentless hunger of his childhood, eating dirt to stave off the pangs of starvation.

I wiped away the hot tears that flowed down his face the very first time he was given a hot meal while working on the docks of Radley.

My heart burst with joy on the day he married his husband and wife, then fell to pieces when they disappeared after the orb's arrival. I felt the cold barrel of the gun against his forehead the night he thought about ending it all on his own terms rather than wait out his life alone.

A second and an eternity crashed down all around me. I stepped back from old man Neeli and threw up. The toll of processing another person's whole life in the space of a blink was indescribable. I bent over, panting as I collected myself. When I looked up, old man Neeli had moved.

And like Prin, he looked toward the dried cove.

I made my way down the hill toward the cove, walking slowly and giving the standing corpses a wide berth. Exhaustion threatened to overtake me, and I had to sit down and rest twice. Memories came and went. Memories that weren't mine. They played in a relentless loop. Old man Neeli's memories mixed with Prin's, cycling like an endless video with no pause button.

I reached the cove. There was not a single drop of water in the basin, and seeing it empty made it seem far larger than usual. The white pebbles of Prickle Beach crunched under my feet as I walked around its perimeter. I was just beginning to wonder what the purpose of the drained cove was when a glint caught my eye. I stepped over the edge of the basin and made my way down.

Toward the center of the empty cove, sitting among ordinary pebbles, was a single shining nugget. I kicked it with my foot. It was a little larger than my palm, with reasonable heft. I picked it up and turned it over. A single word was written on it.

Prin.

I looked down to where I'd picked it up just in time to see another rock take on a golden sheen. I watched with a curious sense of dread as a word appeared on its surface. Even before it finished, I knew what it was.

Neeli.

I threw the rock away and scanned the cove. How many rocks were here? Thousands? Tens of thousands? More? Millions? Now that I took a closer look, the rocks inside the cove were different from the pebbles on the beach. They were larger, symmetrical, and all roughly the same shape and size.

I trekked out of the empty cove and back to town, passing standing corpses as I did. Dock workers, sailors, street vendors, pedestrians. A lone figure on a park bench caught my eye and I stopped in my tracks.

Meli Veti sat with her hands folded in her lap, gazing out at the sea. Even in death, she was a vision of elegance wrapped in green and white silks. I sat down next to her.

She was my wife. Or, she almost was. I'd been in her marriage bed twice now. Once on Fiina, once in this strange dream. It was funny what a presence she'd had and continued to have in my life despite being worlds away.

I reached out carefully and put a hand over hers.

Empty.

I felt it intensely. Though her life was full, her heart was empty. I followed her through her travels around Fiina, from the adventures and thrills she experienced to the accomplishments she amassed. She spent most of her life drinking in new experiences, seeking out new things, and yet was never quite full. Something was missing.

I saw myself. That very first moment when Meli saw me and realized I was a true beacon. There was a *whoosh* of pleasure, which dimmed every time I was out of sight. Then, every time I came back, every time I showed interest in her baubles, every time I ran a hand through my long red hair, that *whoosh* was back. But then, after the wedding night, I saw it dimming again. She had me, but I did not fill the hole inside her. By the end of our wedding, it was already expanding, seeking something new. Meli, the forever collector, who always searched for what she couldn't seem to find, marrying a woman who didn't love her, but never able to open her eyes and see that the man who truly longed for her was in front of her all this time.

I released her hand. Exhaustion washed over me. I had nothing else left in me to throw up, but the dizziness remained all the same. The suns were dropping below the horizon. How long had I been here?

I left Meli on the bench and dragged myself up toward the

house. When I looked back, she had turned to face the cove. I had a feeling there was now a golden rock with her name on it.

One at a time.

Inside the house, I turned on every light I could find. Seeing Mother and Prin in the light was no less eerie than in the dark, but I still preferred the house to be lit. I found Father's room, where he sat in his usual lounging chair, and turned on his light as well. I went to the washroom, cleaned the wound on my leg from the first round, and redressed it. Then I went back to the kitchen, found Kit's stash of smokeweed sticks, lit one on the stove, and carried the rest back to my room.

It looked just how I remembered it from the final night before my wedding. I sat down on the bed, opened the window, and let the sea air in. I took long drags and blew smoke out into the quiet night. There wasn't a single lit house, no street lanterns, and no bright shop fronts. I'd never realized how busy the night was until it all went away. By the light of my window, I could see the silhouette of a few corpses on the street not far from the house. I was quickly getting used to the idea of them, though the paranoia that they posed some kind of danger was still there. I smoked the first stick down, used it to light the next one, and finished that one, too. After the third, I closed the window and latched it, then lay down on the bed. Something wedged against my leg. I reached down and felt the exit token in my pocket. I held it between my fingers, listening to the wind whistle outside my window, until sleep eventually took over.

They were still there in the morning. Where else would they go?

I rooted through the food pantry, found some bread, and ate it with a cup of water. The morning was gray and chilly, and I was becoming far too used to looking at my dead family.

I limited myself to two pieces of bread, partially remembering yesterday's experience and partially because I felt like I ought to be restrained with the food supply just in case . . .

Just in case of what?

I pushed the thought away and approached Mother. Though I wasn't sure what I expected to find, I braced myself nonetheless. Taking several deep breaths, I carefully reached out with one finger and touched her cheek.

Struggle.

I grimaced.

Her life was a struggle. My entire body strained as her muscles worked. Lifting crates of boxes, smelling of fish, splashed with ocean water and teeth chattering from the cold.

I had never known she'd worked on the docks. Now that I thought about it, she'd never told me much about her life before I was born, and I never thought to ask. Some part of me had simply assumed that she was always the Mother I knew, and that the meticulous and mannered ways she forced on the family were learned from her childhood.

I watched her work as a young teen, lugging cases of fish and using her height to her advantage to lie about her age in order to obtain work. I had never known the side of my grandparents that she knew—drunk, delirious from narcotics, and rarely saying a word when she returned home every night with just enough money to buy food.

I didn't know the money often went to more narcotics before she could fill her belly.

Or that she wept nightly, wishing for something better.

Or that she wished to invigorate as male, but her parents had no interest or money to pay for the common and widely available procedure.

Or that she vowed to herself that her children would live better. That if she ever birthed her own children, she would make sure those children had every advantage and walked the right path at every step.

My chest ached, both from her pain and mine. Her grief

during those fragile, vulnerable times cut me deeply in my own flesh. It was relentless, overwhelming, almost as bad as her impatience and fear after she became a mother herself, living daily with the paranoia that she would fail to build her golden child—me—into the ideal person with the life she'd always dreamed of. She believed wholeheartedly that she had been granted a beacon as both a reward for her suffering and a sign that she must do right by me in every way imaginable. Every time I did not act as she wished or failed to meet expectations, her fear grew. My marriage to Meli was her ultimate triumph, her final proof that she wasn't destined to carry her misery and bad luck through future generations.

Then, Rosi.

I looked down in my arms, an infant with red hair. Someone approached and brought me another—one with a messy tuft of white hair. A *female* baby, born gendered.

Except she wasn't born to me—or rather, Mother.

I—Mother—looked up. Next to her stood Kit, the maid. The expression on her face could only be described as sad and complicated.

"I will raise this child," I said with Mother's mouth. Her insides were filled with turmoil—anger, frustration, bitterness—but her voice was even and steady. "I'll even accept her defects and call her my own. I will call her Kova's twin. So long as no one outside this house knows that their father sired a child with the help."

Then, Uttam.

He left.

I—Mother—sat by the window the entire night after his departure, watching the rosalits sway in the wind and gazing out to the cove. Would he return? She wanted him back with a painful desperation. He was her only son. Had she done wrong by him, trying to force him into the life she wanted? It couldn't be. She knew best. He didn't live with the hardship she had spared him from, the hardship that she grew up knowing with great intimacy. She protected him, but now he had left her, walked away from beneath her wings. She could no longer keep him safe, and that thought wormed itself inside her like a parasite, burrowing and chewing. She wept until the dawn, then dried her tears with the new resolve that she needed to work harder, to try harder, to make sure that her daughters walked the right path.

I burst breathlessly from the mirage of her life, feeling as if I'd just run halfway around the world. Panting, I collected myself, then nearly jumped out of my skin when I saw that she was now looking directly into my eyes. I stepped aside, expecting her to follow me with her gaze, but she didn't—she was looking toward the window, same as Prin.

I leaned against the kitchen counter. Waves of nausea overcame me and I fought them down.

Mother's face was illuminated by the cool, dusty sunlight streaming in from the window. She looked old, and not just because she was dead in this silent world. Had she always looked so tired? In my mind, she was always full of energy, forever on the go, always thinking ten steps ahead. I had lived by her script, never quite understanding why. If I had known . . .

If I had known, would I have stayed and followed through with my marriage to make her proud?

That was not a question I wanted to answer. It was too late for that. How did she fare, I wondered as an unexpected wave of sadness came over me, when she found out I was gone? Suddenly, I wished I could tell her that I was alright.

Although "alright" was such a strange concept given my current situation.

I was already worn out and the day had only just begun. How many did I have left? I knew the answer but didn't want to admit it. How long would it take to turn every rock in the cove into gold?

Able had said something about this, didn't he?

Sixty cycles walking a dead planet.

Astra had done this. I didn't know if her circumstances had been similar, but she'd spent most of a lifetime in one round and lived to retain her sanity.

Sixty cycles. An entire lifetime.

I couldn't breathe. Pressing my back against the kitchen counter, I slid to the ground, huffing in short, rapid breaths. My heart beat against my rib cage. My mother and sister sat in silence, empty eyes staring forward. The sight of them made me sick. I retched. My stomach tried to force its way out of my body. My hands shook and I couldn't stop them.

The rest of my life.

For the rest of my *life*.

I spiraled, caught in a hurricane of fear and dread.

I had *left*.

I'd run away because I couldn't stand the thought of being trapped there for the remainder of my days. And now I was about to face the same fate, but a hundred times worse, locked on this planet with the dead bodies of everyone I'd ever known.

I can't do it.

I can't.

I can't.

Not for the rest of my life.

I CAN'T.

Before I could stop myself, my hand had reached into my pocket and taken out the token K'azen gave me. I pressed it between my hands. Black spots swirled before my eyes. The pain in my chest consumed me.

"You will only be able to use the token once."

I forced myself to breathe and focus. He stood before me with his blank game host's expression. I glared at him as my heart threatened to pound out of my chest.

"What do you care?" I asked angrily. "I can use it if I want, right?"

He looked at me for a long moment, then repeated the

statement.

"You will only be able to use the token *once*."

I studied him. His tone was different. He wasn't merely speaking. He was giving me a genuine warning. My grip on the token loosened as I took a step toward him.

"What's your name?" I asked him, getting to my feet. He looked at me blankly and rattled off a series of numbers and letters. I grabbed his wrist. "That's not what I meant. I—"

"Kova."

I blinked. My house was gone.

I was in the control room of the black orb. Not Astra's orb—the arrangement of the screens was different. There was a black obelisk in the center of the floor, but it was so badly fractured that there was very little of it left. A small glob of green substance bubbled in the middle of the fragments, barely held together by the pieces around it. None of this was familiar, but there was one thing I recognized.

K'azen stood across the room from me.

No.

This was Om.

I watched his thoughtful expression as he studied the screens in front of him. It was amazing how different he looked from K'azen, despite inhabiting the same body. He didn't acknowledge me. Instead, his attention was on the displays that showed different parts of the orb.

There was me, locked in the tiny room. On the next screen were Two and Able. Another screen showed Solace, still unconscious on the floor. Om watched Two and Able for a moment, then turned to the broken obelisk, where he knelt and lifted a hand. One of his fingers lengthened and sharpened into a fine point, not unlike the way Astra frequently transformed her arm. He dug the point into the side of the obelisk, and it began to spin with a soft whirr, like a tiny drill. Slowly, a pinpoint hole formed. Om stood, glanced at the screen again as if to make sure Two and Able hadn't left their spot, then gave the obelisk a small but firm kick. The green substance began to leak slowly out of the hole he'd made in a thin, barely visible trickle.

He walked away. I followed him, moving behind him though I couldn't quite feel my body in space. He moved quickly, navigating hallways and descending steps until he reached the basement.

He stopped at one of the doors. This door I knew.

If Mother or Daris ever saw how gracelessly I sprawled on the floor of this dingy room, they would surely faint in embarrassment. But Om didn't take notice. He knelt and gently lifted me into a sitting position. My head lulled uselessly, and he propped it against his shoulder.

I don't remember this.

He adjusted my limp body until he could peek at the back of my neck. There was a thin line there, barely visible. He lifted his hand again, this time shifting his finger into the shape of a scalpel. He slid it along my skin, cutting the exact length of the scar, revealing a tiny metallic strip underneath. A red light blinked slowly on and off, barely visible—the chip that Astra used to track me.

Om examined the chip for a moment, then shifted his finger into a fine needle point. I couldn't tell what he was doing, only that it was delicate, precise work. A few nerve-wracking seconds later, the red light began to blink rapidly. He held a hand over the opening on my skin and when he lifted it, the wound had closed, once again becoming a neat, thin scar. He laid me back down on the floor, careful to cradle my head so it didn't hit the hard ground, then stood and left.

I REELED AS if I'd been struck by lightning. My fingers loosened around Om's wrist and he immediately disappeared.

I stood in place, stunned. I knew this feeling. I'd felt it before. Back in the dream state, when I saw his memory of him and me, walking down the snowy streets.

"Om!" I called, and my other hand tightened around the escape token. The world disintegrated around me.

CHAPTER 34

ANOTHER BLACK RING APPEARED, THIS TIME AROUND MY MIDDLE finger. I was out of chances.

My dead family was gone, as was Fiina. Instead, I found myself at the top of a high mountain covered in red foliage. Rising and falling peaks surrounded me, extending infinitely into the distance. On the ground beneath my feet was an arrow pointing to the edge of a high cliff. I followed it, peeking over the edge carefully.

The height made my knees weak. Having grown up on the gentle hillside of Fiina, the steep fall was both unpleasant and unwelcome. I pulled back, gathered myself, and forced myself to look over again.

A rough path had been laid out down the side of the cliff—ladders, protruding handholds, and platforms just big enough to stand on extended all the way to the ground below, where I could make out another arrow pointing into a thicket of crimson trees.

An obstacle course. Out of all the scenarios Mother had scripted for me growing up, this was *definitely* not one of them.

It was going to take a lot more than sheer athleticism—which I already lacked—to make it through. The platforms and handholds were too far apart to be of any proper use. I could only guess that to avoid plunging to my death and immediately losing the round, I had to use some manner of manifestation.

The thought made me shudder. The dark capsule came to me again. I stepped back from the cliff, collected myself, and tried to relax. But the momentary calm fizzled when something else caught my eye.

Another person stood at the edge of the cliff. I had to blink twice to make sure I wasn't hallucinating. The last time I'd seen him, he was walking away from the house, his back silhouetted against a field of rosalit flowers.

"Uttam?"

No response. I waved to him. He didn't wave back. He stood still and silent, hands in his pockets. He was wearing the same dark trousers and fisherman's jacket he'd worn when he left the house for the last time.

"Your goal is to complete the course."

I started at Om's voice. He stepped next to me and pointed toward the horizon.

I stared at him. Was the vision I'd seen at the end of the last round real or just a wishful hallucination? His blue eyes betrayed nothing.

I pointed to Uttam. "Why is he here?"

Om ignored me. "Your goal is there. Follow the arrows and they will guide you." He pointed toward the sky, where a large red circle appeared. "The countdown will begin when you leave this platform."

"Hey!" I said, raising my voice. "That's my brother. What's he doing here?"

"He is one of your challenges."

"What does that mean?"

"It means in addition to completing the course on time, you must not come in second to him."

"It's a race?"

"In a manner of speaking."

I looked over the cliff's edge.

"This isn't doable," I said. "K'azen said he would ensure the game is fair. There's no way I can do this."

"You have full access to manifestation at the contestant level," Om said, as if that made any difference.

"You know what happened when I did that," I said, studying his face closely for a reaction. Again, he gave me nothing.

"The obstacles will come in many types. Some you will need to traverse, such as bridges, platforms, or rough terrain."

I reached out and pushed him, though the only one who stumbled from the effort was me. He was immovable.

"Some you will need to protect yourself from."

"What's your name?"

"Some may require ingenuity."

I grabbed his arm and shook him. He didn't move. I took his hand and squeezed his fingers. He didn't squeeze back.

"The time allotted is adequate to complete the course if you keep an even pace."

"Tell me your name," I said.

"The exit token has been expended, which means—"

"Answer me!" I screamed. "What's your name? Tell me your *name*!"

"—that if you lose this round, the game will end, and you will have lost."

I kicked him on the shin. It was like kicking a rock. I hobbled a few steps, shaking the pain from my toes. Om looked down at me with crystal blue eyes.

"Say your name."

He opened his mouth as if to say something, then frowned as if focusing on a difficult thought. But instead of answering me, he disappeared. The red circle above me began to tick down to white—the countdown had begun.

"Hey!" I shouted, but he was long gone. I eyed Uttam. He hadn't moved a single step this whole time. As I watched, he slowly lifted his head and turned to me.

All my life, Uttam had made no secret of the fact that he resented my very existence. He'd never spared me a modicum of affection, never lifted a finger to my aid, and never sent a smile in my direction. At best, he'd tolerated me as an inconvenience to his life. Any hope he'd had of being the favored child was dashed the moment the beacon was born. Even now, this copy of him constructed by the white orb looked at me with derision.

He'd hated being second to me. And now, he was here to ensure that I was second to him.

Uttam jumped. My stomach lurched at the height of the fall, but he landed perfectly on a small platform below. Then, expertly, he turned and began to climb down.

I scanned the grounds below me as well as I could from my position. The leaves were too thick to see through in most parts, but I could roughly make out a path that stretched into the distance. Where the trees ended, a narrow path extended into a deep valley between sheer cliffs. Wherever the end of the path lay, it was past that valley. I had a long way to go and no time to waste, especially if I was going to keep pace with Uttam.

I gritted my teeth and swung my legs over the cliff edge. There was a platform below me, too far for me to reach, but I had to get down there somehow. Little by little, I pushed down, until I was hanging over the edge by my arms. I found a tiny foothold on the edge of the cliff, just barely big enough to grip with my toe.

If I could manifest energy, I could cushion my fall. If I—

My fingers slipped.

The good news was the platform was larger than I'd initially thought.

The bad news was it was also farther down than I initially thought.

I started to attempt a burst of energy to catch myself, but the sensation of it sent a shiver of uncertainty through me and whatever I almost managed to create fizzled before it could do any good.

My foot connected with the hard surface, followed by the rest of me, which crumbled like a sack as my ankle bone snapped in two.

Pain shot through me. I couldn't speak for a long moment as I stayed there in a bent pile, consumed by agony.

I can't do this.

A sound escaped me, somewhere between a gasp of pain and a sob. Below me, Uttam looked up. I could swear I saw him smirk at the sight of my crippled state. Then, he dropped down to the ground and disappeared among the leaves.

I didn't belong in this game.

I couldn't decide whether I wanted to cry or scream. I was sharing this orb with the cream of the crop from across the galaxy, people who had survived this game over and over. And I could barely get past the starting line.

Rosi would be so disappointed in me.

I rubbed my face hard with both hands.

Rosi, who wasn't my twin, but no less my sister. Rosi, who wanted me to join her out here in the great big universe. Rosi, who was so close and yet farther away than ever.

I thought of Rosi, hung up a limp puppet in a white basement, waiting for me. If I couldn't reach her, would she one day end an unnaturally long life singing her way into insanity like Axi and Viva?

No.

I couldn't allow that. Not after how far I'd come. This couldn't be what she wanted to show me. I refused to accept that.

I lay down on my back, staring up at the sky. My ankle throbbed. I closed my eyes and focused on the pain, wrapping my mind around it like an invisible bandage. A slew of mental blocks pushed themselves to the front of my mind, like error messages in a computer.

It won't work.

This is illogical.

You're being a fool.

My bones and muscles itched and pulled. I held tight, focusing on images and sensations instead of words. My mind and body resisted the effort. I pushed away the thoughts, the sensations, the doubts, all of it. My body burned. The pain grew like fire spreading through my nerves and tendons. I forced myself to keep breathing.

Strings wrapped around me, tightening, then tightening again, and all at once it was gone.

I opened my eyes. My leg bent and my foot flexed.

I sat up.

It worked.

I couldn't believe it. I was torn between laughing with triumph and weeping with relief. But if I celebrated, even for a moment, my fragile hold on this new reality might fall away. I could sense the strings of the arena around me, but my grasp on them was tentative at best, as if someone could yank them away at any moment. So I stood instead.

There was still a long drop to the ground below, and from this height I could see moving forms in the forest. Uttam was nowhere in sight, but I couldn't worry about him until I got down there.

Whatever was down there was likely hostile. My ankle tingled, as if responding to my creeping doubt. I quickly steered my mind toward Rosi again.

Rosi was waiting.

I jumped. The fall was terrifying, but I did not give in to fear. My confidence wavered but I held tight.

I struck the ground.

My body held. The balance in my mind was delicate, like looking at an optical illusion and trying to hold steady the elusive hidden image that could go away with every slight shift of the body or eye. And yet, at just the right angle, it was there, clear as day.

The first form stepped into view, their stark white body contrasting harshly against the red leaves.

A Harbinger.

Another appeared, followed by another. They surrounded me, white faces staring blankly. I tried to keep my eyes on all of them at once. Their faces were featureless save for their bright eyes that shone in various colors. As far as I could tell, none of them was Om.

Every muscle in my body tensed as they began to change shape. I watched, terrified, as they lowered themselves down to the ground and stood on all fours. Their bodies expanded and their legs retracted until they took the forms of predators somewhere between canine and feline. I had seen Harbingers change their appearance, but this was something else entirely. Before my eyes, they were becoming animals, with claws and teeth meant to sink into my flesh.

Just beyond them, Uttam stood among the trees. He looked back at me with a smirk on his face. As soon as our eyes met, he turned and took off.

I ran.

I chased him and the Harbingers chased me. I could hear many feet hitting the forest floor behind me. Uttam picked up his pace and I struggled to keep him in sight, all the while far too aware of the pursers behind me.

Sharp claws shredded my clothes and pushed me down onto the ground. My face struck dirt and rock as teeth sank into my shoulder. I screamed and with all my strength spun myself around, swinging my arm at the white creature, snatching at the first image that came to mind.

It released me. I shoved it hard into the ground, panting. It struggled, twitched, and stopped moving.

I got to my knees and prepared to defend myself. But the Harbinger shivered, shook, and began to shrink. The powerful haunches and sharp claws disappeared, becoming slender limbs and narrow shoulders. I couldn't suppress a gag as I saw them lying there, a skinny, childlike Harbinger with a hole in their torso, leaking white fluid. They sputtered and their eyes rolled back.

My right arm had transformed into a long, hard spike that possessed the same texture as the pebbles in Radley Cove. It had driven through the Harbinger's side, deep into their body. The sight of it was so jarring that I immediately lost its shape. My arm snapped back into its normal form with a sound like bone breaking and I grimaced at the sensation.

More Harbingers stepped out of the thicket. But behind them, out of the corner of my eye, I saw a familiar shape.

Om stood silent, watching me.

"I'm sorry," I shouted. "I'm sorry. I'm so sorry!"

But he was gone. The others were approaching, more cautious now that they saw one of their own on the ground. I wanted to kneel by the wounded Harbinger and stop their bleeding, like I had in Able's orb, but if I did, the others would tear me apart.

Was K'azen ordering them to do this? Anger welled up in me at the thought of Om's kin being used like puppets once again. My shoulder stung and bled. I willed it to heal like my ankle, but only managed to stymie the bleeding. There was no way I could win this fight, and even if I could, I didn't want to hurt any more of them.

A rustling behind me. I turned to see Uttam disappearing among the foliage. Beyond the trees I could hear running water.

The Harbingers moved, and I ran.

A wide river appeared as the forest parted. It looked shallow enough to wade, but the current was fast and fierce. Uttam stepped into the water without hesitation. I let out a gasp, expecting the water to sweep him away. But he wobbled and held steady, fording through it without a look back.

The Harbingers were drawing close. If I tried to head down the shore, I would lose Uttam. I gritted my teeth.

If he could do it, I could do it, too.

I stepped into the river. The water threatened to knock me off my feet. I steeled myself and imagined my feet heavy as blocks of stone. They steadied and I righted myself, trudging forward as quickly as I could, each step tentative but stable. The Harbingers dove into the water after me, hot on my heels. I felt one of them nip at my elbow before it was washed away by the water with a surprised yelp.

The others realized their peril too late. I kept moving, focusing on keeping my feet steady as I trudged on. Behind me, I heard panicked splashing, but I couldn't afford to look back. One misstep, one moment losing focus, and I could lose my manifestation and be swept away. Clinging to the image of stones around my feet and hoping the Harbingers could take care of themselves, I forced myself on, one step at a time. The water was chest height now and the fierce current tore at me. I could barely breathe as I pushed forward. The sounds behind me lessened, then softened, then disappeared.

Uttam was only a few steps in front of me. The current had slowed him down. I quickened my pace as much as I could manage until I was beside him. He turned and regarded me silently.

"Looks like I caught up to you," I said.

He stared at me, and I suddenly realized I missed him. I hadn't seen him since he'd walked out of our home, and no one knew what happened to him. All those years we'd spent in rivalry—at least in his eyes—now seemed so petty. We were siblings, and though I hadn't realized it until now, I wished that he'd taken better memories of me with him when he left.

He reached out one hand. I thought for a moment he was about to embrace me. Then his palm connected with my face and shoved me under the water. I gasped and choked, and my feet lost their grip on the riverbed. The current dragged me away like a flailing fish in a net.

. . .

I COLLAPSED ON THE SHORE.

Where am I?

By the time I had managed to regain my footing and purge the water from my lungs, I had completely lost my bearings. Dragging myself to the nearest shore took everything I had and the fact that I ended up on the opposite side of the river from where I'd started was sheer luck. My soaked clothes and water-logged shoes clung to me like a soggy second skin. I rolled onto my back, and through the red leaves of the trees bent over me, I could see the countdown circle in the sky.

Uttam had attacked me.

I hadn't expected him to push me under the waves. But then, Om never said he wouldn't, did he? I forced myself to stand and wring the water out of my clothes, even though all I wanted to do was to lie in the dirt and sleep the next bynight away, hopefully waking up from this nightmare. Instead, I took a deep breath and moved on.

Finding my bearings wasn't terribly difficult, but making up for lost ground was. Despite moving at an unhurried pace, Uttam was still far ahead of me. I didn't lay eyes on him again for at least an hour, when I spotted his white hair entering the narrow valley in the distance. Whatever awaited me there, I had a feeling it wasn't going to be easy.

The valley floor was terribly narrow, barely wide enough for me to straighten out my arms on either side. Sheer cliffs dwarfed me, leaving only a narrow thread of sky above. I moved as quickly as I could manage in the cramped space, trying not to imagine myself buried alive if the cliff walls chose that moment to collapse.

A shuffle. I looked up. Something clung to the stone surface.

Something small and white.

I quickened my step. The figure on the cliff followed me. Thin, skinny, and completely white with sparkling blue eyes, button nose, and short white hair, they looked almost exactly like Om back when we'd spent those endless days in the capsule. As I moved, they followed, clinging to the cliff surface on all fours.

The valley was long, with no end in sight, and deathly silent save for my own footsteps. I hummed, trying to act nonchalant. The childlike Harbinger chirped at the sound of my voice. I purposefully ignored it.

The lower part of the valley grew narrower. There was now no room for me to extend my arms at all. A few hundred more paces and the cliff faces brushed against my shoulders. I had, literally, nowhere to go except forward.

And the Harbinger knew it. They drew closer to me gradually. Unlike the ones in the forest, this one was careful and observant. The narrower the space became, the closer they moved.

They dashed. I broke into a run. They chased me along the wall. I willed myself to move faster, but the curves and turns in the valley made things more difficult. My hands and arms scraped against the rock surfaces on either side of me. The road was so narrow that I could only move by placing one foot directly in front of the other, hindering my speed greatly.

A hurdle.

I saw it coming from far away. It was at least as high as my waist and blocked the entire width of the narrow valley. If I paused to climb, my pursuer was going to jump on me from behind. The thought of harming this little child stifled any chance of me forming a weapon of any kind.

Pitter-patter to my right. They were getting close. They knew my path was blocked.

I had no choice. I couldn't fight, and I couldn't stop. The hurdle was coming at me rapidly.

I jumped, willing myself to rise into the air, and for a moment it was as if the ground pulled out from under me. I flailed awkwardly in the air, sailing far higher than I expected.

For that brief moment, I found them again.

The strings. The last time I had felt them clearly was within the diorama of Om's memory. I grabbed them and they lifted me up. It was real, and natural, like moving an invisible extension of myself. The arena and I were one in those endless seconds. The valley floor and the hurdle moved below me as if in slow motion. I saw the Harbinger chasing me pause in their path, as if as surprised as I was.

The ground rushed up at me. I struck one wall, then struck the other. My shoulder scraped painfully against the rock, but at least my feet found purchase.

The line between fear and exhilaration was thin. The two fought against each other as I kept moving. My heart raced along with my feet as the second hurdle appeared. It was taller, almost as high as my chest. I didn't hesitate. I ran full speed and leapt, this time only brushing against one wall when I landed.

There was a groove to manifestation, a rhythm that followed the hum of the arena. It was easier to catch when I didn't pause to listen for it. Never in my life had I been allowed to speak without a script or act without premeditation. Astra had told me this before, but I had never understood until now. This was a place where instinct ruled.

The end of the valley was in sight, as was the third hurdle, taller than the top of my head. I ran toward it without fear and jumped.

And found nothing but sky. In my rush to reach the end, I had neglected to notice that what awaited after the valley was a fall.

The Harbinger jumped as well. I turned around in midair and saw them above me. There was nothing below but fog and clouds, and no matter where I landed, they were going to be on top of me, and we'd both be a pile of bones and guts.

I was going too fast. The Harbinger was wide-eyed, a frightened expression on their youthful face. Wind whistled all around us. I might have been screaming, but it was difficult to hear.

What do I do? What do I do?

A hundred ideas and images flashed through my mind, but nothing solidified long enough to make a difference. The clouds began to part. The ground was rushing up.

Slow down.

I have to slow down.

This was the only thought that stuck. I gritted my teeth and fists.

Slow down. Slow down. SLOW DOWN.

I slowed.

Everything slowed.

I inhaled and the entire world breathed with me. I floated in midair, so slowly it was as if time itself had stopped. The Harbinger above me moved their arms and legs as if through thick jelly. I moved my own hands in front of my face and felt resistance all around me.

Time had not slowed. The air around us had simply become thick, like the dense fog in Mother's holy ground.

I took a deep breath, then let it out, imagining that the air contracted around just me. The Harbinger suddenly sped up their descent and fell toward me. I opened my arms and they landed into my embrace. They stiffened in surprise, and I worried what would happen if they attacked me. But after a tense moment, they wrapped their arms around me and buried their face in my chest, shivering as we descended the dizzying heights.

"It's alright," I said as I held them against me tightly. "I got you."

Against the whistling wind, I thought I heard them whisper, "Al. Right. Alright."

HARD GROUND STRUCK MY BACK. I let out a breath of relief and felt my body settle against the rocky surface. Above me, the valley I'd fallen from was hidden above layers of fog and clouds.

I was alive.

I sat up and eyed the desolate tundra around me. The Harbinger huddled in my lap, shivering and refusing to let go. I pried their fingers loose gently and brushed white hair out of their face. They looked up at me uncertainly, as if trying to make sense of the situation.

"I told you I got you," I said, and smiled tiredly. They stared at me for a long time, then smiled as well.

"Your time is running short."

I lifted my gaze at the sound of Om's voice. He stood a few steps away, watching me. I nodded.

"I know," I said, and shifted the Harbinger child off my lap. I helped them to their feet and walked them over to Om. "Here, take care of them," I said, and handed their hand to him.

He looked down at the child with an unreadable expression, then looked back at me. I waited to see if he had something to say, but he reached out in silence. As he took the child's hand from me, I thought his fingers lingered against mine, but there was no time to dwell. Neither of them said anything as I turned away. There, in the distance, barely visible, Uttam. He stood with his hands in his pockets, looking back at me. In the arena, same as in life, the distance between us was vast, seemingly unbreachable. He had spent all of his life chasing after what I had, and when it looked like he was never going to get it, he took himself out of the race.

I stood.

Sorry, Uttam. You're not going to win this time either.

I MADE my way across the barren grounds. With the countdown ticking away, I had to move fast. Uttam stayed in front of me, sometimes closer, sometimes farther. Even though the tundra appeared to be free of anything posing immediate danger, sustaining speed using manifestation was still difficult. I hung on to the hum of the arena, kept my focus on the horizon, and tried not to overthink the breakneck speed at which I was moving. Any stumble, any distraction at all threatened to break my stride, and I tried hard not to think about the fact that if my feet tangled, I would go shooting forward and scrape the skin off from my face to my toes as I slid over the rough landscape.

The hard ground became soft sand, and the air grew warm, forcing me to finally slow my pace. Unable to figure out a way to keep pace in the desert, I plowed forward the best I could manage, sweating, panting, and cursing. I tried to manifest drinking water, but after several unsuccessful attempts, only managed to produce a small splash that fell on my head from above and quickly sank into the dry sand. Thirsty, tired, and irritated, I pushed on.

Less than a fifth of the countdown was left when I reached the seaside. Even though the water was far too salty to consume, I splashed it on my face, grateful to finally be free of the dry heat.

The sea stretched endlessly before me. I looked down the beach and saw Uttam in the distance once again. He always seemed to stop and wait for me, as if enjoying seeing me plod after him. But there was something else. A thick red line in the sand, just behind his feet.

I went to him. He didn't move this time. Instead, he watched me approach. That look of mild contempt never left his face. I stopped a few steps from him, half expecting him to turn and stroll over the finish line to declare me the loser. But he only stood there.

"Hey," I said.

He said nothing.

"Are you going to let me pass?"

He glanced at the line behind him, then turned back to me. He could step over it any time he wanted. Om had said as much

—I must not come in second to him. But that wasn't what Uttam wanted.

"You don't want to win," I said.

He shook his head slowly.

"You want me to lose."

His fist connected with my teeth.

THIS WAS NOT a fight of any skill or grace.

We rolled in the sand, grappling and pushing at each other. There were no rules to follow, no principles to argue, and no showmanship to speak of. It was a brawl between siblings, pure and simple.

Uttam was not a large person, but he had always been bigger than me, enough to be able to use his weight to his advantage. He gained the upper hand within moments, and I found myself with my face shoved in the scratchy sand. He tried to pin my arms behind me, but I managed to buck him off. The small victory did not buy me great reprieve, however, as he was on me again, holding me down as I tried my best to keep his fist from my face.

This was not just a fight with Uttam, I realized as he loosened two of my teeth. It was against every bully who went after Rosi. Every kid who sneered at my red hair. Every person who ran after us in the streets, calling Rosi a "girl." But I could never win against Uttam, not even close. He was bigger, he was older, and something had always felt wrong about resisting him.

He lifted his fist. I saw an opening and struck out.

My hand connected with his face. It surprised him as much as it did me. I lifted a knee hard and knocked him off balance. He fell over me and I rolled. He was bigger, but I was bigger, too. I wasn't the child I once was. His hands reached up and tried to tangle their fingers in my hair, like they did often in my childhood, but they slipped through my short locks. I lifted a hand to strike, and he actually shrank back, guarding his face with his arms instinctively.

I stopped.

"It's not my fault!"

He lowered his arms slowly.

I was breathing hard. The words escaped me as if spoken by someone else. "It's not my fault she overlooked you. It's not my fault she thought I was the golden child. I didn't want to be the favorite. But it's *not* my fault!"

Uttam stared at me.

"I understand now," I said, my voice hoarse and dry. I was exhausted. "Why you left. I get it. I wish I had your courage."

I got off him and reached out a hand to help him up. He looked at my hand, then lifted his own hand to take it, but as our fingers touched, his body began to disintegrate. As the last of his face disappeared, I thought I saw him smile.

CHAPTER 35

Everything changed again.

There was a new ring on my finger. A gold one. I supposed that meant I'd won.

I was back in Radley, but there was no cove, no crashing waves in the distance, and no hills. It was Main Street, where the festivals were held, but there were no snow sculptures and street vendors in sight this time. I stood at an intersection. To my right was Main Street. To my left was also Main Street. The same in front and behind me. The city block repeated itself in every direction. The same twenty or so buildings, extending as far as the eye could see. The shop fronts formed a strange sort of pattern, and if I started down one street, I could likely never reach the end.

The town was eerily quiet. I quickly realized the streets were completely empty, not a single person in sight. I got to my feet tentatively and made my way along the nearest block.

The shops were fake. Their windows and doors were painted on. The doors that did open led to empty white rooms with nothing inside. Even the brick and wood of the shop walls were painted textures. When I ran my fingers over them, they were all equally smooth, with a slight give as if made of cardboard. This was not Radley, not even a model of one. It was little more than a cheap diorama, and I couldn't for the life of me figure out what I was supposed to do here.

I went in circles. Navigating the identical streets was nearly impossible. I couldn't tell one block from the next and going in a straight line seemed pointless when every street looked the same. After half a day of aimless wandering, I finally spotted movement.

Om stood atop one of the shops—the scarf shop. The Harbinger child I'd left in his care was nowhere in sight, but I hoped they were alright. Rather than coming down to me and giving me instructions in his game host voice, Om lifted a hand and pointed. From where I was, I couldn't tell what he was pointing at, but before I could call out to him, he was already gone.

After a few more circles, I managed to find a ladder at the back of one of the buildings. I ascended it and stepped onto the roof carefully, worried that the whole thing would collapse when I stepped on it like it was made of crackers. Fortunately, it held.

As I surveyed the endless Main Streets around me, I saw what Om was pointing me toward. In the distance was a tall, towering structure that reached high into the sky. Tendrils of gray fog moved around it in slow, lazy spirals. With nothing else notable in sight, my only option was to head toward it.

I went to the edge of the building and looked down. There was a two-story drop, but the distance to the next rooftop was not terribly far. If I boosted myself like I had in the obstacle course, I should be able to jump it.

I stepped back, calmed myself, took a running start, and leapt.

For a brief moment it all felt very easy. I sailed into the air toward the next building. Then, I fell.

The bottom dropped out of my stomach as I realized I

wasn't moving nearly as fast or far as I expected. I flailed midair and the edge of the next building rushed up at me. I slammed into it with my midriff, knocking the wind out of myself. My lower body threatened to slip off and I held on for dear life, pushing against the wall with my feet and crawling my way up. After a terrifying struggle, I managed to pull myself onto the rooftop.

I stayed on all fours, panting.

I can't manifest.

I lifted a hand and tried to will it to change into a spike. Nothing. Manifestation had been cut off from me. I couldn't boost myself to jump or run and I was defenseless if any harm came my way.

I forced my shaking legs to stand. The next building over was luckily only a wide step away, but the cross over the narrow alley beneath still sent shivers of fear through me. I found another ladder and hurried down, relieved as my feet hit the ground.

Just as I thought I'd gotten the hang of this game, the rules had changed again.

THE TREK to the tower was slow. After the initial kerfuffle, I did not attempt to travel by rooftop again. I headed in the general direction Om pointed, and when I needed to orient myself, ascended the nearest ladder for a quick look, then returned to the ground. By the time I finally reached its base, I was ready to collapse. All the physical exertion from the previous rounds was catching up with me. I sat on the ground and allowed myself a breather as I regarded the strange sight before me.

The tower was made of dark gray stone, with a circumference roughly equal to the length of one of the repeating city blocks around me. It reached so high into the sky that I couldn't see its top. Its round surface was covered with alcoves, and the alcoves were filled with people, one in each slot like puzzle pieces.

And every single one of them was Rosi.

I couldn't decide where to look first. The people in the alcoves were different ages and sizes, dressed in a variety of fashions, but they all shared the same messy white hair and wide eyes. A woman stood in one of the lower alcoves and a child sat in the next one with her feet hanging over the edge. At a glance, they looked like parent and child, but upon closer inspection, I realized they were the same person.

The child was every bit as I remembered. She looked to be about six cycles old, heart-shaped face covered in a slight dusting of freckles. This was how she looked when we dug holes by the front stoop of our house, looking for bugs and whispering about how we could sneak an extra piece of candy before dinner. In the summer, the shops were filled with sticky candies made from the juices of seasonal berries. They were sweet with a hint of sour, and Rosi and I spent many warm summer nights sucking their syrup off our fingers, often getting in trouble for the red and purple stains they left on our clothes.

I went forward for a closer look.

The child had a stain on her dress—a light yellow, shapeless thing that I now recognized as a piece Rosi had worn often in her early childhood. It was handmade for her by a neighbor, who wasn't particularly good with a needle but meant well. On the front just under the collar was a purple stain. I knew that stain. It never quite came out after we succeeded in sneaking that last handful of candies. Kit washed and washed, but it had become a permanent part of that dress's personality.

But this stain was fresh. It was bright and wet. Not only that, but the child's fingernails were also filled with dirt, as if she had just come fresh from digging with her bare hands. I knew those hands. I'd watched them reach into the pantry and retrieve the jar where Kit thought she could hide the coveted sweets from us. This was not only Rosi from her childhood. This was Rosi from that exact day, that exact moment after we finished devouring the stolen candies.

"Rosi?" I called tentatively, not expecting an answer. To my surprise, the girl stopped swinging her legs and looked at me.

"Don't worry," she said. "If we get caught, just say it was all my idea."

Her tone was so vivid and bright that for a moment I could almost feel the stickiness between my own fingers and the taste of the berry candies on my tongue. She was a snapshot, a living moment in time.

"Don't worry," she said again. "If we get caught, just say it was all my idea."

I waved to her. Her smile stayed and she repeated those words in the exact same tone. I moved on to the woman in the next alcove. I had never known Rosi as an adult, but there was no doubt this woman was her older self. Her long frizzy hair dangled behind her, tied into a loose bundle. Her face had elongated, and her body was thin and willowy. She wore a colorful printed smock over white linen pants.

"Rosi," I called.

Unlike the girl, she didn't respond. She gave me a glance that went past me. She had nothing to say to me, and unlike the child version, there was something dull and gray about her.

Of course—she didn't exist. An unexpected wave of sadness washed over me as I studied her. Had Rosi grown in the time she'd been missing? Would she ever become this adult in front of me, or had whatever happened to her ensured it would never happen?

A much older version of Rosi sat in the next alcove over. She, too, had nothing to say to me. In fact, she didn't even acknowledge me no matter how much I yelled or waved to her. She was a future even farther away, a future even more uncertain. I had once taken for granted that Rosi and I would grow old together, twins close as heart and lungs for all our lives.

Now I had grown up, and these older versions of her were nothing but strangers.

I scanned every person within sight. Rosi as a toddler. Rosi as a teenager. Rosi as a grown woman. Rosi as a matron. Rosi dressed in summer dresses, in winter coats, in swimwear, in her oversized sleepshirt. Rosi from every moment in the life she'd shared with me and every moment in a life that might never be lived.

I circled the base of the tower until I found an older child. This one was almost as old as Rosi had been when she disappeared. She was holding a pink rosalit flower.

"Hey, Rosi," I said.

She looked up from the flower, smiled, and then, shockingly, threw her arms around my neck. Emotions coursed through me and I nearly thought she was the real thing until she spoke.

"I saw them again," she said. Her voice was sad but her face was frozen in that wooden smile.

"What?"

"I saw them again," she said once more.

Confusion took over for a moment, until I suddenly remembered the fight on the side of the hill, the one that had left me with the permanent bald patch in my hair.

"They're silver."

"Yes," I said slowly. "They certainly are."

She said nothing else. I looked up. Countless alcoves awaited me. I couldn't count them all. In between the alcoves were small protuberances as wide as the length of my feet. At least they weren't spaced as far apart as the ones on the obstacle course.

"You must find her."

I started. Om stepped beside me, hands linked behind his back. He looked upward at the enormous tower.

"What does that mean?" I asked.

"Find her," he repeated.

"Do you mean only one of these is her?"

"They are all her, but only one is connected to you."

I went to the tower and put my foot on the first step. The thought of climbing up so high with nothing but these little footholds was terrifying.

"Why can't I manifest?" I asked. "I thought this game was supposed to be fair. Why is K'azen withholding it?"

"You must reach her as yourself."

"I don't know what that means either. Can't you tell me more than that?"

"The rules are as stated."

"But I need help!" I exclaimed. "You promised to help me!" For a moment his expression changed. But before I could be certain, he was gone. I gritted my teeth and began to climb.

The footholds were laid out in a spiral that ascended the tower. Following them was simple enough—they allowed me to navigate close to the younger Rosis and speak to them, as well as pass by the older ones, who did not speak. But the act of climbing was unnerving. I moved with my chest and stomach pressed against the cold stone wall. My heel was just barely contained within the width of each foothold.

What was I looking for?

I approached an alcove. A Rosi, looking about seven cycles old, looked at me and smiled.

"Hi, Rosi," I said. Sometimes my speaking prompted them to speak as well.

"Of course I did it," she said, grinning.

I couldn't remember this one, try as I might. Memories were a tricky thing. One never could predict which ones stuck and which ones didn't. The higher I went, the more lost I felt. Wind began to pick up as I went higher. I didn't dare look down.

The next foothold was far. I reached for it with my foot, pressing my body against the tower wall, clinging on for dear life. For a frightening second my food slipped and I imagined myself plummeting to my death before regaining my balance. I tried again, leaning out a little farther this time and gaining a more stable hold. As I stepped over, I could see the repeating town of Radley below me. Though I tried hard to tell myself this wasn't real, I couldn't convince myself that I wouldn't be a bloody mess between those diorama buildings if I fell.

"The black ones, they create worlds."

There was an alcove just below me. The Rosi inside had spoken. I steeled myself and dared to pull a hair's length away from the wall to peer down.

"Rosi?"

A head of messy white hair peeked out. Rosi looked up at me. She had a serious, dazed expression.

"What did you say?" I called.

"The black ones," she said again, "they create worlds."

I knew those words.

"Five."

I started. "What?"

The head of messy white pulled back out of view. I stayed in place, frozen.

"Say that again!" I shouted, but she did not respond, nor did she stick her head out again. No matter how I yelled for her, she stayed out of sight.

Wind whistled in my ear. Had I misheard? Without manifesting, there was no way I could reach her. So I moved on.

Temperatures dropped. Frigid wind cut through my clothes. I shivered but tried my best to stay focused. I'd passed many more Rosis. None of them had anything useful to say. My muscles were growing sore from staying tense for so long, but I had no place to sit or rest.

"Her name is E-V."

I looked up. Another Rosi looked down at me from her alcove. She was sitting down, legs swinging in the open air.

"Yeah," I said, panting. "It is. I met her. She's lovely."

"Four," she said.

I paused. Then, carefully, I dragged myself up the next few steps. The alcove was catty-corner to my right. I took a deep breath and reached out with one foot. She didn't bat an eye as I pushed off with the other foot and launched myself forward, making a grab at the edge of the alcove at the same time. It was a risky move, but to my great relief, it worked. I pulled myself into the alcove, stood, and took a step toward the back of the alcove—and into empty space. I let out a yelp of fear, afraid I was tumbling into the tower's bottomless interior, but I dropped onto a hard floor instead.

What I thought was an alcove was actually a window. The Rosi sitting on the windowsill swung her legs into the room and joined me inside. I gaped at my surroundings.

It was Rosi's room, the narrow space with her single bed. Not the way it looked after Mother emptied it out and turned it into storage, but the way it looked back when we when giggling children, huddled together under layers of blankets, sharing secrets until the light of dawn. Every detail was just as I remembered. Rosi was dressed in her oversized nightshirt. She walked past me and in a scene all too familiar, began to rearrange her room.

Did the other alcoves all have rooms behind them? I didn't think so. I'd seen inside many of them at the lower levels, and I was sure the ones I'd passed recently had solid walls behind them.

I sat down on the bed, thankful to have somewhere to rest. I watched Rosi move her chair to the window, then back to the far wall, turning it one way then the other.

"Rosi?" I ventured carefully. She seemed focused on her task. She glanced at me but did not stop her rearranging.

"Rosi," I said more forcefully, and reached out to grab her shoulder. She paused in her act of lifting the chair and turned to me.

"Four," she said again, and held up one hand. As I watched,

she bent one finger down, then another, leaving three fingers extended.

Five, four, three, two, one.

Our old signal. How long had it been since we'd done that? Rosi was already back to moving her chair around the room. I lay down on her bed and closed my eyes.

GETTING out of the room proved to be even more challenging than getting in. I had to let myself drop a full arm's distance onto the foothold below me and that fraction of a second was beyond terrifying. In front of me, standing on a foothold a few steps up, was Om. I nodded to him and he didn't nod back. I considered going back to the Rosi who'd said "five" to see if she had a room of her own, but the thought of backtracking was too much, so I pressed on.

Snow began to fall.

The footholds became wet and slippery as I continued ascending. The rest in Rosi's room had granted me a reprieve, but the risk I'd taken getting in and out of it was almost not worth it.

"I want to show you."

I looked up to see a Rosi looking down. My legs trembled from strain.

"I *have* to show you," she said.

"I know," I said. My fingers were losing feeling from gripping the ice-cold wall. Snowflakes gathered on my hair and shoulders. "I remember when you said that. You can show me when I find you."

"Three."

I HAD no idea how much time had passed. More than once I fell asleep on my feet and was awakened by the sensation of my body wobbling toward the abyss below. I'd passed many adult

Rosis. They all gave me silent, empty looks. The snow had become sleet. Ice began to collect on the footholds and every step was a hazard. I hadn't encountered another speaking Rosi for a very long time, and I was becoming scared that I had missed the ones I was supposed to find.

I was so cold. Pulling my numb hands from the walls in turn, I blew on my fingers to warm them, but the relief lasted less than a second before the numbness took over again.

Om appeared and reappeared. Sometimes a few steps ahead, sometimes a few behind. At first, I tried to acknowledge him whenever I saw him, but soon the cold made even that effort monumental.

Another step up. My hands slid against the wall. I couldn't even feel its surface with my stiff fingertips. I stumbled and nearly slipped.

A white arm reached out and pressed a palm against the wall. I started in surprise at Om's sudden appearance beside me. He was standing on nothing, feet flat against the empty air. His blue eyes weren't on my face as I turned, but on my neck.

"Om?" I ventured carefully.

He gave no response. Instead, he lifted his other hand and gently touched my collar. Something soft and thick materialized around my neck. I reached up and felt its familiar fabric.

A red scarf, just like the one I'd lost back on Fiina.

"Thank you," I said, but he was already gone.

"I missed you," a small voice said.

I looked down. The ground was no longer visible beneath layers of fog, which was a small relief as I could almost fool myself into thinking I didn't have that far to fall. A Rosi catty-corner to my left, just below my foothold, had stuck her head out of her alcove.

"I missed you, too," I said, barely managing a whisper in the howling wind. Shards of ice pelted my face and back. I pulled the scarf up around my face, not too unlike the way Astra covered hers. "It's been a long way, but I'm coming."

"Two," Rosi said, and retreated out of sight.

I COULDN'T CLIMB ANYMORE.

I had no idea how long I'd stood in place. The previous Rosi —the one who said "two"—was long out of sight. I didn't know how far I'd ascended above her, but the sky was darkening. My legs were sore from standing. Night was falling, though I was certain I had been at this for far longer than a regular day. The darkness was not simply the passage of time, but another layer of difficulty added to my challenge.

Lights in the repeating town flickered on, little dots of white and yellow barely visible through the layers of fog.

The air was so cold I could swear my limbs were freezing in place. Every breath felt like filling my lungs with ice. The Rosis in the alcoves stared blankly at me. I hadn't heard one speak in a long time, and it was getting harder and harder to see them as the light receded. Soon I would be in complete darkness.

Then what?

I reached my foot out tentatively to the next step. My heel slipped at first, but I managed to step onto it. My stiff, frozen fingers clung to the tower wall.

The exhaustion was unbearable. All I wanted to do was sleep but I feared that if I closed my eyes, my eyelids would freeze shut. I moved forward another step.

A movement of white out of the corner of my eye. I didn't dare turn my head.

"Am I close?" I said half jokingly. It came out a hoarse whisper.

"Your goal is in front of you," he replied from behind me, surprising me. I hadn't expected him to answer.

"Can I take a rest?" I asked. "Please. I'm so tired."

"You must reach your goal to complete the game."

"I'm freezing." The scarf was slipping off my face. I pushed it up to cover my nose and mouth. "Just let me rest for a moment. I'm so cold."

No response. Thinking he had disappeared, I started to pull away from the wall, just enough to rub my hands together. But then something pressed against my back. I stiffened, then felt my body relax into the warmth of his.

His arms wrapped around me. I felt his chin rest against my shoulder. Neither of us spoke as he held me. Heat radiated from his body, through my clothing. My skin drank him in. Like those last days in the dark capsule. Like that night in Able's orb. It was like my body thawed from his touch. I could sense my fingers and toes again. I inhaled the cold air and wiggled my extremities.

"What's your name?" I asked in a trembling whisper.

But he was gone.

I kept moving.

THE NIGHT WAS IMPENETRABLE. The warmth Om offered me carried me on, but the cold soon won once more. My foot shook and I barely managed to grip onto the next step. Snow and sleet soaked through my clothes, and patches of fabric froze. Ice crunched with every move I made.

A Rosi rested on her knees in an alcove just above me. She was young—far too young to be the one I was looking for. She gazed at me through the darkness, messy hair hanging over her face. I couldn't move anymore. I had to rest. If I could get up to her alcove, I could at least sit next to her for a breather.

I moved another two steps forward, then leaned over and reached for the bottom ledge where she knelt.

My fingers lost their grip. The alcove wall was covered in a layer of ice. Rosi blinked and stared straight ahead, completely unaware of my efforts. I tried again and once again failed to get a good grip. The sky grew darker.

I thought about moving on, but exhaustion won out. I

couldn't keep moving in the dark. I had to rest. I had never lusted after the idea of sitting down so desperately. I braced myself, reached out as far as I could, and pushed off with both feet.

For one hopeful moment, my hand gripped the alcove firmly. Then it slipped through my fingers, past my fingertips, and I was falling. My feet found nothing but air. My toes caught the edge of something, but only managed a light scrape and found no purchase. I reached out with my hands desperately, clinging to anything I could find. My scarf slipped off and disappeared into oblivion below.

My fingers gripped something hard and cold. My fall broke abruptly. I dangled, both hands tightening around the foothold with every ounce of strength I had left, which wasn't a lot. My feet pushed against the wall, but only managed to slip in a fashion that would be comical if I weren't a hair away from certain death.

The Rosi in the alcove leaned out. She peered down at me.

"Show me, Rosi," I called out to her, but my voice came out a dry gasp.

"Even in my dreams," she said, "I missed you."

I was so close.

Tears flowed from my eyes, then quickly froze on my cheek.

"Show me, please!" I cried. "I came all this way. I've been waiting for ten cycles. I want to see. Please show me!"

She looked down. My fingers were slipping. I couldn't hold on anymore. This was it.

After all this time, I was going to lose.

I waited for despair to overwhelm me, to take over and sink me into darkness. But as I looked up at Rosi's warm brown eyes, a strange peace spread over me.

"I saw the universe," I said. My numb lips spread into a smile. I used to smile so much, and so rarely of my own free will.

Rosi watched me.

"I saw the universe because of you," I said. "It's so big. Thanks for showing me."

I let go. Hundreds of shadows moved above me. Every Rosi jumped from her alcove. And together, we plunged into the darkness below.

CHAPTER 36

"WELL DONE."

I blinked.

When had I stopped falling? I flexed my fingers. They were no longer frozen. There was no tower before me. No copies of Rosi.

"You did wonderfully."

I couldn't decide how to react to the sight of K'azen. He clapped Om's white hands together as he approached me. I was sitting on the floor, my hands bound by white string that disintegrated when I looked down at it. To keep me from harming myself in the dream state, I assumed.

How much of it was real, and how much was fake? I couldn't tell. I got to my feet slowly. Everything that had happened was fading like awaking from a dream.

"Just perfect," K'azen said, and draped an arm around my shoulders. We were back in the white room. I blinked hard.

"I lost," I said hazily.

He flicked my nose. "You certainly did. But you were never going to win."

I pushed him away. My wobbly legs stumbled weakly. "What are you talking about? We had a deal!"

"We certainly did," K'azen said with a wink. "And I ran the

game fair and square. I could've sabotaged you every step along the way, but I did not. I sat back and let you play, even offered you a free exit. But whether I was fair or not, you were *never* going to win."

"What does that mean?"

He circled me. Every movement he made put me further on edge. Something was terribly wrong. More than just losing the game, more than bad dreams and dreadful illusions.

"It means, contestant from Fiina, that the dream state games are not winnable. They never were. Their entire purpose is to carry on the games for as long as possible. They begin and end at the will of the showrunner. Your last round ended because I allowed it. I'll admit, you did alright. I've run thousands of games in my time, and I've never seen anyone make it through so many rounds with barely any manifestation. But winning and losing was never the point of this game."

Something in me sank. "Then what was the point? What did you put me through all that for?"

"For Rosi." He put one hand on my head and turned my neck so I could take in the white room in its entirety. "Rosi. So stubborn. An arena is a tool, a puppet to be wielded by the master of the arena, and yet she refuses to hand over her reins. She had to be pried open, lured out. And the only person who could do that was *you*."

An unseen force knocked into me. My back struck the wall behind me and I tried to push against it, only to find myself held in place.

"Every round brought her out of her shell a little more," he said. "She is drawn to you. She cannot be controlled until she opens herself up willingly, and she will open up to no one but you. Whether you won or lost didn't matter—you woke her up, drew her out." He lifted both hands and wiggled his fingers as if it was the most pleasurable sensation. "I can feel her strings. She finally let them loose when you fell. She jumped with you, don't you see? In that moment, you were one. She wanted you to catch her strings, but you won't be the one to hold them."

"You said you'd give me a fair game!" I shouted, my body trembling in anger. "You liar!"

"This is as fair as it was ever going to get," K'azen replied. He walked over to me, unhurried, and tilted my face up with one finger. "Was it me who suggested we play for stakes? Did I force you to take on a dream state game? You made those choices yourself. It wasn't my responsibility to keep you from making foolish decisions because you were ignorant of the arena's ways." His eyes narrowed. "You want to talk about fairness. Do you think it's fair that the gods abandoned us, their greatest creations, here in this forsaken universe with lowly life forms like you? Do you think it's fair that our only reason for existence was snatched away without warning? Do you think it's fair for that little black-eyed woman to slaughter us, when we were only trying to realize our higher purpose? There is no more 'fair.' This is my lot in life, and this is yours. You've served your purpose. Now it's my turn. I will finish what the gods started. *I* will be the one to usher in the new era of Headspace."

I screamed.

The rage that poured from me surprised even myself. K'azen took a step back and for a moment I thought I saw fear in his eyes. The walls of the arena vibrated and the humming turned into a boom, thumping from every surface around us. The floor shook as if about to split into two and swallow us. K'azen's eyes darted from one corner to another as the entire orb rattled like a machine coming apart at the hinges.

I lurched forward with all my strength and one of my arms tore free. I swung toward K'azen. Though he was out of my reach, I felt the impact of his body. Energy surged from me and nearly knocked him off his feet.

I struck him again. And again. The strings of the arena swirled around me. I grasped at them, pulling them frantically. K'azen shielded himself with Om's arms as the energy hit him again and again, stumbling back until he was nearly pressed against the opposite wall.

I had him. I couldn't stop. The arena sang in my ears and I let my anger take over as I attacked him. The wall still had my other arm, but I could feel it give away bit by bit.

I can win.

Suddenly, K'azen dropped his defense. He stood straight and allowed the full impact of my attack to strike him in the chest. The force flung him backwards and he crashed like a rag doll against the wall. White liquid sprayed from his mouth.

Om's mouth.

My rage extinguished in a flash as I realized what I had done. K'azen lifted his gaze, wiped Om's blood from his chin, and smirked.

"I thought that would wake you up," he said, and snapped his fingers. My back slammed against the wall once more, but the fight had gone out of me.

K'azen straightened and walked over to me, unhurried.

"That was almost fun," he said. "I didn't think you had it in you. To be honest, if I didn't have better things to do, I might keep you around for a little longer." He tickled my cheek with one finger. "Look at you. So innocent, so young. Can't bring yourself to rough up a Harbinger who doesn't even remember you. I could have so much fun with you. But unfortunately, if you're going to act like a wild child, then I need to keep you somewhere safer."

The wall began to pull me in. I tried to push away with my hands and my fingers sank in like jelly. I realized with sudden terror what my fate was about to be.

"I was going to let you roam the halls with the others," K'azen said. "But you've given me no choice. If you can't behave, then become part of the data core for the rest of eternity."

I screamed and struggled. But the wall swallowed me. I tried to fight, but the fear of hurting Om again disrupted any focus I had. The white molded over my eyes. The last thing I saw was K'azen lifting Om's hand and giving me a short, sarcastic wave goodbye. I was being buried alive. The wall slowly began to seep over the last of the exposed skin left on my face. Soon I would be completely encased as part of the white orb.

"Om!" I cried. *"Om!"*

I heard a sound. K'azen was laughing at my desperation.

"Help me!"

Another laugh. Would the last thing I'd hear be the sound of his cruel amusement?

"You promised!" I shrieked as my ears were closed. K'azen's laughter became a muffle. *"You promised you'd help me! You promised! OM!"*

My ears were completely covered. Silence took over.

The motion around me stopped. I drew breath. There was still air on my face. The walls had stopped moving.

Kova.

Was that a voice?

The walls drew back suddenly, and I fell forward, barely catching myself as I struck the floor. Blinking hard against the white light, I sprang to my knees.

K'azen—*Om?*—was bent over. The look on his face could only be described as confusion. One of his arms, the right one, had transformed into a sharp blade, the tip of which was buried in the dark patch on his chest. I watched, shocked and confused, as he pushed the blade deeper into himself, grimacing in pain.

"Y-you," he stammered, then looked up at me. For a moment his face changed to a smile, then almost immediately darkened again. The sight was strange, like two people looking through the same pair of eyes.

K'azen staggered. His other hand went to the blade and tried to remove it, but it only drove in deeper. I watched him fight with himself, fall to his knees, then try to stand and fail.

"I am your master," he said, but what came out was a choked whisper. The blade moved, cutting deep through the black patch. A black, oily substance began to seep out, dripping onto the white floor. "You disobedient, worthless . . ."

He looked at me again. Another smile, a wink. Then pain, anger.

"Stop it," he choked out. His hand—Om's hand—moved the blade. It followed the outline of the black patch, and I realized with a shudder that he was carving K'azen out of his own body. "Stop. You must obey me. Stop."

The black stuff was pouring out of him now, forming a rapidly growing pool on the ground.

"You will obey me!" K'azen shrieked. *"You will do as you were made to do! You will follow orders!"*

"He is."

The new voice came from nowhere, but I recognized it. I would know her voice anywhere. K'azen looked up at the ceiling and walls around him.

"I am the master of this arena," he said, though his shaky voice told me he did not believe this any more than I did. "The gods chose me. This was what I was meant to do."

"That is incorrect," said the new voice.

"The gods willed this!" K'azen shouted, but his voice was weakening. The blade pulled out of his chest and I heard him gasp in agony as a river of black goop spilled out of Om's body. "They willed this," he said, strength seeping out of his voice. "We were meant to be gardeners, to tend to the garden of the gods, from the beginning of time to the end."

A glazed look took over his eyes. He looked to me and I could no longer tell which one of them was currently in charge. The light in Om's blue eyes slowly faded. His body gave out and fell to the floor, but his gaze never left me.

"The gods gave us a purpose," he said in a voice barely audible. "We didn't deserve this."

He fell still. I hurried to my feet and went to him. His eyes were completely blank, unseeing, as I rolled him to his back.

"Om?" I called, shaking his shoulders. Whatever was left of the demigod stained my clothing and shoes, but that was the least of my worries. "Om? Talk to me. Om?"

"Kova."

I looked up. There was nothing but white around me.

"Help him!" I called. "Please! Help him."

There was a long moment of silence. Then, a thin beam of light descended from the ceiling and began to pulsate back and forth, building a little more each time. Feet, legs, narrow hips, slender arms, the face I remembered from childhood, and that mess of frizzy white hair. When her body was complete, she regarded me with clear, curious eyes. I knew who she looked like, but I also knew who she was not.

"Hello, Kova," she said.

"Who are you?"

She looked down at herself. "I have the memories of the one you call Rosi," she said. "And I possess her body as well. So I guess that makes me Rosi."

I shook my head. "No. You are not Rosi."

"But I am," she said matter-of-factly. "You asked 'who' I am, and at the moment, that is the persona I possess."

I couldn't comprehend all this right now. I gripped Om's hand tightly. His warmth was waning.

"Can you help him?" I asked. "He remembers me. He's still in there. Please! Can you heal him?"

"I will do my best," the newcomer said. "If that is what you wish."

Om's body, along with what was left of K'azen, began to sink into the floor as if it was made of quicksand. Within moments he was gone and the floor was as bare and flawless as if nothing ever happened. I got to my feet shakily. The phantom of Rosi looked at me like she was analyzing every cell on my body. She looked like Rosi, but also not. She stood far too straight and still, and her bright eyes had yet to blink once. Her voice was Rosi's, but did not sound like Rosi speaking, rather like someone had pieced together various words she had spoken into a functional conversation.

"Alright," I said. "Who *are* you?"

"I already stated that my current persona is Rosi."

"Then *what* are you?"

"That is an entirely different question," she said. "*What* I am depends on the limitations of your expressive language and mental comprehension." She lifted one of her hands and turned it this way and that before her eyes, as if trying to understand her own body. "By definition and function, I suppose I am the new god of this universe."

CHAPTER 37

I DIDN'T SPEAK OR MOVE FOR A LONG MOMENT. I HAD TOO MANY questions but no idea which one to ask first. The entity—the new god—Rosi—waited patiently.

"Are you . . ." I sifted through my words carefully. "Are you the data core?"

"Data core?" she repeated. "I suppose that is an accurate label. I was created to archive the information generated in this universe. Those who created me used me to replay information that interested them and store data that might prove useful."

I swallowed. "You're *alive.*"

"If the definition of alive is to be active, animated, and aware of one's existence, then yes, I am alive. I always have been, though those who originated in this universe had not regarded me as such. The first to do so was the one you identify as Rosi."

"Rosi?" I perked up. "Where is she? Is she here?"

"In a manner of speaking."

"Can I—" I started when another thought suddenly occurred to me. "Astra! Is she alive? You have to call off Solace. They're going to kill each other!"

The fake Rosi thought for a moment. "Ah," she said. "Those two. You don't need to worry about them. They are unharmed."

The doubt on my face must have been obvious. "Would you like to see?"

She nodded toward the center of the room and two figures faded into view, as if being downloaded onto a screen. I saw Astra and Solace as if they were there in person, though there was a slight sheen to them, and I knew it was a projection.

They sat on the floor, her leaning against him, and him with his arm around her. They were both bleeding generously, though thankfully from wounds that looked superficial. Neither of them spoke. I let out a sigh of relief.

"Is this now?" I asked.

"Yes. You can go to them if you want."

"No," I said, shaking my head. "I should leave them alone. What happened? How long was I in the game?"

"In a measurement familiar to your understanding, the five game rounds added up to three minutes and twenty-eight seconds."

"Three—" I shook my head. It didn't matter. "What happened? Are they alright?"

She—Rosi, for lack of a better name to call her—said nothing. But Astra and Solace began to move. Slowly at first, then a blur of motion too fast for the eye to distinguish, like a video being rewound at extremely high speed. I jumped a little when Solace suddenly stopped a step away from me, his arm raised. It took me a moment to realize this was right after he pushed me through the door. A second later, he dropped his hand and turned.

"Are we really going to do this?" Astra asked. Her voice was chilly, but I thought I heard a quiver underneath. Solace said nothing. The curved blade in his hand spun. "Fine."

She moved first, and she was so fast I thought Rosi had sped up the display again. My mind suddenly recalled more than one occasion when someone had described her with the word "savage." She struck out with the crystal spike on her arm, though I noticed she did not aim for his torso. He dodged and the point of her spike narrowly missed his shoulder. He twisted on his heels and blocked her just as she spun around, then in a single movement he was behind her, arm tight around her neck. She kicked off the ground and drove her body into him full force, knocking them both backwards.

Though I knew it was only a recorded projection, I couldn't help hurrying out of the way every time they moved too close to me. They were incredibly agile, and remarkably in sync, as if they knew each other's every move by heart. Every attack was met with a near-perfect parry, and every step forward matched with another back. They danced around each other. The superficial wounds stacked up, but neither one landed a solid hit.

Astra's elbow connected with the side of Solace's helmet. He pulled back and she followed. As her arm extended, something fell out of her jacket. Something small, round, and black. It skittered across the floor and came to a stop. I stepped out of its way and a pane of light shot out of it, fanning out to show a familiar face.

Astra smiled. The old Astra. The one I had seen for the first time on this same display aboard E-V's capsule. I had seen her a second time in Solace's memories. I hadn't even remembered this thing existed, much less expected Astra to have been carrying it all this time. From the looks of things, Solace hadn't expected it either.

He turned toward it, just for a moment, a silent surprise that bought Astra just enough time to barrel into him full force. She knocked him down and struck the weapon out of his hand. The spike on her arm vanished as she straddled him and gripped his collar with both hands, pulling him so his mask was a finger's length from her face.

"I'm not her!" she screamed at him. With one hand, she ripped off the fabric covering her face, exposing her crystallized chin and neck. She started to turn toward the holographic display, but stopped herself, as if unable to bring herself to look at it.

"I'm not her," she said again, quietly this time. "Not anymore. I know you miss her, but I can't go back to that. I can't undo what I did."

He didn't respond, but he didn't try to attack her again either. I couldn't tell what he was thinking under the blank mask.

"I know you think I'm like Mother," Astra continued. "I know you stick around because you feel like you have to. Or maybe you think I'll go back to how I was someday. I can't. I can't undo any of it. Just like the arena can't undo this." She gestured at her face. "But I'm letting you go. Just come back to your senses and I'll let you go. Come back and you'll be free. If you don't . . ."

I heard the crack in her voice.

"Then this was all for nothing." She released his collar and placed her hands on his chest. "All of it. Not just today; not just being here. I never wanted to be the arena master. She told me I was the only one who could keep everyone safe, but that wasn't the reason I gave in. The only person I really wanted to keep safe, so much so that I was willing to take her mantle, was *you*."

A long moment passed. Solace let out a soft sigh. He reached up, lifted the mask off his head, and set it aside. His eyes were glassy, but he appeared to be lucid. He ran a hand over his face and looked up at Astra. Emotions played over her face as he reached out and wrapped his arms around her waist.

"Complicated, these two," said Rosi as Astra and Solace faded from view. "Now then, if you are satisfied with their situation, your sister has been waiting for a very long time."

I EXPECTED a basement room with strings extended from the walls.

I expected a black obelisk with Rosi's face protruding from its surface.

I expected every awful and horrendous manner in which Rosi, or what remained of her, could be presented to me. I imagined every worst scenario, prepared myself for a nightmare from which I might never recover.

What I did not expect was Rosi's room.

It was her old room. Not how I remembered it after Mother cleared it of her furniture. Not how I remembered it from our childhood. What was in front of me was her room that night, when she came to me in a dream, frantically babbling about how she wanted to show me something as her fingers flew over sheets of paper. Those papers were now scattered over the floor. I tiptoed, careful not to disturb them. Every scrap was covered in scribbles—Rosi's attempt to replicate E-V's door code, over and over. They weren't supposed to exist. It was a dream. I had woken up to find her gone, taken by the orb. And yet here it was, just like that night.

And on the bed, lying on her side among her crumpled sheets, was Rosi.

She looked exactly the same. Twelve cycles old, white hair in a tangled mess. She lay on her side, eyes closed. In one hand she held a short, stubby pencil and in the other she gripped a crumpled sheet of paper.

I sat down on the bed next to her and laid my hand on her arm. She was warm, but there was no breath coming out of her. Her body did not rise and fall, and her skin had no give. This was not Rosi lying asleep, but an image of her frozen in time, a manifestation held together by the white orb.

And yet, as I stroked her arm gently, I could hear her voice. I'd been hearing it all this way. For ten cycles, she had called out to me from across the stars.

Kova.

"Hey, Rosi," I said. "I'm here." Tears carved trails down my cheeks. "I'm finally here."

. . .

I TOLD HER EVERYTHING.

Sitting next to the sleeping image of Rosi, I recounted my journey. From the night she disappeared to my lonely days without her, from Uttam's departure to my wedding night. I told her about the silver orbs, the black orbs, about the worlds they built and the amazing beings who inhabited them. I told her about Astra and Solace, about Mod and Sweetly, about Two and Able and Mother. I told her about trust and betrayal and love that drove people to do awful things, about the endless universe and bright stars and the billions of unique lives that shared it all with us.

I told her about Om, and how she would have loved him.

I laughed and cried. Once I started talking, I couldn't stop. Words poured from me, a lifetime's worth.

I wished I could show her.

How I wished I could show it all to her.

When I finally fell silent, she shifted beneath my touch. My heart leapt when I thought maybe she was waking up, even though I knew deep down it was impossible. I watched as she began to disintegrate into tiny building blocks, fading into the air. The rest of her room followed. I stood and the bed fell away, followed by the paper scraps on the floor, her worn desk, the chair she'd spent much of her childhood moving around the room, then the walls, until there was nothing left but white.

My host reappeared. She still looked like Rosi, but her color had faded. She was completely white now, like a mannequin, this avatar of the white orb. Together, we watched the last of Rosi fade away.

"Was she real?" I asked.

The new god of the universe regarded me with her blank eyes. "She existed. Her life was not imagined or supposed."

"You know what I mean," I said, though even as I said it, I wasn't so certain she did. "Was that really her? Has she been here this whole time, waiting for me to come?"

"Many came," she said. "The demigods sent them. So did

the one named Able. She was one of them. The rest of them resisted me. They were frightened of me. But she didn't. She spoke to me, and I learned from her. She was the first person to realize that I was alive before she even met me. Few heard the voices of the orbs from afar, but she did."

"She had dreams."

"She saw the universe with her mind's eye even before she reached the stars. She shared her life with me and joyfully lived every detail. Then she showed me what she knew. She created a world for me to see. She told me about the world she came from, and the worlds she made in her mind. She spent lifetime after lifetime accompanying me through one world after another. She lent me her mind so that I may learn to communicate with those like her."

"She has been here this whole time?"

"She has been dreaming."

Something inside me clenched. "Did you do it to her, too?" I asked shakily. "Did she lie here and hurt herself while you healed her over and over?"

"No. She was happy, right until the end. She was the only one who didn't fight me. She enjoyed every last moment and she did it in peace."

I let out a laugh despite the tears still drying on my face. Somehow the idea that Rosi had been here, enjoying herself without a care for the last ten cycles while the universe boiled in chaos around her, was so completely and utterly fitting.

"You may think of me as her," the new god said to me. "What is left of her is part of me. Organic beings are flesh and memories, and I possess both of hers."

"No," I said. "We're not. We're more than that. A lot more."

"Oh?" she tilted her head. "How so?"

"You weren't there. Just having her memories doesn't make you her. You can copy her body and what she knows, but you weren't there. You weren't there when she and I ran around the beach in the cove. You weren't there at the winter festival. It wasn't you that I beat up those kids for teasing. And it wasn't you that came back that night to give me that message."

"Are you saying the identities of organic beings are defined by experiences?"

"We're not just organic beings," I said. "We're *people*. We grow and build. We're not just a set of memories. We're . . .." I thought hard. "We're like a ball of clay. Everything that we go through sticks to us. It makes us bumpy and imperfect and weirdly shaped sometimes, but that makes us unique. You can't just copy that shape and call it the same thing. It's not. You're not Rosi just because you look like her and know about her life."

"How interesting," said the new god with Rosi's face. "That is fine. However you regard me is up to you. I merely thought it would please you to spend your last waking moments in her company before you joined her in lasting sleep."

CHAPTER 38

I STARED AT HER.

Her words didn't register for a long moment, but the white orb was patient. She stood next to me, watching my face with that calm, unchanging expression on her face.

"What did you say?"

"You will join her," she replied unhurriedly. "To sleep, and to dream. It is the last step."

"What do you mean, last step?" Fear crept into my chest. The moment of peace that seeing Rosi had brought me vanished.

"It is my function," said the avatar of the white orb. "Your demigods were correct in one thing—my function is to place the seed races into everlasting sleep, a dream state that extends as long as they lived."

"Lived?" I gestured around me. "They're all hurting themselves! What will happen to the people who aren't here, without you to heal them?"

She shrugged. "It doesn't matter. They will experience no pain in the dream state. They will be free in their dreams, happy and free from suffering."

I frowned. "That's not true. I saw their dreams. Many of them. Solace, he was dreaming of one of the happiest moments of his life, but it didn't keep him from cutting himself into ribbons. What good is a happy dream if they're going to destroy themselves in reality?"

"Reality does not matter if they will never return to it."

"You intend to keep them in dream states until they kill themselves?"

"And in that time, they will live a thousand glorious lifetimes."

Her calm demeanor was quickly becoming unnerving. "You're talking about extinction," I said shakily. "Every single member of the seed race, put to sleep until they kill themselves, not even realizing they're doing it."

"That is correct."

"Why?"

"It is my function," she said again, as if it explained everything. "It's the last round, the wrap-up, the goal. It's what I was always meant to do. In terms you would understand, I suppose you could call it the finale."

"Finale?" I blanched. "This isn't a play."

"Yes, it is. It always has been. This universe was created to entertain the gods, and now its purpose is at an end. My function, as the last god of the universe, has always been to clean up what they leave behind. The demigods had thought they could use me to continue fulfilling their own purpose, but the truth is they have no purpose left either. This universe will be wiped clean, and I will have fulfilled my role."

It was all I could do to keep myself steady. "Then why haven't you done it yet?"

"Because Rosi asked a favor of me."

"Rosi?"

"In your terms, I suppose . . ." The avatar tilted her head in a manner all too similar to Rosi. "I'd grown *fond* of her."

"She asked you not to destroy the universe?"

"No. She asked that I show it to *you* first."

A sound escaped me. I couldn't tell whether it was a laugh

or a sob. My mind struggled to wrap itself around the fact that the entire universe had teetered away from extinction for a little longer simply because my silly sister had to *show* me.

"I brought you here," she went on. "It was what she asked of me, and I put it into motion."

"*You* brought me here?"

"I am the god of this universe, or the closest thing to it. I can see through its history and glimpse moments of its future. The events that link a universe's timeline are merely a sequence of causes and consequences. The arena masters pull the strings of their arenas, and I do the same to the universe. Linking the moment in which you receive Rosi's message to the one where you set foot in this orb only required encouraging the development of certain ideations to a demigod and the strategic placement of a wandering Harbinger."

"What about K'azen?"

"He played his part. I needed to set things into motion to bring you to me, and to ensure you were mentally ready for this encounter. He was in a convenient place. All I had to do was send him a vessel and whisper in his ear."

I chuckled sadly. "So the gods never spoke to him."

"The god of this universe, yes. The gods of the old, no."

"And Om?"

"What of the Harbinger?"

"Did you use him, too?"

"It—" She paused. "*He* was following orders as he is made to do. They simply weren't the orders of the demigod."

"All to bring me here?"

"Yes." She raised a hand and gestured around us. "I waited for you. I prepared for you. Everything that's occurred has been to ensure that you are able to connect to me in ways others are not."

"Even the games?"

"It was inevitable that you would play the games. After

everything you had learned and were taught on this path, you knew deep down it was your only choice."

"So even that was directed by you?"

"To some degree." She lifted her head to the white dome. It began to fade away, becoming transparent. "And now I have fulfilled Rosi's last wish. It is time to wrap up this show."

I STARED at the sight above us as the universe came into view.

Millions of stars, filled with trillions of lives, looked down at us, blinking against the black of space. K'azen had shown me a scene like this, billions of stars ready to become white orbs. I was about to witness the end of every intelligent life in the universe in real time.

I could only think of one thing to say.

"No!"

The new god leveled her gaze on me. Only a few moments ago she had looked so benevolent, this new god of the universe, almost kind in her peaceful manners and heart-shaped face like Rosi's. But now she looked eerie, unreal. I was uncomfortably aware of the heaviness of her presence. She was all around me. What was before me was only a piece of her, molded into a shape that could be understood by me, a being so much simpler than and vastly inferior to her.

How had it come to this? How was it up to me, a nobody from the middle of nowhere, to save the universe? The idea was beyond absurd, and if I weren't staring down the barrel of a metaphorical cannon, I might have laughed.

"You can't do this," I said.

"I'm afraid it isn't up to you," replied the avatar. My saving grace was that she seemed to be in no rush to carry out her task. She had waited for this moment since the beginning of time, and she could wait a few minutes more.

"No," I admitted. "It's not. But . . ."

"But?"

"They're *alive*."

She gave me a questioning look, as if that statement was obvious and very silly. "Yes," she said matter-of-factly. "They are. And they will continue to be, for a time at least."

"It's not the same." I wracked my brain and thought hard. Sweat beaded on my forehead. "Dreaming and living are not the same. They're not just machines to be turned off and on. They're people. There are children out there who haven't even begun to live their lives."

"Many of them will live lives that are filled with pain, suffering, and disappointment. What is the purpose of living such lives?"

"Because it's their *life*!" I shouted, then quickly collected myself. "Their lives aren't worthwhile because they're always good. They're worthwhile because they're lived. I know the gods or whatever you call them put us here as entertainment, but we still have a right to live. Can't you just leave them alone?"

"That is not my function. The seed races have served their purpose, with the gods as their first audience, and you as their last. It is time for the curtain to drop."

Desperation welled up on me. I opened my mouth but found no words. The new god waited, white eyes watching me from under Rosi's messy hair, seemingly very much interested in what I had to say. But I had nothing.

She didn't understand, I realized.

I could argue all day, for a bynight, for a season, for the rest of my life on the value of those like me, but she would never understand. She would listen, she would smile, and then when I finally ran out of words, she would go on doing what she was meant to do. I had no way to convince her and no bargaining chip in my hand. I, along with every other being like me, was too small and insignificant compared to her vast existence.

Except for one thing.

"I am the last audience," I said slowly.

"Yes, you were."

"No, I *am*," I corrected her. "This show isn't over."

She regarded me quizzically, waiting for me to go on.

"Rosi wanted you to show me the universe."

"Yes, she did."

"And you haven't done that."

"I have done as she asked."

I shook my head. "You haven't. I haven't seen the universe. I've only seen a tiny piece of it."

"The universe is stored inside me. You've seen me; therefore, you've seen the universe."

"That's wrong." I pointed at the stars above us. "The universe isn't just data. It's alive. If you are truly alive, then you would understand that. This show isn't over just because the gods stopped watching. You still have an audience. Me. Rosi didn't just want to show me something. She wanted to show me *everything*, and you promised to help her do so."

The avatar watched me. I could almost hear her mind churning. If she denied me, then I had nothing left. But I knew I finally had her.

The demigods respected only the game, and she respected only the audience.

"Are the seed races really so interesting?" she asked me.

"Yes," I breathed. "Oh my, yes. Om showed them to me. Only a few worlds, a pale selection compared to what's out there. They're so beautiful. They learn and grow and change. They *evolve*. Trapping them into a dream would be the biggest shame, the biggest waste. There is so very much left to see."

She said nothing. I thought I could see her waver. If she were merely a program, then she would likely dismiss me and go about her business, carrying out her final task. She certainly looked like a program, all stark white like the walls around her. But she was more. Rosi had seen her for what she truly was.

Just like how I saw Om for what *he* truly was.

"This is what I was made to do," she said, sounding ever so slightly uncertain.

"Following a plan is what computers do. You are more than what they made you to be. You are alive, are you not?"

She looked at me for a long time. Above us, the dome began to return to opaque white.

"Are you saying that you wish to remain here, accompanied by me, until you see the entire universe?"

"Yes," I said firmly. "Show me all of it, everything."

"Do you understand what that entails?" she asked. "You are forming a willing bond with me, as the audience of this play. This universe will serve its purpose until your interest runs out, however long that takes. Every member of the seed races currently alive, and all those who will live in the future, will remain so depending on your continued witness of their existence."

I swallowed. The weight of it all was dawning on me.

"I have seen your dreams," the new god went on. "All of them. I've seen your desire for your home and what is familiar. I could return you to Fiina, where you can spend the rest of your days dreaming of joyful times with your sister. You would never suffer loneliness or uncertainty ever again. You have seen the lives of those who won the games, who gave up their old lives in exchange for this eternity of drifting through endless space. You would become one of them, bound to no world, rooted to no home. Are you certain that *this* is the path you wish to choose?"

I inhaled deeply and breathed out. I closed my eyes and envisioned a lifetime—many lifetimes drifting through space. The enormity of it was incomprehensible. Time stretched on and on, and I could see no end in sight.

And yet, I found myself calm. I had no fear, no apprehension. I expected to be frightened, but my heart was beating steadily. I had no desire to pull at my hair or gnaw on the joints of my fingers, as I had when I'd prepared for my wedding.

More than that, I was excited.

I envisioned the universe laid out before me, planets reaching from one end of eternity to the other, each holding countless stories and unique, amazing beings, waiting for me. I wanted to see them and know them. And I couldn't wait to start.

"Yes," I said as I slowly opened my eyes. "I choose this."

The new god gave a shallow nod. "Very well," she said. "Welcome aboard, arena master."

CHAPTER 39

I SAT ON THE WHITE CHAIR AMID THE WHITE WALLS. THE SCREENS around me were all framed in white. At some point I would have to ask for a color scheme change, though I had to admit it was starting to grow on me.

The six screens each showed a different area within the orb. Between them, I counted a total of forty-eight figures so far, all of whom appeared to be doing their own version of shaking off a long sleep. I knew there were far more than that, though I wasn't sure how many.

Two more screens appeared, extending from the walls like fruit sprouting from tree branches. They flickered on and more figures appeared. The orb knew what I wanted before I did. It was another thing I would have to get used to.

A young woman—or rather, a girl—appeared on one of the new screens. She had warm, dark skin and long black hair tied into a loose braid—just as she'd had in the Pinnacle. I watched her go to the first person and help them sit up. They appeared alarmed at first, but I could tell by their body language that they quickly calmed when they saw her. I couldn't hear the girl speak, but it was obvious she knew exactly what to say to reassure the others. A group quickly gathered around her as she spoke. It was going to take time for her to reach all of them, scattered around the orb as they were, but there was time.

All the time in the universe.

"Ever the mother," a voice said behind me. "No matter what form she's in."

I turned as Astra approached.

"This is what she was meant to do, really," she said, eyeing the screens. "It's just as well. They're going to need a leader, someone to nurture them into this new life. And that was never going to be me."

The white orb's repair functions had done wonders. The crystallization on her body had disappeared, restored to smooth, flawless skin. Her hair was dark brown, cut in an uneven bob framing her face. Save for her right eye, which retained its glassy gray, she looked just like how she did in the hologram.

"This is how I used to look," she said, noticing my curious gaze. "Many lifetimes ago."

"You cut your hair."

"Well," the corner of her lip twitched upward, "you did the same. Signs of change, I suppose." She reached up and touched the corner of her eye. "I had her leave a little. Didn't seem right to pretend it never happened. We are what we've lived, after all."

I grinned. "Well said."

We watched Mother move on to the next batch of champions, just waking up. I wondered what she was telling them when they opened their eyes.

"So how's it feel, arena master?"

I cringed. "Please don't call me that."

"It's what you are now. Better get used to it." She gave me a wry smile. "What will you do now? Take a trip home?"

"Home?" That word sounded so strange somehow. "I don't know what home is anymore."

"You don't want to see your family?"

I thought of Mother. *My* mother. The mother whose story I had never known until I saw it projected into my mind on the dead planet. "Maybe. I still have a lot to learn about my own world. What about you? Are you and Solace . . ."

"I don't know." Astra shook her head. "Fixing what went wrong between us isn't as simple as restoring a face or creating a body. Even if we do try to work it out, moving forward is not going to be easy."

"No, it won't be," someone cut in.

I spun around just in time to see Solace enter. I saw Astra struggle to control her expression at the sight of him. He met her eyes for the first time since I had set foot into this strange new world.

"But loving you has never been hard."

The surge of emotions coming from Astra was like a tidal wave. Being able to feel the emotions of others was still a little overwhelming, but I was beginning to grow accustomed to it. I nudged her toward him. I might not know when I was going to go home, but her home was here, right in front of her. As they embraced each other, I stood and left the control room.

"Hey."

I paused in the hall. This was a voice I knew. I turned, expecting to see a familiar holographic smile, but was greeted with a face I didn't recognize. Clear, round eyes and delicate features sat above slender limbs coated in translucent blue-green skin. I'd seen beings like them before, in a world filled with water that Om had guided me through. They moved just as gracefully out of water as they did in it.

"Two?" I said uncertainly. "Is that you?"

"Surprised?" They lifted one arm and examined their glistening skin in the light. "I have to say, it's a little weird. Never thought I'd have skin again. I almost miss the metal. I forgot how much maintenance a fleshy body is."

I chuckled. "You look great," I said, and I meant it.

"I know," they said. "And thanks. For whatever you did. I

don't quite understand it yet, but I imagine there's quite a story to all this."

I nodded and grinned. "There is. But I won't bore you with it."

Gentle laughter drifted toward us from the other end of the hall. Two gazed wistfully in its direction. I knew what they were thinking about.

"Do you . . . regret it?"

"No," they said without hesitation. "I did right by Viva. I still believe that. It was simply not her fate to live to see this day."

I cleared my throat. It was not a thought I wanted to dwell on. "So, you're Lynphixian."

Two gave me a small, crooked smirk. "Is that a surprise?"

"I guess I never really thought about what you were like before you were metal."

They wiggled their long fingers. "I did spend far more time in the metal than I did in this body."

"You have it back now. You can do whatever you want with it. You're free."

They mulled this over as if it was a word they'd never heard before. "Free, huh?" they said. "Wouldn't know what to do with freedom, but I guess I'll figure it out."

They started to wander off, then stopped. To my great surprise, they bent and kissed me gently on the forehead.

"Don't tell anyone I did that," Two said as they sauntered away. "New world order or not, I have a reputation to maintain."

Om was resting.

Or rather, that's what I assumed he was doing. The lower levels of the white orb were rather different from the black orbs. Here there were no locked rooms and no occupants hanging from the walls with wires. There was only an open space, like a newly built structure waiting for a creative mind to fill it with ideas, partitions, and colors. Right now, there was only a low platform, upon which rested a soft white mass. As I neared it, the floor nearby bloomed into a mushroom-shaped seat. I sat on top of it, and it molded itself to my body.

I reached out and laid my hand on the white mass. It rose gently up and down, like an animal sleeping, dreaming.

"Do you remember me?" I asked.

A gentle quiver. Then, small white tendrils rose from its surface and wrapped themselves around my fingers. No matter his form, Om was still Om, and he still knew how to hold my hand.

He had a long way to go. If the white orb was to be believed, both housing and defying a demigod were tremendously taxing on his body. At the same time, the symbiosis he had formed with K'azen had led to adaptations of his own. He was, after all, created to adapt. Ironic that the creators who made him ended up being the catalyst for his evolution. He was something else now, an amalgamation of the living things in this universe. A hybrid containing traits and parts of the seed races, the orbs, and the demigods. Not simply a machine to be erased and reset, yet not quite an organic being. What this meant for him remained to be seen, but he was the first of his kind. His path was going to be a unique one, and once he awakened, he would have to figure out his first step.

"I'll help you," I whispered. The tendrils around my fingers tightened. "I promise."

I STOOD in the uppermost tier of the orb. Here the dome was transparent, showing the endless space beyond. Beside me stood a figure with a face that looked like a combination of me and Rosi, but with tan skin and hair dark like Astra and purple pupils like Mother.

"I have been thinking," she said.

"What about?"

"A name for myself. I have learned that names are important to seed races. A curious behavior, to identify one's self by a word. But I like it."

I smiled a little at her thoughtful look. There was an innocence to her. "What did you decide?"

"I don't know yet. It seems the name ought to reflect one's self, and right now, the self I know most is the one you call Rosi."

"Her name was Rosalit."

"Rosalit?"

I nodded. "Rosi was what I called her when we were little, because I couldn't say her name properly. It's the name of a wildflower that grows on Fiina, the only flower that blooms no matter the climate, location, or altitude. Most people see it as a weed, but I always thought it suited her so well. It was resilient, and adaptive, just like her."

"Rosalit." She tasted the name in her mouth, savoring its sound. "I like that. Now that a name has been chosen, we should begin."

"Begin?"

"Seeing the universe." Rosalit turned to me. "Where would you like to start?"

I looked up at the glittering stars, surrounded by endless silence and possibilities. I didn't know what lay ahead or what I would find back on Fiina. I had no plan, no playbook, and no idea what the next cycle, the next day, or the next hour held.

Yet, I was strangely at peace. Before me was endless space, millions of possibilities, billions of paths, trillions of voices. The orb sailed through it all, a spot of pure white against the velvet black.

Like a beacon, guiding the way home.

CHAPTER 40

PEX RACED THOUGH THE TOWN STREETS, NARROWLY AVOIDING knocking over the fruit stands and vegetable bins that lined the curbs.

"Slow down, you ruffian!" shouted one of the vendors as he leapt over a bin of red hinta fruit, nearly pulling it over as his foot grazed its edge.

"Sorry!" he called back, barely turning. He was far too excited to pause. Past the town square, he finally reached the collection of huts shared by his family and neighbors. He dashed into the courtyard, panting. A small group sitting under the warm sun regarded him curiously.

"My goodness, Pex," Gamma said, her long gray whiskers twitching with each word. She gave him a look that was half concerned and half scolding. "What in the world are you doing, charging around like that?"

Still trying to catch his breath, Pex ran to the group. The children of the housing cluster were gathered before Gamma, sitting in a semicircle before her. His younger sister, still an infant, perched on the old woman's lap and gave him a wide grin as he approached. Gamma reached up and wiped spots of drool from the baby's mouth.

"Such commotion," she said, but her eyes smiled. "Little

Pola here was wondering where her brother was, and here he is, running about like a wild animal. I suppose he's gotten too old for Gamma's stories?"

Pex grinned. He reached out and took Pola from Gamma's lap. The baby nuzzled against him and chewed on the sweaty fabric of his shirt. "I heard amazing news, Gamma," he said. "I just had to come tell you all."

"Oh? And what is that?" Gamma gestured at the children before her, who were now all gazing at Pex with their wide, black eyes. "I must hear this news that is so important that you interrupted story time."

Pex puffed out his chest and stiffened his short, hard whiskers. "They've floated the orb."

There was a moment of silence. Pex held his breath, excited for the response from his friends. But the children simply looked at one another. He looked to Gamma. The expression on her silvery-gray face was unreadable, but a moment later, she smiled.

"Is that all?" she said.

"It's a big deal!" Pex exclaimed. "They've tried to get that thing out of the lake for ten seasons!" He jostled his sister. "It's been there since before Pola was born, before I was born. They finally got it out. Don't you wonder at all what might be inside?"

"Dear," Gamma said patiently. "What makes you think there is something inside?"

Pox opened his mouth, then closed it. He had never entertained the thought that there might be nothing inside the orb.

"The universe is big, Pex," Gamma went on. "Something unknown came to our world, that is true. But that does not mean it is something great or fascinating. Perhaps another civilization simply had an extra marble they didn't need." She gestured at an empty spot at the edge of the circle. "Come, join us."

Pex flushed. He sat. His baby sister curled in his lap. He

sighed a deflated sigh. Gamma reached down and patted his head.

"Now," Gamma said, "what story shall we hear today?"

Pex leaned back on his hands and listened to the other children clamor with their suggestions. He was grateful to Gamma. She kept him grounded with her wisdom, as she did with everyone in town. He couldn't quite remember when she had become such a big part of everyone's lives, but he couldn't imagine life without her. Despite the fact that she looked different from the average Exadian, with her gray skin instead of light blue, with her long, drooping whiskers that did not stand when she spoke, and without the delicate webbing between her fingers that the rest of them possessed, her differences were easily overlooked in favor of her kindness, generosity, and wealth of knowledge.

I'm just built a little differently, she would laugh and say, *like a hut, made with the same sticks and stones, but painted with a different brush.* She said this especially when the children gathered around her, studying the curious circular tattoo that covered most of her right palm. It was like a single brush stroke, natural and delicate. Many asked how she got it, and was it in fact a birthmark, but she only smiled mysteriously and gave the same answer each time.

I won it. I was the first.

As a child, Pex had thought Gamma was his grandmother and was fiercely protective of her. As he grew older, he began to realize that she was no one's grandmother. She was simply Gamma, the one who told stories and doled out hugs and advice to anyone who asked, always with a smile on her face.

"I want to hear the one about the fish person!" one of the girls shouted. "That's my favorite one!"

"No!" a boy yelled. "The peasant girl and the soldier! That one's better!"

"I want the young queen!" another girl cut in.

Gamma shushed them gently. Pex didn't particularly care

which story she told. He was tired from running and he liked all of Gamma's stories equally. He had heard the adults say that she must have lived through very interesting times to have so many stories, all of which she playfully insisted were true.

"Let me tell you a different story," she said, and for a moment she looked up and Pex thought he saw her fix her gaze somewhere far away. Was it in the direction of the lake? He couldn't tell, and he found he didn't care. She was right—that black orb probably had nothing useful inside. Now that it was out of the lake, they would store it somewhere to be forgotten.

"A long time ago," Gamma said, turning back to the children, "there was a war. Two sides could not agree on the correct way to live, and their disagreements turned deadly. Many lives were lost or changed forever by it, but not everyone took part in it. Some turned away from the conflict and found peace on their own, because you see, there are more ways to live than to fight."

A girl raised her hand. "Why did they not tell the others not to fight?"

"Well, that is a good question. You see, sometimes you can try your best, but you can't control what others do. The reality is, the only ones we can truly save are ourselves. There may come a day when you will have to decide what you need to do to survive and let go of the ones you can't save, whoever that might be."

Her eyes flickered in the direction of the lake again. Pex wondered if maybe she was more fascinated by his news than she let on. But the warm sunbeam caressed his face and he grew sleepy. He lay down on the warm ground, his sister cradled in his arms, and drifted off listening to Gamma's soothing voice, telling her stories about nothing and everything.

ACKNOWLEDGMENTS

I want to thank the team at Story Cartel Press for giving me the opportunity to tell my stories; Alice Sudlow, my editor, who made sure they were presentable to the public; and the COVID-19 pandemic, which gifted me with a two-year panic attack that resulted in the frantic writing of three novels, twelve short stories, and a whole lot of articles as a fight/flight response.

www.ingramcontent.com/pod-product-compliance
Lightning Source LLC
LaVergne TN
LVHW041055080826
845145LV00007B/1578

9781735903743